The Sea Peoples

The
Sea Peoples

A NOVEL OF THE CHANGE

S. M. STIRLING

ACE
NEW YORK

ACE
Published by Berkley
An imprint of Penguin Random House LLC
375 Hudson Street, New York, New York 10014

Copyright © 2017 by S. M. Stirling

Map by Jade Cheung

Library of Congress Cataloging-in-Publication Data
Names: Stirling, S. M., author.
Title: The sea peoples: a novel of the Change/S. M. Stirling.
Description: First edition. | New York: ACE, 2017. | Series: Change series; 11
Identifiers: LCCN 2017019825 (print) | LCCN 2017024613 (ebook) | ISBN 9780399583186 (ebook) |
ISBN 9780399583179 (hardback)
Subjects: LCSH: Regression (Civilization)—Fiction. | Quests (Expeditions)—Fiction. | BISAC:
FICTION/Alternative History. | FICTION/Fantasy/Epic. | GSAFD: Science fiction. | Fantasy fiction. |
Alternative histories (Fiction).
Classification: LCC PS3569.T543 (ebook) | LCC PS3569.T543 S43 2017 (print) | DDC 813/.54—dc23
LC record available at https://lccn.loc.gov/2017019825

First Edition: October 2017

Printed in the United States of America
1   3   5   7   9   10   8   6   4   2

Jacket art by Larry Rostant

To Jan, for being wonderful

ACKNOWLEDGMENTS

To Robert W. Chambers, author of *The King in Yellow*, one of the seminal texts of modern fantasy and horror, and pioneer of the unreliable narrator. If he was good enough for Lovecraft to be inspired by (aka "steal from"), he's good enough for me to do the same!

Thanks to Kier Salmon, unindicted co-conspirator, who has been my advisor and helper on the Change since the first.

To Gina Tacconi-Moore, my niece, flower girl at my wedding twenty-nine years ago, Queen of Physical Fitness and owner of CrossFit Lowell, who gave me some precise data on what a really fit young woman, such as herself, could do.

To Steve Brady, native guide to Alba, for assistance with dialects and British background, and also natural history of all sorts. He saved me from an embarrassing error about vultures this time, for example!

Pete Sartucci, knowledgeable in many aspects of geography and ecology.

To Miho Lipton and Chris Hinkle, for help with Japanese idiom; and to Stuart Drucker, for assistance with Hebrew.

Diana L. Paxson, for help and advice, and for writing the beautiful Westria books, among many others. If you liked the Change novels, you'll probably enjoy the hell out of the Westria books—I certainly did, and they were one of the inspirations for this series; and her *Essential Ásatrú* and recommendation of *Our Troth* were extremely helpful . . . and fascinating reading. The appearance of the name Westria in the book is no coincidence whatsoever. And many thanks for the loan of Deor Wide-Faring and Thora Garwood, on whom she gave fresh advice and help for *The Sea Peoples*.

To Dale Price, for help with Catholic organization, theology and praxis.

To John Birmingham, aka that silver-tongued old rogue, King Birmo of Capricornia, most republican of monarchs.

To Cara Schulz, for help with Hellenic bits, including stuff I could not have found on my own.

To Lucienne M. Brown, Pacific Northwesterian and keen wit, for advice and comments.

To Walter Jon Williams, Emily Mah, John Miller, Vic Milan, Jan Stirling, Matt Reiten, Lauren Teffeau, and Sareena of Critical Mass, for constant help and advice as the book was under construction.

Thanks to John Miller, good friend, writer and scholar, for many useful discussions, for lending me some great books and for some really, really cool old movies.

Special thanks to Heather Alexander, bard and balladeer, for permission to use the lyrics from her beautiful songs which can be—and should be!—ordered at http://faerietaleminstrel.com. Run, do not walk, to do so.

To Alexander James Adams, for cool music, likewise: http://faerietaleminstrel .com/inside.

Thanks again to William Pint and Felicia Dale, for permission to use their music, which can be found at www.pintndale.com and should be, for anyone with an ear and salt water in their veins.

And to Three Weird Sisters—Gwen Knighton, Mary Crowell, Brenda Sutton and Teresa Powell—whose alternately funny and beautiful music can be found at http://www.threeweirdsisters.com.

And to Heather Dale, for permission to quote the lyrics of her songs, whose beautiful (and strangely appropriate!) music can be found at www.heatherdale .com, and is highly recommended. The lyrics are wonderful and the tunes make it even better.

To S. J. Tucker, for permission to use the lyrics of her beautiful songs, which can be found at http://sjtucker.com, and should be.

And to Lael Whitehead of Jaiya, http://www.broadjam.com/jaiya, for permission to quote the lyrics of her beautiful songs. One of which became the Montivallan national anthem.

Thanks again to Russell Galen, my agent, who has been an invaluable help, advisor and friend for decades now, and never more than in these difficult times. I've had good editors, but none who've helped my career and work as much.

All mistakes, infelicities and errors are of course my own.

The Sea Peoples

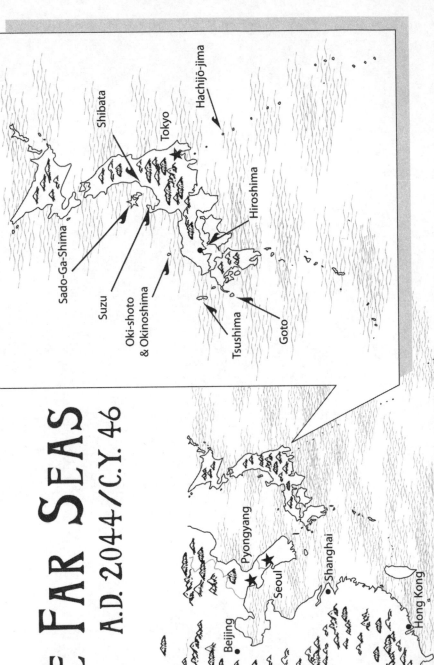

THE FAR SEAS
A.D. 2044/C.Y. 46

Shibata
Tokyo
Hachijō-jima
Hiroshima
Sado-Ga-Shima
Suzu
Oki-shoto
& Okinoshima
Tsushima
Goto

Pyongyang
Seoul
Shanghai
Hong Kong
Beijing

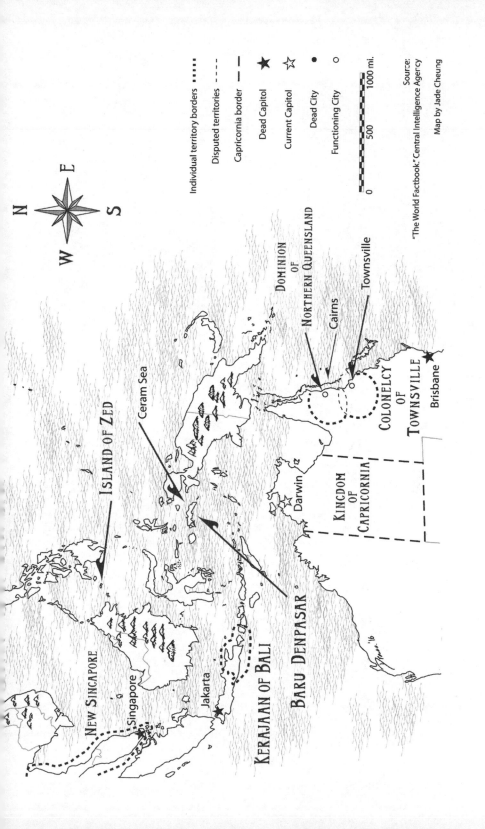

NEW SINGAPORE
Singapore

ISLAND OF ZED

Ceram Sea

DOMINION
OF
NORTHERN QUEENSLAND

Cairns

Townsville

Jakarta

KERAJAAN OF BALI

BARU DENPASAR

Darwin

KINGDOM
OF
CAPRICORNIA

COLONELCY
OF
TOWNSVILLE
Brisbane

N
W E
S

Individual territory borders ••••••
Disputed territories – – –
Capricornia border — —
★ Dead Capitol
☆ Current Capitol
● Dead City
○ Functioning City

0   500   1000 mi.

Source:
"The World Factbook," Central Intelligence Agency

Map by Jade Cheung

PROLOGUE

Where am I? Prince John Arminger Mackenzie thought. *I was at the fort . . . we stormed the wall . . . something fell on me. . . .*

Something loomed ahead of him, then vanished again in the blur.

Is that Carcosa?

Thinking about the ramparts glimpsed for a moment was a distraction from the pain, as John stumbled along with his feet bleeding on the ruts and rocks of the roadway and his shoulders screaming every time the two pulled on the pole.

I don't know what they are but they have hands.

His hands were tied in front of him, and the stick was run between his elbows and his back, an arrangement which made it impossible to look up without straining his neck muscles and impossible not to stumble if he didn't.

What's different? he thought. *Why am I having so much trouble concentrating? Apart from being in the enemy's hands . . . and how did that happen? Why can't I remember?*

There had been windup record players in the places he lived most of his life, they were expensive but gave a reasonable sound . . . unless something happened to make one skip. That had always jarred his natural ear for music with a sense of discontinuity, like being startled out of a deep reverie by a flick from a wet towel.

Now his awareness itself was jumping like that needle. Was there really nothing but dank mist around, except for a stretch of roadway beneath his feet? Had he been plodding through a fog forever?

The world became clearer, fading into solidity again, and he wished it hadn't. A gibbet stood by the side of the highway. The corpse hanging from it was withered and blackened, and one arm was tied out with a stick and string as a pointer, but what it pointed to was nowhere because it swayed and turned in the wind. The eyes moved and looked at him as the face came around, teeth forever bared by withered lips in a silent scream. A crow plucked at its rib cage.

The crow was dead, with white bone showing through tattered feathers. So were the flies clustered around those eyes.

The pain hovered, always there, but John's mind didn't seem to be. A heavy scent filled the air, like roses and rot at the same time. The light was bright but directionless and he felt as if he were locked in a closet despite being able to see clearly.

They'd been winning, and then the flaming tower had broken apart and fallen towards him just as they came over the wall. He'd thought, *I'm going to die*, and . . . then there had been the ruined temple in the jungle and the . . . woman-thing called the Rangda and her horde of little men with huge eyes . . . and the temple had split and the Pallid Mask had taken him through . . . and . . .

Am I dead? Surely I haven't been that bad . . . but I haven't had a chance to make confession. . . .

Pain. There was always the pain; the pole thrust between his elbows behind his back dragging him along, and looking down and seeing the sweat and blood drop into the white dust of the road. The muscles in his shoulders and arms ached as if they might snap like rotten string, and his feet were swollen lumps of fire.

He'd seen the castle-city-whatever that its dwellers called Carcosa as the *Tarshish Queen* approached the harbor of Baru Denpasar. It looked weird enough, a fantastic concoction of walls and turrets, tall slim bulbous-tipped towers and domes, all made of coral rock that varied from cream to crimson. He hadn't studied it much since; local belief was that if you looked at it too long, then . . . things . . . could happen to your mind.

Not that I have much choice now, he thought, and closed his eyes.

Instantly something slammed into his back. It felt like a whip of barbed steel.

"I could not bear to think you did not behold your new home," that soft voice said.

Still in the Old French that only one trained to be a troubadour . . . and this, whatever it was . . . would know.

What he saw resembled that castle on the shore he'd seen a few days ago, but it was different as it loomed up to the south. The fields around it were a mixture; sometimes he was looking at rice paddies not much different from those around the city of Baru Denpasar, sometimes at something more like Montival or tales of Old Europe, with reaped sheaves and tattered-looking buildings of half-timbering and slate, and sometimes . . .

A child stood beside the road with a dog in its arms, watching the approaching cavalcade. As they drew closer, he could see that the dog had no legs, only seared stumps, and it cried endlessly and silently as the child reached down and tore off another mouthful with his pointed teeth, raising a bloodied smile as the Pallid Mask's party rode by.

The impulse to close his eyes again was overwhelming, but he didn't dare. Instead he started to pray silently:

Sancte Michael Archangele, defende nos in proelio, contre nequitiam et insidias diaboli esto praesidium!

John blinked. For an instant, before it faded into a mist, he was looking at a ceiling. Why would he be looking at a ceiling? He wasn't even in the world right now, as far as he could tell.

As if I were back home, with nothing to worry about but Órlaith trying to make me do some work.

His mind was skipping again. This time it was filled with a familiar mix of love and fond exasperation.

She's a devil for work, my big sister!

CHAPTER ONE

Crown Princess Órlaith Arminger Mackenzie looked south and shoreward towards the Hawaiian capital of Hilo, shading her eyes with a hand. The planks beneath her feet were the quarterdeck of the frigate RMN *Sea-Leopard*, pride of the Royal Montivallan Navy and new-built in the Astoria yards; eighteen hundred tons of Douglas fir and Garry oak and Sitka spruce, cordage and sailcloth and copper sheathing and brass and steel salvaged from the dead cities, at nearly three hundred feet from bowsprit to rudder the most powerful warship afloat in the Pacific.

It had also been packed to the gunwales with double its normal complement on the trip across from Montival, nearly seven hundred souls, since there weren't enough transports to spare the warships. The *Sea-Leopard* wasn't as busy or as crowded now: the sails on the three towering masts were furled as she lay at anchor, and all the extra personnel plus the liberty party were ashore. Most were members of the crowd whose surf-murmur carried over the thousand yards or so to the docks, apart from the ones whose main ambition on dry land was to find a bottle and go from upright and sober to horizontal and unconscious with the least possible interval in between.

After this trip I find that a wee bit attractive, Órlaith thought dryly. *Sure and it would be the more so if I'd been sleeping in a hammock in the hold with two inches' space on either side and someone on a pallet on the deck below and nobody washing much for that there's not enough fresh water for anything but drinking. Even the rats are probably swimming for it.*

She'd been in a bunk in the Captain's cabin, sharing the space with the Admiral and six others, and had gotten admiring looks for not taking the whole for herself. Now everything on board was squared away and shipshape, down to the neat coils of cable and hawser, and the pyramids of roundshot and racks of bolt next to the long rows of massive catapults on the gun-deck below. There had been a good deal of coming and going by everyone *except* Órlaith herself; her setting foot on Hawaiian soil was a political matter, and had to be staged with due ceremony.

Shore leave or no, the *Sea-Leopard* could still be ready to sail and fight in the very short time it took the topmast hands to run up the ratlines and reach the gaskets on the sails; the catapults would be cocked and loaded by then and the anchors cast off with empty casks to float the ends of their cables for later attention. The Montivallans were among friends . . . but it never hurt to be ready.

Admiral Naysmith had been standing with her hands clasped behind her back, hard-featured square face with the little blue burn-mark of the Bearkiller A-List between her brows impassive above the white linen tropical-service uniform jacket and gold-braided epaulettes. Now she nodded at the signal-flag that went up a mast rigged on the dock ashore and turned to the ship's captain.

"We're ready to proceed, Mr. Edwards," she said. "Make it so. And a signal to that effect to the Japanese flagship, in the Crown Princess' name."

Naysmith cocked an eye at Órlaith, who nodded approval. The orders ran down the chain of command, more and more specific as they did. Signal-flags of their own went up the halyard to the mizzen-peak.

Órlaith politely ignored the exchange, studying the town instead; she liked and respected the blunt-spoken Bearkiller's professionalism but they weren't close, and she was careful not to infringe on her area of authority. As overall commander of the expedition Órlaith was entitled to tell her what she wanted to accomplish, but how to do it was the Admiral's business.

She *suspected* that the middle-aged Naysmith had doubts about someone of the same twenty-two years as her own eldest child—who was a lieutenant somewhere in the fleet—being in charge of a major expedition, bearer of the royal Sword or no, though of course she'd never say a word to that effect. Looking at it from the outside she had something of a point. Órlaith had grown up watching famously good strategists in action, but she knew she wasn't equal to either of her parents.

Yet. And they started as young as I am now, overshadowed by their famous parents . . . two of whom . . .

Her maternal and paternal grandfathers had been deadly enemies from the Change on and had ended up killing each other in single combat with several thousand witnesses in their respective armies whooping them on.

Ah, well, youth is the one disease age always cures . . . and we of House Artos are not a long-lived breed, anyway . . . and besides, it's an interesting view. It's my first time off the mainland, even if I'm not traveling just for the pleasure of it.

Hilo was a very substantial if not huge city of more than twenty thousand souls, low-built and spread out amid trees and greenery and gardens ornamental or practical or both. White walls and roofs of tile or palm-thatch showed through the greenery and even at this distance you could see the purple and blue and crimson of banks of flowers and blossoming trees, citrus and tropical fruits, jacarandas and flamboyants and flame trees.

Southward loomed the peaks of massive mountains, not steep but very high; snow glittered from the tops of Mauna Kea and Mauna Loa. The sight made the hair prickle on the back of her neck, and she felt a return of that sense . . . a feeling of chambers within her mind open-

ing . . . that she'd felt when she first took up the Sword of the Lady after
her father's death. Her hand went to the crystal pommel at her side, the
symbol of the High Kingship that Rudi Mackenzie—not yet Artos the
First, High King of Montival—had won on the Quest of the Sunrise Lands.
In form it was a knight's longsword, save that the guard was shaped like
a crescent moon rather than a cross, and the pommel at the end of the
double-lobed horn-and-silver hilt was moon-colored crystal cradled in a
stag's antlers rather than a metal ball.

Beneath that seeming . . . it could be and do many things, and you
could never entirely disregard the sheer presence of it even when it was
quiescent. She'd often thought that it wasn't really a thing of matter as
most understood such things, but a thought in the mind of the Goddess
made manifest in the world of common day.

Now it let her sense . . .

That's sacredness, she thought.

She inclined her head towards the peaks of the volcanoes and made
the Old Faith's gesture of reverence with the back of her hand to her
forehead.

As she did, images flashed through her mind: a great canoe's prow
grinding ashore on a beach of blinding white sand, its grotesquely carved
figurehead *alive* somehow; a giant figure roaring in mirth as he wrestled with
a huge eight-eyed bat; a man of stern kingly majesty raising a carved staff
as his black hair blew around a tattooed face and the sea broke at his feet
in a storm of terrible power; a woman of unbearable beauty whose eyes
were the fires at the core of Earth, walking atop the surface of a river that
ran with molten stone . . .

But a sacredness that is not mine. *Not hostile and not bad, but Powers fierce and
wild and strong and . . . foreign. Stories I haven't heard, walking the ridge of the world
once more. The Change opened many doors, and the world is very wide.*

The warm moist air from the shore fluttered her long hair beneath its
plumed Scots bonnet, locks yellow-gold with a slight hint of copper. It bore
scents from the land, some homely enough from cooking and people, others spicy and sweet and wild, welcome amid the usual war-fleet smells of

tar and smoke, bilgewater and imperfectly clean sailors and troops packed in too tightly and rancid canola-oil smeared on armor and blades against the corrosive salt of the sea-spray.

And the overpowering stink of the horse-transports, which was like a badly-kept stable on a huge scale no matter how many times the bilges were flooded and the animals were put to work on treadmills pumping them out. Rank gave her a bubble of space on the warship to enjoy the contrast.

Some of Hilo's buildings were from before the Change, though none of the really tall ones you still saw now and then on the mainland, even in living cities like Boise or Portland. Those had probably been dismantled for their metal and glass, since without artificial ventilation and cooling they'd be even less practical in this climate than at home. More were new, and the great stepped stone platform in the middle distance was just finished, judging by the remains of bamboo scaffolding and hoisting cranes still being taken down. That was a heiau, a temple to the Gods who were worshipped here once more.

Unlike all of the cities and many of the duns and towns and steadings she knew at home there was no encompassing defensive wall to make a sharp distinction between dense-built settlement and open countryside, despite the obvious technical capacity to build one. The plots around buildings just got bigger, until you could say they were small farms and country villas rather than houses with gardens, and they started to include pastures for cattle and horses and runs for swine.

Which means they haven't had war here lately, probably not since right after the Change; not great wars with massed armies and strong siege-trains, at least, Órlaith thought. *Lucky them!*

There had been little peace in what was Montival-to-be until her parents and their comrades had brought the High Kingdom's order with the Sword of the Lady. She had grown up among the veterans who'd fought the long grim death-grapple of the Prophet's War across half a continent, starting with her parents, and there had been the wars against the Association before that in the time of her great, wicked maternal grandfather. Her generation had lived in a spreading peace, but the memories remained.

The most familiar single sight was a massive modern fort on the peninsula to the westward where the maps of the ancient world showed a golf course, not much different save in details and decoration from the castles in the northern parts of Montival. An orca-shaped observation balloon hung high in the air above it, tethered by a long curve of cable.

Form follows function, she thought. *Everyone makes their wheels round and everyone puts a pointy stabby thing on the end of a spear.*

The towers there flew the bright striped flag of the *Aupuni Mōʻī o Hawaiʻi,* and as a courtesy the green-silver-gold banner of the High Kingdom of Montival and the *Hinomaru* of Japan.

Órlaith knew that the kingdoms of Hawaiʻi and Montival had been friendly as long as they'd been aware of each other's existence. Since not long before her father Rudi Mackenzie's accession—as Artos the First— in the year of her birth, in fact. There had been a king again in Hawaiʻi well before that; since right after the Change, as folk turned to ancient things as an anchor in a world gone mad. Their current ruler, Kalākaua II, was his grandson and only a few years older than Órlaith.

But that friendliness had been confined to good wishes, resident merchants who doubled as ambassadors, growing trade and a little cooperation against the pirates and raiders who grew right along with the traffic they preyed on. Just exchanging messages at this distance was hard and slow, despite a more or less common language, and the chances of misunderstanding vast.

It was a good sign that the vanguard of the fleet and army of Montival— frigates, smaller warships, scores of merchantmen turned troop-transports— had been welcomed within the long curving breakwater that guarded Hilo's harbor. Many were already tied up at the wharfs, and boats and barges plied busily back and forth to the others. And there was other shipping here too, dozens of hulls and a forest of masts, the Royal Navy of Hawaiʻi and traders from here and around the world and others down to little fishing boats and outrigger canoes, all amid the raucous swarm of gulls and seabirds that marked a rich port.

"I wish we had more troops ashore," her liege knight—and aide-de-camp and Head of Household and childhood friend—Heuradys d'Ath grumbled beside her.

Heuradys was trying to look everywhere at once without being obvious about it and preparing to be even more overburdened ashore, with the mixture of irritation and slightly self-mocking amusement of a hypercompetent person in a position where they knew full well no amount of competence could ever be enough. In a sense it was easier for Órlaith to ignore the prospect of assassins popping up with daggers in their teeth—or waiting with concealed crossbows and poison darts—than it was for those around her. All she had to fear was death; they had the much stronger terror of living long enough to know they'd failed in their duty.

After all, the Crone comes for us all, soon or late, she thought. *I don't expect to make old bones myself, even if the Powers haven't warned me about it the way they did Da. Either I'll have children by then to take up the Sword, or one of the sibs will.*

Then she went on aloud: "We've got thousands of troops ashore," she pointed out cheerfully. "And glad to be out of the transports they are. The horses especially, poor things. We'd have lost half or better if we couldn't stop here to let them pasture and run, and the survivors would have been useless for weeks on the other side."

Heuradys snorted. "To clarify: more troops besides the ones in their shirtsleeves seeing the sights . . . and chatting up the better-looking locals . . . and trying to eat bananas without knowing how to peel them . . . and sucking rum out of coconuts in the shade of the palms . . . and frolicking on the beaches."

"The beaches are wonderful here. *And* the oceans. The levies deserve some time off after the voyage. Fair winds and a quick passage, but it was hard sailing at times. Four hundred cases of seasickness at the same time . . ."

"Seawater warm enough to swim in! Athana witness, that's just not right, proper or natural."

"You just want some company for your ironclad misery, Herry," the Crown Princess said with a smile.

Though to be fair most of Montival's coasts did have an Arctic current running down them from Alaska; you had to go down near the ruins of Los Angeles before you could swim in it without a wet suit, and even there it wasn't like Hawai'i.

"That *shirtsleeves* remark was a blazon, so."

Heuradys was five-ten to her liege's five-eleven, with tightly braided red-brown hair of the shade usually called auburn and catlike amber eyes, slightly older in her mid-twenties but with much the same leopardess build. She was also wearing full knight's harness of white plate armor— hers was a titanium-alloy suit that had been a royal gift when she turned twenty-one and gained the golden spurs four years ago—with her visored sallet helm in the crook of her left arm and her teardrop-shaped kite shield slung over her back.

"Oh, rub it in, Your Highness-ness, rub it in," she said.

In a staccato north-realm accent much like High Queen Mathilda; Órlaith had picked up the Mackenzie lilt from her father.

Salt rivulets ran down Heuradys' high-cheeked face, one with an underlying hardness but comely in a way blunter than her liege's sharp-cut good looks. It wasn't so very hot, no more than a warm summer's day in much of Montival, but it was unrelenting and the air was very humid. This was the sort of weather that was pure comfort if you were lying naked save for a flower wreath in the shade of a palm tree and watching the surf. . . .

While sucking a rum drink out of a coconut through a straw and thinking about a swim and then dinner, Órlaith thought.

In armor . . . you sweated whenever you wore plate. Not so much from the weight, which was only about fifty or sixty pounds and less with one of these titanium-alloy marvels that only monarchs and great nobles could afford, and well-distributed over your whole body. But it and the padded doublet underneath cut your skin off from the air and trapped the body's heat very effectively. You could manage to work up plenty of perspiration even in cold weather, and there were good reasons it wasn't a very common style of protection in areas that grew sugarcane and breadfruit, starting with the risk of heat exhaustion. Órlaith had suffered enough in plate herself—she wasn't a north-realm Associate like Heuradys but she *was* a knight and entitled to the golden spurs—to be glad it wasn't necessary today.

Besides her own bonnet with its silver clasp and the Golden Eagle feather that marked the totem of her sept, the Crown Princess wore a sleeveless shirt of saffron-dyed linen embroidered in green and blue at the hems, chased gold bands pushed up each arm, a pleated knee-length kilt and a fringed plaid pinned at the shoulder with a broach of swirling knotwork in silver and gold and niello and hanging behind nearly to the ground, both in the Mackenzie tartan, knit knee-hose, and silver-buckled shoes.

The gear was not particularly martial and certainly not aristocratic. In fact, it was simply what Mackenzie clansfolk wore back in Montival, albeit of the sort you saw brought out on the festival days of the Wheel of the Year, not the set kept for mucking out a pigsty. Or the plaid you wore wrapped tight over a jacket to keep warm in the Black Months while you stood under a rain-dripping tree leaning on a shepherd's crook and staring at sheep who were even more miserable than you were.

But with the Sword of the Lady at your side, you never lacked for majesty; there was no need to stick a thumb in any Hawaiian eye by way of toploftiness to make them take notice.

"I'd be saying it's just pleasantly warm," Órlaith grinned. "And by the Powers, doesn't everyone know that a knight of the Association laughs at hardship as they do at danger?"

Her friend made a slight sound that would have been a loud raspberry in less public circumstances; they'd always teased each other.

Heuradys was properly respectful of the Sword, but not in the least intimidated by its presence, having grown up as much at Court as in her own family's manors and castles. Her father Lord Rigobert was Count of

Campscapell and her birth-mother Countess Delia was a leader of fashion in the Association territories. Her other mother Lady Tiphaine d'Ath was Baroness of Ath in her own right, and a commander of note who'd been Grand Constable of the Association for years and Marshal-Commander of Montival for even longer.

"Ah, and here we go," Heuradys said, watching the Hawaiian dock. "At last! I've already got the impression that driving, compulsive urgency is not the local vice of choice."

"Boiseans and Corvallans say that sort of thing about Associates, you'll remember."

"Yes, but they're just being prejudiced and tight-arsed; when *we* say it, it's true."

A pair of stately barges rowed out from the largest Hawaiian wharf, the one reserved for their King's vessels; they were decorated lavishly with flowers in colors ranging from brilliant white to a red so deep it was almost black. The one heading for her had the Montivallan and Hawaiian flags prominently displayed. The crew of the *Sea-Leopard* poured on deck and lined the rails to the commands of the petty officers.

"To Her Highness . . . general . . . *salute!*" a bosun barked and then trilled out a call on his pipe.

Hands snapped to brows, the old-style gesture that the RMN used. Órlaith returned Admiral Naysmith's salute—and the crew's through her—then put fist to her heart towards the national flag at the mizzen-gaff. A pair of trumpeters sounded a peal as she walked to the gangway—an extensible stairway with a rope rail that could be lowered down from quarterdeck to the waterline.

"For Her Highness and Montival—three cheers!" the Admiral called, raising her fore-and-aft hat.

The ship's officers on the quarterdeck did likewise, and the crewfolk standing in rigid lines along the bulwarks lifted their plain round caps.

"*Hip-hip—*"

"*Huzzah! Huzzah! Huzzah!*"

Órlaith gave a cheerful wave and took the first step. Her dog Macmac had been stretched out in the shade of a bulwark. He rose and padded over panting slightly as he fell in at heel—he was a typical Mackenzie greathound, forty shaggy inches at the shoulder and weighing more than she did, with a head like a furry barrel full of fangs and bright brown eyes. Macmac was too disciplined to frolic in public like this, but he was even more eager to get ashore than she. The close quarters were hard on an active beast his size, even with a run on the treadmill daily.

In his way, he was a bodyguard as effective as Heuradys and didn't have any other duties to distract him.

"And sure, it would be beneath my dignity to climb down a ladder like common mortals," Órlaith murmured.

When you lived your life in public, which she mostly had since babyhood, doing and saying things because they had to be said and done, you learned how to talk so that you weren't overheard. All the kin of House Artos had to be ready to die for the land and the folk to whom they were bound, in battle or at the hand of Fate when the Powers judged it was time that the King's blood must be shed to renew the land.

You also had to be ready to dance *this* dance of symbols and gestures, like it or not, and whenever she grew impatient with it she made herself think of all the other callings. A farmer didn't necessarily think spending a day pulling and topping turnips in the cold mud and week-long drizzles of a Willamette November was better than mulled cider and apple-cakes with cream in front of the hearth, but it was necessary if humankind was to eat.

Órlaith knew; she'd done it now and then. King's work was just as necessary, so that farmers could sit safe by their hearths and reap what they'd sown in due season.

"A ladder . . . That would be interesting for anyone who wanted to look up your princessly kilt, too," Heuradys said dryly from behind her; she was, of course, wearing hose beneath the armor.

"My underwear's clean just this morning," Órlaith replied in a tone equally pawky, and they both suppressed grins. "And my princessly arse is in very viewable condition, mark you. Nicely trim."

The Hawaiian crew of the barge were tall stalwart muscular young men, clad in loincloths and with the wraparound skirts that seemed to be the other main part of the local garb laid aside and folded as padding on their benches. Flowers glowed in their long hair and sweat sheened on the taut curves of their bodies; Órlaith and her knight both cast sidelong appreciative looks without being too obvious about it.

And you have a lover the now who's better-looking than any of them, and a man of wit and grace forbye, Órlaith reminded herself happily.

Though she hadn't seen Alan Thurston since they left Astoria, since he'd made the crossing on one of the troop-transports with his cavalry troop, and frankly missed his company.

Soon, Alan, soon!

Am I mad? Alan Thurston thought.

It was a thought that he often had during the dreams, and that flitted away *like* a dream when he woke, leaving only a shadow of unexplained fear to haunt his darker waking moments. He could remember that, with an odd detachment, remember so much more than he did when he was awake though he couldn't, didn't think about it . . . the knowledge was simply *there.*

In the waking world he wondered without knowledge, and in dreams he knew without pondering. In an abstract way it was interesting, raising the question of whether there *was* an Alan Thurston, rather than fragments and masks that fooled even whatever it was that wore them.

This wasn't one of the really bad dreams, either. They came in series, like sets of linked tales, like those of the Knights of the Round Table or King Conan's wanderings or the Quest of the Ring or the epic of Captain Call and Gus McRae from Texas to Montana.

This particular set of dream-tales was perhaps the oddest of them all. He thought it was of an ancestor of his, another of the lost Imperial Dynasty of America; the man called himself Hildred Castaigne.

Certainly it was from before the Change, since in it he saw machines that no longer functioned—steamships and locomotive engines and flying ships like giant observation balloons with engines that were a droning buzz in the sky. The bits and pieces were from different points in the dream-man's life, in no particular order, sometimes new, sometimes maddeningly the same over and over, night after night, sometimes with a doubled view as if he were seeing what the man saw and also what was really there . . . if *real* had any meaning in a dream.

It's like talking to a lunatic in your own head, he thought. *A lunatic who's also a God.*

In the old days there had been special places for the insane, asylums. In the world the Change had made, few places or families had resources to spare for someone who couldn't earn at least part of their keep, not if it went on for years. Functional madmen were tolerated, and the other types tended to have accidents or just quietly pass away unless some religious group took them in as an act of piety and sacrifice.

Not that I've got all that much experience with lunatics, but it's the way I've always imagined it.

This time he/they looked out from a window over a city, many of the buildings newish and looking much like the Capitol buildings in Boise, all columns and domes and marble. Others reared grotesquely high, dozens of stories, but even the tallest weren't glass-faced like the ones you still saw sometimes where they hadn't been taken down for salvage. These were sheathed in more natural stone and brick but looking the odder for that, because he had enough engineering education to know that you couldn't possibly build load-bearing walls that high.

Castaigne—the man he dreamed of being—was sitting in a soft-padded chair in a book-lined study not altogether unlike the one in the ranch-house back home, reading a book between glances out the window. The slightly stuffy smell of velvet and leather-bound books contrasted with the fresher air through the open panes, but that had a tinge of metallic smokiness too as well as the concentrated town-smell of horses.

The hands that held the book weren't his own—thinner and paler, not the hands of a man who'd ridden as early as he could walk and handled bow and reins and saber, lariat and branding iron, or pitched in with the ranch-hands at roundups and the endless rounds of chores in the lonely estate on the shores of Lake Hali in the mountains of what had once been Idaho.

These were a city man's hands, and a scholar's, he thought. The words on the page were familiar both to the man he was in the dream and to his waking self—it was the play he'd read so often, *The King in Yellow*. There was an eerie detachment to the scene; he knew the words, and the man he was in the dream knew the words, though he was more frightened of them than Alan. The thin fingers trembled as they traced the lines of text, and Alan could hear the way his mind spoke to itself and what it felt, like a faint echo in his own, a tale told so often that it had become part of him:

I cannot forget Carcosa, where black stars hang in the heavens; where the shadows of men's thoughts lengthen in the afternoon, when the twin suns sink into the lake of Hali; and my mind will bear for ever the memory of the Pallid Mask. I pray God will curse the writer, as the writer has cursed the world with this beautiful, stupendous creation, terrible in its simplicity, irresistible in its truth—a world which now trembles before the King in Yellow.

Castaigne slammed the book shut and sat shivering and sweating, tears trickling down his face as he laughed shrilly for a moment. The leather cover bore an embossed figure in gold, the outline of a tall man robed and hooded and masked in yellow with the shadow of ragged crimson wings behind him.

A ghost of pain shot through the man whose shaking hands held the book, focused at the back of the neck; Alan recognized the sort of ache you felt from a bad thump on the head, the sort he'd had occasionally after a horse threw him or a sparring-match with wooden sabers got out of hand and someone bounced the ashwood blade off his helmet too hard.

Then the dream-man rose and walked into a luxurious if fussily-ornamented bedroom, and then to a picture on the wall, an oil-painting of a woman in an elaborate uncomfortable-looking dress that left most of her upper body bare. It swung aside to reveal a safe with a combination lock of curious design. The thin fingers were deft on it, and Alan could feel the ridged metal beneath them.

Dream-man waited for three minutes or so, his mind a golden reverie, an ecstasy of waiting, and in it Alan found his mind more and more one with the man he dreamed. It was hard to resist the feeling of exultation, of power beyond imagining in vistas of rule and glory. The safe clicked and chimed like a musical clock, and he swung back the solid steel doors when the safe opened . . .

. . . *and I lift, from its velvet crown, a diadem of purest gold, blazing with diamonds. I do this every day, and yet the joy of waiting and at last touching again the diadem, only seems to increase as the days pass. It is a diadem fit for a King among kings, an Emperor among emperors. The King in Yellow might scorn it, but it shall be worn by his royal servant.*

I held it in my arms until the alarm in the safe rang harshly, and then tenderly, proudly, I replaced it and shut the steel doors.

The pleasure of the crown was infinite, but somehow also repellant; it blazed with life and power, but made him feel as if he'd stumbled into a tomb and found it on the head of a mummified corpse stretched out on a bier over which black beetles scuttled.

Dream-self walked slowly back into the study, and leaned on a window sill that overlooked a great square. The afternoon sun poured into the windows, and a gentle breeze stirred the branches of the elms and maples in the park; from the buds and tender new leaves it was spring, wherever this was. A flock of pigeons circled about the tower of a Christian church, swirls of them alighting on the purple tiled roof or wheeling downward to a bronze fountain cast in the semblance of a lotus blossom in front of a marble triumphal arch. Gardeners were busy with the flower beds around the fountain, and the freshly turned earth smelled sweet and spicy. A familiar style of lawn mower drawn by a fat white horse clinked across the dense velvety green, and watering carts poured showers of spray over the roads about.

Children in odd clothing—miniature suits shaped like the uniforms sailors wore, or flared gauzy skirts for the girls—ran and played in the spring sunshine amid the banks of bright flowers, and young women in modest long-skirted costumes that reminded him of what the more conservative Mormon ladies wore back home wheeled elaborate baby carriages. They chose paths that let them exchange flirtatious glances with men lolling on the benches; from their boots and spurs and sabers they were horse-soldiers, though the uniforms of gold-slashed blue jackets and tight scarlet pants and polished tasseled boots were far more colorful than most he knew. Only Associates among the peoples he knew were such peacocks at war, and the cut was different from theirs.

Through the trees, the triumphal arch of the monument at the park's heart glistened like silver in the sunshine. On the other side of the square were handsome-looking barracks and stables of white stone, three stories of regular windows above pillars and arches, enough for several regiments and alive with color and motion. It all seemed like a vision of a land strong, contented and at peace as its folk went about the business of their everyday lives, earning their bread and raising their children.

Yet he felt—unsure if it was himself or dream-self—an irresistible impulse to lean out and scream warnings of what crawled hungrily beneath the surface and waited to emerge.

Warnings or threats? Of the doom that falls from the darkening sky?

"Cassilda's fate shall be yours! You cannot escape! None of you can escape! *None of us can escape!*"

Alan Thurston woke gasping. His troop-sergeant lifted a hand from his shoulder.

"That must have been a doozy, sir!" he said. "It's all these heathen fruit you ate giving you collywobbles—not a decent apple in the place."

Alan sat upright on his cot, head nearly brushing the hot canvas of the tent and smelling the stuffy scent; it had cleared up outside, only a few piled white clouds in a dome of blue sky broken by the white tips of the volcanoes. The sides of the tent were rolled up to show that, and the vivid green of the grass that the encampment of the 1st Latah Volunteer Cavalry (Army of the United States of Boise) was busily treading into mud. Memory tattered away like wisps of yellow thread, sliding through the fingers of his attention, and he shrugged his bare shoulders.

Instead he remembered what day it was, and a long slow smile lit his face.

Órlaith! he thought, conscious of a tightness in his throat. *And we actually should have some time for each other.*

Sergeant Creveld was a weathered man in his thirties with several scars on his tanned face and close-cropped sandy hair; he looked at Alan with avuncular fondness beneath the disciplined respect. Order was strict in all the Boisean forces, but the cavalry were less formal about it than the heavy infantry . . . and this was a volunteer unit anyway, raised for the campaign to avenge the High King's death. Creveld was a Regular, though, one of the cadre transferred to see that the reservists who made up the rest of the force came up to scratch. Everyone in Boise did his three years in the service and drilled regularly for the next twenty, of course, but cavalry came from ranching areas where folk were born and raised in the saddle.

And it took a lot more than three years to make a first class horse-archer; you had to be practically born at it.

"You wanted a bath, sir? Don't blame you after wiping down with salt water for weeks. And since you've got a date with the local bigwigs *and* you-know-who . . ."

He grinned, a friendly male expression that knew no rank and grew wider as Alan flushed and cleared his throat.

Alan had worked hard helping get the unit settled in, and everyone was proud that their commander was dating the Crown Princess, who had neither shouted it to the skies nor made any attempt to conceal it. They were *more or less* proud that the President's nephew was their commander, too, especially since Frederick Thurston was leading the Boisean contingent personally and had made it plain he wasn't holding Alan's father against him. Quite a few of the troopers were his neighbors or retainers or neighbors' retainers back home, which helped since they'd been used to seeing him at county fairs and barbeques and round-ups and militia musters all their lives.

Most of the time he and his mother were just well-to-do neighbors, not internal political exiles, the more so as memories of the Prophet's War faded and a new generation grew up very tired of hearing their parents' stories.

Everyone was glad the First Lady was back in Boise watching the store, too. Virginia Thurston had never forgotten or forgiven anything about anyone, as far as anyone knew, and it was widely thought that included anyone descended from her husband's dead traitor of a brother. She'd have been far more unpopular if it wasn't equally true that she never forgot a friend or supporter or hesitated to help them when they needed it.

Well, Mother's more or less the same way—maybe it's something women with blue eyes have in common, he thought.

He'd been sleeping naked under a light blanket, all you needed here in the heat that also explained why the sides of the tent were rolled up under the eaves—though you did need a roof, since it had rained hard twice in the twenty-six hours they'd been ashore. He ducked out with a towel around his waist—that hid the unmistakable physical evidence that he was thinking about the date too, since he didn't want to give more help than he had to to the cavalry's bawdy sense of humor—and found a folding canvas bath steaming and ready, and slipped gratefully into the hot warmth. Working through most of the night had made the afternoon nap just enough, even for someone only twenty-two and in hard good shape. It was nothing he couldn't handle, as he'd handled spending twenty hours in the saddle on a roundup.

"We've got a good spot for drawing water, too, sir. Upstream of that mob from the CORA," Creveld said.

Alan snorted and nodded agreement. The levy from the Central Oregon Ranchers Association were individually tough plainsmen and mountaineers, hunters and herders who were good riders and handy with blade and their saddlebows; they even had some coordination, at a friends-and-neighbors level. At anything beyond that they were all anarchists by Boisean standards, and while he didn't *really* think they pissed in the same places they drew drinking water he wasn't altogether sure that the company sergeant was just being prejudiced, either.

A freckle-faced HQ clerk with red braids who doubled as an orderly brought him a cup of coffee, and he thanked her absently. Since they grew it here it was the real thing, too, not the mixture of chicory and toasted grain that went by that name in most of Montival unless you lived near navigable water or a railroad or were very wealthy or both; he'd only tasted it two or three times a year before he left home. He could feel it making his heart beat faster, unless that was just anticipation. He certainly felt alert enough by the time he'd drained the last of the sweet black liquid.

He sipped and watched the business of the camp, though he could have followed most of it with his eyes closed—the thudding of hooves as a troop galloped past the targets, the snap of bowstrings and whistle of shafts and thud of points hitting piled-earth targets, the clatter of wooden practice blades against each other or on the pell-posts hammered into the ground or the flatter crack on the varnished bullhide of a shield. Fainter and farther he could hear iron on iron from the blacksmith-farrier.

Getting the unit settled in hadn't been a problem, just familiar hard work, since competitive pitching and breaking camp was a popular youngster's school sport in Boise and second nature to anyone grown. Neat rows of tents along regular laneways marked the streets of the camp; coils of barbed wire on slanted, sharpened steel stakes marked the perimeter; the center held the larger tents that held HQ, infirmary, armory and portable forge. Off to one side were the wagon park and rope corrals for the regiment's horses, which had taken far more shipping space than those who rode them. A crew was working on a disassembled catapult, the sort of light scorpion that galloped along with horse-soldiers.

If you knew horses, which he did, you could tell that the mounts were still very happy to be ashore, though not quite as hysterically glad as they had been yesterday. The campsite a few miles outside Hilo was only gently sloping, but it was thin-soiled and rocky and had been used as cattle-pasture; everything more fertile was densely cultivated with fields and groves of crops he only knew from books, like oranges and limes, or didn't know at all like breadfruit and cassava and taro. The Montivallan expeditionary force was paying the owner generous rental fees, fertilizing his grass, and had paid premium prices in cash for most of his herd except the picked breeding stock to boot.

Several of them were roasting over fires somewhere within smelling distance right now, and the scent of meat basted with barbeque sauce made his mouth water after a long time on ship's biscuit and salt meat and canned goods. Everyone craved greens even more.

As of the morning's roll call, the regiment had had four troops plus the HQ company, with five hundred and ninety-six effectives—one luck-less individual had fallen overboard in the middle of the night four days out from Astoria, unless he'd been carried off by a very large seagoing owl, and six were currently on sick report. Several hundred were on leave with thousands from the other contingents, wandering around Hilo and seeing the sights and just stretching their legs.

The rest were mostly working; grooming the horses, going over their tack, or drilling with weapons and practicing moving mounted in groups to the commands, by word or bugle. The tink-tink of the farrier sounded in the background, the panting wheeze of the bellows, and the screech as someone sharpened a saber on the pedal-powered grindstone.

When the water had cooled a little—and he had too, which made standing up a bit less embarrassing—he dressed in field uniform: riding boots made so they'd be fairly comfortable for work on foot too, baggy linsey-woolsey trousers of light summer weight, pullover short-sleeved shirt of knit linen, and four-pocket uniform jacket. He'd left off the mail shirt and the steel helmet modeled after the one the old American forces had used, but buckled on the belt with bowie knife and curved stirrup-hilted sword as automatically as he put on his hat or boots; he'd have done that at home, too. You didn't go beyond the front verandah unarmed once you were an adult, unless you were of the small minority who lived in big cities. That was true most places he knew about, not just Boise.

At least it's a better uniform than one with crimson tights, he thought, then wondered for an instant *why* he'd had the thought before it slipped away.

The only people he knew who did wear crimson tights were from the Portland Protective Association, and they didn't do it in the field, just when they were peacocking around their castles and manors and at court.

"I'm going to practice a little more, sergeant," Alan said.

The sergeant's eyebrows quirked. "That crazy Mackenzie dancing?" he said. "And you'll wear a *kilt?*"

"I wouldn't want to look clumsy," Alan said; the clansman's costume was bundled up in his tent on top of his footlocker, and fortunately there were a couple of men in the Crown Princess' train who were close enough to his size. "But if I do, I'll cut my foot in half without making all Boise look bad in front of foreigners. Remember, that dance is done over naked steel, sergeant."

He looked up at the sun; a little past noon. "I've got some time. Her Highness ought to be coming ashore about now anyway."

CHAPTER TWO

The Hawaiian commander made a sweeping gesture of respect and greeting as Órlaith stepped onto the barge and barked an order as the last of her entourage came aboard. The boat hooks that two men had hooked in the gangway were released, the long oars pushed the craft away from the great warship's side, and they bent to row in trained unison.

He called out:

"I ku mau mau!"

The Sword gave her command of all tongues as she needed it, a skill most useful to monarchs. Words and the intricacies of their patterns poured into her mind. That meant:

"Stand together!"

The crew replied in a roar as they poised their oars: *"I ku wa!"*

Stand and shout, with action suited to the words.

The leader cried out again:

"I ku mau mau—

I ku huluhulu—

I ka lanawao—"

She knew: *Stand together—haul with mighty strength—under the great trees!*

The barge surged under her feet as the oars bit, but the acceleration was smooth and even, the work of hands that knew their task intimately. Admiral Naysmith would be coming ashore later, and so would Edain Aylward Mackenzie, her chief of staff and Bow-Captain of the High King's Archers. Her commander of ground forces Lord Maugis de Grimmond was already there, overseeing the encampments in the places the Hawaiians had staked out and keeping the touchy pride of contingents from all over the High Kingdom's wildly varied member-realms in check.

She was keeping her . . .

Grim, middle-aged and formidable.

. . . military commanders out of the picture right now, for diplomatic reasons, the same ones that meant no complete regiment or battery of field artillery had gone ashore formed and armed, and the broadsides of the frigates were aimed anywhere but at a potential target.

For that they have faces like clenched fists when they're at their jobs. A face like a fist is entirely right and proper, when you need a fist. Which we will, but not here and not now.

It was all a matter of which face you wanted to be seen.

Montival was much, much bigger and much more populous and, when it cared to be, much stronger in arms than Hawai'i. As far as she knew they were stronger than anyone this side of Hinduraj over in the Bay of Bengal, or possibly some of the larger kingdoms among the fragments that made up the wreckage of China, currently occupied fighting one another and Mongol and Tibetan and even Amur-Russian invaders pouring into the shattered chaos of flood and famine that still reigned there.

There was no need to be rude about flaunting the fact. She was here to woo and not threaten; if any intimidation was necessary at all it could be accomplished by inference rather than action. The Hawaiians weren't fools, to need an obvious fact shoved up their noses on the point of a blade.

She wanted Hawai'i as an ally, but "friendly quasi-neutral" allowing her forces to base themselves here would do. Hostility would ruin everything. Not even Montival could fight a war across the Pacific from its own ports.

There was a sufficient entourage with her to keep a minimum of state, a minimum which had the added advantage of not overshadowing Reiko; she'd managed to convince the stewards and house-mistresses at home that she should have only what was called a riding household, one stripped down for war. Sometimes her mother, who was an Associate, forgot to remember that Órlaith wasn't . . . and that North-realm ideas of what was due a person of consequence sometimes grated on other parts of Montival where rank and title didn't count for quite so much and where folk remembered the old wars of her grandparents' day and resented the fact that the Portland Protective Association was the largest single member-realm of the High Kingdom.

Fortunately High Queen Mathilda was also a knight, and had been on the Quest of the Sunrise Lands in her youth and knew in her bones you couldn't always lug crates of cotte-hardies and a twitter of dressers along to make you look like the Princesses of ancient storytellers like Malory or Froissart or Disney.

There were Heuradys and Sir Droyn Jones de Molalla, also a North-realm knight of the Association and also of her personal household, in charge of the dozen men-at-arms from the Protector's Guard; Karl Aylward Mackenzie and a half-score of longbowmen from the Clan Mackenzie *dúthchas*; the young Dúnedain Rangers Faramir and Morfind, who were the son and daughter of her father's twin half-sisters; and Susan Mika of the Lakota *tunwan* and until recently of the Crown Courier Corps. Diarmuid Tennart McClintock was there too, with a like number of his tattooed caterans from the wild hill lands south of Eugene and the valley of the Rogaire, draped in their baggy Great Kilts and assorted ironmongery. All had accompanied her and Reiko on the journey to the Valley of Death.

And they're my sworn followers, not just under my orders by Mother's command as Queen-Regent, she thought.

She loved her mother Mathilda dearly, but they had had their quarrels, and Órlaith would not be High Queen in her own right until she turned twenty-six, which was still several years away. Until then the High Queen-Regent's word was final, which was fair enough. . . .

When she's there to give it. I spent half the last year carefully not being there when someone showed up waving a Crown Writ I knew I didn't want to read, even if it meant hiding in a cave with the bears or lying underwater and breathing through a hollow reed. It's something I should remember when I take the Throne, if I get delusions of omnipotence. As an added boon, they're all about my age, give or take.

Órlaith looked over to the *Arī no Okurimono*, which was her friend Reiko's ship . . . and more importantly in this context, the ship of her friend's other hat: as *Shōhei Tennō*, the Empress of Dai-Nippon, Sovereign Majesty of Victorious Peace. Haring off into the wilderness with a band of young scapegraces to help Reiko recover the Grass-Cutting Sword had been the occasion of one of those quarrels with her mother, and the worst of them.

Not dying, success, not dying, and picking up a few new signatories to the Great Charter of the High Kingdom along the way down in South Westria while not dying counted for much, as did not dying . . . but Mathilda hadn't forgotten that her daughter defied her either, even if she'd avoided violating the letter of the law. Or that her brother Prince John had been along and was still missing.

Da's loss has made her . . . grasp at known things and fear change, Órlaith thought. *Nor can she altogether forget that if the Japanese had quietly sunk in a storm up in the Aleutians or arrived two days earlier and been killed in Westria by the Koreans chasing them before we turned up, Da would still be alive. She doesn't let it affect her actions much, but it's there. I saw Reiko lose her father at the same time as Da, and that . . . makes a difference. And I knew he was fated, had for years. . . . Mother's a Christian and they think differently about things like that.*

Órlaith had given Reiko the ship, which was a three-masted topsail schooner much the same size and armament as the one which had originally borne her from Japan to Montival . . . and her father to his death there, where Órlaith's own sire had died at the hands of the same foe in the same fight. Three Nihonjin warcraft of similar size from the *Dai-Nippon Teikoku Kaigun*—the Imperial Japanese Navy—had joined them here in Hawai'i.

The schooner was the product of a private yard in Newport, and had been built for Feldman & Sons, who were willing to take Órlaith's word that they wouldn't lose by the transaction in the long run. That was why it was called *Gift of the Ally*.

I miss you so, Da. And your advice . . . that too. I knew you were a very wise man, but I'm only realizing how wise now that it's not there for me to lean on. The foe took you from us, and not the least of it that they robbed us of the wisdom of your deep age. The responsibility is something I have to bear now, will I or nill I. Nobody else can do it, so the Powers have decreed, but it's fair frightening.

Reiko's barge was setting off for shore at exactly the same moment, with a united barking scream of:

"*Tennō Heika* banzai! Banzai! *Banzai!*" from the crew of her ship and its consorts.

To the Heavenly Sovereign Majesty, ten thousand years!

Órlaith couldn't give her a ship the size of the *Sea-Leopard*—the Crown Princess wasn't in a position to dispose of a frigate, didn't want to since even mighty Montival couldn't spare them, and the Imperial Japanese Navy couldn't easily spare the massive crew needed for one anyway—but strict formal equality had to be observed.

Not that either of them cared that much personally, though Reiko was more easily shocked by breaches in decorum than she. But the modern Nihonjin were a proud and touchy people, fiercely warlike and suspicious of outsiders, and that pride centered in the person of their *Tennō*. The more so as their country had been hit so hard and fallen so far in the time of the Change, and had had so little contact with outsiders until recently, except their Korean enemies. In Reiko's life, even more than in her own, you were rarely just yourself, personally.

You savor such moments, then put them away and get on with the day's work of being what your people needed you to be.

The pier where they disembarked was solid and built of dark stone.

The barges came in to either side and the crews latched on; Heuradys and Droyn helmed themselves and flicked the visors of their sallets down, going from human beings to metal figures covered from head to toe in smooth curves of shining metal, like the fabled robot-men of the ancients with only the dark cavity of the thin horizontal vision-slit across the visors to mar it.

They went up the stair ahead of her with a rattle and clank of plate and steel sabatons on stone, moving with catlike ease in the war-harness weight of metal and leather and wood. They took stance to either side, sliding their big kite-shields onto their arms and drawing their longswords to lay over their shoulders. Then they stood motionless in a glitter of steel and plumes and colorful heraldry, family arms on their shields quartered with the Royal crest marked by a baton of cadency.

Órlaith followed. Reiko was just stepping onto the stones opposite her, close enough for them to exchange a look—not a smile, their faces both stayed grave, but it was there beneath. She had friends, some close as her heartbeat, but she and the young Nihonjin woman shared things besides the bonds of battle and shared peril, beyond even the pleasures of conversation and simple company. Things that only the heir to a throne that had come to them with the death of their fathers could.

They were equals, in a life where both had known only their sovereign parents on one hand and vassals, however beloved, on the other.

Two of the Nihonjin samurai preceded Reiko, carrying *naginatas* with the shafts tucked under one arm and the blades pointed down; both were in that bright lacquered armor of silk cords and lames of lacquered steel whose blacks and crimsons and yellows looked almost liquid. Grimacing black-and-silver metal masks adorned with fierce horsehair mustaches covered their faces below the broad helmets, and staffs in holders on their backplates held small banners aloft marked in the angular characters of kanji script.

Reiko was in a short dark kimono with a subtle black-on-black pattern, her hair pinned up beneath a woven straw hat shaped like the top of a mushroom, held under her chin by a complex knot of soft silk cords. It and the gray-striped *hakama* that covered her legs and the dark gray *haori* jacket were crisply perfect but gave a note of sober formality to the occasion, along with the five *kamon* that showed the stylized chrysanthemum *mon* of the Yamato dynasty. She moved with a quiet dignity so graceful that it took a moment to realize that she was as tall as most of the Nihonjin men around her, and that the quietness was complicit of a promise of savage speed at need.

Behind her two bannermen carried poles with the white-and-red *Hinomaru* flag of Dai-Nippon—the Rising Sun sigil of the reborn Empire of Great Japan—and the red banner with a sixteen-petal golden chrysanthemum in its center, the personal standard of the *Tennō*. Beside her and a little to the rear was Imperial Guard commander Noboru Egawa, a man in his forties with a brutal-looking scarred thick-featured face and fireplug build and missing left hand. His gray-shot hair was shaven back in a strip across the pate to the complex topknot at the rear, the mark of the warrior caste in Japan once more.

Behind him came a brace of ladies-in-waiting in dark *kuro-tomesode* kimonos embroidered with a pattern of cranes and a double file of more samurai bearing *naginatas* or long asymmetric *higoyumi* bows, their faces bare but as immobile as their brothers' steel masks beneath their helmet-brims.

At the rear was another lady-in-waiting, leading a small child by the hand—in Nihonjin clothing, but with a pale freckled round face and reddish hair, looking around her with solemnity that occasionally broke into the delighted gap-toothed grin of a brave, bright child who loved new sights and had just been presented with an infinity of them. Reiko had rescued her from the lost castle in the Valley of Death when she found the Grasscutter, and it appeared that had been early enough to spare the child lifelong damage from its horrors.

Most of the Japanese carried the two swords thrust through their belt-sashes, long katana and the shorter close-quarter *wakizashi*. In modern times that was the other Nipponese mark of one whose trade was war, rather like a knight's spurs. Egawa's katana was an ancient masterpiece from the smithy of the legendary Masamune, the Honjo sword that they had recovered in the Valley of Death. Reiko had gifted him with it as a mark of great honor. The Grasscutter that was one-third of the ancient Imperial Regalia had been there too, in fragments born within living bodies. Those had been *absorbed* somehow as she fought her way through that place of horrors and the union of them with the *Kotegiri* Masamune blade she used was . . .

The Grasscutter reborn, Órlaith thought with an awe that never faded, looking at the sheath of black lacquer in which golden flecks moved very slowly, with an illusion . . . perhaps an illusion . . . of stars in an endless black depth that you noticed only if you stared.

The gift of the Sun Goddess to Her descendant and chosen daughter.

In Nihon they'd long had a story that the Yamato dynasty were Her descendants. Apparently in a way that mere human minds could not fathom that was *literally* true, not just a metaphor for how the ruler stood for the folk before the Powers that warded land and dwellers, and at times embodied them.

Perhaps I alone of human kind besides Reiko can sense that blade's true might, since I bear its equal. And that gives me new ground to stand on to understand what it is that I bear. This war is not just a contention of kings, or even against the tyranny of evil rulers, though the Goddess knows it is both those. More is at stake, much more.

She and Reiko fell in beside each other, each with their two armsmen ahead and the rest of their retinue behind.

"John?" Reiko said softly.

Órlaith shook her head, her lips thinning as her hand rested on the pommel of the Sword. It linked all of her line, the descendants of her father and mother who'd mingled their blood on its point and driven it into the living rock of Montival at the first King-Making. Unfortunately that usually just gave you flashes, not . . .

Actionable intelligence, she thought, and went on aloud:

"Nothing since we left Astoria. Just that he's alive and in peril, and to the south and west of here," Órlaith said.

She spoke Japanese as they usually did together; Reiko's English was now passable but no more. The sounds were difficult for someone who'd grown up speaking nothing but *Nihongo*.

Reiko sighed slightly, and her steel tessen war-fan made a graceful gesture. The Sword had given Órlaith a native-born speaker's command of her language, and also of those things its speakers did that conveyed meaning without words.

I am so very sorry.

Reiko's face was calm, but her eyes conveyed her trouble; it was sincerely meant, too . . . and with the Sword, Órlaith didn't have to guess at that, as all others did. Her father had warned her that could cut her off from human-kind if she weren't careful, and it had been one reason he didn't carry the Sword unless he must.

"Not your fault," Órlaith said.

Which is . . . true. Yet and perhaps not altogether so.

Reiko hadn't *meant* any harm to Órlaith's brother. She'd met her own brother there on that beach, heir to the Chrysanthemum Throne and long thought dead, revealed as a prisoner and puppet of the enemy. She'd turned the Grasscutter over to him, and when he'd drawn it the gift of the Sun Goddess had burned him to a drift of fine ash in an instant. The Immortal One Shining in Heaven had shown who was truly Her child.

Then Reiko had taken it up and danced by the sea's edge, a dance of anger and summoning . . . and become *one* with her Ancestress for an unimaginable instant as that strong and ancient Power reached from the world beyond the world into the land of common day. Órlaith had used the Sword of the Lady to shield Montival from it, but the grief and burning wrath of *Amaterasu-ōmikami* had fallen on the sea with a terrifying might, like an avalanche falling down from forever.

"Yet I unleashed the forces which drove his ship so far from your shore," Reiko said.

Órlaith's eyes flicked to the Grasscutter.

No, she thought, her mind turning to its older, original name. *That's*

Ama-no-Murakumo-no-Tsurugi, the Sword of the Gathering Clouds of Heaven. The blade that commands the spirits of fire, of sky and storm and air, when the Tennō wields it and the folk of Nihon are threatened.

"You did what you must," Órlaith said. "The enemy were strong and had fell powers of their own to command, and the outcome of the battle was uncertain. Many who walk the ridge of Earth today would lie stark if you had not. John *and* myself, it might be, and you, and all the hopes of our peoples with us."

But I miss you, Johnnie, and I fear for you.

She couldn't let worry for him consume her day-to-day; that would be as much a breach of duty as running away in battle. She needed her unhindered wits about her, and that required a balance in the soul, not grieving memories of toddler-John stumping around chortling or crying over a broken toy or even being an annoying broody spotty-faced brat at thirteen, convinced he was a musical genius and that nobody understood him and (to his credit) wondering whether girls really liked him or just his rank.

But sometimes the fear and sorrow returned, strong and harsh.

How do you fare today, my little brother?

CHAPTER THREE

"Where *is* he?"

Lady Philippa Balwyn-Abercrombie—Pip or Cap'n Pip to everyone here—kept the panic out of her voice with an effort of will that felt as if she was squeezing her own throat shut with both hands. Running around screeching would *not* help. Then she stood back and let the professionals dig for a moment. And Evrouin, John's valet-bodyguard, who kept at it grimly, using his glaive as a lever to get debris out of the way.

She was sweating in rivulets with the usual damp heat of Baru Denpasar added to tons of flaming hardwoods ignited by napalm shells, the salt stinging savagely in her cuts and scrapes and scorches and plastering strands of her tawny hair to her face and neck, turning her white shirt and shorts black as her boots and suspenders and steel-lined bowler hat and streaking the tawny light-gold tan of her naturally fair skin. Smoke made her cough, and turned the spittle black when she spat aside. Pip sucked eagerly at the canteen her second-in-command Toa handed her, the two-liter bottle looking tiny in the big Maori's huge, tattooed brown hand, and wiped at the black mascara running down from the circle drawn around one eye.

The burning central tower of the Carcosan fortress had collapsed in the moment of victory . . . but John couldn't be just gone. Even if he'd been crushed and burned, a big young man in full plate armor couldn't just disappear. . . .

Could he? The things I've seen since I got here . . .

Other bodies had been there, dead or wounded, and more over the rampart where the Baru Denpasaran forces had stormed the wall, and more still in the open ground below where catapults and arrows and then spear and parang had done their work. Enough to hide the ground in places for a dozen yards at a time. Stretcher-parties from the victors were bearing their wounded back to the field hospitals in the siege camp, while others gave the mercy-stroke to the enemy hurt.

Neither side in this war took prisoners; not for any good purpose, at least.

There was a thick stink lying over the whole bowl made by the earthwork walls of the Carcosan fort, of the bad-cooking smell of burning and burnt human flesh from the tower and a chemical taint from the rain of napalm that had set it alight, the coppery salt of blood like the time she'd visited the municipal slaughterhouse outside Townsville. And the shit stink from the thousands of bodies slashed open in the fight or smashed open by catapult bolts and prang-prang darts and great burning net bags of cantaloupe-sized rocks from the trebuchets that had burst in mid-air and come down like endless lethal hail on the heads of the enemy formations massing to resist the attack.

And already a hint of corruption, the rot so quick in this hot jungle valley far from the sea-breezes, and a buzzing of innumerable flies.

The humid, hazy air overhead was filling with red-winged, white-breasted kites and crows and birds of prey not too proud for pre-killed food, though they were going to be frustrated as the Baru Denpasarans were digging mass graves with their usual beaver-like energy. She wasn't squeamish by nature and she'd been in fights before. But that had been mostly at sea where the clean ocean swallowed the results, and never on anything like this scale. Fortunately, she couldn't take the time to pay attention to the full apocalyptic horror of it.

Prince John had not only been beneath the fragments of the tower when it fell. He'd *vanished*.

I've got to stop thinking that. It's getting repetitious and it doesn't do a bloody thing.

The pain of her own numerous but minor hurts was utterly distant. Pip felt her mind gibbering in shock, which was a rare experience for her so far in her twenty years on earth. Absolute self-confidence was her inheritance on both sides. From her mother's distinguished, if also severely raffish and dodgy, English aristocratic blood; Mummy had been in Australia eluding the bailiffs because her father had gotten caught in some roguery or other shortly before the Blackout hit. And Pip's own father was heir to the Colonelcy of Townsville, a King in all but name—and there were rumors he was planning to correct the name when her granddad finally released his iron grip on life and her father took over.

She knew he'd had a crown designed and kept it in a safe and took it out and looked at it sometimes when he thought nobody was watching. That would have bothered her much less if she thought *he* thought she was capable of holding it on her own without some prestigious man about the place. Despite the fact that she seemed to have stumbled upon a very prestigious young man indeed . . .

Two thoughts went through her mind:

This is hitting me so hard because I'm more in love with Johnnie than I thought.

She'd known she was falling for him as well as being instantly and seriously in lust, but she'd never thought of herself as a sentimental woman . . . even when she'd still been a girl. Mummy hadn't encouraged it, and she had been about as sentimental as a cat herself. Granted that John was tall and handsome and had big soulful brown eyes and nice hair and plenty of musical talent and a nicely off-beat sense of humor and was *not boring* and was inventively unselfish in bed . . .

Deep beneath that, in anger and rage and unacknowledged fear:

Bugger this sodding nightmare of an island! I can't say I wish I never came here, but it's close. Maybe England wouldn't have been that bad—it was the family home from 1066 on and all that.

She'd left her family's country estate . . . run away from Tanumgera Station in the dead of night with half a dozen of her father's best racing camels and her late mother's old retainer Toa and sundry other knick-knacks including but not limited to her adventurer mother's prized pair of kukri-knives . . . because her father was bound and determined to send her off to Court in Winchester, on the other side of the world in the capital of the Empire of Greater Britain to acquire some minor Windsor royal for stud purposes. The knickknacks had been fair and just recom-pense for . . .

Daddy being such a fussbudget about winding up Mummy's will early, as if twelve months on a calendar made a real difference when I'm obviously an adult now and should have the trust funds and the Darwin and East Indies Company stock.

She'd gotten possession of the neat little armed schooner *Silver Surfer* in Darwin with some of those knickknacks, which had included the mod-els and plans for rapid-fire Townsville Armory catapults that King Birmo of Capricornia had been very very tangibly and materially pleased to get. Plus a bit . . .

Just a teensy bit . . .

. . . of sort-of-nepotism from her mother's old and now rich and re-spectable (or as respectable as anyone got in freewheeling Darwin) partners-in-crime from her days as a seagoing not-so-quasi buccaneer, salvager (royally licensed), explorer and trader-at-catapult-point. Uncle Pete and Aunt Fifi were always ready to help, and she suspected it was as much the fact that she reminded them of their younger selves as her mother's memory.

And she'd gained the respect of the crew she'd recruited from the dockside dives by her own efforts, by showing she could do the job. *And by personally and very publically whaling the stuffing out of a few con-venient fools who thought they could treat the rich girl as a joke.* Then it had been off to the romantic wilds of the Ceram Sea, to make a killing in quasi-legal high-risk and high-return frontier trade and do something *herself*, with the pitch of her own quarterdeck under her feet to fulfill a thousand childhood dreams born of her mother's stories. And Aunt Fifi and Uncle Pete's even more lurid versions, since they'd never been constrained by English understatement . . . and they'd probably been more accurate, too.

So that Daddy would have to take me back on my terms, if I wanted to go back to Townsville at all. It is a stuffy sort of place.

Such a promising start, before they'd been trapped here on Baru Denpasar until the *Tarshish Queen* sailed in with John aboard . . .

Bugger that. And bugger losing John! If he was dead, that would be one thing, but he's not. I just got him and I'm not giving him up, not even to the refugees from a bloody bad horror novel running that pink-coral abomination they call Carcosa!

She forced herself back to her feet as the rest of the Montivallans came up. Even if you were young and very fit, a day like this made you feel like a grandmother. The two she was interested in were nearby anyway, and had been dodging the chunks of falling tower along with the rest of them. Deor Godulfson was staring, his gray eyes looking . . . as if he was seeing things that might not be there.

And perhaps he is.

The wiry black-haired bard was wearing a blood-splashed mail shirt and carrying a red-dripping broadsword, but his primary occupation was what his eccentric little homeland in what had been called California called being a *scop*, musician and minstrel. She'd heard him perform fluently in any number of styles including ones she'd never heard of. He was very very good—as good as John but with a great deal more experience and single-mindedness. Among his people that also meant being some sort of medicine man, evidently; they took the *Magic of Art* thing rather seriously.

His companion—they were the same age and sort of platonic life-partners and had been since their teens apparently, since she liked men and so did he—was Thora Garwood. *She* was a rangy handsome red-haired woman in her early thirties in a suit of plate armor subtly different from what John had been wearing, one with a face-on snarling bear's head in dark reddish brown on the breastplate. She was also absently cleaning her long single-edged, basket-hilted sword with a cloth; fighting was *her* specialty, and she was terrifyingly good at it.

Fortunately she hadn't wanted to fight over John and they'd come to a mostly-unspoken understanding, though Pip still walked warily around her. In Pip's already fairly wide experience absolutely nobody *liked* you for stealing their boyfriend, even if they'd been planning on parting ways soon.

Deor frowned. "Why haven't you taken Prince John up?" he said. "He's injured!"

"Because we can't bloody find him!" Pip snapped. "Can you?"

"But—"

She'd meant the question rhetorically and sarcastically, yet Deor was staring at a spot where two of the huge smoldering timbers lay crossed, leaving a space between them. The clutch of armored Montivallan crossbowmen—from something called the Protector's Guard back in their home—had already been through there with fanatical thoroughness, and were spreading out around into less and less likely spots, while their commander Sergeant Fayard sat with his splinted leg outstretched cursing them on and cursing the local doctor who was finishing up on it.

"Oath-sister?" Deor said, in that rhythmic accent that made everyday speech sound a little like chanted poetry.

"I can't see a thing," Thora said, sheathing her sword. "But you can?"

He caught her right hand in his and—

"There—" he dropped to one knee, fumbled at something on the ground.

No, above it, as if someone was lying there, Pip thought with a chill mix of terror and hope.

She felt her vision blur as she glimpsed a ghostly shape beneath his hands. A helm came suddenly into focus as he eased it upward and tossed it aside, a flare-necked Montivallan visored sallet with the stubs of ostrich plumes still in the holders at either side that she recognized instantly. It was chrome steel and had been burnished like a mirror only a few hours ago . . . and had been on John's head as they went up the scaling ladder. An instant later his four-foot kite-shaped shield was there too, lying as if it had been lying across his . . .

That's John! He's curled up under his shield!

Chills ran up her spine despite the damp heat and the sticky sweat that never dried here.

Something's making me not see him. Bloody hell. It's adventure if you're reading about it back in Townsville. Here it's . . . bloody hell.

Carcosa's evil name wasn't just because they and Baru Denpasar fought over this island. The Balinese conquerors who'd founded Baru Denpasar in the first year after the Blackout had been desperate and ruthless themselves and like so many others they'd been self-exiled and looking for a new home to feed their families. The passengers and crew of the sail-powered cruise ship turned corsair vessel *South Sea Adventure* had been perfectly ready to help them fall on the locals here with fire and slaughter and take some of the spoils in return, rather than face a voyage back across the Pacific to a homeland in even worse condition because it had more big cities and fewer peasants who knew how to grow food without machines.

With infinite local variations, things like that had happened all over the world in those years of chaos and blood, as nations died and new ones rose from the ruins and adventurers carved themselves kingdoms at the sword's edge. The consequences were still echoing down the generations.

What had happened when the captain of the *Adventure* stumbled across . . . something . . . in the interior years later had been very different, by all accounts. He'd come back to his little pirate sub-kingdom as something very much *other*, and soon his followers were too. The Baru Denpasarans were much more numerous, but that . . . otherness . . . had more than compensated.

Back in Oz this sort of thing was rumors, mysterious happenings in mysterious places, people in the far Outback wandering into the Dreamtime, or exotic islands or some underground temple or the usual unverifiable miracles people had always talked about. I had to go and find out for myself, didn't I just!

They called the former Captain the *Yellow Raja* now, from the color of the rags that always encased him in public. Nobody saw his face, or had for decades, if it was the same man . . . or, according to some speculations, if he still *had* a face. His chief henchman was called the Pallid Mask, from what *he* wore. They'd renamed their ship the *Hastur* and their stronghold as *Carcosa*. Things had gotten worse from there.

Deor eased back on his heels, stripped off the glove from his left hand and held it, palm down, a foot or so above the ground, then began to move it back and forth. As he shaped John's invisible form, it began to solidify. Deor grasped Thora's hand, pressed it downward.

"His skin is clammy," she murmured, experienced fingers searching for wounds with her eyes slitted, almost closed. "But the pulse is there."

"Bloody hell!" exclaimed Pip, crouching opposite him. "When you touch him, I can see, but before . . . I saw rubble, and my eyes . . . just slid away. I can feel them *trying* to slide away now. It's as if someone was saying *nothing here, don't look* at the back of my mind."

"A seeming, and a wicked one," Deor said, sliding back into a sitting position and cradling his head in his hands. "Wicked and strong. Woden, lend me wisdom!"

Pip set her hands on either side of John's face, smoothed back the sweat-soaked hair.

"He's solid enough, but so cold!" Her fingers went to the throat under the jaw. "And his pulse is steady, but slow."

"He's not bleeding that I can tell," murmured Thora. "Maybe a blow to the head?"

The sallet helm bore several dents and dings that had not been there before.

"A coma?" Thora went on. "I've seen them, from head injuries."

"He breathes, but he doesn't feel unconscious," said Pip. "Even when he's asleep, you can feel that he's *there.*"

For a moment the two women's eyes met, and Pip felt the sudden vibration of shared awareness between them.

Thora was frowning. "Is the armor shielding . . ."

"No," said Deor. "You know how a dead body feels—an empty sack of meat in the shape of a man. This is something like that, not quite as bad, but nearly. John's body is breathing, but—"

Deor put his hand to John's forehead again: "His spirit is not there, the thing that makes us what we are. Not asleep, not even the deep sleep that comes of a blow on the head. It's *gone*, gone elsewhere. There's a link, but it's faint. And—"

He jerked the hand back and seemed to slump, taking a shuddering breath.

"—and it has gone to no good place. We may have his body, but the enemy has still taken him prisoner. This is less of a victory than we thought."

Thora took a deep breath of her own and got to her feet, looking around her.

"Well, wherever his soul is wandering, we need to get his body out of here."

Evrouin's swarthy face had gone grayish-pale as he stared at the Prince's suddenly visible body and murmured a Latin prayer; then he crossed himself, shook his shoulders like a dog coming out of the water, and helped them strip off John's armor and clothing. In the background Fayard was yelling at his crossbowmen, who scrambled back to glare in bewilderment at the man lying where they knew nobody was, then faced outward in a defensive circle. Most of them crossed themselves first, amid a mutter of Catholic prayers in Latin—she was Anglican Rite herself, and used to hearing them in her own language.

Pip knelt beside the fallen man and as Deor held his head slowly, carefully dribbled a little water into his mouth; you had to be very cautious getting someone to drink when they were unconscious because it was so easy to get water into the lungs.

"You've found him!" said a lilting voice full of relief. Then sharply: "Don't move him! Let me past!"

That was young Ruan Chu Mackenzie, one of John's Montivallans from the *Tarshish Queen*—hence the joy—and Deor Godulfson's boyfriend.

He wore a kilt, had an accent that was almost a parody of Irish speech, and altogether seemed implausibly Celtic for someone from what had once been the United States and who obviously had at least one Chinese grandparent judging by his looks and the Chu part of his name. But Pip knew odder things had happened since the Blackout—what they called the Change where he came from.

More important, he'd been trained as a medic, what his people called a healer, as well as an archer. He unslung the baldric that held his yew longbow and quiver and set them aside as he knelt at John's side and gave him a quick, competent once-over that included taking his blood-pressure with a little kit from his haversack.

That made Pip reassuringly confident of John's physical *presence* again. He was her own age, just twenty, broad-shouldered and long-limbed, four or five inches taller than her five-six, with brown hair and green-brown hazel eyes that showed as Ruan's thumb pushed back an eyelid. His pleasantly smooth features were just losing the last of the adolescent puppy fat.

But she was also acutely aware of how the *personhood* was gone, that lively sense of humor and the ear for music and the ability to see the absurd that had delighted her and were somehow there *in potentia* even when he slept. Now even their shadows were gone from his face, and he hadn't had enough years to groove them into skin and flesh.

"Nothing! Pulse slow but normal, and the pupils contract, and that evenly. Sure, and it can't be a concussion," Ruan said. "His skull is sound as a bell, see?"

"You're right," Deor said.

"And head wounds *bleed*," Ruan added.

They all nodded without thinking, having plenty of experience. They did, like bastards, even if they weren't serious at all. The skin under the scalp was full of blood vessels, and even without a cutting edge they broke easily if a blow hammered skin against bone.

"I can't feel any place where the bone's depressed, either, and it's not spinal damage," Ruan said. "It's not a healer of bodies he needs, but a *bhuid-seach.*"

Seeing Pip and Toa uncomprehending, he translated: "*Bhuidseach.* Spell-wreaker, one who walks with the Powers. Like Deor. This thing with the Prince is ill-wreaking, not the natural course of things on the ridge of the world as wounds and illness are, but a bending of the shape of things. Sent of a living will to harm."

Toa grunted thoughtfully; Pip swallowed. Her Uncle Pete had been fond of pre-Blackout adventure stories of a type she privately called *Men with Swords and Things with Tentacles* after something her mother had said. She'd read a few from his collection herself on visits to Darwin and found them amusing, though often wrong about how swords were actually used.

She sincerely *hoped* they were as wrong about the Things and their appendages, but you could never tell.

Then Ruan grabbed a pair of passing stretcher-bearers. They came willingly enough, since the foreign allies were popular. The whole Baru Denpasaran army knew that it was the catapults of the *Tarshish Queen* and the rapid-fire prang-prangs from the *Silver Surfer* and the knowledge of siegecraft that came with both that had made it possible for them to take this fort without crippling losses. And the fort squatted on the main water channels to the rice paddies of the western half of the island. It had been a hand around their throats.

In the final assault, besides their Raja Dalem Seganing's name, as a battle cry the locals had shouted: *For the food our children eat!* as they charged home through the killing ground and over the ramparts in an unstoppable wave of desperate and merciless ferocity.

The agile and nearly-naked Baru Denpasarans with the stretcher negotiated the tumbled remains at the top of the fort's outer wall nimbly, amid the shattered smoking timbers of the palisade and the churned-up earth. Then they brought their load down one of the heavy metal-shod siege ladders that had been flung up against the sloping surface of the earthwork, adroitly enough that the unconscious man's body would have stayed on it even without the straps across chest and thighs. The surface was firm beneath their feet, since spade-like shoes on the bottom and long curved crowbeak spikes at the top nailed it to the surface of the earthwork where they'd first been flung against it.

"And *you*—" Thora gripped Deor's arm and hauled him upright to help him along. "You aren't much better."

Deor shook his head. "Wherever the Prince went, it . . . draws. Draws strongly."

"Drink this!"

She handed him her canteen of sweet tea and he gulped at it, coughed, drank again. Pip took something from Toa and nearly choked as it turned out to be a flask of *arrak* this time rather than water, distilled from the sap of borassus-palm flowers. Aged in halmilla-wood casks for years it could develop subtle flavors; Uncle Pete and Aunt Fifi's Darwin and East Indies Trading Company had a warehouse full of it that they called Mendis Brandy and shipped all over Oz with profit for them and delight for the purchasers.

Nobody had bothered with aging this very recent batch of the local white lightning, and it was ninety proof. It didn't taste of anything in particular except vaguely turpentinish and it hit her empty stomach like a napalm shell, and went from there out through her veins. For a moment she could feel those veins, as if her body were outlined in a threadwork of fire.

"Did I ever tell you how I met your mum?" Toa rumbled quietly under the cover of her coughs. "And Pete and Fifi?"

"Not the details," Pip said.

She knew it had been on the North Island of New Zealand, on a salvage trip to the ruins of Auckland in one of the last runs the three of them had made together on the old *Diamantina*. After that the Darwin and East Indies Trading Company had become a major player and they'd been reduced, against their wills, to mostly directing other people's voyages.

The South Island of New Zealand had come through the Blackout years rather well, being mostly rural and not having any cities bigger than modestly-sized Christchurch. The northern half of the island nation had held Auckland, the biggest city, on the northernmost peninsula and the old capital of Wellington at the southern end. Between them they'd taken down most of the rest, and grim things had happened there until the southerners finally got around to taking the place in hand and resettling it. Not as bad as around, say, Sydney—not nearly as bad as near London or Tokyo—but bad enough to finish off most of the people near the cities or the roads between them, and if you died the disaster was personally fairly total.

She took another swallow, a modest nip this time, and handed it back. The Maori tilted it back and let his Adam's apple flutter before he screwed the cap back on and tucked it into the pouch on the elaborate woven belt-and-loincloth arrangement that was all he wore besides a cloak of feathers on a linen backing. He had the mass to soak it up easily, being six-foot-six, a brown block of three hundred pounds of solid muscle covered in writhing tattoos from head to foot, interrupted by plentiful dusty-white scars, his stiff graying black hair drawn back in a bun through a carved bone ring at the back of his head.

His gargoyle face frowned and he used the heavy Macassar-ebony shaft of his eight-foot spear like a walking staff as they followed the stretcher-bearers; the long palm-broad steel head had already been scrubbed clean and tended with file and hone. Toa was fairly casual about most things; *she'll be right* was a saying he'd taken to heart. But weapons and gear weren't among them and he could move with a speed and grace astonishing in so huge a man.

"Well, let's just say your mum and Pete and Fifi didn't just save me life. There was something like this—"

He nodded forward at where Prince John's form was being manhandled down the slope.

"—that was part of it. Proper mess, and I don't remember all the details . . . never did. But enough, enough. That's why I never wanted to head back to ol' NZ. Well, that and those bleedin' Pākehā from Christchurch running all over it trying to *civilize* us years and years after we could have used some real help. Civilize us *again*."

Below, John's soldiers—the dozen crossbowmen of the Protector's

Guard in their battered half-armor—were forming up around the stretcher, their faces anxious under a stiff discipline. As Pip understood it, John stood to inherit the position of Lord Protector of the PPA through his mother, while his eldest sister Órlaith took the Throne of the High King- dom as a whole; and they were specifically *his* guards, part of an elite unit with all the usual sworn-to-the-death oaths and so forth.

"Let's get him back to town," Pip said. "And then we'll see what Deor can do. I'm not letting this one go, Toa, old boy, not if I have to sacrifice goats to the Great JuJu and dance naked by the light of the New Moon to get him back I'm not."

"Too right," he grunted. "Want to see you settled for your mum's sake, promised her and all."

More softly: "And . . . straight-up, because I wouldn't leave a bloody crocodile in the sort of place I think he may be stuck."

"Hail!" Deor Godulfson cried. "Hail, Moishe! Over here!"

Moishe Feldman greeted them not far from the gates of the city of Baru Denpasar, almost unnoticed in the roaring crush of celebration as flowers flew in multicolored rain from either side onto the—now stalled—column of victorious troops, less the militiamen who'd peeled off to their villages on the way back. His left arm was still in a sling; he'd taken the wound in the sea-fight when the *Tarshish Queen* arrived in the harbor nearly sinking, and the Carcosans swarmed out to attack her.

Deor gripped his good hand wrist-to-wrist, glad to see that the olive-tanned face looked better than when they'd departed even if there was a sprinkling of new white hairs in the man's close-cropped black beard. An arrow through the arm was no joke, even if it didn't hit anything that wouldn't heal eventually.

"Good to see you, old friend," he said.

"And you and Thora, safe back from battle. *Barukh ata Adonai Eloheinu, melekh ha'olam, hagomel lahayavim tovot, sheg'molani kol tov.*"

They'd known each other off and on for more than half their lives, since Feldman's father's ship had found shelter in Albion Cove, the fishing village on the coast of the Barony of Mist Hills; shelter from a storm and from a three-thousand-mile running fight with a brace of Suluk corsairs who'd jumped the *Ark* off Hawai'i, the first outsiders to visit since the Change.

"The ship's sound as new," the Corvallan merchant said.

He meant that literally and knowledgeably; his firm sailed out of Newport, Corvallis' window on the Pacific, and his family had hands-on investments in the shipyards there. He'd seen the *Tarshish Queen* grow from builder's plans and fresh timber.

"Provided we can get our catapults back and keep the . . . steel ship . . . off somehow, we can head home," he added.

The quick dark eyes grew thoughtful as Deor told him what happened, and the more so as he came to the two-wheeled carts that held John and their other wounded.

"I can't help you with this," Feldman said.

Deor nodded; the Law by which his friend's people lived forbade them certain arts and knowledge; anything that smacked of *seidh*.

"What I *can* do is tie up the Raja's people in negotiations," he said briskly. "We need to keep this very quiet until the Prince is . . . better."

"Too right," Toa rumbled. "They think anyone who gets the Evil Eye put on 'em by you-know-who may be working for them on the quiet afterwards and the only sure way around it is to scrag 'em. Pip and I trust you can do the needful for Prince Johnnie, mate, but they wouldn't."

Pip nodded vigorously. "My ship?" she said.

"Ready to go," Feldman said. "Down to fresh sails and cables in the lockers; and the Raja loaded that cargo he promised you—and my goodness but it's tasty. My First Mate saw to it with your helmsman and had her towed to a berth next to ours."

Pip nodded, which didn't surprise Deor at all. First Mate Radavindraban of the *Tarshish Queen* was very competent.

"Your quartermaster Kombagle knows everything there was to be known about stowing a hold properly," Feldman said. "Even if he looks a bit . . . alarming."

Pip snorted. "You mean the *asgras* and boar's-tusk through the nose?"

Deor frowned. "Isn't that the way his people dress?"

"More of a caricature of a Papuan warrior," Pip said.

"By way of a statement, you could say," Toa rumbled. "You can square ol' Dalem S?"

"For a monarch, the Raja is . . . relatively honest."

"Do you think you can keep him from getting too inquisitive, Moishe?" she said.

"The Lord willing and nothing too drastic happens over . . ."

His head went eastward though you couldn't see Carcosa's ramparts from here.

". . . there."

Then he patted the well-worn hilt of the cutlass where it hung by the side of his brass-buttoned blue coat.

"I've dealt with pirates and with kings, I think I can keep him talking, and he's not barefaced enough to steal our catapults after we just won the battle he hired them for. Just . . . get *this* finished as fast as you can."

He looked down on John's motionless face, put a hand to his own forehead, and recited softly:

"*Mi Shebeirach avoteinu v'imoteinu, Avraham, Yitzchak v'Yaakov, Sarah, Rivkah, Rachel v'Lei-ah, hu y'vareich et hacholim John Arminger Mackenzie. Amen.*"

The folk of Baru Denpasar lined the road to both sides, and Raja Dalem Seganing's elephant glittered in its coat of jeweled mail, turning to a blaze in the sunlight on the carved gilding of the howdah. There were elephants in the expeditionary force's train too, but they were at the rear . . . probably because *Tuan* Anak Agung, the commander of the little army, had origi- nally been accompanied by what the locals called *Pedanda*, a High Priest and Priestess of their people's Hindu faith. They'd ridden on one of the elephants . . . and they'd been killed by Iban mercenaries working for the enemy in a night raid.

And I think that may have been to clear the decks for this . . . abduction of Prince John, Deor thought.

Deor also thought that Anak was a competent man of war, but that he was very, very worried about how his ruler would balance the loss of his holy man against the admittedly crucial victory.

The *Tuan* dismounted from his horse and knelt in the dust of the road, bowing his head before the elephant and the figure in the howdah and holding his ivory-hilted parang-sword across the palms of his hands. The elephant trumpeted again, and the mahout tapped it with the goad. It sank down into a kneeling position—rather imposing since the beast was of an African breed and twelve feet at the shoulder—and Raja Dalem walked down a sort of extensible ladder-stair that let down from it.

"Courtesy of Uncle Pete and Aunt Fifi and Mum," Pip whispered. "They shipped the elephants of Oz—feral zoo stock. Twice."

Deor nodded, knowing the story. That had been necessary because the original shipment to Bali had mysteriously disappeared . . . courtesy of the *South Sea Adventure*, back when its owners had still been fully human and merely piratical.

The Raja was a slight-built man in his sixties, but the human being nearly disappeared behind a towering crown of gold fretwork and golden leaves, a jacket of black silk riotously embroidered in threads of precious metal and jewels, gold-and-emerald earrings, and a sarong of shimmering batik. Guardsmen only slightly less gorgeous shaped up around him; *Tuan* Anak looked dusty and plain beside them.

The Raja took the parang from Anak's hands, and the crowd's noise died away in a ripple as those who could see passed on the news, as if they were holding their collective breaths. Then he reached behind him and took another weapon, similar but with a blade of watermarked steel and a hilt fancy even by the standards of what he was wearing, and presented it to the warrior.

The crowd's roar rose again, louder than ever, and *Tuan* Anak rose and bowed deeply as he tucked the mark of favor into his sash.

Kings will forgive a good deal, for victory, Deor thought.

"And that's my cue," Feldman said. "I'll handle the Raja. Now get him to the villa and get him back for us!"

CHAPTER FOUR

D eor sighed, looking down at the body on the snowy cotton sheeting of the carved teakwood bed, stripped and washed and dressed in a light cotton robe.

"Not injured at all," Pip muttered. "But . . ."

No one was counting the chafing and scrapes and bruises that mottled the fair skin. That was just the cost of doing business when you fought in full plate, and better than the alternative.

They'd politely rejected the offer of Raja Dalem Seganing's personal physician; luckily victory had the Baru Denpasaran court preoccupied enough that they weren't suspicious and Feldman had stepped in smoothly. Even giving the servants here leave to go join their families for the ceremonies of thanks and the riotous celebrations you could just hear in the distance over the whisper of the palms shouldn't arouse too much comment. The folk of Baru Denpasar hadn't seen any outsiders save enemies in two generations now; few remembered the world before the Change. Perhaps the foreigners were kind, perhaps too grief-stricken that their Prince was badly injured, perhaps both and who could say?

Toa had grunted satisfaction at that. "Better if we're sodding careful about who we let see him."

He jerked a thumb over his shoulder in the direction of Carcosa.

"I wasn't having you on when I said *Scrag 'em and let the Gods sort 'em out* is their motto. If they realize he's not just had a thump on the noggin we've got problems, gratitude or no gratitude."

Deor nodded. "Not to mention that Timorese sailor you mentioned, the one they found drifting and mad after his ship tried to escape from here."

Pip and Toa nodded, both looking uneasy to a degree that was alarming in a pair so fearless. According to them, the man had been strangled in his sleep . . . either by his own hands . . .

. . . or possibly by his own shadow.

Fortunately Prince John had been given the use of a villa of the Raja's outside the palace compound, one built before the Change with its own gardens and stretch of beach, blinding white sand where the waves broke in blue and foam. That made it less desirable to the local folk if anything; they'd brought from Bali itself—which he and Thora had visited—the conviction that *kelod*, evil and chaos, came from the sea while virtue and right order ran down from the mountains.

Evrouin rose from John's bedside, tight-held frustration on his olive-skinned face.

"I'll go check on Sergeant Fayard and the guard detail, then, my lords, my ladies," he said unhappily.

Fayard commanded the detachment of the Protector's that had followed Prince John to the *Tarshish Queen*. After the battle at the Carcosan fort he'd be doing his commanding on crutches for a while, but only one of his men was too badly hurt to walk. Deor thought they were all happier to be serving their Prince outside this room, being Associates and strong Catholics to a man and uneasy with . . .

What they know I must do, he thought. At least that I must call on Powers their faith forbids.

John was Catholic too, of course, but he was of House Artos and . . . broad-minded. Deor and Thora were both heathen and offered to the northern Gods, though they called them by slightly different names.

Deor's folk in Mist Hills used the Saxon names, Woden and Thunor; the heathen half of Thora's Bearkiller kindred used the Norski ones and called their faith *Asatru*. And while Thora gave Them due honor and the seemly offerings and paid respect to the land-wights wherever she dwelled—she'd had the Hammer on a thong around her neck since he'd first met her—she was content to leave it at that.

Deor was Woden's man and had been since childhood. The All-Father gave battle-fury and victory to His chosen warriors, but He also sent the mead of poetry to inspire men . . . and to some, the knowledge of *seidh*, the workings of things beyond common ken. After all, had He not given His eye for wisdom?

The villa was private enough, brightly open, cool with the sea-breezes and comfortable, though odd to Montivallan eyes since it was more a matter of pillars of coral limestone than of solid enclosing walls, columns holding up a high steep roof of shining black-streaked borassus timbers covered in neat palm-thatch. Inside the rooms were partitioned with bamboo, and the floors were smooth cool cream-colored marble over the concrete slab foundation.

"We don't have all that much time," Thora said. "They'll suspect, if we wait too long."

"And Johnnie can't eat solid food," Pip said.

You could see the slight shadow of wasting on him already. They'd all had bowls of rice and spiced fish; the body and the spirit strengthened one another.

"He's not getting enough fluids, either," Ruan said. "I may have to intubate him. But that's risky in itself. Infection . . ."

Prince John had not regained consciousness during the long days of the journey, though there had been times when he stirred and moaned as though his spirit were still fighting somewhere far away. The rest of the time that sense of absence was, if possible, even more apparent, if one could say that of a negative, although his body had stayed visible, perhaps because Pip had never let go of his hand if she could help it.

"But there has to be *something* we can do!" Pip exclaimed.

A knock at the door showed Captain Ishikawa. The Nihonjin sailor had shepherded the catapults back and was overseeing their repair in the Raja's machine shops and remounting on the ships.

"Is there anything I can do?" he asked quietly.

Pip started to shake her head angrily, then snapped her fingers. "Ishikawa-san, I think there is. You can go to the machine shop and stage another fight with the Raja's chief engineer."

The local engineer did not like foreigners in general, or ones from Nihon in particular; there were memories of great war of the last century current here, even after a full hundred years. The hand of Dai-Nippon had rested on these islands then, and not lightly.

He was startled into a grin. "Ah so *desu*! You seek a distraction! That will be easy!"

The bow he gave her was both courtesy and a genuine gesture of respect. She returned it, then sprang up and paced, her vital energy in almost shocking contrast to the absolute immobility of the man on the bed, who made no movement but the slight rise and fall of his chest.

"Well, if his spirit isn't here, we'll just have to seek him elsewhere," Thora replied.

"I know." Deor felt his flesh pebble despite the heat. "Watch my back."

"Always . . ." she said. Then briskly to Evrouin: "We need you to keep everyone local out of here."

The valet-bodyguard nodded. "I'll see to it, my lady, my lords."

Thora added: "But it has to be done quietly. We don't want them wondering why, either. Moishe . . . Captain Feldman . . . is taking care of the Raja, but he's not the only pair of prying eyes on this island."

Evrouin grinned; he was exhausted enough that he looked twenty years older than his true early thirties, or possibly newly dead.

"That's why I'll go help Sergeant Fayard," Evrouin said. "He's a brave man and a good soldier and loyal to the death, and they don't let dunderheads in the Protector's Guard, but tact isn't his strong point. The Queen Mother picked me for this job, and for my wits as much as my quick hand with a blade."

Deor nodded. *And you're glad that your duty takes you out of this room, know-ing what we must do,* he thought. *Strange folk in truth, Christians.*

Even though his eyes were closed, Deor could feel Thora's spirit, though veiled by the vivid envelope of flesh as through closed lids one can still see a candle burn. And he thought it was a little brighter because of that added point of radiance that was the child.

"I want you with me in the link," he said aloud to Thora. "I will have to journey to find him, and that will help."

"And me?" snapped Pip.

"I'll need your help too"—Deor looked from Thora to Pip and back again—"because of your connection, and—"

One eyebrow lifted as his focus sharpened. In her womb, tiny but intense, was another point of light.

He coughed. "And because you are carrying his child. . . ."

For a moment Pip's gaze went inward. "You can see that?"

"He saw it for *me*—" Thora said dryly.

Deor sensed consternation, but Thora had always been able to hide her reactions, and to take a joke.

Pip's eyes widened. "You mean that he's knocked up *both* of us?"

Pip glared first at Thora and then at Prince John; then her eyes crin-kled and she loosed a bark of half-willing laughter.

"Busy little bastard, isn't he, our Johnnie!"

Some creatures, thought Deor, *are compelled to reproduce when death is near. . . .*

He thrust it away.

"Understand," he said aloud. "We will have to journey to find him. A man's spirit—or a woman's—is not a single thing. Parts may be absent, though the man walks and speaks and eats. If more is gone, as with Prince John, then the body is an empty shell . . . but always until death bound to the spirit with a cord that some eyes can see and follow."

"And me—" growled Toa. "I don't let her go alone."

"Have you done this before?"

"Close enough," Toa grimaced. "Not something I went looking for then, or now."

His eyes went inward for a long moment. "Her mum saved more than my life, once," he said. "And I promised her I'd look after Pip."

"Very well."

Deor looked down at Prince John. It was one of the moments when the prince's wanderings had brought his spirit nearer. His face creased with an echo of suffering, like one of the shadow plays they were so fond of here, where puppets lit from behind cast silhouettes upon a screen.

"Make yourself comfortable," he said. "Time is . . . different, where we're going, but it won't be a matter of seconds."

He paced around the room, pausing at each corner to reach out to the house-spirits and pour a little arrack on the floor.

"Wights of this steading," he murmured, "hail to you. Bless and ward our work today."

"Is this another of your Norse magics?" asked Pip when he had done; her head turned a little to one side in lively curiosity.

Well, John wouldn't be that attracted simply by a pretty face, Deor thought. *Not for long, anyway. Though she's very comely.*

Women didn't arouse him, but he could appreciate beauty in the female form, as he might in a hawk or horse. Pip was striking by the canons of his folk, who prized that fairness and regularity of feature; their tales and poetry had praised it since their most ancient days. After all, she was of the old blood, the Saxon and Norman kindreds whose ways his father Godulf had followed in the Society for Creative Anachronism and had drawn on to found Mist Hills afterwards. Like a golden cat who'd wandered far from the home-ground of their folk to find a new place in these sunlit seas. She moved well, too; like a dancer and warrior both, and with an inner confidence.

There's a mind there, a shrewd one that's always observing, and a strong will. And a ruthlessness in getting what she wants . . . but then, John was always attracted by strong women. Thora for one! Considering who his mother is, and her mother, no surprise there. High Queen Mathilda is strong; Lady Sandra was terrifying.

"Norse?" Deor shook his head, and wasn't going to waste time making fine distinctions among Heathen. "I learned this skill from the Macken-zies."

From his chair in a corner where he'd be watching over them, Ruan spoke: "I thought I recognized some of it. I never went deep into the Mys-teries myself. No knack for it, but all my clansfolk learn a little."

Deor nodded: "My folk at Mist Hills had none who'd gone deeply into the lore before the Change—apart from a little runecraft and such—and I fumbled at it untaught, until Lady Juniper took me as apprentice. I learned still more in Norrheim on the Sunrise sea, where they did have those deep into *seidh*, and then in Iceland, but Dun Juniper was the core and beginning of it for me."

Involuntarily he smiled, remembering the flicker of sunlight filtering through fir branches and Lady Juniper's murmur as she led him out of the world. He had been strung taut as a bow with mingled excitement and fear, wondering if he would fail, or more frightening still, succeed.

"Lady Juniper taught me to journey by seeking a part of myself lost when my father died."

Memories surged—the darkness in Duke Morgruen's torture cham-ber, the vivid crimson of blood, and the wrenching grief as his father fell.

Godulf died for me! That was all I could see at first.

What Lady Juniper had brought back for him was his father's ring, the same ring Deor's brother had passed on to him before he and Thora left for Montival.

I wore it, he thought, remembering, but I did not think I deserved it. It healed my heart, to hear her tell me what she had found. How better for a man to die, than for his son? His duty was the core of him.

"After that," he said aloud, "I learned to journey for others."

"But this is different." Thora still looked troubled.

Deor nodded. "This time we have to bring back the whole man. He is neither dead nor alive now, body and spirit sundered, and we must make him whole."

He looked at Ruan. "Be careful, my heart, and take no action unless you are very certain that there is no choice. If a body is woken while the spirit lingers elsewhere . . . what comes back may lack parts left behind. Or it may be . . . partly something else."

He tried a few taps on the hand drum he had bought in the bazaar of Baru Denpasar. It was made of a ring of coconut wood and the skin was from a goat; it throbbed with a staccato beat that sank into bone and blood as his skilled fingers evoked the rhythms at the heart of life.

"Then let us get on with it!" snapped Thora.

"You sure you want to use that?" Toa nodded towards the drum. "We might get 'em suspicious about the Prince."

"They already know I'm a spirit-walker," said Deor. "They will only think I work to heal."

I hope, he thought.

The bedframe creaked as Pip sat down on the bed and then swung her bare feet up onto the sheet that covered John's body. Most would have said she was calm, with even a slight smile on her curved lips.

She's strung as tight as a Mackenzie bow.

Toa settled himself on the floor by her side and they clasped hands.

"What do you want us to do?" Pip said.

"Be close; take his hand."

She did, in her left.

"You are linked as closely as by blood, now."

Thora's swordbelt clanked as she hung a loop of it around a bedpost and lay down on John's other side.

"Wherever he's wandering, I don't think he's enjoying it," she observed as the Prince's firm lips parted in the ghost of a groan.

Deor nodded, arranging himself cross-legged at the foot of the bed. "Get comfortable. We may be here for a while."

He began to tap on the drum, locking his muscles into the rhythm. "Try to relax—" Viewing their tense faces, he forced a smile. "This has got to be easier than storming that fortress."

"I'm not so sure," Thora replied. "When someone comes at me with a sword at least I can hit him back."

"If you need them, spirit weapons will come to you," Deor answered. "Remember the weight of your sword and it will come to your hand."

"A sword made of thoughts?" she said.

"Thoughts have power even in the waking world," Deor said. "You've seen the Sword of the Lady, oath-sister. In the place we go, thoughts make the very substance of things."

She nodded soberly, and he continued: "And call on your allies. Mine is a meadowlark. You may see him when we're in the Otherworld. Thora's protector is the Bear, the Grizzly."

He looked at Pip, who shook her head in bafflement.

"She's a lion . . . lioness, if you want to get technical," growled Toa from the floor. "Mine's *te Kiore*, the bush rat—that's what my lot call the war-party's scouts who go out through the forest in front of the main force."

"So—" Deor tapped the drum until they had all settled once more.

Tha-ba-da . . . tha-ba-da, sinking into bone, into blood, into pulse and gut.

He relaxed his throat muscles, let his voice go smooth. "Sink down . . . let each limb relax . . . The bed supports you, the floor is Earth, our guards protect you, the wights—"

He reached out, felt a watchful, if slightly confused, awareness.

"—grant permission for our work this day. Let your eyes close. . . ."

As he shut his own he felt awareness begin to alter, at once expanding and shifting focus. He could feel Thora's steady disciplined strength and Pip's vivid energy, reached to add them to his own. As he touched the sparkle that was Pip he felt her surprise.

She's more sensitive than I expected, he thought. *Maybe more than she herself knows.*

Show me your love for John, he sent. *Make your yearning a beacon!*

He reached deeper, searching for the point of light that was the child, and then for the brighter blaze cradled in Thora's womb, seeking the vibration of identity they had inherited from John. He brought to mind his memories of the Prince and Thora sparring, laughing as they danced with steel and each other. He had tried not to imagine them in bed together, but he opened his awareness now. John would need some powerful memories to come back to.

And what about my own feelings? Deor thought wryly.

By the time he met Prince John, he had known all too well how to tell when a man, however unwillingly, felt interest—and when he did not. The Prince was as completely a man for women as he had ever seen, but that did not change Deor's own appreciation, only its expression.

Remembering, he brought to mind all his admiration for John's intelligence and his feeling for the complexities and delights of music, the occasional, well-hidden, diffidence, his love for his family and for Montival and that youthful eagerness for the sight of new lands and peoples that reminded him so much of his own self half his lifetime ago. And that sudden burst of wild raw courage that had led him over the rail of the *Tarshish Queen* to rescue First Mate Radavindraban from the great saltwater crocodile; not for kinship or oath, but because it needed doing for a comrade.

Thora and I followed him then, and we returned despite the terror beneath us in the waves. Now we'll lead him back. Láwerce guide me . . . Woden guard me . . .

He began to build up the visualization of the path. He drew on his feeling for these lands, the times he'd sailed these waters and walked jungled hills like these. Bits and pieces came from the trip inland to the fort; the triangular gateway of a temple, the sight of a great drum hanging below a carved spire, the smell of paddy and the rustle of palm leaves.

"So"—he began to tap a little more quickly—"let us fare forward. Think of it as a long patrol."

His expanded awareness could feel each of them behind him now. Toa added a bass note to it, something deep and massive, scarred by wounds within but stronger for it. A fluttering rose around him, as of a bird with a white body and a red beak. And something peeked out from behind a massive log, something with beady eyes full of cunning.

"See in your mind's eye the jungle through which we came, but now the path we are following dips down beneath the earth."

BETWEEN WAKING WORLD AND SHADOW

He could smell the mingled scents of the jungle, both fetid and fertile, moist earth and the heavy perfume of frangipani blossom. And as they went farther, a reek of old blood and the alkaline dust of drying bones.

Suddenly those scents were alive in his nostrils, carried on a hot moist wind. There was rutted mud beneath his feet and wisps of mist in the jungle to either side. He was in Mist Hills dress, a linen tunic and cross-gartered hose, leather shoes and seax and sword at his belt and his harp in her case of tooled boiled leather slung over his back. A rift in the fog showed a tall building on a hill nearby with a tower at one end; for a moment he thought it was a Christian church because of the field of grave markers at its foot, until he saw that atop the tower was not a cross but a circle, and within it a spiky three-armed symbol in black on gold. Then the drifting tendrils showed it again.

The Yellow Sign. The sign that was on the crocodile's armband when we fought the great beast of the waters.

"Come to me, comrades," he said, feeling the strings of their fates in the fingers of his mind. "Come to me in my need!"

A meadowlark circled about his head.

"Come! For the Prince!"

"Well, here I am, oath-brother," Thora said.

She was in a simple Bearkiller jacket and trousers and boots, unsheathing her sword and looking around. The gesture had some of a grizzly's arrogant assurance, though.

"Come!"

"Come on, you scheming yellow-headed bitch, I know you're not timid, at least," Thora added cheerfully. "Front and center!"

"I'm here, I'm here," Pip said. "Let's not be catty, shall we?"

Deor turned; for a moment he thought he saw a great tawny she-cat indeed, and then it was Pip—not in the robe she'd worn to lie on the bed, but in the odd outfit of round-topped black hat, white shirt and shorts, suspenders and boots and knee and elbow-guards, the kukri-knives and slingshot at her belt and the ebony cane with its two silver-gold heads. A circle of mascara marked one eye.

"Bloody hell," she murmured, looking around her. "It really happened. Now this is a fair suck of the sav! Uncle Pete will love hearing about this, even if he doesn't believe a word of it."

"Come! Come!" Deor called, with his voice and spirit and the thunder of the drum sounding . . . somewhere.

Something rustled in the undergrowth. Something flitted through the tall alien trees. The Maori was there, leaning on his spear and panting. Then he held up a hand to silence Deor's greeting.

"What's that?" he said very quietly.

It came from the place that might or might not be a graveyard. A hollow sound, like a horse's hooves on dirt, or now and then harsher on stone. Slow, though, and irregular. As if it were a horse ancient and sick and weary unto death. They all peered, trying to make out the threat.

Pip's eyes went wide. "Don't look!" she said. "Turn around, *now!*"

They all obeyed, Thora last; it was against her deepest nature to turn her back on an enemy.

"Something that John said to me . . . an old legend. Old, from Europe . . . something from a ballad he recited . . ."

Then she nodded and winced as the memory came back fully: "The beast that grazes among the graves. The Hell Horse."

Thora touched the Hammer slung around her neck and started to turn.

"Then why in Almighty Thor's name are we facing the other way?" she snarled.

Pip caught her arm. "If you *see* the Hell Horse you die!"

The hooves sounded again, slow and dragging . . . and nearer.

CHAPTER FIVE

The Hawaiians were waiting as Órlaith and Reiko approached; bright feather cloaks, crested helms, tall carved staffs and a glitter of spearpoints among the guards. A rumble of pahu-drums pulsed in the background as their players' hands slapped in unison, long narrow instruments made of carved coconut-wood with their heads covered in sharkskin. To the fore were grave older men and a few women, probably generals and noblemen and *kahuna*—priest-diviners.

Their liege was much younger, only a few years older than Órlaith, which gave her a stab of sympathy—he'd be surrounded by those who barely recognized him as an adult, as she was.

The tall figure of King Kalākaua II in the center was made taller still by the golden crest on his golden helm—both were made of yellow feathers, and the cloak hanging from his broad shoulders was of the same, though patterned with red as well. Apart from that and sandals, his only garment was an elaborately folded loincloth that ended with a broad vertical panel before and behind, and there was a heavy battle-spear in his hand with a circle of leaves fastened just below the head, evidently a symbol of peace.

Kalākaua was an impressively muscular brown-skinned man, mostly of the blood of the canoe-navigators who'd first settled these islands, though his features were aquiline and eyes hazel, and he was about Heuradys' age. Queen Haukea was a little younger, and judging from her milky freckled complexion the startling red of her hair was natural. Several maidens dressed like her in colorful kikepa wraps tied to leave one shoulder bare waited with leis of frangipani and sambac-jasmine flowers to bestow on the guests.

Órlaith had no objection to that, but decision formed as she determined to alter the procedure a little. She took a step forward, stooped to raise a clod of earth to her lips, and spoke formally with a tone pitched to carry without shouting . . . and in the ancient language of the islands.

English was the tongue most common here for everyday use, albeit in a wildly eccentric form that Montivallans often strained to follow, but they remembered the 'Ōlelo Hawai'i and used it for worship and for the most solemn occasions of State.

"I come as friend, as ally, as a stranger who asks leave of the King and the Gods of the land and of the *aes dana*, the spirits of place, asks their permission to sail their waters and walk upon their shore. With respect I bow before the Powers who rule here! I bow before Pele of the fire, Lady of Kilauea, whose flame draws land from sea! I bow before Her father Kāne of the forests, Lord of supreme Hunamoku, whose might separates Earth and Sky! I bow before His brothers Kūof the mace who bested Apuhau, and Lono whose tears make fertile the earth! Before Laka of the red lehua flower, who brings love and beauty, I bow! Before dread Milu of the dead, I bow!"

There were nods of approval from the elders . . . and from the tall figure of King Kalākaua II she thought a slight nod of craftsman's acknowledgment. From one performer to another, as a murmur of astonishment and pleasure ran through the watching crowd, the news traveling from mouth to ear beyond the reach of her own voice.

"That was well-done, Your Highness," he said after the greetings, as they exchanged bows and shook hands.

"It costs nothing to be polite, Your Majesty," Órlaith said cheerfully.

Heuradys coughed; that had been a favorite saying of Sandra Arminger, Órlaith's maternal grandmother and Lady Regent of the Association for a long time before the High Kingdom.

The full form she'd generally used was: *Even when you have to kill a man, it costs nothing to be polite.*

"We've a good deal to talk about," Kalākaua said. "Hawai'i's suffered from piracy . . . based in Korea and elsewhere . . . but we haven't been able to do much about it. Now maybe we can."

"Indeed," Reiko said. "And relations between Hawai'i and Dai-Nippon could be fruitful for us both. Soon we will be in a position to break the Korean blockade of our homeland permanently, and we have very rich sources of salvage material."

Which is a polite way of saying a lot of Japan is covered in ruins, Órlaith thought.

The Hawaiian monarchs nodded; their land depended on trade to a degree unusual in the modern world. The islands were self-sufficient in essentials—anyone who'd survived the Change was—but they needed outsiders for the rest and had lively entrepôt dealings as well.

"But first I suppose your people have to get a good look at us," Órlaith said. "What was that thing the ancients had for exotic animals . . . a zoo?"

Queen Haukea grinned, which evidently alarmed some of the Royal advisors. "Or a museum of curiosities."

Órlaith chuckled, which lack of offense relieved them in turn. From their point of view she *was* a curiosity . . . and a dangerous foreign beast . . . and they had to be torn between the twin perils of looking weak and giving offense.

The rest of the afternoon was about what she had expected. A ride through the streets of Hilo in open carriages with cheering crowds on every side, including plenty of her own forces on shore leave and countryfolk in from round about. The locals kept surging against the barrier of spears and bamboo-laminate longbows held horizontally in the hands of their king's armsmen, trying to throw her flower wreaths to add to those already piled around her neck officially, and dancers and musicians performed at street corners.

Once beyond the inevitable tangle of warehouses and forges and shipyards at the docks, the buildings were the usual city-mix of places to live, places to make things and places to sell things you'd made or brought from somewhere else or combinations of the three, combined with taverns and service trades, but all in a style of big arched windows and courtyards and high-pitched roofs obviously intended to shed rain but catch every available breeze. The roads were well-kept, the buildings in good repair, the folk looked well-fed, and you couldn't mistake the genuine enthusiasm they showed their King, the smiles on the shouting faces and the rain of flowers before the hooves of his carriage-horses.

Not the sort you get when someone's metaphorically standing in the background with a spear directed at the crowd's livers, which is unmistakable too. No doubt there's the usual share of human misery and wrong-headedness, but it's a happy enough little kingdom in the main, well recovered from the Change. 'Tis pity I come as the herald of war.

She remembered looking into the eyes of the enemy *kangshinmu* in south Westria, that whirl of dissolution . . . war was needful. Not just for Montival's sake, either, or for revenge for her father's death at the hands of foreign men who'd come onto the High Kingdom's land uninvited with weapons in hand, though that would be ample cause for war in the normal course of things.

Something had gone very wrong in Korea in the aftermath of the Change, something as bad as the Prophet her parents had put down in Montival's far interior, and the people there didn't deserve it any more than the hapless inhabitants of Montana-that-was had. Much good had come through the doors the Change opened, and much evil had also been set free to walk the ridge of the world . . . and the world hadn't yet seen the whole of either.

After the procession, there was a religious service with much blowing of conch-shell trumpets and drumming and more dancing, this a lot more decorous than the impromptu versions on the street corners; the local priesthood seemed to be willing to let her have the benefit of the doubt, and she hoped the Powers they followed did too.

Hawai'i had religious toleration, and she'd seen various flavors of Christian and Buddhist and Shinto shrines in the city. The reports said there were a couple of covensteads and Asatruar hofs for visitors from Montival, too. Most folk seemed to follow the traditional pantheon, though, and they were rather touchy of the dignity of their Gods and of the servants of the divine.

And especially touchy about the mainland, *as they call us,* she thought.

That wasn't surprising; Hawai'i had been part of the United States so recently that a few living oldsters remembered it from their youths, and Montival was the giant among the multitude of successor-states on the old Republic's territory and occupied the whole of the western front of North America above Baja. From what she'd read of the history the American annexation here a century before the Change hadn't been universally popular, especially among the descendants of the folk who'd originally settled the islands.

You could tell from looking that the people here were of much the same mixture of heritages as Montival's, albeit in greatly different proportions—there were fewer who looked like Órlaith and Heuradys and more who resembled, say, Sir Droyn's blunt features and light-brown skin, and *quite* a few who had Reiko's fine-boned build, narrow tilted eyes and pale umber complexion—but apparently in the generations since the Change they'd blended and mostly taken on the heritage and attitudes of the firstcomers.

This island kingdom was simply small, though; populous as some of Montival's member-realms, compact and well-governed and rich from fields and sea, trade and crafts, but still a little nervous about possible ambitions from its giant neighbor. Soothing those was part of her task.

And besides, I could feel it if this were destined to be Montivallan soil . . . and I don't. It's . . . not ours, even in potential. I get the same feeling as I do stepping across the border to, say, the Dominions or Iowa.

The journey ended with the fortress Órlaith had seen from the

Sea-Leopard bulking to the east. They clopped west of it, along a road turned into a tunnel of green shade by towering multi-stemmed banyan trees. An arched wrought-iron gate opened onto a walled enclosure of many acres; a squad of lightly-armored Hawaiian spearmen guarded it, and a detachment of soldiers from the 1st Brigade, United States of Boise Army. The tropical sunlight was harsh on the curved hoops of their *lorica segmentata* armor, the long iron shanks of their pila and the eagle and crossed thunderbolts on their big curved oval shields. And on the stiff taut curves of their faces, blank as machines. One blinked, very slowly, as a fly crawled along his eyelid.

The Boiseans were in a column of twos; they snapped their shields up, smacked the heavy six-foot javelins on them in a single echoing *crack* of salute, did ninety-degree turns to face each other and stepped back four paces in stamping unison to line the roadway on either side. Each pila's butt grounded with a thud at parade rest.

Órlaith nodded gravely. Her father had always thought of—and in strict privacy with her and Mother called—this sort of thing *dancing a fight* or simply murmured *Osprey Men-At-Arms Number 46*, but he'd also given unstinting praise to the Boiseans who'd fought with him through the Prophet's War and at the Horse Heaven Hills. And professional respect to the ones who'd fought on the other side, whatever he thought of their political judgment.

Past the gateway, and the carriages were in parkland scattered with buildings that were mostly new since the Change, connected by roads of white crushed shell amid very beautiful gardens with sweeping velvety-green lawns, groves of many different trees, bright flowers, reflecting pools with golden ornamental fish . . .

"Nice," Heuradys murmured as they were shown to their quarters; a subtle touch was the absence of noise and numbers. "Not that straw in a stable wouldn't be a relief from that barrel of sardines packed in oil they call a ship."

Órlaith felt her soul stretching a little too, and there was a murmur of agreement from her followers as they swung down from the mounts the

Hawaiians had provided. All of them were countryfolk, born and reared among fields and forests and rangelands. Cities were alien environments they visited or occasionally worked in, and the ships had been a shock.

Faramir Kovalevsky of the Dúnedain frowned in thought as the carriages and horses wheeled away, his blue-gray eyes going distant for an instant beneath the brim of the spired Ranger helm he wore for the occasion, along with a black jerkin marked with the silver Tree, seven stars and crown.

"A ship is like a jail, with the chance of being drowned added," he said.

There was a general laugh, which he disclaimed with a raised hand:

"Not me! That's some ancient sage Mother is fond of. Not in the Histories, I think, some Fourth Age philosopher."

Histories was what the Rangers called the works that described ancient Middle Earth and the Quest of the One Ring, the traditions on which their founders had modeled their scattered, wilderness-dwelling nation.

Of course, Great-Aunt Astrid always claimed that she was descended from the Dúnedain in the Histories, from the House of Hador. She was a great warrior and hero, by all accounts, but Da told me many who knew her in person thought her barking mad. Though he used to say too it didn't really matter much in the end, because she made her mad dreams sober truth.

Non-Dúnedain were more likely to regard the Histories as fanciful tales, though less fanciful than some from the ancient world. The folk in them lived more or less as real people did in modern times, after all, not flying to the moon or sailing beneath the sea. That old sage Faramir quoted had a point, too. A crofter's cottage or even a barracks back home usually had more room than even the commanders had enjoyed on the trip out, with the added advantage that the world was just out the door. Most of them had spent as much time as they could at the mastheads and bowsprits, or hauling on ropes whenever the sailors would allow them to help, for distraction as well as keeping in trim.

"And I'm glad we're within a perimeter, at least," Heuradys added.

Reiko actually smiled as she dismounted from her carriage in turn and looked at an arched bridge over a pond.

"That is in our style!" she said, pulling her folded *tessen* from her obi and making a sweeping gesture with the steel war-fan.

The polished-looking Hawaiian guiding them—a brown, bronzed young man who showed that you could look immensely aristocratic wearing nothing but sandals, a brightly printed sarong-like wraparound they called a kikepa here, a ten-inch knife through your belt and flowers in your raven hair—smiled and bowed slightly.

"These are the Gardens of Queen Lili'uokalani, Majesty," he said; he had less of the strong local accent in his English than most of the people they'd met, too, just enough to give it a pleasant soft tinge.

He made a graceful gesture. "She was our last great Queen before the Change, but this park was laid out by Nihonjin gardeners; there is a teahouse in the fashion of your people also, Majesty, and we have equipped this mansion with tatami and fittings you will hopefully find familiar. The island to the west along the black-sand beach has a temple of healing, but for the duration of your visit we are keeping the common people out. We hope that all is satisfactory, and as we indicated His Majesty of Hawai'i bids both of you—"

He managed to bow politely to both the foreign royals in the same gesture.

"—to a feast an hour after sunset."

His gesture was almost as tactful as the fact that the rambling structures that would house the Montivallan and Nihonjin parties were almost identical. Reiko bowed politely to Órlaith, who matched the gesture with a slightly deeper one—her friend was a reigning monarch, while she was only an heir-apparent.

"Until sunset, Orrey-chan," Reiko said.

That was startlingly informal, enough that several of her more recently-arrived courtiers showed that absolute absence of expression by which Nihonjin *shi*—gentlefolk—conveyed disapproval of a superior.

"Until then, Reiko-chan," Órlaith said, matching it.

The two ladies-in-waiting opened the door, another made a just-barely successful snatch at the young girl she'd been escorting as she tried to make a break for the gardens.

"Come, Kiwako," Reiko called to her in *Nihongo*, taking her by the hand and then laughing and sweeping her up on her right hip, across from the two swords. "Time for your nap!"

Her samurai stepped out of their sandals—and discarded the fragrant flower leis that they had tolerated only with a massive effort of self-control—and fanned out inside and around the edges of the house. The women sank to their knees and bowed their heads almost to the floor as Reiko shed her footwear, set Kiwako down to do the same and entered with Kiwako's hand in hers. Órlaith thought she sensed the very faintest of sighs, as Reiko vanished once more into a world of ceremony and protocol far more ancient and rigid than that which often carked the heir to Montival.

Heuradys and Droyn and Karl Aylward Mackenzie and their followers—including Karl's greathounds Fenris and Ulf—did a sweep before *she* got past the front door of the house they'd been assigned, and then Morfind and Faramir and Susie Mika did it again, while Diarmuid Tennart McClintock spoke to his caterans:

"Scit th' groonds. An aye be cannie aboot it."

She didn't think that the handsome young McClintock tacksman was more conscientious because they'd been lovers once, briefly and long ago; he'd been her first man, at a Beltane festival in the usual way among those of their branch of the Old Faith. He was a settled man now, with a handfasted wife and a newborn babe down south in his clan's *dúthchas* where he was a minor chief. He'd come along to the Valley of Death for friendship's sake, and because he agreed it was the will of the Powers that it was very needful. But it probably made him feel the responsibility more intensely, and his followers might well be more enthusiastic because they knew it and considered it an honor done their folk.

The McClintocks fanned out through the nearby groves and flower beds, sometimes visible only by the flapping of their bunched-up Great

Kilts. Órlaith winced a little at their trampling. And at the way one swordsman with sinuous blue tattoos on this face, arms and legs, and a beard like a burst pillow stuffed with ginger-colored straw drew the four-foot claidheamh-mòr slung across his back and used it to poke into hidden spots in the shrubbery.

You just couldn't convince a McClintock cateran that anyone else knew how to find things amid vegetation, even if it was vegetation they'd never seen before and a very, very long way from the forests where they hunted deer.

Any more than you can convince them stealing the neighbor's coo-beasties or *wooly* ship *isn't harmless rough fun or that they shouldn't drop by a little past midnight to burn down the barn of someone who punched out their second cousin in a drunken brawl at the Samhain games and lift his horses while they're at it,* she thought resignedly. *Grandmother Juniper says we should blame all those Highland adventure novels old Chief Hamish liked so much before the Change, but are tales really that influential?*

She snorted to herself: *Of course they are.*

From the briefing packets that High Marshal d'Ath's office had prepared for the expedition, mostly culled from interviewing merchants who made this run, Órlaith suspected that the guesthouses were usually kept for visiting *ali'i*, the subordinate nobles who ruled various parts of the seven major islands that made up the Kingdom of Hawai'i. As such they had to be big enough to accommodate their staffs and guards, which was convenient. Two statues stood on plinths beside the main doors, at first grotesque to Montivallan eyes and then showing their own beauty, snarling protective *ki'i* of the sort she'd seen at the *heiau* temple earlier in the day.

"First watch," Heuradys said to Sir Droyn, who nodded and set his men-at-arms in their places at the door and around the edge of the big rambling structure.

The construction was set around several courts and struck her as ingenious on several accounts; crushed coral rag mixed with a little cement and water and mineral pigments and pounded in frames, then left until it dried into shapes like monolithic blocks of coarse rock run through with pleasing patterns of waving horizontal lines. The walls were thick but only navel-high, with pillars of the same material carrying the high ceilings that showed rafters of Douglas fir imported from Montival, and the underside of the steep palm-thatch roofs above. Between the rooflines and the low walls were moveable curtains and screens of woven bamboo dyed in colorful patterns, and more of the same made up the interior partitions. Marble that had probably come from salvage expeditions to dead Honolulu on Oahu covered the floors, and brick from the same source was laid as pathways in the courtyards.

The party went in, and by the time Órlaith reached the main common-room a swift efficient unpacking had begun, with a little quiet push-and-shove about who got barracked where. Heuradys settled that and the guard register with brisk authority—it was part of her job as Head of Household to see that Órlaith didn't have to worry about details—and picked a room beside the master-suite Órlaith would be using, which had a small private garden and fountain of its own.

"Nice," Órlaith said judiciously as Macmacon lapped noisily from one of the pools, jumped up on a cushioned chair and circled until he was a ball of fur and dozed.

She looked around the central lounging room's cool airy spaciousness, with walls open on the shaded verandah and an interior court fragrant with jasmine and frangipani and drooping blue sprays of Queen's Wreath, the splashing of a fountain in a pool big enough to swim in sounding pleasantly in the background. The sound made her want to strip off her clothes and jump in, which she intended to do just as soon as possible.

Hilo had plenty of rainwater from cisterns and more still piped in from the slopes of the mountains southward, for drinking and sanitation and to power the machinery she'd sometimes heard whining and thumping while the parade went through the streets. The mansion's layout was also cunningly sited and planned to catch every possible breeze by moving the screens and partitions. They weren't backwoodsmen here, and from the looks of things must have good engineers on call.

The furniture was comely but functional, mostly of laminated bamboo and white cotton, some of polished stone tops or hard attractive woods she didn't recognize. Susan Mika flopped down on a sofa and tossed a few fried *poi* chips from a bowl into her mouth after dipping them into a spicy red sauce. Like a lot of short, thin wiry energetic people she had a bottomless capacity for food when it was available.

"Nice? You can say that again, Orrey," the Lakota girl said. "Of course, back home on the *makol* they think it's not really a home unless you can put wheels on it and haul it around with you while you shear sheep and punch cows and steal horses—that part's fun, I gotta admit—and harvest *tatanka*."

Makol was what the Lakota—the people outsiders often called Sioux—named their own territory on the high bleak prairies beyond the Rockies on the realm's eastern borders. It was part of the High Kingdom and the realm bore the title of *Guardian of the Eastern Gate*, but sheer distance from anywhere else meant it was even more autonomous than most of Montival's members.

Heuradys raised a brow as she shed her armor with Órlaith's help, a groan of relief and a strong smell of sweat.

"You don't agree, Susie?" the knight asked. "Do I detect a note of skepticism?"

"I left, you may notice. Glad I did, too, even if I miss my family. All that nomad virtue and hardiness and buffalo pemmican and ancestral chants around the fires in our freezing fucking winters . . . *bo-ring!* Not to mention we copied the gurs we actually live in from that Mongol friend of my granddad, so much for ancient tradition. Yeah, they've got tipis beat all to hell, especially in cold weather with a nice airtight stove, but you know what I mean."

One thing the Sword of the Lady did was tell you whether someone was speaking truth, or more precisely whether they thought what they were saying was the truth. Outright lying with intent tasted like metal foil clenched between your back teeth. In this case the answer was yes . . . and no; a sensation like what you felt waiting for someone to complete a sentence when they paused, only much stronger.

That response was one reason Órlaith thought there had been some sort of scandal involved in the wiry little easterner's departure from the high plains of the realm's borderlands too—they were a straight-laced lot there—but had never pushed for the details. You had to be careful when you carried the Sword. Her father had said that if you weren't you'd become impossible for ordinary people to be around without hatred.

"*Lila washté!*" Susie exclaimed, going down the corridor and sticking her head into a room, her broad-cheeked brown face splitting in a grin. "Totally excellent! Nice big bed, and it's perfectly positioned for guarding Her Immense Importantness. Dibs on the right-hand side."

"Left-hand for me," Faramir Kovalevsky said quickly, grinning and running a hand through his pale-gold curls as he shed his helmet with a sigh of relief.

"*Amarth faeg!*" his cousin Morfind Vogeler said as she did likewise, which was a complaint about the woes of one's fate in Sindarin, then added: "*Uff da!*"

Rangers from Stath Ingolf insisted that that was Sindarin too; if pressed they'd admit it was from the Wisconsin Kickapoo Valley sub-dialect of Elvish, which was where Ingolf Vogeler had originally come from.

Her hair was straight and black; she was a handsome young woman of his own twenty years, a little taller than the blond Ranger, with a bad ax-scar down one side of her face that was only a year old and still purple-colored.

"Why do I always get the middle spot?" she went on; Órlaith was glad to hear the teasing in her voice, since she tended to be quiet and brood.

"Because he and I both get up to pee more often than you do, my beautiful Ranger lady of the capacious bladder," Susie said. "I'm just minimizing the waking-you-up-by-climbing-over-you-in-the-dark stuff."

They shouldered their duffels and weapons and went inside the room to unpack, bickering amiably as they went. Órlaith reflected that they made *her* feel very adult sometimes, and she wouldn't reach the quarter-century mark for another eighteen months. The relationship they'd settled into seemed to suit them. Though it would be at least mildly frowned on by Ranger custom, Faramir and Morfind being first cousins.

"In bed two is glad company, three is choreography and boring," Heuradys said ironically . . . and softly.

"I heard that! You're simply jealous!" Susie called, sticking her head out again for an instant.

"It's not natural the way she picks things up," Heuradys grumbled.

"Makes her a good scout." Órlaith grinned and shook her shoulders back, thumbs in her swordbelt. "Settle in and familiarize yourself, everyone; then a swim for those who want it, your best clothes, and dinner."

That raised a cheer. They were here on serious business, but Heuradys was the oldest of them in her mid-twenties, and they were perfectly ready to have some fun along the way.

The which behavior is a good model for life, not so?

CHAPTER SIX

BETWEEN WAKING WORLD AND SHADOW

Deor spoke crisply: "Run!"

"Run away from a *horse*?" Thora said.

"It's a *crippled* horse," Deor said. "And it isn't going to trample us. From what Pip says, we have to see it first before it can wreak harm!"

"Which way?" she asked.

Deor felt inwardly for a direction; as far as his eyes . . . you could call them eyes . . . could see they were on a featureless dirt road through scrubby countryside extending in both directions. But there was something like a silver thread running with light in his mind, or at least that was how his consciousness interpreted it.

"This way," he said crisply, pointing down the roadway. "The Prince lies in that direction."

It was the logic of a dream, or a nightmare, but that suited the place they were. Thora trotted off in the direction of his finger even as she complained; they'd been together a very long time, and she trusted his judgment in these matters as he trusted hers when it came to fighting.

"Watch where we're going," Deor said as the four of them moved off. "We'll have to retrace our steps to return to the world of common day."

It was like running in a dream, too. There were moments when he felt as if he were flying, not running; as if he were Láwerce hovering above a great yellow cat and the shambling sleek menace of the cinnamon-colored bear, and the cunning silent beady-eyed menace of the bush rat. Instead he forced himself to travel as a man, booted feet on the dirt of the road and sword slapping against his thigh.

The road stretched ahead through mist, and when the mist cleared the scenes to either side were never the same twice—nor were they ever something you wanted to see—but there was little sense of motion. It was as if they trotted on a strip that moved beneath them.

Toa lengthened his pace effortlessly, the huge muscles rolling like pythons beneath his tattooed skin as he moved ahead but his feet making little sound on the rutted mud. He held the great spear underarm, moving with his trot and ready to flash out in a gutting stroke like a frog's tongue.

"If this isn't the real world, why do we have to run?" Pip said, her pale eyes turning angry yellow for a moment. "Why can't we just imagine bicycles or a nice well-sprung four-horse carriage with a cooler full of Saltie Bites Lager like King Birmo's?"

Thora chuckled, and Deor grinned at Pip's indignation. Her face had a certain rigid quality that showed how she was holding it thus by main force, but he liked the guts she was showing.

"That's why we have clothes and weapons . . . and bodies . . . here," he said. "But ours aren't the only will and mind involved. Think of it . . . think of it as walking in someone else's dream, one that only becomes fixed as we see it. Or the world of someone else's mind . . . and that one, or Ones, are not of human kind. Not now, not for a very long time if ever. I wouldn't recommend climbing into any carriage we found here."

"Because we might not like where it went or what was pulling it. This is Someone's dream that has that Hell Horse in it," Thora supplied. "Hi-ho, we're off to meet them, too. Johnnie's keeping bad company."

"And do not take food or drink that any we meet offer as a gift," Deor added.

Pip nodded. "I've heard those stories too. Oh, what fun. Some things are better kept in books."

"Or sagas," Deor agreed. "But we live in a world where such things walk. Perhaps our grandparents did also, though they denied it."

The air around them grew darker as they wolf-trotted—jog a hundred paces, walk a hundred, repeating over and over again, the pace that humans could use to run to death any other beast on the earth. Then the mists parted for a moment. Black cindered stars moved through the sky above, slowly, in chaotic patterns pregnant with meanings that plucked at the edges of his mind.

On a hill in the middle distance a tall fire burned, and stick-thin figures like a cross between human form and that of a praying mantis danced around it, heads thrown back in ecstasy as they pranced and whirled. Limbs raised on high moved twig-like fingers in unison, drawing patterns in lines of dark intensity. Within that white-crimson heat was a pillar, and other figures chained to it writhed against the bonds, shrieking ceaselessly in a high shrill note that scraped at his ears. A wild discordant music of flutes and drums and something that sounded like a steel barrel being pounded by a hundred tiny hammers wove through and around the screams of pain, and the dance went on without end.

Fit for the halls of Surt, Deor thought, as the mist mercifully closed in again.

But he knew some corner of his self was storing images for the song he'd make of this one day. He shook his head as he dodged around the rusty wreck of an automobile lying canted in the roadway, at the foot of a heroically nude statue, headless and holding aloft the stump of a broken sword.

More and more of them cluttered the way ahead, a sight familiar enough to anyone who'd seen the lands around the dead cities of the ancient world. Hand-bones gripped a wheel seen dimly through dirty, impact-starred glass. Wisps of hair clung to the skull between them, and something seen dimly retracted itself into a gaping eye socket. An ancient tang of rust and decay long contained in sealed places crept under the scent of acrid dust.

Ragged thornbrush crowded close to the sides of the road, a wall the height of a man laced together with oddly swollen, lumpy vines with thorns like bone claws; dead trees reared above the thickets. Tendrils of fog crept through the brush, and they had to slow to weave their way through more piled wrecks, sometimes clambering cautiously—there was nothing like rusty iron to give you lockjaw if you cut yourself on it.

Something else crawled through the brush, many things, with a faint rustling and chittering. If you looked closer you saw that wrecked automobiles were scattered through the undergrowth as well to either side, as if they'd swung wide to try and dodge the pileup themselves. The charred trunk of a great tree lay across the crushed remains of one, where the impact had brought the oak down and they had burned together. The trunk of the car had burst open, revealing many small bones.

Ahead Toa swung up a clenched left fist like a small beer keg, and they all stopped. Fog hung over the path before them too, like a sluggishly moving gray wall pouring over the dead machines. The Maori went to one knee, peering about.

"Stuff moving in the bush," he said. "Around those busted cars."

"Toa, did you notice the cars are all pointed in one direction?" Pip said. "As if they were all trying to get away from something up ahead of us."

"Right," Toa said. "Didn't work, though."

"And they look burned," Thora said. "Half melted, some of them."

Deor blinked and looked more closely, narrowing his focus for a moment from the wide-spread alertness you used in hostile country. Usually you didn't notice wreckage of the ancient world much, not enough to see detail unless there was some reason to, when you were looking for valuable salvage or for something hidden among it.

The young woman from Townsville was right: they were all headed in the same direction, on both sides of the road, though he knew it had been the custom for streets this narrow to have two lanes moving traffic in opposite directions, keeping to the left or right—living cities used the same pattern where traffic was dense enough.

Thora is right too.

The rear ends of the cars were scorched and buckled and sometimes steel and glass had run, as if some flash of fire brighter than a thousand suns had hammered them all in an instant. Others were tumbled and crumpled by some great storm-wind that had accompanied the light. The ground crunched beneath their feet, as if littered with something thin and fragile. Looking down he saw that it was, but irregular and sometimes in the shape of the road's ruts, earth itself seared to brittle glass.

"Odd-looking autos, too," Pip observed. "Not like any wrecks I've seen. More like really old pictures or paintings of autos, from well before the Change."

They didn't look much like those he'd seen in his home in Westria or around the world amid the wreckage of the old world. In dry areas some were still unworn enough that you could get a good sense of how they'd appeared. These were boxier, more angular, and the wheels were narrower and higher—the way two different schools of craft might make the same thing, say a wagon or ship, the variance of tradition and place always there within the boundaries imposed by function.

"They didn't just stop, either, I think," Deor said thoughtfully.

That was why the roads of the world he'd grown up in were still littered with such; on that day nearly half a century before they'd simply ceased to function as the Change flickered around the globe in an invisible wave of alteration. Plenty had crashed as their controls and engines died, and burned then or later; then time and rust had had its way with them, or human hands looking for spring steel for blades, or mechanisms to be incorporated into a watermill, or glass to be melted down and blown into bottle and plate and sheet metal to be beaten into shield-covers. In lands still peopled they'd long since at least been pushed aside to free the roadways for the modern world's animal-drawn vehicles, and most salvaged down to the scraps.

But these looked as if they'd been undisturbed since they were caught moving and beaten with a lash of fire. Or a wave of it. The word *wave* sparked a comparison in his mind.

"They fled from Death with all the speed they had, and Death followed them still faster," he said. "Not just foemen, but something terrible beyond common thought. Remember the beach at Topanga?"

They glanced at each other, remembering. Remembering the storm clouds gathering in a clear sky like a churning funnel as lightning slashed through it in an endless flicker. Then it toppling towards them . . . not only the cloud, but the scourging wind, and the water towering higher and higher and crashing down as the ship's stern rose and rose in a world gone black and actinic blue and the Korean warships tumbled and smashed like toys beneath a boot. . . .

Deor remembered more; he had had the Sight to see what lay behind the physical things, and it had been like staring into the Sun, blinding the eyes of the spirit.

Vaster than worlds, he thought, and recalled tension like a steel band around his head until it snapped and left him feeling like a dust-mote tumbling in a hurricane. *The wrath of a Goddess.*

"I think . . ." he said. "I think we walk among memories as well as dream. Memories of what was, or what might have been . . . perhaps what might be, also."

Pip's head came up, and then Thora's and Toa's. Deor heard it too.

Clip-*clop*, clip . . . clip *clop*, slow and maddeningly irregular. Toa's thick lips curled back from his teeth, and he glanced towards the brush and then back over his shoulder.

"Let's go," he said. "Neighborhood's getting too soddin' crowded for comfort, straight up, and it's not the types who show up for a vicar's bunfight."

Pip opened her mouth and then hesitated. A sound came from nearby, a metallic clunking chunk accompanied by a groan.

"What was that?" Thora exclaimed.

Pip spoke, slowly and her voice very flat. "That sounded very much like an automobile door opening and closing again. One of my granddad's cronies kept an old Jag from before the Change in mint condition on his Station and had it pulled around by horses now and then while he tooled behind the wheel. It sounded just like that when he got out. Except not so rusty."

"But there's nothing in those cars except—"

The same sound was repeated, this time with a loud screech as of rust-bound metal breaking free into movement. And again, and again. The stink of ancient decay grew suddenly stronger.

"—nothing in them but the long dead," Pip finished. "Let's bloody *go*, shall we?"

"Too right!" Toa said, and trotted into the fog.

Deor took a long breath and plunged into the mist behind him. It seemed to press into his mouth and nostrils, choking; then there was an instant of unbearable heat and they were through it, skin still tingling from what wasn't—quite—scorching damage. The heat had been full of screaming, too, as if from multimillionfold deaths that never died.

The others exclaimed—or in Toa's case, grunted and cursed in his own language—as they felt pavement beneath their feet, and an unfamiliar brilliant cool light leaking into the narrow dark place they stood. They were in a city, a living one from the lights and murmur of voices and wheels amid less familiar noises; in an alleyway smelling of uncollected trash in sheet-metal bins. He looked around; small red eyes looked back and then scrambled away. Scrawled on one surface of sooty brick in tall reddish-brown letters barely legible because of smearing and long dribbling trails was:

NOT UPON US, O KING! NOT UPON US!

Then they all exclaimed again, and louder, as they realized their clothes had changed as well. Deor felt something choking him and his hand flew up to it. Some very conservative parts of Montival still sent emissaries to the High King's court in what the ancient world had called a *suit and tie*, and this was like that, only worse—the collar was starched and dug into his neck, and he had on a wool jacket and waistcoat too, and a hat much like the one Pip had called a *bowler* when she wore one. A quick look showed that Toa was wearing blue denim, a suit of loose pants with a bib-like extension that covered his chest over a collarless gray shirt and rough shoes and a flat floppy cloth cap with a bill over the eyes; he'd seen something very similar worn by farmers in New Deseret. The two women were in dresses that extended a little below the knee, light color-ful fabrics and impractical-looking shoes with buckled straps bearing distorted skulls, and hats like bells made out of cloth with wool pom-poms on top.

"Where's my damned *sword?*" Thora snarled. "I thought we could call weapons to us!"

Her left hand clapped against her hip on that side, groping for a scab-bard where there was nothing but a narrow belt of cloth instead of the frog for her backsword. But there was a large embroidered handbag over her arm, and it clinked metallically. The red-haired Bearkiller froze, and then reached within it. They all recognized what she pulled out; it was a revolver, a massive thing with an eight-inch barrel.

What they'd never seen was one that would work as the old tales described, of course.

"Be careful where you point that, here, oath-sister," Deor said, and she tilted it up. "Think of it as a loaded crossbow."

Toa had something in his hand too, a wrench a yard in length ending in a knob crusted with stains they all recognized as well, and from their own experience. Pip was still carrying something very like her double-headed cane, and she looked inside a haversack-like thing slung over one shoulder.

"Mummy's kukri-knives are in here," she said.

Deor felt a catch under his left shoulder. He reached beneath the woolen jacket, and felt the butt of a weapon like the one Thora had just tucked away again in a complex holster arrangement designed to make it easy to draw but well-concealed.

"I think we have equivalents," he said. "Ones that . . . fit . . . with wher-ever we are."

Pip looked rebellious. "How did we *imagine* things we'd never imag-ined?" she said.

Deor was tempted to brush the question aside, but she might . . . would . . . need to make decisions in split seconds. A mind in turmoil was less likely to make the right ones.

"The High King, High King Artos, once told me that *he'd* been told by those who knew that time isn't an arrow. Time is a serpent. Our world is one of many through the cycles of the universe. Many . . . many iterations. Some very different, some much the same, some just different enough to be like an image seen in a distorted mirror. Deeds and persons and places echo from one to the other; sometimes what is dreams or tales in one is sober truth in the next. And within each . . . iteration . . . more Powers than one, or more powers than two, many more, push to bring the cycle of things more to their liking."

"That's bloody indefinite!"

"That's as definite as I can be; he said that the Ones he spoke with more or less told him that was all he could understand, and Artos thought it was for the same reason you can't explain arithmetic to a dog, that the reality is simply beyond what we can grasp. But we're not alone here, let's say, and we're not entirely alone with the One whose place this is."

Thora stepped forward and ducked her head outside the entrance to the alleyway for a quick glimpse either way.

"Those are streetlights," she said, her voice soft with wonder for a moment. "*Electric* streetlights."

They all stared at that light, so unlike the flicker of flame or even the glow of gas mantles. It was like stepping through into an ancient tale of wonders.

Deor closed his eyes and felt for the thread of connection that had tugged at him from the Prince's side.

"I think we should keep moving," he said.

Pip nodded and took a deep breath. "Look as if you own the place," she said crisply, in that drawling accent. "Best rule in a strange town."

"Yes, it is," Thora replied dryly.

She'd seen full many of them, as she voyaged the world around in Deor's company, and had fifteen years on the tawny-haired youngster.

Was I ever that heedlessly arrogant? he thought. *I hope not . . . but then, after I left Mist Hills for the broader world, I wasn't the Baron's son anymore—not even his odd younger son who liked boys. I was the bumpkin, the yokel, the hayseed from the place in the wilderness nobody had ever heard of; I had to earn every grain of respect I ever tasted.*

The street outside was fairly broad, running between brick-faced buildings four or five stories high, floridly decorated in terra-cotta moldings, many with wrought-iron balconies. Cars—moving autos—dashed by, and crowds dressed much as they were moved thick on the pavements beneath light-stands shaped like vultures holding globes of light in their beaks. The folk moved quickly, faces down and closed, avoiding one another's eyes, and if you looked closely most of the autos, heavily laden, were heading in one direction.

The air had an odd chemical smell, like some laboratories he'd been in here and there, and an acrid burnt tint a little like forges or smelters. There was none of the usual urban scent of horse manure and stale horse-piss.

And fear, I know that smell. It smells of fear.

A man in a brass-buttoned blue uniform stood on the corner, with a pistol at his side and a yard of truncheon in his hand, a curious helmet like a cloth-covered fireplug on his head. Occasionally he would trot over when the autos got themselves into a snarl blowing a whistle and waving; once hauling a man out from behind the wheel and beating him bloody before throwing him back in. The passengers pulled the unfortunate man into the backseat, and one of them moved up to take control.

There was a stand nearby, much like those used in some cities he'd seen to sell newspapers. Posters plastered the sides of it. One bore large letters:

NEW YORK HERALD

"New York!" Pip murmured.

They all glanced at one another; that fallen city was a name of terror, at the heart of one of the greatest and worst of the Death Zones created when the world-machine stopped.

"Is this New York before the Change?" she said. "It's not much like anything I've seen or read about it. Not in the details, at least—no hundreds of giant glass-walled buildings for starters."

Toa was looking upward. "Take a dekko," he said, his bass voice rumbling softly.

Not far from them—though perhaps farther than it appeared—was a towering structure like an elongated pyramid, stepped in at intervals and glowing with innumerable windows, and topped with a yellow-lit spiky three-armed sigil. Beams of light like gigantic spears picked out something at its peak just below the Yellow Sign, like a huge finned whale-shape floating in the air. As they watched, it cast off and turned away with a purposeful motion unlike any balloon, a buzzing coming from it that still cut through the throb of street-noise.

"Anything about those in that fancy school, Cap'n?" he asked.

"That they weren't around in 1998," Pip said, but gave it only a glance.

She fished in the bag at her side and tossed a coin to the attendant in the booth, who sat in a wheeled chair behind the counter. He grabbed it and yammered; Deor saw the stub of a tongue in his mouth, and a line ran from a collar at his neck to a staple in an iron post at the back.

The captain of the *Silver Surfer* scanned the paper in her hands; it had more pages than any Deor was familiar with, even in Portland or Winchester or Sambalpur, a fantastic extravagance given what paper cost in most places.

"March 17th, 1998," she said.

"The day of the Change!" Deor exclaimed.

They crowded around her to read the headlines.

CZAR'S BOMBARDMENT SUBMERSIBLES OFF THE COAST! one exclaimed. WAR AT ANY MOMENT! UPRISING IN SUANEE, SPECIAL ACTION GROUPS SENT IN!

Pip began to read the print below in a murmur: "*From our correspondent in the Capitol . . . which is apparently Yhtril, DC . . . District of Carcosa . . . Eternal Emperor Castaigne proclaims that in this time of crisis, all loyal subjects must come together and make sacrifices for the nation.*"

She stopped, and her brows went up, and he could see her throat work as she swallowed and continued:

"He proclaims that one's own children are the most desirable sacrificial burnt offer-
ing, though self-immolation in the Lethal Torment Chambers is acceptable. All patriotic
Americans must kneel in servile adoration and worship before Divine Uoht and glut His
hunger, that He may intercede for us with the King in Yellow and send the Pallid Mask
against our enemies as He has before."

They paused. "I really don't think we want to stop here," she said. "As
you said . . . not a good place, eh, what?"

"I never thought we'd agree on so much, girl," Thora said with a
taut grin.

"Deor?"

"This is *a* past. Not ours, I think. Or the image of a past that might
have been, or in some cycle of the greater worlds once was. The ideal to
which that which rules here aspires, or something close to it. And for
which it needs Prince John."

"So, which way, oath-brother?" Thora said, and the others nodded.

He closed his eyes for a moment.

"This way," he said. "The feeling of the Prince is stronger here."

So is the fear, he did not add aloud. *We're growing closer to whatever it is that*
creates and sustains this place.

They walked down the street, and turned onto another. That was a
much broader highway, at least a hundred paces across. The sidewalks
were broad too, laid in patterns of colored brick, with a double row of
trees clipped into rectangular shapes on each. The buildings were all
seven stories and faced with faded white stone, with a common cornice
line but a pleasing variety of form and detail. Most of the ground floors
were broad brightly-lit shop windows.

It would all have looked much *more* pleasing if several of the lamp-posts
hadn't had ropes flung over them and nooses holding bodies dangling
and slowly turning as they hung swollen-faced and bulge-eyed. The pe-
destrians ignored them, faces tight with fear, or occasionally paused to
spit and laugh.

Toa's head snapped up. "Something bad coming . . . hear those voices?"

Deor listened. Savage shouting and pounding feet, but not those of battle. Pip turned an enquiring face to Toa, but the scop answered first, memories taking him back to a place of fear and flight, and whitewash peeling from blank walls along narrow streets. Thora pulling his arm across her shoulders as he staggered reeling with blood running down his face, the sword naked in her other hand, and their desperate panting breaths loud in the alien night.

He answered: "That's a mob, the snarl of a hunting mob, and it's coming our way."

Thora nodded, her lips narrowed to bloodlessness at her own recollections. There were a fair number of people ahead of them, and they were turning to look at the noise as well. Most of them ignored it, walking quickly towards wherever they were going. A few pointed and called out, mostly wooping wordless cries. Others laughed and put hands beside their necks and jerked them upward, miming strangulation with heads to one side and lolling tongue and eyes.

A figure burst through the spectators. It was a man with blood running down his bearded heavy-featured olive face, matting one of the long curls trained into his hair before his ears to the side of his face. He wore a version of the male costume that seemed to be standard here, but darker and with a longer coat.

Despair flooded his face as he saw Deor and his party standing in his way. He tried to halt, windmilling his arms, and a broad-brimmed black hat fell off his head as he stumbled and began to fall. He spoke then, in a choked whisper, words Deor had heard before and understood:

"Sh'ma Yisrael Adonai Eloheinu Adonai Eḥad!"

Toa caught him easily, one huge fist knotting in the shabby black coat and whirling him around behind the Maori's massive back. Deor caught what was almost a throw and found the man was lighter than he would have thought, skin and bone beneath the heavy cloth, smelling of blood and old sweat. What had looked like bulk of body was parcels beneath the coat, parcels wrapped in paper from the way they crackled.

"Quiet!" the scop snapped. "Behind me!"

He found the heavy pistol from the shoulder-holster was in his hand;

it was the same impulse that would have drawn his sword, but transmuted.

As our clothes were, Deor thought.

And thought of One who was also patient and cunning and bided His time. He grinned, a fighting snarl.

Thora had also drawn her pistol, and then hesitated and looked at it.

"Oath-sister!" he said. "Don't think about it, just *use* it as you would your blade."

Pip and Toa poised, cane and wrench ready in their hands.

Other figures pushed through the crowd on the sidewalk. Some where men and women in ordinary street dress for this time and place, carrying baseball bats and a knotted hangman's rope, and a can of liquid that smelled like the rock-oil they used for lanterns in some places. Leading them were two in yellow robes, with blank masks like a sketch of a face strapped across their visages. Another similarly masked was in front, but wore only a twist of yellow rags around his loins, and carried a seven-tailed whip whose strands were tipped with sharp-edged beads of pale gold. Blood dripped from them, and from his own back and sides where he'd lashed himself.

Deor looked into the masked man's eyes and decided. He leveled the weapon, felt his finger squeeze carefully on the trigger. There was a loud *crack* and the pistol bucked painfully against his hand, startling him with its suddenness and the brutal power. A jet of flame split the night from its muzzle, and a black spot appeared between the brows of the masked man with the whip. The back of his head exploded in a spray of brain and blood and bone splinters, spattering into the faces behind him. The impact jerked the man he'd killed like no bow he knew, as if he'd been kicked in the head by a horse or hit with a war-hammer.

Reflexes he didn't know he owned brought the pistol down again to aim, but Thora had her own pointed already. She fanned the spur of the hammer with the heel of her other hand, an astonishingly swift strobing *crack-crack-crack-crack-crack* and then *click.* Men twisted and fell under the brutal impact of the heavy bullets, and one struck the gallon can of rock-oil. It ignited in a gout of crimson flame that sprayed burning liquid across a dozen more.

Screams and blood and fire in the night, and one woman tossing aside the noose she'd been waving aloft and running away beating at hair like a flaming torch itself.

"Come!"

It was the dark-clad man they'd rescued. He plucked at Deor's jacket. "In His name, come with me now or you die! Don't run, but walk quickly."

Deor did, and the others followed; the man guiding them sank back behind the scop, looking at them in bewilderment then shaking his head as if putting something aside in a greater urgency. Deor found that he'd thrust the weapon back into its holster.

"Grab me by the collar," the stranger hissed, when they were among crowds who had only heard the brief fight in the distance. "As if you dragged me along. Now, or someone will suspect!"

Quick-witted, Deor thought, as he obeyed.

The man led them away from the brightly lit thoroughfare, randomly at first to throw off any pursuit. Their path ran through streets like the first they'd found; the buildings grew taller and shabbier and the ways between them narrower as they went on. At last he turned down an alleyway where sagging iron stairs zigzagged up the sides of the buildings between blank windows, and thumped at a metal door in what Deor's musician's ear recognized as a complex rhythm.

It opened. A man's face showed in a dim blue light, with the same strange hairstyle and a family resemblance to their guide, though his locks were a frizzy reddish-brown.

"These are Righteous Ones, Jacob," the man said. "They saved me from the servants of the faceless."

"Praise Him, Moses."

Jacob's hand came out from under his coat and he stood back. They all hurried down the stairs within into a damp cellar. A lamp was lit as soon as the door was shut and bolted behind them, honest flame rather than the eerie legendary brightness of electricity. Faces peered up at them from pallets on the floor, divided by blankets hung from cords. There was a heavy smell of wet brick and misery. A child began to cry, and was quickly hushed. The man his friend had named Moses unbuttoned his coat and handed out the parcels underneath, which turned out to be loaves of heavy dark bread and blocks of some pungent-smelling cheese.

The faces that had looked at Deor and his companions with fear now focused on the food with an intensity he recognized, that of folk very hungry indeed. Moses looked at him, weighing a chunk of the rye bread, and Deor shook his head.

"Thank you, but we have no need and you do."

There were murmured blessings, and the food was divided with haste but scrupulous care. The children began to eat as their mothers handed out portions.

"What can we do to repay you, then?" Moses asked. "You're welcome to share what refuge we have."

"Guide us," Deor said, trusting instinct. "Help us to escape."

The man's full-lipped mouth quirked. "Where is escape, in the world as it is? But I will do what I can, if you want to get out of the city before the end. Our little ones will have food today, at least."

He turned to his companion. "Get them all down to the sub-basement, Jacob."

"We shouldn't wait for the warning sirens?"

Moses shook his head. "That might be too late. It can't be long now. Make sure of the water, and the tools for digging out."

He turned to the strangers. "Come, follow me."

Lantern light showed a stairway; they went down, and through a se-ries of doors. From the way the levels varied and the look of the walls of narrow parts, they were being taken through a maze made by digging passages between the cellars of buildings. Once from the stink and the round shape, through a disused sewer.

Moses frowned. "Odd. There's fog . . . well, the ladder and cover are just ahead. May the blessings of the Lord, King of the Universe, go with you."

"And with you, my friend," Deor said, and waved the others forward.

Their guide turned and disappeared around a corner, the light bobbing and fading. Near-total blackness fell.

"Link hands?" Pip suggested. "And let me go first. I've got good night vision."

"Sees like a cat," Toa agreed.

They did; Deor felt one hand vanish in the Maori's huge paw, and the other grip Thora's familiar long-fingered callused strength. Occasionally he could hear the chink of Pip's cane against a wall, then a more metallic sound.

"There's an iron ladder set into the wall here," she said softly.

Deor opened his mouth to reply—to urge caution—when an eerie screech sounded, muffled by the stone and brick around them but still shatteringly loud. For a moment he thought it was some huge beast scream-ing in rage and fear, and then he knew it was a machine, probably the warning sirens Moses had mentioned. The city above was about to meet its fate. Their only hope was that the trapdoor above led somewhere *else*.

"Up!" he shouted through it. "Now, now, *now!*"

CHAPTER SEVEN

Órlaith had heard the far-faring merchant skipper Moishe Feldman of Newport describe Hawaiian feasts, and had prudently eaten nothing but a few ship's biscuits and some local fruit bought from the bumboats that clustered around the fleet that morning . . . though it had been hard to stop with one when she tasted her first mango.

Restraint was advisable, but those smells are making me dribble, the which would not be dignified!

The *lū'au* was held outdoors, though she noticed that there were big pavilion-style tents ready to be deployed in an instant. Hilo had a wet climate, even by the standards of Montival's own coast where it went stretching up through rain forest miles into Alaska. Tonight the sky was clear and the stars were many and bright; torches and baskets of burning wood on poles cast a flickering light, beneath the more prosaic glow of incandescent-mantle pressure lamps.

The tables were low and flanked by cushioned wicker benches that were only about six inches above the short-cropped green grass and the woven-leaf mats that covered it; fragrant mounds of sweet-smelling pink and blue frangipani and almost overpoweringly sweet night-blooming jasmine and musky guava blossoms competed with the smells of food. Palm trees rustled overhead, and there was a chattering that died away as a herald entered and boomed in Hawaiian and English:

"The King comes! The Chief!"

Musicians struck up, and the crowd went to one knee briefly before they rose and sang. Órlaith's Sword-trained ear translated:

Hawaiʻi ponoʻī,
Hawaiʻiʻs own true sons,
Nānā i kou mōʻī,
Be loyal to your king,
Kalani aliʻi,
Your country's liege and lord
Ke aliʻi!
The chief!
Makua lani ē,
Father above us all,
Na kaua e pale,
Who guarded in the war,
Me ka ihe!
With his spear!

The band then politely added the themes from Nihon's "Kimigayo" and Montival's "Voices Speak of Home," which latter meant they'd really been paying attention since it had been adopted very recently.

One song that was first heard in Japan when Charlemagne was King of the Franks, one that was made in Queen Victoria's time, and one that was written by my aunt Fiorbhinn last year, Órlaith thought. *The which is the respective antiquity of our three dynasties and kingdoms, too. Ah, well, all traditions are new when they start and they all start somewhere.*

Kalākaua II's entourage entered between the lines of cloaked and ceremonially bare-chested spearmen; their working dress that afternoon had included light torso-armor of leather and steel, practical domed helmets and stout round shields. A tall noblewoman reverently bore the folded yellow cloak that was too precious to risk by actually wearing very often since it was fashioned from the feathers of the long-extinct mamo bird, and another had the golden ring of state on a cushion. Men carried the dove-headed staff that symbolized the royal line, and the two tabu-staffs crowned with black and white cloth that showed his sacred link to the Gods of the land.

Kalākaua himself was dressed in a kikepa of shimmering blue and gold silk knotted over one shoulder and leaving the other bare. He was a good-looking man in a leonine fashion, though she thought he'd be thickset in later life unless he worked very hard at it. Both he and Queen Haukea wore flowers in their locks, apparently a sign of informality and festival here.

They also both wore *niho palaoa* around their necks, hooked ivory ornaments made from sperm whale teeth strung on human hair, a symbol of noble blood like an Associate's woven-wire ring or jeweled dagger.

Protocol governed the almost-identically-equal bows the Hawaiian monarchs exchanged with her and Reiko. Apparently that ended the formalities, for then the local overlords sat with her and Reiko to either side, and much more lively music started. The dancers that swept in between the tables certainly looked festive, with a style that switched between a fast rhythm based on swift stamping and hip-movements that made their grass skirts quiver and a slow languorous one with swaying and hand-and-arm gestures that probably meant something complex. It was certainly pretty even if you didn't know the conventions.

"We're about as private here as possible," Kalākaua said as the first course was served. "And it doesn't draw the eye like closing a door."

The starter was bowls of *poke*, very fresh cubes of raw ahi tuna tossed with soy sauce, sesame oil, a touch of honey and chopped sweet onion, garnished with dried green seaweed and scallions. Órlaith signed hers with the Pentagram, murmured the blessing that ended:

"... and blessed be those who toiled with You
Their hands helping Earth to bring forth life."

Then she made an appreciative sound at the rich almost-meaty taste,
and the second journey of Reiko's chopsticks was much more enthusiastic
than the first. At the table just beyond her Nihonjin followers were
showing—if you could pick up on very subtle expressions and then
dawning smiles—profound relief at being served something edible and
not having to pretend to enjoy some loathsome barbarian swill.

*Reiko's more flexible, but I've rarely run across a group more conservative about
things like food than the Nihonjin,* Órlaith thought.

Once they'd gotten back from the Valley of Death and the first exchange of boats had brought a Nihonjin chef for Reiko she'd thoroughly
enjoyed the products of his art, the skill of which was the more remarkable for its disciplined restraint. The world was very wide and varied;
even Montival alone was, and she'd traveled over most of it with her
parents, enjoying the local dishes all her life, from buffalo-hump steak to
the complex fantasies of Associate court cuisine.

*And they're very relieved there's rice—to them that is food, and everything else a
garnish. And there were plenty of Nihonjin here in the ancient days; this dish is probably
partly the legacy of their foodways.*

The alternatives were the same dish with octopus, which was equally
popular; there was also fruit-juice, beer, sake, various rum-and-fruit con-
coctions, a brandy distilled from pineapple that was a truly vile waste of
a delicious fruit, and wine. Heuradys grinned and leaned in to turn one
of the wine bottles in their coolers towards Órlaith; the label read Cha-
teau d'Ath and it was the '40 Pinot Noir red.

"If your un-esteemed maternal grandfather had known how valuable
those Montinore vineyards were going to be, he'd never have enfeoffed
that estate to Mom Two," she murmured.

"Ah, well, that was Lady D'Ath's reward for kidnapping my father,"
Órlaith replied, also sotto voce.

"Turn about is fair play," Heuradys said. "It was also her reward from rescuing your lady mother."

Which was true; Mackenzie raiders under Grandmother Juniper's personal command had captured Órlaith's mother Mathilda, first, and Lady d'Ath had led the party which got her back and took Rudi Mackenzie in turn . . . thus introducing the future High King and High Queen to each other as children, despite their parents' bitter enmity.

The memory heartened her. The old wars against the Association had been desperate enough in their day, but now she united their blood and Montival dwelt at peace with itself, and Heuradys was her boon companion and good right arm.

The red wine went well with the succulently rich, herb-infused, melting-tender pit-roasted whole pig that was the main course, served steaming on the leaves that had wrapped it in the imu, the underground oven. Many other dishes accompanied it or followed.

When everyone was nibbling bits of sweet fresh pineapple and banana on slivers of bamboo and sampling little bowls of mango custard, Kalākaua moved on from the generalities.

"We've had a fairly sheltered life here in the islands since the Change," he said.

Queen Haukea snorted. "If you don't count Oahu," she said, and explained to Órlaith and Reiko: "My grandparents made it out . . . just before the rest of the islands sealed it off."

"It was . . . necessary," Kalākaua said.

"It also meant driving a million people back to die," she said. "You know what they found in Oahu afterwards."

Órlaith nodded; allowing for local details it was a conversation she'd heard before, though more among her grandparents' generation than her own. Oahu and its great city of Honolulu had held most of the dwellers in these isles before the Change, utterly dependent on food shipped in from the rest of the world. The result had been what folk in Montival called a Death Zone, where there were few survivors except some who'd hidden very well, and others who'd lived by hunting and eating their fellows when everything else findable or catchable had been devoured. Most of human-kind had died in the twelve months after the Change, of violence and above all of hunger and thirst and the plagues they bred, and more than half of the remainder in the next few years. In some places it had been worse; the main islands of Japan, for example.

Reiko made a sign of affirmation with her fan: "We also on Sado-ga-shima, and the other islands of refuge," she said. "The times were very hard, and called for very hard measures everywhere."

Reiko turned the fan towards her Guard commander. "General Egawa-san's father, Egawa Katashi, brought my grandmother across Honshu from Tokyo, a month after the Change. He and the Seventy Loyal Men; and so the Yamato dynasty was preserved and our Empire founded anew. But they fought with the others to turn back the starving who followed. Else those fleeing death would have carried it with them, and brought everything down in wreck."

The Hawaiian monarch sighed, looking troubled. "It could have been worse. From what we're hearing about Korea, it *was* worse there."

Órlaith nodded. "When we were in South Westria . . . southern California, on the old maps . . . I watched one of the Korean warships through a telescope."

She was silent for a moment before she described the officer on the enemy warship's deck looking back at her through a pair of binoculars . . . and chewing idly on a smoked hand, spitting out the little finger-bones now and then.

"You're serious, aren't you?" the King asked; his Queen put down her spoon and took a gulp of the wine.

"I'm glad you told us that one *after* dinner," she said.

Órlaith nodded. "I don't suppose Koreans are any more or less wicked than other folk by nature," she said.

Reiko nodded, if a little unwillingly, which said a good deal for her, considering what her folk (and she personally) had suffered at the hands of that dark kingdom. Lord Egawa would never publically disagree with his *Tennō,* but Órlaith felt a moral certainty that he assuredly did in his innermost heart. To him an enemy was simply an enemy, and the only good one was a dead one.

For now, that makes no practical difference, Órlaith thought.

Her own first impulse was the same, to turn the place over to sword and flame from one end to the other and not just because its warriors had killed her father.

But a monarch must have justice in their soul, or else you're nothing but a bandit chief with a fancy golden hat. Also in the long run it's more practical, if you want peace, or at least as much peace as a quarrelsome tribe like human kind is ever likely to get.

"But they've been ruled and corrupted by darkness for a long time now," Órlaith said. "The longer it's left to fester, the worse for the world."

Kalākaua hesitated, and then nodded; so did the Queen. Órlaith merely nodded in return. Agreement in principle was the crucial step. The rest was detail work, and could be left to those whose business it was. She certainly wasn't going to endanger it by trying to push for too much right now.

"And the worse for those unlucky enough to dwell there, too, the ordinary people, who I'd like to see set free and helped if we can do it," she added. "That's not the most important of my aims, mind you. The Powers have entrusted House Artos with Montival and its folk, first and foremost. After that we're allied with Dai-Nippon now, bound by oath and honor to pursue this war to victory for us both. But it's something to be kept in mind."

Best leave things there for now.

She turned her head to Karl where he and the other Mackenzies sat a table away, with the McClintocks beyond. Clansfolk often drank deep at a feast—the McClintocks certainly were sampling the local tipples, and Diarmuid had had a couple of them dragged off and was reduced to clouting the heads of others with his bonnet now and then to remind them of the fact that he was their war-chief and that they weren't at a Yule feast back home with nothing to worry about except hangovers and brawls, if not of the principle of moderation. Karl had seen that his fellows hadn't done more than grow a little merry, and now he caught her eye. She gave him a slight nod and a hint of a wink.

Then she turned back to the Hawaiian monarchs. "You've shown us a glimpse of the riches of your folk's songs and dances," she said. "Let us return the favor!"

Kalākaua grinned and nodded, obviously glad to change the subject for a bit, and looked his youthful age while he did. He clapped his hands and called in his own language. The local instruments—nose flutes, xaphoons, drums and bamboo xylophones—died away. Most of the Mackenzies drew their leaf-shaped shortswords and the guards tensed imperceptibly, then relaxed again as they set them down in the turf between the main tables in a broad circle divided into eight parts, one edge up and the points inward. Firelight glittered on the honed steel. That symbolized the divisions of the Wheel of the Year, the Old Faith's sacred calendar.

Gwri Beauregard Mackenzie had had a set of bagpipes bundled at her feet and now she brought them out. Not the great hoarse *pìob mhór*, the war-pipes that could cut through the clamor of battle and whip fighters to a frenzy, but the smaller and sweeter-toned Uilleann variety. Gwri sat cross-legged and strapped the instrument's belt around herself; Uilleann pipes were inflated by a bellows arrangement under the elbow. She was grinning as she did, teeth white against her creamy brown skin, the long braids of her hair tipped with silver balls that glittered as she bent to the pipe's mouthpiece.

Karl bowed and addressed the assembly; he was Órlaith's age or a little less, a tall young man with a handsome squarish face and an archer's broad shoulders and wheat-colored hair worn past the shoulders, loose for the feast rather than braided battle-style. The Mackenzie lilt was stronger in his voice than in his liege's, though he'd spent plenty of time outside the *dúthchas* since his father commanded the High King's Archers. He wasn't quite as guileless as the wide blue eyes suggested, but he was young and the grin was wide and friendly.

"Friends and hosts, our thanks to you for the hospitality, and to the Powers by whatever names They are most pleased to be called here. We

were after thinkin' we'd make some small recompense by showing you a
dance of our own, and a song of the season to go with it—little though
this fair land of yours resembles the Black Months at home, where it's
chill and dark this time of year!"

The pipes sounded, high and sweet like the horns of Elfland in the
distance, and the crisp rattling buzz of a bodhrán-drum held in the left
hand and played with the little double-headed striker stick in the right.
A lively six-eight double jig rhythm sounded, and there was a murmur of
interest and appreciation from the audience that quickly died away.

Sure, and you can tell the Clan Mackenzie was founded by a musician! Órlaith
thought, remembering her grandmother kindly. *Lady Juniper left her mark
for good and all, right enough.*

All her father's folk learned song and an instrument in Moon School,
since it was an important part of their strand of the Old Faith. And it was
notorious that an impromptu céilidh broke out wherever a few of them
were set down without something more urgent to do.

Though if it were the war-pipes and Lambeg drums . . .

Karl and his brother Mathun, who looked very much like him with a
few years subtracted, faced each other motionless across the circle of
swords for a moment. Then they began to dance, left hand on hip and
right up so that the crooked fingers were above the blue flat beret-like
Scots bonnet; they were both from Dun Fairfax and of the Wolf sept, and
had a swatch of the gray fur of their totem in the silver clasps above the
left eye.

The rest of the clansfolk took up the words of the song, strong young
voices in expert harmony:

"Yule is come
Now beat the drum
And light the Solstice flame!"

The sword-dance kept the upper body almost still, save for when left
and right hand switched positions, but the feet moved in a skipping

rhythm that sent kilt and sporran and the tail of the plaid swaying; every six beats there was a quick stamping jump to the right, that left the dancer in the next of the eights into which the swords divided the circle.

If you made a mistake, it also meant you were stamping a foot down on the upraised blade of a sword, which would be unfortunate for the sole of your shoe and the foot within. Back in the Mackenzie *dúthchas*, the Clan's grave elders waged a continual battle to try and make everyone use dulled blades for this dance; at the major public festivals and for practice among those too young to be Initiates they even succeeded.

"Tonight we'll raise
A hymn of praise
For the Sun returns again!"

Two more of the young Mackenzies fed themselves into the dance, Boudicca and Rowan, moving in perfect unison.

"Hail to Yule, the longest night
Of all the turning year—
Await the resurrecting Light
That banishes despair!"

Then Karl surprised her a little; he signaled her to come over if she wished, but she was willing enough. Without undue modesty she knew she was a striking dancer. And she'd seen enough to know that here, as in much of Montival, dancing was considered suitable for those of high rank, particularly with a religious element. Which wasn't a problem, since pretty well everything Mackenzies did had a religious part to it; the Old Faith didn't make much distinction between the everyday and things of the spirit.

And besides that, I like dancing, and this is a chance to do it!

You needed an even number of dancers for the sword-ring, and it got more difficult with every pair; six was as high as it usually went, with eight reserved for the great feasts of the Quarter Festivals and even there for teams who'd practiced together often.

Órlaith wasn't surprised when a man in Mackenzie dress stepped up opposite her, but she almost missed the beat when she recognized Alan Thurston. That took only an instant despite his wearing kilt and plaid and bonnet rather than the tight blue copper-riveted trousers and tooled boots and Stetson of a Boisean rancher, or the bleak gray practicality of the USB Army's uniform.

Alan was the nephew of the President-General of the United States of Boise but had only a vague resemblance to his uncle Frederick, though more to his cousins; the family's men ran to a tall, broad-shouldered, long-limbed build and squared-off chins, and he had all of that. His father Martin was long-dead, and had also been a traitor, parricide and collaborator—later mindless puppet—of the Prophet of the Church Universal and Triumphant, and the reason the Prophet's War had been a civil strife in Boise. That was also the reason Alan had grown up in quiet exile on a remote ranch with his mother Juliet.

He was also . . .

Gorgeous, she thought happily, returning his grin. *If he'd ever gone on the stage, there wouldn't be a dry seat in the house. Mine all mine! Well, yes, Da killed his father . . . but then, Da's father killed Mother's father long before they were married, and that never bothered them much. All the better for the Kingdom's peace that they wed, in fact, to be a symbol of the burying of old feuds and to produce . . . me.*

Curling honey-brown hair sun-streaked with his mother's gold, eyes of sage green rimmed with a darker color, nose straight and slightly flared, high cheekbones tapering down to a square chin with a cleft, full lips smiling and showing even teeth against skin that was a creamy olive tint just on the pale side of very light brown.

For a moment she worried that he'd have trouble with the dance; square dancing was the closest thing the wilds of rural Boise had to this. Then he took up the tune and the step outside the circle without missing a beat. He must have been practicing.

And Karl must have been helping him, the scheming lout! Órlaith thought with fond amusement. *Not that it would have worked if he wasn't quick and graceful by nature.*

She sang with the rest, noticing Alan's sharper accent, with its eastern across-the-mountains hint of a twang:

"For now the tide will start to turn
Night will yield to Day
And the waning Year will shed its skin
And cast the dark away!"

As she moved, she admired the smooth play of muscle in the young man's legs. He had the strong thighs of a horseman, but good calves as well; in fact, he'd told her that he'd deliberately trained by running alongside his horse for an hour or more every day, vaulting across the saddle now and then.

Which is why I'm not bandy-legged like a lot of people in my neck of the woods, he'd said with a grin.

Moving into the circle in mid-dance was hard, and Órlaith concentrated on letting the music take her body and move it as if it were playing directly on muscle and nerve. She turned a gliding side-step into a skip forward, and that meant instantly doing the high-knee sideways motion into another wedge. Alan matched it effortlessly, and then they were fully into the rhythm. Everyone followed Karl into a pirouette, turning in a complete circle in a wave of plaids one after the other without changing the pace and then ending with another shift:

"Pile the bonfire
Join the dance
Come raise your voices high—
Lord Winter can no more advance
His hold on Earth and Sky!"

The pipes and bodhrán picked up the pace, and she could feel the unified scuffing of six pairs of boots on the turf as if the soles of her feet were the skin of the drum:

"For soon the sap will rise again
The mute once more will sing—
And the heart will wake anew
To the promise of the Spring!"

With the last note they all stopped, then bowed deeply by extending the right leg back and extending the right hand, first to each other and then turning and repeating the gesture outward to the audience half-glimpsed in the light of the flames.

The gathering broke the silence after the last dying note of the pipes and tap of the bodhrán with a storm of laughter and applause. Órlaith returned to the upper table, parting from Alan with a long glance and a wink; Karl would get him into the villa easily enough later and she could sleep late tomorrow.

The smile died on her face as she saw the expression on the messenger who'd knelt behind the Hawaiian monarchs and was speaking urgently as they leaned in to follow him. The more so as their faces took on the look of his.

Kalākaua turned to her. "A courier boat from Australia has arrived," he said. "From Darwin. They say they've a message from your frigate *Stormrider*, and then to you personally from King John . . . King Birmo . . . of Capricornia."

Órlaith hissed between her teeth and exchanged a glance with Reiko as the Hawaiian handed her an envelope. She nodded slightly to the *Tennō* who was also her friend. The *Stormrider* had been blown in John's wake by the same blast, but evidently she'd lived up to her name and survived the journey to . . .

All the way to Capricornia!

That was a very long way indeed. There was some direct trade between Montival and Capricornia, but only recently and only by the more daring skippers . . . such as Moishe Feldman of the *Tarshish Queen*. Most were content to use Hilo as an entrepôt, paying higher prices to the Hawaiian middlemen in recompense for lower costs and risks on the long dangerous voyage to the pirate-infested Asian waters.

The message was certainly on Royal Montivallan Navy stationery, and sealed with blue wax and the stamp of an RMN captain, a stylized ship's wheel and sextant. The seal looked intact. . . .

"We've had it brought directly to you, Your Highness," Kalākaua said. "The Capricornians are standing by for you to interview."

The Sword of the Lady rested by her side, sheathed and with the belt wrapped around it. She knew he spoke the truth . . . as far as he knew it.

He was frowning a little, too. That was one of the better-known abilities the Lady's gift conferred on the one of House Artos who bore it, but she wasn't sure how much of that was known here. Or believed, even if the facts were known. Back home everyone knew it, and virtually everyone believed it right down in their bones, too—by the time her father reached his second decade on the Throne, men had been known to flee to the wilderness or jump from high places rather than face a monarch who couldn't be taken in by even the most cunning and convincing lie, because he could sense the *intent* to deceive.

That was one reason he'd used it less than he might have. As he'd put it, having that ability required restraint if you weren't to convince a fatal number of people that the only way to make life tolerable was to kill you.

"Thank you, Your Majesty," she said soberly. "That's appreciated, and it will be remembered."

She took a deep breath, then cracked the sealing-wax and opened the eight-and-a-half-by-eleven structure of heavy water-resistant cream-colored paper.

Her eyes went quickly down the lines of text—it was typewritten, but had Captain Russ' signature at the bottom of four single-spaced pages.

Another was from King John I of Capricornia—or King Birmo as he was more commonly known, apparently.

"*Stormrider*'s intact," she said; her own party had their ears cocked, and so did Reiko and her commanders. "They took some damage from the storm off Topanga, but they've been repaired in Darwin's own naval yards . . . which means we owe the King of Capricornia a favor."

Her eyes went to the date-stamp.

"Goddess gentle and strong, they made a fast passage! And they have news of the *Tarshish Queen*, hence of John. No direct contact, but strong circumstantial evidence that she was afloat recently, and where that was. The Korean warships chasing them have definitely all been destroyed, apparently by the *Tarshish Queen*'s catapults and by . . . chance circumstances, about which they've sent evidence. They and a supply ship from Darwin are heading for the area to search further."

Reiko's face was impassive as she nodded and smiled slightly. Nevertheless her polite:

"Very good news, Orrey-chan," was entirely sincere; and it held an element of relief.

Órlaith thought hard. "We'll hold a conference tomorrow," she said. "Time's short, but not so short we won't do better after a good night's sleep."

CHAPTER EIGHT

BETWEEN WAKING WORLD AND SHADOW

Pip looked around the chamber where she and Toa emerged, poised for threats and then feeling a rush of relief when it proved empty. That didn't make the environment actually as unthreatening as it looked—she'd absorbed that lesson quite literally at her mother's knee, listening to her stories—but it was nice for a start. Thora boiled up out of the trapdoor on Toa's heels, pulling Deor who followed and promptly collapsed into a sprawl, panting, with Thora beside him putting a steadying hand on his shoulder.

Presumably this is harder on him, since he's the one who knows about this and has to pay attention to the bits behind the scenery, Pip thought. *Amazing how real this all feels . . . right down to the splinter in my thumb. Except the parts where I sort of see a lioness in the background, or feel as if I am one. Best not to think about that. God knows what Mummy would have said about her daughter turning into a large beast of prey. Of course, metaphorically speaking Mummy was a large and very successful beast of prey herself, but I think literalizing the metaphor would have offended her sense of the fitness of things.*

She dug the splinter out with her teeth as she took in their surroundings. It was daylight, at least, bright beams through shuttered windows and around the edges of the door. That didn't mean the situation was any better than in the doomed and nighted city of madness and hatred they'd left, but it made her feel a bit more cheerful, and she'd take any sort of cheerfulness going. It was also distinctly cool, as cool as she could ever recall being except for a trip to Tasmania once where there had actually been *frost*, but fresh and comfortable enough with the long-sleeved dress.

She prodded at the wall with her . . .

"It's an *umbrella* now?" she asked—rhetorically, but with genuine anger in her voice. "I liked that cane! I had it made specially and developed my own techniques for whacking at people with it!"

I got my own ship so I could be in command, she thought. *Now I can't even control what I'm wearing. And I'm preggers . . . always thought I would, someday, but not unexpectedly! Think of the trouble it's going to take to find a decent nanny God-knows-where!*

Then with an effort of will:

Now, don't let that make you testy, Miss Philippa. Manners Mayketh Woman.

The last part of the thought had the tone of one of her teachers at Rockhampton Girls Grammar School, a place which was supposed to give you polish and where she'd undoubtedly learned a good deal, not all of it on the official curriculum.

I never liked Miss Gresham. Rather a sour old bitch, as I recall.

Closer examination showed that the umbrella was still a stout stick of Makassar ebony with a heavy ridged knob on one end, and that the ferrule of the brolly was a triangular steel spike; she could use this if she had to, either for hitting or like a fencing épée. Looking down she saw that the dress was much the same as it had been in the first vision of New York, except that there was a petticoat beneath it, the skirt was a bit longer, and the buckles on the shoes weren't silver skulls but just silver buckles.

Which is all to the good. I've no objection to skulls as a fashion statement, but I suspect they were more in the nature of a mark of your religious commitment back there.

Toa went straight to the door; he was still in dungarees, but this time his spear was more or less a long-handled navvy's shovel . . . which would do nicely for gutting and cutting if needs must, almost as much as the original. The more so as the edge bore the telltale waving line that revealed it had been carefully sharpened.

"Still in town," he said.

There was disapproval in his gravelly Ocker-accented voice; he disliked cities, having grown up where the only ones around were ruined and deserted. Cities made it too easy to sneak up on you, though he did approve of the broader variety of pubs.

"Cities have their points—bloody *hell*, I'm wearing a *corset!*" Pip said; a quick investigation with a finger revealed that it was a light cloth one.

But still! This is ridiculous.

"You've got a corset at home," Toa pointed out. "Saw it on that stand once when you came back from that school. All frilly grundies, with ribbons and those little chiming bells."

"That was a theatrical *costume*," Pip said loftily. "And for needlework practice."

In fact you might say it had been sporting goods, since she and a friend had taken turns wearing it at Rockhampton in amateur theatricals of their own devising. The boarding school had been rather isolated out in the sleepy countryside, and you had to make your own entertainment after classes. She'd enjoyed chess and open-air perspective drawing and the Mathematics Club, but it didn't do to be completely cerebral and you could only steeplechase or play Extreme Field Hockey or haunt the salle d'armes so many times a week.

"So's that droog thing with the suspenders and bowler hat a costume," Toa said, keeping his eye to the slightly open door.

"No, that's working clothes," Pip said lightly, touching her hair, which was worn rather long and piled up in an elaborate do under a broad-brimmed hat this time. "I've won fights on land and sea wearing it, haven't I? It's nicely terrifying. Well, *I'm* terrifying when out on a bovver but it helps."

"Makes the opposition fall about laughing. That helps when you put the toe cap into their ghoolies."

She'd been surveying the room while he kept his eye to the shutters and watched the outside. They were definitely in a workman's storehouse of some sort, bare brick walls with racks and shelves, half-empty sacks of plaster with labels in English, buckets of paint, boxes of nails, and sundry brushes and trowels and boards and other tools, along with folding ladders, giving the air around the supplies an atmosphere turpentinish and medicinal. And another earthy one beneath it, the scent of setting mortar. Someone had been building. The smell was familiar since, like any substantial station, Tanumgera had carpenters and masons working on something at any given time.

A grimy newspaper lay on one of the shelves. She looked at it; the *New York Herald* again, but the date was in early April of 1920. Reading it without conspicuously marking what she was wearing required holding it out at arm's length since it was very dusty and spattered with dried daubs of paint.

Though the headlines were less apocalyptic they were still very strange. History hadn't been her favorite subject, particularly not the deeply boring history of the last pre-Blackout century or so, but she knew that her version of 1920 hadn't seen a Russian invasion of Sweden, or a civil war in Austria-Hungary, or anything meriting a *Communards Storm Paris, Louvre in Flames* leader. Nor had there been a President Winthrop in the United States.

She was *pretty* sure he'd been named Wilson; either that, or Williams.

Still, this feels less . . . less as if the tentacles are showing. It's more like what led to me. I think something terrible happened here, something to throw the world on the path to . . . what we saw in the last place.

Deor still looked fairly rocky as he knelt on the round metal trapdoor, and Thora had stayed beside him as he recovered from his last glimpse of the place they'd escaped.

"Fire," he whispered. "A world of poisoned fire. The powers of Gods, in the hands of men less than beasts, worse than *eoten.*"

Well, that's very poet-y and Northern and doomy, Pip thought; she'd read *Beowulf* and the *Prose Edda* . . . in translation. *I'll just say that place gave me the galloping creeps, nearly as much as the one with all the wrecked autos.*

"Like the sword of Sutr, carried burning to Vígríðr plain on the last morning of the world," Thora said quietly.

Then Deor shook himself and smiled crookedly. "No point in grieving for something that never happened . . . not in our cycle of the worlds," he said.

He was wearing a suit that differed only in details from the one he'd been in before; if anything the collar looked even more uncomfortable, which was revenge for the corset. From the way Thora had started twisting and running a hand inside her dress to find out what was strapped around her, she'd never worn one even to play Distressed Victorian Maiden in Lecherous Hands, though compared to armor it couldn't be *too* bad.

"This is still New Nightmare City, pardon me, New York," Pip said holding up the newspaper. "The same one, I think, but a lot earlier."

Deor grinned at her a bit crookedly. "And for the question in your mind, Captain Pip: why are we being led through the ages here, as well as across continents and seas, as we journey towards the Prince? I don't know. Let's just say that paths in the Otherworld don't follow the rules of those in the world of common day. There are more purposes than ours at work here, and they may be very subtle."

"I'll keep thinking about that for consolation as we're devoured by monsters," Pip said, and smiled back at him.

"Looks like we could get out of here without anyone much noticing," Toa said. "Crowd looks safe enough if you don't mind they're all Pākehā."

"You're very tolerant that way," Pip observed ironically.

"Too right, I never even mention the Pākehā smell or the bad teeth or the no-chins bit or the way they're mostly hunchbacked midgets. They're all looking at some bloody parade or other out there right now."

Pip gave the room one last glance-over. "Why don't you carry that package?" she said, pointing to a large one wrapped up with string. "It'll make you less conspicuous."

The Maori grinned, an alarming expression. "You mean they might not notice the *Tāmoko*?" he said, flicking a sausage-like thumb at the swirling patterns on his face, as individual as a fingerprint. "I'll blend right in."

He lolled his tongue and made his eyes bulge for a moment, like the beginning of a war-haka. Then he hefted the parcel, which clinked dully, and hoisted it on one shoulder and put the shovel over the other. That did make it necessary to really peer closely before you caught the full effect of features, tattoos and scars.

"Ready?" Pip said.

I hope this works. No matter what his mother's mother was, nobody's going to mistake Toa for a Pākehā. The people we meet seem real, but are they? And if they are, are they really seeing us, or are we part of a backdrop to them?

Deor nodded, settling the bowler on his head; it really didn't look right for someone named Deor Godulfson. Toa swung the door open and Deor led them out; Pip followed, with Toa bringing up the rear. She approved of that. He had a sense for when he was being followed, and it had saved both their lives more than once.

Outside the sky was clear, and the little building they'd been in was shown to be a simple brick rectangle with a slate roof and *Parks and Maintenance Department, Municipal Government of Greater New York* in cast-iron letters above the door. It was mid-morning and they were on the south side of a broad treelined street, with a park to its north; over the tops of the elms there she could see a great triumphal arch. The city-rumble was there in the background, the familiar modern sounds of horses and wagons and carriages, thickly interspersed with the growling of motor vehicles like something out of an old storybook.

The traffic's been blocked out of these streets, though, Pip thought.

She recognized the signs from occasions in Townsville City with her parents or grandfather, though this metropolis was vastly larger.

Parade or something else official.

The southern side where they stood was also a park, but you could tell that it was a newer one, and from the look of the rest of the neighborhood she suspected that buildings had been torn down to make room for it—the layout was a regular north-south grid, and the architecture of the blocks she could see was a curious mixture of busy-looking and sooty brick and newer, lighter-colored structures in a much more uniform neo-Classical style.

The flower-banks of the new park were very pretty—a blaze of for-
sythia and crocus and yellow daffodils, and the fountains raised skyward
in graceful arcs, but the trees were new and smallish, the pathways still
pristine, each of the blue and red bricks beneath their feet sharp-edged.
A fairly dense crowd was scattered through the park, but they were obey-
ing signs that read:

It Is Forbidden To Walk On The Grass.

And all focused on the ceremony going on in the center of the open
space. The whole city block was enclosed by an ornate gilded iron railing
about head-high on her, with a line of outward-leaning points in the
shape of leaves and vines at the top, and broad paths met in the center of
it like a Greek cross. Where they joined stood a small circular building
of glistening white marble, topped by a shallow copper dome and sur-
rounded by thickets of flowers. It stood on a six-foot circular platform of
the same stone, worked in shallow relief with figures of robed and hooded
women with their arms before their faces in a gesture of mourning. In
front of the stairs was a sculptural group, three female figures in ancient
Greek robes: one spinning out a thread, the second measuring it, and a
third about to make a cut.

The Fates, she thought; even tense and looking for threats she could see
it was fine work if you liked a naturalistic style.

Either the Fates, or the Sixth Form prefects at work.

Six Ionic columns supported the roof, and the single door was a tall
sheet of worked bronze at the top of a graceful semicircular staircase.
Each half of the door held a design of a pomegranate tree. A temporary
speaker's platform draped in the flags of the old . . .

Well, not so old in 1920, she thought.

. . . American republic stood behind the statues, with a group of dignitaries on it; all men of middle age or more, some in archaic-looking rigs
of black cutaway coats and waistcoats and top-hats, some in elaborate
military uniforms, both types she recognized from history books.

A regiment's worth of cavalry was drawn up in a hollow square around
the building, sitting their mounts silently with the sun bright on the pen-

nants and the blades of their lances, which might account for the extremely orderly, not to mention silent, disposition of the crowd. None of them wore armor except for rather odd-looking brass helmets, polished and with horsehair crests, and they all had revolvers at their belts as well.

Their uniforms were blue with gold piping, elaborate with corded decoration, and their jackboots polished to a mirror sheen. Those were as nothing compared to the smaller group of cavalry around the speaker's platform itself; hussars in tight red breeches that fastened up the outside seam with jet buttons, boots with gold tassels, short fur-edged midnight-blue jackets worn slung over one shoulder in the style of a cape, clasped with a woven-silver cord adorned with gold and silver braiding and several rows of multiple buttons. Under *that* was a dolman also decorated in braid, on their heads were tall fur busbies, and their embroidered saddlecloths had four long points. It all made the pictures she'd seen of the King-Emperor's court in far Winchester look drab, or even the Pope's in Badia.

Well-mounted, though, she thought.

The horses were long-legged hunter types, their coats gleaming with health and good grooming, the leather of saddles and tack as immaculate as the uniforms of the troopers. It was undoubtedly a ceremonial occasion, but the lancers and hussars looked as if they knew how to ride, at least. Being the granddaughter of Townsville's Colonel meant she'd grown up around horse-soldiers. All the successor-states in Oz had plenty of empty country covered in grass.

But why lances and sabers, if they have working firearms here?

One thing that *was* familiar was the sonorous politician's blather of the speechmaker delivered by one of the top-hatted dignitaries, at least in tone if not content.

"The laws prohibiting suicide and providing punishment for any attempt at self-destruction have been repealed. The Government has seen fit to acknowledge the right of man to end an existence which may have become intolerable to him, through physical suffering or mental despair. It is believed that the community will be benefited by the removal of such people from their midst. Since the passage of this law, the number of suicides in the United States has not increased. Now the Government has determined to establish a Lethal Chamber in every city, town and village in the country. It remains to be seen whether or not that class of human creatures from whose desponding ranks new victims of self-destruction fall daily will accept the relief thus provided."

"Well, if someone wants to do away with themselves . . ." Pip murmured dubiously.

"There is ill-wreaking here," Deor said. "This thing . . . somehow it's tied to Prince John's loss. How, I do not yet know, but it is."

The politician paused, and half-turned to indicate the round columned building behind him. The crowd had been quiet; now the silence in the street was absolute.

"There a painless death awaits him who can no longer bear the sorrows of this life. If death is welcome let him seek it there."

Aha, she thought. *Painless death . . . but in that later New York, the Eternal Emperor said Lethal* Torment *Chambers. I suppose this is what they mean by a slippery slope, what?*

The speaker turned to one of the uniformed officers on the platform: "I declare the Lethal Chamber open."

Then to the crowd: "Citizens of New York and of the United States of America, through me the Government declares the Lethal Chamber to be open."

An officer barked a command, a bugle echoed it—Pip even recognized the sequence of notes—and the hussars fell in behind the carriages that drew up to take the dignitaries and commanders. The lancers wheeled neatly, the tall steel-tipped shafts swaying and reforming like a thicket of reeds bowing to a breeze, and clattered off with an endless rumbling clop of shod hooves on pavement. The crowd began to break up, voices slowly filling the void.

"There," Deor said quietly, pointing out one nattily-dressed young man. "Him. Follow him."

"That I can do," Pip said. "Mummy had the Police chief in Townsville City run me through an urban surveillance course once and gave me pointers herself—said you never knew when that sort of thing would come in handy."

The man Deor had pointed out wasn't remarkable. About thirty, medium in stature—an inch or less taller than Pip, who'd inherited much of her father's height—with reddish-brown hair worn trimmed above the collar and parted in the center and a clipped mustache, and faded green eyes. He was handsome in a slightly wasted way, but slim in a manner that suggested he'd been more active once and with the pallor of someone who spent most of his days indoors. His clothing was black except for a silver-gray waistcoat, and a dark-gray homburg hat, but fitted as if it had been done by a very good tailor.

He was ordinary for this time and place, until you saw his eyes. They skipped over Pip without acknowledging her, then lingered for a moment on Toa as if slightly puzzled. Once you saw those eyes he didn't look ordinary at all. They seemed to open on vistas, across a sea whose waves were cloud. . . .

Pip fought down a snarl and made herself retract her claws. . . .

Wait a minute. I have claws? she thought, startled. *I mean, I literally have claws?*

For a moment she thought she did, claws like curved knives that could rip flesh apart with a drive of shoulders stronger than Toa's.

Pip would have liked to dismiss the idea as a fancy, but she wasn't fanciful.

And I'm in a place where the usual rules don't apply. Though after months on Baru Denpasar I was starting to think those are a bit more elastic than I'd always assumed anyway.

The man walked on, walking with the stride of someone who knew where he was going but wasn't in a hurry.

"Bunch around me," Pip said quietly. "Talk a bit. You don't think a group is following you."

"You don't?" Thora asked conversationally.

"Not on a city street. One tail is more conspicuous there. It's completely different from countryside tracking, according to my instructor."

Thora and Deor closed up, with Toa still bringing up the rear. He was attracting the odd glance, once from what was apparently a mounted policeman, to judge from his cloth-covered bobby-style helmet and long riot-stick, but then the eyes flicked to the folk ahead of him and lost suspicion.

Bet if he was here alone it would be a difficulty, Pip thought. *Though more of a difficulty for anyone who tried to accost him!*

The man they were tracking moved through the crowds easily. The clump with Pip had a little more difficulty, but she'd noticed before that if you moved without the slightest doubt that people would get out of your way, they usually did. It helped if you were well-dressed, too, and judging from the passers-by the clothes they'd . . . arrived in . . . were the local equivalents of the gentry's costume.

Pip noted the street signs and memorized them; they crossed one called South Fifth Avenue, and walked along its western side to a Bleecker Street. There was the same mix of older and newer buildings she'd noticed around the Lethal Chamber, and then it was solidly older; five or six story brick buildings divided into apartments and attached shops. The crowds were thicker, and less well-dressed, with many more cloth caps and women in dowdy, tired-looking dresses longer than what she or Thora wore. Now and then the man they were following attracted sullen-hostile glances, or jeers from ragged urchins, and the narrower streets had a number of pushcarts selling anything from sausages she wouldn't have tried on a bet to old clothes.

Beside one door was a row of signs. The first and largest read:

HAWBERK, ARMOURER

Thora snorted, and Pip spared her a glance and a raised eyebrow: they were both inwardly groaning at the obvious pun, since hauberk was precisely what you called a mail shirt . . . though she thought the term was more common in everyday use in Montival, which from what she'd heard and John confirmed had a taste for terminology culled from history.

Or historical novels, she thought, with a slightly snide edge to her mental tone. *Whereas in Oz, we call it a mail shirt or a fence-wire jumper.*

The man they were following went through the part-glass door, giving a glimpse of a long dim hallway ending in a stairwell. The entrance rang a bell as it opened. On its heels came a hearty voice crying:

"Come in, Mr. Castaigne!"

Then a continuing murmur of voices as it closed, ringing the bell again; she thought she could hear another voice, a man's, and then a woman's, but too muffled to catch what was said.

Pip slowed, dawdling, watching the street for a little until she could see out of the corner of her eye that their target wasn't loitering just inside, then held up two fingers and went through the door. Deor followed, while Toa leaned on his shovel and held the box so that it shadowed his face, while Thora pulled a piece of paper out of her handbag and pretended to read it . . . or possibly really did.

It would help if I knew what I was supposed to do with this thing once we catch it, Pip thought. *As the dog said when he took out after the stagecoach!*

The dim hallway within had a door to the armorer's shop, left slightly ajar; the distinctive tinka-tinka-tinka of a metalworkers' hammer sounded within, absurdly familiar in this alien place, and then voices. On the wall opposite was a list of other establishments, not terribly different except in detail from Townsville or Cairns or Darwin or even Hobart; tailors, cobblers, a used and antiquarian bookshop, a maker and repairer of musical instruments (at which she could feel Deor twitch with interest) and one truly strange one reading:

A. Wilde, Repairer of Reputations, 3rd floor.

Deor didn't twitch at that one; he stared at it fixedly, then slowly lifted his gray gaze to the stairs.

"Carefully," he said, his voice almost a murmur. "We're in the right place, but gang very carefully from here. There is that here which might know what we are, and destroy us if we're unwary."

Pip nodded.

"That is a lovely piece of embroidery," the voice of the man they'd been following said through the doorway to the armorer's shop.

"It's the arms of the last Duke of Burgundy," a woman's voice said. "See, I'm doing it from this colored plate in the Metropolitan Museum's collection of European royal families' arms; it will go with a suit my father has restored."

Someone about my age, Pip thought. *And sounding genuinely enthusiastic.*

Pip had a better-than-nodding acquaintance with heraldry, through her parents. The Abercrombies had a perfectly genuine and rather complex coat from the College of Heralds which they'd brought with them to Queensland when Queen Victoria was middle-aged; the Balwyns' was so old it was simple, a red lion rampant dexter. One of her ancestors had worn it on his shield when he followed Godfrey de Bouillon over the walls of Jerusalem in 1099 in steel cap and hauberk, screaming *Ville Gagne!* with the best, slaughtering anything that moved, wading ankle-deep in blood and looting the place bare.

Embroidery, though . . . I'd rather fight giant squid in a bathtub full of large-curd cottage cheese.

"See, it's Philip the Bold's."

"Complex arms," the man said again.

"Yes, they became very elaborate then, towards the beginning of the Renaissance. One and four quartered azure, semé-de-lys or, a bordure compony of argent and gules; two per pale, bendy of six or and azure, a bordure gules and sable, a lion or, armed and langued gules; three per pale, bendy of six, or and azure, a bordure gules and argent, a lion gules, armed and langued or. Overall, or, a lion sable armed and langued gules. Distinguished from his father's because it's brisured by a label argent."

Heraldry attack! Pip thought. Then: *She's nervous, but chattering because she's trying to hide it.*

The young woman spoke under the sound of the other man's hammer, and then a metallic clicking and rustling; adjusting tiny bolts and rivets, she thought, and the jingle of mail, and the *scuffa-scuffa* of a polishing cloth and emery used to remove rust.

"Who is this for?" the first man asked.

The deeper voice replied, listing a complex search for a suit that was apparently of historic value to some collector; it all sounded a bit old-country and odd, since Pip had been brought up in a world where armor was a new craft patterned on designs pulled from books, and valued for its ability to keep your hide unpunctured by the slings and arrows and lances and spears and boomerangs and whatever of outrageous fortune. As embodied in your more outrageous neighbors.

And he's nervous too. An older man . . . and he's got a different accent. Rather like Mummy's or mine, in fact. English, and very wellborn. Odd, here in New York, and working at an artisan's craft. But then again, Mummy spent most of her life after the Blackout until she married Daddy on the opposite side of the planet from England, doing some rather déclassé things, or ones that would have been if buccaneering weren't such an old tradition in our family. The girl sounds the same way; the Yank sounds like a Yank, except a bit plummy and old-fashioned, like a book talking. No contractions.

Pip knew what pre-Blackout American accents sounded like; Auntie Fifi had a twanging one that she proudly described as *Original Western Trailer-Trash*, and there were a variety of others sprinkled thinly about the parts of Oz she'd seen, mostly rather elderly by now. The people with John mostly had very distinctive and different patterns of speech, apparently grown up since the Change, though Captain Feldman's was more like the pre-Change standard.

The American continued to the English armorer: "Did you continue the search so persistently without any certainty of the greave being still in existence?"

"Of course," the posh Englishman replied coolly.

"It was worth something to you."

"No," the older man with the English accent replied, laughing. "My pleasure in finding it was my reward."

"Have you no ambition to be rich?" the American asked, with a sly smile in his voice.

The tone put Pip slightly on edge, as if it were a cat toying with something small and helpless.

"My one ambition is to be the best armorer in the world," the Englishman answered gravely.

The conversation ended and Deor hissed: "In here! He mustn't see us!"

They opened the door on the opposite side and entered. Pip gave a brilliant smile at the proprietor, sitting at a desk piled high with the musty-smelling books that crowded the shelves all about. They were ancient-looking for the most part, the leather of their binding wrought in ridges or tooled, often cracked and dried with age. They were the sort of thing the Bunyip aristocracy of Station-Holders in Townsville would have paid through the nose for if some salvager could get them out of the dead cities.

He peered at her over reading glasses with narrow lenses and cackled. "Not often we see a young miss like you in here! What might I help you with?"

Behind them the door to the armorer's shop clinked open and shut. Footsteps went down the hall to the stairwell, and then up it with a tap of shoe-leather on boards and a creak.

"What's that you have there?" Deor asked, nodding his head at the slim volume the old man was reading.

"Oh, just something French," the man said, smoothly sliding another book across it.

From the brief glance at the page it was a printed play with stage directions and dialogue.

And with naughty pictures, probably, Pip thought; though what she'd seen had been only a chastely-robed woman gesturing wildly. *Now what?*

"Follow," Deor said.

They filed out with the merchant staring after them in bewilderment—Toa reluctantly putting down a book on Gothic cathedrals, a style for which he had a passion, which had also astonished the proprietor—and went to the stairs. Pip put her hand into the bag over her shoulder, reaching for her slingshot. Somewhat to her surprise, it was still there rather than being transmuted to some fascinatingly archaic firearm of the ancient world.

Deor put a hand out as they filed up the stairwell, Toa walking crabwise next to the wall so the steps would creak less. Pip paced up quickly on quiet cat-feet, the slingshot clamped in her hand. The building was strange, obviously old and run-down, but equally obviously built in the modern fashion for natural ventilation and lighting from windows, lanterns and candles, though electric lights had been added later in a slapdash fashion.

Deor stopped at the top of the stairs. Thora followed him, hand on the gun in her handbag as it would have been on the hilt of her sword, and pointed to a door. Deor nodded, then made a sign towards the next one down the corridor; it had a disused air, and he listened at it and then nodded again.

"John," he said very quietly.

Thora tested the knob, then began to lean against it, her leanly muscular arm tensing. Pip stepped forward:

"Let's be subtle, shall we, eh?" she said.

Thora stepped aside, frowning faintly. Pip felt slightly abashed for a moment at the implied professionalism.

Tsk, tsk, girl. Mind on the prize, what?

She pulled her lockpicks out of the bag—they were there, and in the same chamois-leather wrap she usually kept them in, an identical replacement for her mother's.

Perhaps it's better that I'm not Supreme Goddess after all, she thought mordantly as she unlimbered two of them; the lock was a straight French, the antique straight-through type with two studs on the end of the key and much easier to jigger than a Yale style. *I seem to be rather unimaginative even when I'm in a sodding spirit realm and can make things by thinking about it!*

Her fingers moved carefully, slow steady pressures and then . . .

Click.

Picking locks is not for the nervous, as Mummy always said, she thought, rocking back on her heels as Thora went through with a nod and her hidden hand undoubtedly still clenched on the gun-butt.

They all followed, Toa last and closing the door delicately, with a hand that made the chipped glass knob look like a bead. Then he braced the door with his long-handled shovel, digging the point into the battered, splintered boards of the floor.

The others fanned out to search the suite of rooms. Most of whatever furniture it had had was gone, or draped in dingy sheets. There were four rooms, and one included a toilet and tub. The water wasn't connected, and the tub was coated with a thin film of what Pip thought was actual marble. Thora exclaimed from another room, and she went into it. The Bearkiller woman was looking at a flower in a vase. . . .

Except that it wasn't a rose, as she first thought. It was a carving, done in marble too, a creamy white color. The work was exquisitely detailed, and she wouldn't have thought it was possible to catch the fleshy delicacy no matter how skillful you were. She looked at it in fascination and reached a finger out towards it.

"No!" Deor said sharply, his eyes fixed on the rose.

"It's a dangerous carving of a rose?" Pip asked in exasperation.

"It's not a carving at all," Deor said. "That *was* a rose, and it has been changed. So it begins, here, and leads to that day we saw, the day of fire."

Pip snatched her hand back.

He found a set of wineglasses on a table. "Toa, keep watch. The rest of you, listen with these. We'll all get something, and we can put what we hear together."

Pip took up the tulip-shaped glass—rather dirty, with red-wine crystals at the bottom—and set it against a spot where the plaster had fallen off the lath of the wall. A murmur of voices came through as she pressed her ear to the base.

She caught a name. *Castaigne*, she thought. *Might be useful.*

CHAPTER NINE

Alan Thurston dreamed. A cat was singing in human words, but not to him, its voice as sweet as clover honey dripping from a comb of beeswax on a hot August day. Honey of the type his mother had given him, smeared on a hunk of fresh bread as a treat when he'd done his lessons well:

"Hush, child
The darkness will rise from the deep, child
And carry you down into sleep, child
The darkness will rise from the deep, child
And carry you down into sleep."

Alan stirred, and felt chains clink. He was in a bare room, brick and boards, sitting with his hands above his head and manacled to the wall. The prison around him was dim, the details strangely indefinite—as if it were somehow a generic representation for the concept of *prison* itself. Alan knew he'd been here for a very long time. Perhaps he'd been there always, though he'd never been aware of it. Or one of him had always been here.

One of me was always here. One of me lives a man's life elsewhere. They are coming . . . coming together . . . I feel it . . . as if the halves of my soul are becoming one, for the first time. Will be one.

He could see another man in the dimness, hanging in bonds that fastened his wrists to a bar of wood hung from the ceiling at a height that made him stretch his toes to touch the floor. The cat sat at his feet and crooned:

"Guileless son,
I'll shape your belief
And you'll always know that your God is a thief
And you won't understand the cause of your grief
But you'll always follow the voices beneath—"

The animal swayed, and the hanging man's eyes followed it, brown-green and haunted, staring into the yellow ones:

"Loyalty loyalty loyalty loyalty
Loyalty loyalty loyalty only to me
Guileless son,
Your spirit will hate her
The flower who married your father the traitor
And you will bring them the only true savior . . ."

Then he was . . . elsewhere.

Ah. I recognize this, the city of New York more than a hundred years ago. No, Hildred Castaigne recognizes this; I dream him again. This is the armorer's chambers he visits sometimes.

He was looking at a young woman; a very pretty one, with light-brown hair piled in an elaborate halo-like manner framing delicate features.

Constance Hawberk, he thought, not sure if the name came to Alan Thurston or the man he dreamed he was. To—

Hildred Castaigne, Alan reminded himself: that thought at least he knew was his, because you didn't think of your own name very often so he must be thinking it himself, against the other one.

The man who will be Emperor of America as royal servant to the King in Yellow, who will rule even the unborn thoughts of men.

Probably the girl's name was in the dream-man's mind, because the man was looking at her with concentrated dislike and no hint of desire. But it was an oddly abstract hatred, directed at her as an object rather than a person, as a bundle of potential problems. Less like that you felt towards a person who'd done you an injury, and more the way you cursed a landslip that blocked a droving-trail and thought about how many days of sweating work it would mean to get it shored up again. Though Alan hoped he'd never feel that spiteful simply because something or someone was in the way.

I really don't like Hildred Castaigne much, even if we're related, Alan thought with the detachment of dream. *And there's something very strange about him.*

"Did you see the opening ceremonies at the Government Lethal Chamber, Mr. Castaigne?" Constance asked. "I was out on Broadway this morning and saw the cavalry passing, but I needed to get this banner finished for the Museum's exhibit."

"You mean that I imposed on you, dear," her father said, giving the greave a final buff of the chamois cloth.

He was a thickset man with muscular shoulders, arms and hands but a bit of a belly on him and a brown beard that reached his chest. Every one of the tools his battered callused hands used was familiar, which itself was strange in this dream-place.

"Helping you with your work with my needle is not an imposition, Father!" she said with a chuckle. "It's not as if we were gentlefolk of leisure, with nothing better to do than stroll about and see the sights."

"I was there, yes. Rather boring speeches, though the Chamber is a nice piece of architecture," Castaigne said. "Thank God this city has finally developed a sense of aesthetic decency."

Then she hesitated and looked at him and quickly away again, flushing: "Did you see your cousin, Lieutenant Castaigne, there?"

"No," dream-Castaigne said carelessly; inwardly he was snarling like a rabid wolf.

That's very odd. He's almost ready to murder her because she loves his cousin, but there's no . . . he doesn't want her himself, but the thought enrages him utterly. What a strange man!

He'd seen people willing to kill over jealousy, and ones who'd done it—Boise was a fairly law-abiding sort of place even in the rough remote parts he'd lived in, but people were people. This was different.

"Louis' regiment is maneuvering out in Westchester County," Hildred said.

Castaigne rose and picked up his hat and cane. There was a flash of disturbing images; holding Constance by the throat and smashing the silver hilt of the cane into her face again and again, blood spattering into his mouth and eyes as the fragile bones crunched and an eye popped out of its socket. . . .

"Are you going upstairs to see the lunatic again?" Constance's father said with a laugh.

At the word *lunatic* a flash of white fire went through Alan's mind, or rather that of the man whose body he shared. The thoughts that followed made his desire to beat the young woman's face in look like a gentle caress, and they started with a red-hot knife-blade. Alan tried to pull away. He wasn't a squeamish young man, and he'd grown up around the normal accidents of herding and logging and hunting dangerous beasts, with a couple of brief brushes with bandits. He hadn't flinched when the only thing to do was give the mercy-stroke to a man who'd had a horse stumble and fall and catch his pelvis between the saddle and a boulder.

But there were things you didn't want to know human beings were capable of, even in imagination. The dream held him, in bonds that were no less unpleasant for being imperceptible. Hildred Castaigne didn't just want to kill, he wanted screams and begging and pleading and to gloat over despair. The agonies of a continent wouldn't satisfy his lust for revenge.

"I think I shall drop in and see Mr. Wilde for a moment or two," Castaigne said quietly.

How can they not know? Alan thought. *How can they listen to him and not know what he is?*

"Poor fellow," Constance said compassionately, with a shake of the head. "It must be hard to live alone year after year. Poor, crippled and almost demented. It is very good of you, Mr. Castaigne, to visit him as often as you do."

"I think he is vicious," her father said, beginning again with his hammer.

"No, he is not vicious," Castaigne said. "Nor is he in the least demented. No more than I."

Alan's dream-mind laughed aloud. That was rare enough in these dreams that he enjoyed the moment threefold, because Castaigne *was* demented, like a large barrel full of starving coyotes fed on locoweed and kicked downhill.

And *vicious* didn't begin to cover it.

Hildred went on: "His mind is a wonder chamber, from which he can extract treasures that you and I would give years of our life to acquire."

Hawberk laughed, and Alan felt a kinship with the bluff Englishman. Hildred amplified:

"He knows history as no one else could know it. Nothing, however trivial, escapes his search, and his memory is so absolute, so precise in details, that were it known in New York that such a man existed, the people could not honor him enough."

"Nonsense," muttered Hawberk, searching on the floor for a fallen rivet.

Where Alan came from the word would have been *bullshit* with an added horse-laugh.

"Is it nonsense," Hildred said, suppressing another vivid image of the heel of his shoe crushing Hawberk's jaw so that he choked to death on his own blood: "Is it nonsense when he says that the tassets and cuissardes of the enameled suit of armor commonly known as the *Prince's Emblazoned* can be found among a mass of rusty theatrical properties, broken stoves and ragpicker's refuse in a garret in Pell Street?"

That hit, Alan thought, watching the shock on the middle-aged man's face. *That really hit.*

"How . . . how did you know? Know that they were missing?"

"I did not know until Mr. Wilde mentioned it to me the other day. He said they were in the garret of 998 Pell Street."

"Nonsense," Hawberk said again, but his hands trembled under the leather artisan's apron.

"Is this nonsense too?" Castaigne said, with a smile that felt as if it could cut like a razor. "Is it nonsense when Mr. Wilde continually speaks of you as the Marquis of Avonshire, and of Miss Constance as . . ."

Constance leapt up, her face gone pale and sweating; the embroidery fallen unheeded to the floor. Hawberk smoothed his leathern apron; Alan saw his face settle into the mask of a brave man facing danger.

"That is impossible," he said quietly. "Mr. Wilde may know a great many things—"

"About armor, for instance, and the *Prince's Emblazoned*," Castaigne said, grinning.

"Yes," Hawberk continued, slowly. "About armor also, maybe. But he is wrong in regard to the Marquis of Avonshire, who, as you know, killed his wife's traducer years ago, and went to Australia where he did not long survive his wife."

"Mr. Wilde is wrong," murmured Constance.

Her lips were pale and her fingers clenched, but her voice was sweet and calm.

There's a girl with nerve and grit, Alan thought admiringly. *And we have something in common—she and her father are political exiles too. Maybe she's an ancestor as well?*

"Let us agree, if you please, that in this one circumstance Mr. Wilde is wrong," Castaigne said.

Inwardly, Castaigne was laughing. Cackling, rather, and reciting to himself:

When from Carcosa, the Hyades, Hastur, and Aldebaran . . . and through a long line of names, too: *the Last King . . . Hildred de Calvados, only son of Hildred Castaigne and Edythe Landes Castaigne, first in succession . . ."*

"Wakey-wakey, sweetie."

Alan started up. For a moment he had no idea where he was; someone had flicked him on the backside with a towel. Memories fled through his mind as he grasped at them, like eels slithering between his hands. He shook his head, rolling over and sitting up.

He felt tired, which turned out to be as much a feature of a field soldier's life as it did of a working rancher's except that it was less seasonal. This time he had no objection, because it hadn't been a case of staying up late to make sure the tents were pitched and the horse corrals in the right place and the chow line would be ready for breakfast.

Órlaith stood grinning at him, as nude as he, his own height of blond comeliness and reminding him of a cougar he'd seen running up a rocky slope once, moving like falling water from boulder to boulder with casual ease. Though she also reminded him of a Golden Eagle swooping down a valley.

Good God, what a woman! he thought; his dreams might be troubled and vague, but he remembered the waking part of last night vividly. *I wasn't a virgin, but I might as well have been.*

And that has nothing to do with who her parents are. Well, she takes after the High King's looks, I'll admit.

He'd been about eight when Artos the First had visited their ranch; it had been very much High King Artos, and not Rudi Mackenzie. Brief and formal and the High Queen hadn't been with him, but it had been intended to show that his mother was fully forgiven as far as Court was concerned, and it had. And he'd never forgotten the meeting, or the moment of unaffected kindness to the small boy he'd been.

And it's not just his height and complexion she's inherited. He was . . . very alive, and she's the same way.

"Time for a swim," she said.

"It's dawn," he said blurrily, peering at the morning sunlight falling in narrow slits through the woven bamboo walls of the room.

"That's why it's time for a swim," she said. "I've got to be at the conference very soon. As my father said to me, on campaign always take an opportunity; it may be your last chance."

She winked. "And he said you'll be short of sleep anyway, but you can sleep in the Summerlands."

He smiled back; Summerlands was what Órlaith's version of the Old Faith called the afterlife. Even if there weren't many witches in Latah County, everyone knew a little of the stories behind the High King's religion. Then the smile faded slightly for an instant. . . .

Is she testing me by mentioning him? he thought. *Her father killed mine, after all, even if I was still in the womb at the time. No, probably not.*

Everyone in Montival who listened to the epics, and more particularly every educated person whose family was involved in the politics of the High Kingdom, knew the history of House Artos and House Arminger back in the War of the Eye—the Protector's War, people from the Association called it. And how the son of the Bear Lord and Lady Juniper had ended up marrying the only child of Norman and Sandra Arminger.

And from the stories, the High King did my father a favor, there at the end. Even Mother thinks so, though she's just said it was very bad after he came under the Prophet's control and that he wasn't himself anymore. But he tried to kill her when she defected, after all, and in front of hundreds of witnesses, and while she was pregnant at that. If that crossbow bolt had hit it would have been a short and unmerry life for me. I think Orrey just doesn't hold him against me, which I like. Very much.

He laughed and stretched. "I was just thinking, one generation with a history of getting together after mutual homicide by their parents could be happenstance, but twice . . . that's a pattern there."

She grinned back at him, tossed him one of the towels she was carrying and led the way out to the villa's courtyard pool. Several of her close household were already splashing around, or watching and letting the mild warmth dry them off. And none of them thought wearing clothes to swim in was a good idea.

He wasn't shocked, though he'd been raised in a conservative part of a conservative part of Montival. Most of the people he'd grown up around were old-fashioned Protestant Christians, with a scattering of Mormons. The ruling Boise City branch of the Thurstons were of the Old Faith—Asatru heathen specifically, not Wiccans like the Mackenzies or McClintocks. His uncle Frederick had taken to it on his trip to the Sunrise Lands with the High King, and his mother and sister had followed when he came back. It had spread widely through Boise's territories in the generation since because of the prestige of that association with the victorious General-President, but not yet to many in the remote backlands of Latah County.

You got over being body-conscious in field service, though. The heavy infantry brigades of the US of Boise Army were all-male, but the support echelons and the light cavalry weren't.

And I don't want to look like a bumpkin from the back of beyond, anyway. Even if I am a bumpkin from the back of beyond, for now. I've got a brother to take over the ranch, and Tom never wanted to leave.

They all nodded to him as he followed Órlaith out, most of them smiling. One medium-sized man with long brown hair and mustache gave him a considering look, walking a few paces to take in all of him. He had a wildcat build, a thin torc of twisted gold around his neck and tattoos all over his otherwise naked body; apparently what they said about McClintocks was true, though Alan had never met any before he came east for the war. Latah County in the US of B and the hill lands south of the Willamette down by the old Californian border where the Clan McClintock laired were both mountain-and-valley, but apart from that they were about as far apart as possible in every imaginable way.

Diarmuid's his name, Alan reminded himself.

He'd been working on learning who was who in the Household.

Diarmuid Tennart McClintock. Personal name, family name, clan, like the Mackenzies. He's a tacksman, sort of like a rancher or squire, and in his mid-twenties, oldest man here.

Diarmuid gave Alan a final close examination and spoke to the big blond young Mackenzie, Karl Aylward:

"Nae scrat up. Ye owe tha' price ay a scuttle sheeps," he said cheerfully; his accent was thick even compared to the way Mackenzies spoke, and much rougher. "Ah tauld ye she wasnae given tae claws."

Two women—the short slight Sioux girl and the tall black-haired Ranger with the scar—quietly stepped up behind the McClintock. Each planted a foot against her side of his bare butt and shoved in neat unison, and he went windmilling forward to land in the water with a shout cut short in a gurgle and a huge splash.

Karl Aylward Mackenzie apparently thought that was hilarious, which was the sort of rural sense of humor Alan was familiar with. Heuradys d'Ath grabbed Karl's arm while he was standing helpless with bellowing laughter, put it in a lock and spun him neatly into the water after the southern clansman with a move Alan recognized but thought he might have had trouble countering. Diarmuid promptly tried to hold his head underwater.

Alan had never swum in anything but rivers and ponds in his home-range, though in plenty of those; they were handy and fun, especially if you didn't mind sharing the water with beavers, trout and the occasional muskrat.

This pool was an oval of marble occupying most of a courtyard, with water running into it from a wall-fountain shaped like a bronze lion's mouth; like the marble, it was probably salvage. The fancy villa was the best the locals had and they'd quite rightly provided it for the Crown Princess' party. He'd thought the expeditionary force was being more deferential to local sensibilities than was strictly necessary, considering that the fleet and the army it escorted numbered rather more than the entire population of the island's capital city.

I have trouble taking Hawai'i all that seriously, he thought, watching with appreciation as Órlaith dove in with scarcely a splash and began doing an underwater lap. *Maybe I should try harder.*

In the days of his grandfather Lawrence Thurston the United States of Boise—back then, they'd just called it the United States of America because they hadn't cared how it read with the neighbors—had aspired to recreate the United States from sea to sea. That hadn't worked out despite President-General Lawrence Thurston's fanatical dedication— he'd been a soldier of the old Republic and took it very seriously—but Montival incorporated the western third of what had been the United States and what had been British Columbia as well, which had made Boise's membership go down a lot easier. It was a reunification of sorts, even if not the one their first General-President had had in mind.

Granted that large parts of Montival's vast expanse were empty, or empty of anything but a few neo-savages living on deer and collecting their enemies' heads, or had scattered hamlets and herding camps whose contact with the High Kingdom were entirely theoretical, but it was still hard for him to take this little miniature toy of a *kingdom* in mid-Pacific very seriously. You could drop it into Boise alone a dozen times over without making much of a splash. And while the USB was probably the second most populous part of Montival—the other possibility was Boise's neighbor New Deseret—it wasn't the biggest in area by a long shot. He'd known Montival was huge before he left home, and after traveling overland on horseback and by rail and barge all the way to the coast he appreciated it down in his gut in a way that only watching countryside crawl by for weeks could bring.

The official and even more the unofficial briefings they'd gotten before landing had repeatedly made it crystal clear that anyone in the USB Army who let the locals see that sort of dismissive attitude was going to be very, very sorry, and so were the NCO's and officers who allowed it. He supposed that the other contingents of the Montivallan expeditionary force had received the same message, in appropriate ways; some of them came from places where *heads will roll* wasn't necessarily a metaphor.

Alan dove into the sun-filtered water himself. It was a big enough pool that there was still plenty of room even with several of Órlaith's Household making determined attempts to drown each other in it. One end was around four feet deep, and the other twelve, and it was all just deliciously, comfortably cool given the warmth of the local climate.

He came to the surface and shook back his head, the honey-brown of his curls darkened by the water. The contrast with diving into a mountain lake fed by glacial runoff was startling. The closest he could think of was a stock-watering pond in summer, without its disadvantages, starting with what cattle and horses and sheep did whenever and wherever they felt like it.

"I could get used to this!" he said.

Swimming pools were luxuries for the very wealthy in some places;

feudal ones like the Association, or rich city-states like Corvallis. The US of Boise had its share of rich men, but it discouraged ostentation and display, usually with swingeing taxation, on the theory that if you could waste money that way you should be paying more.

There were plenty of towels for drying off afterwards. He'd brought along a set of his dress greens, so he had a uniform that didn't look too out of place even after he'd settled his beret on his head. Boise was a conservative sort of place, so they weren't much different from what the old Republic's soldiers had worn on formal occasions, except that they had a Mandarin collar rather than the open one with shirt and necktie and boots rather than shoes.

He did tuck a napkin into the collar while they all took a brief break-fast from a table, especially since a lot of it was fruit helpfully cut up—though he was glad of that, because many of the types were delicious but so unfamiliar he wasn't sure how to eat them. He'd never seen a banana until the day before yesterday, for example, and he'd assumed from the few pictures in yellowing heirloom books and magazines that you just bit into them like an apple.

Heuradys d'Ath was doing the same, though she was in an Associate's getup of hose, shoes with turned-up toes and points at the ankles, jerkin, loose-sleeved shirt and—across a chair for the moment—houppelande coat with great dagged sleeves and roll-edged chaperon hat with a dangling tail and heraldic livery badge over the brow. By Associate standards it was fairly restrained; the hose wasn't particolored, there weren't little golden bells on the toes of the shoes, and the houppelande was a subdued maroon with only a little gold embroidery around the cuffs and buttonholes.

Of course, Boiseans had always mocked the PPA's selective medieval revivals, though he supposed when you thought about it following 20th-century Pre-Change official fashions was only slightly stranger than using 15th-century ones. He suspected that part of it was that the Port-land Protective Association had been too strong for even Lawrence Thurston to feel like tackling back in the old days, though both parties had spent twenty years preparing for the final confrontation that never happened. Satire had been a harmless outlet for the tension.

"At least you're wearing something even more uncomfortable than I am, Herry," he said.

She winked at him. "No I'm not, gorgeous," she said. "This is a special outfit I had done up in a hurry before we headed out, all cotton and linen and silk. That's official-issue-as-specified-in-field-regulations linsey-woolsey you're wearing, isn't it?"

He grinned back, though he was also feeling slightly uneasy. If things had worked out just a little differently when he and his retainers showed up at one of the d'Ath manors on their way to Portland—she and Órlaith had been quasi-exiled there while the High Queen was angry—he might have ended up with her, at least for a while.

Instead of just for one night, and then I threw myself in front of that tiger—which I swear I didn't think about, I just did it when the damned things came jumping out of the brush—and Orrey and I sort of collapsed into the sack and then I was sorry I'd been with Herry. But God, I'm twenty and healthy and I was unattached at the time— if a good-looking woman made it plain, what the hell was I supposed to do, say: Get your well-shaped ass out of here, and take that damn bottle of wine with you? *Guys just don't do that, we're not made that way. At least I'm pretty sure by now she wasn't checking me out for her liege, which is an icky thought. Associates are weird but I don't think they're that weird.*

Though the total, cheerful absence of jealousy on the part of either of the young women was a bit . . .

Deflating, he thought. *Not literally, though, thank God, and if I were getting swollen-headed over my looks—*

He wasn't vain but he'd had enough direct experience to know that he hit women fairly hard

—it would be an ego corrective that Herry thought once was enough.

He finished with a couple of rolls—spicy pork sausage in a crust made of some local tree-grown-thing that mimicked bread or potatoes quite closely—and fell in with the rest. He'd pitched in during the landing precisely so he'd have some leave time now, and nobody seemed to mind that he was tagging along.

The conference was outside under canvas, but considerably more serious than the *lū'au* in the same place had been last night; all the senior Montivallan military commanders were there, for starters, including his Uncle Fred, aka General-President Frederick Thurston, looking very serious.

They exchanged salutes after the elder Thurston had paid his respects to Órlaith; nobody in the US of B was surprised that their head of state was personally leading the national contingent, since he'd commanded in the field with distinction during the Prophet's War.

"Hello, Lieutenant," the older man said, shaking his hand after the exchange of military courtesies. "You haven't met Alice and Lawrence."

He'd met his uncle *Frederick* Thurston five times, briefly and counting only the occasions where he'd been old enough to remember it as an adult. His mother had told him that his uncle and his father had resembled each other closely, down to the light-brown complexion and loosely-curled black hair worn short. His children were just old enough to be in uniform—as newly minted Second Lieutenants on their father's staff—and looked a good deal like their cousin in turn. Each regarded the other curiously.

Except that they look more earnest and serious than I usually do, and that one of them will probably be General-President, Alan thought. *And I won't.*

The current incumbent wasn't *quite* a king and the position wasn't theoretically hereditary. Boise had free and open elections for President every seven years, and had since the New Constitution was adapted right after the Prophet's War and the founding of the High Kingdom.

On the other hand, nobody *not* named Thurston had ever ruled in Boise since the Change, and in the last election the second-highest total of votes had gone to someone who ran as the official Presidential candidate of the Gibbering Lunatic Party, on a platform that included making transport cheaper by having all roads run downhill both ways and replacing all taxes with royalties from the Big Rock Candy Mountain. That candidate had worn a large red artificial nose, floppy shoes, and a buttonhole carnation that shot water, too, and had been given to shouting:

I'm the most serious alternative you've got!

"You're moving in more exalted circles than ours, I hear, cousin," Alice Thurston said, with a slight smile and a raised brow.

Alan shrugged and grinned. "An army's pretty gossipy."

His uncle laughed as well. "Oh, yeah. Worse than the tavern crowd at a crossroads village."

"I'm a lucky man," Alan said. "It sort of just . . . happened."

"I heard something about a tiger," Lawrence said. "*Two* tigers, actually."

Alan's smile was a bit tight, remembering the great striped shape rising up before him and the impact of the paw against his spear, like a blurring-fast trip-hammer flipping him through the air, the carrion smell of its breath. And the voice at the back of his mind, the monkey part of his brain yammering:

This thing eats men!

"I didn't actually kill either of them," he said. "I sort of delayed one after Órlaith's horse threw her. Then the Crown Princess . . . stepped in with the Sword and . . . *that* was sort of alarming, really, in a way that was different from the way the tigers were. And Lady d'Ath—I swear to God she was as fast as the cat, and then everyone piled in."

Frederick Thurston nodded, his eyes distant for a moment. "I remember seeing Rudi . . . the High King . . . use the Sword of the Lady. That first time in Norrheim, on the Sunrise Sea. He was . . . terrifying when he fought with his own hands even before that. And the Sword was—"

The General-President stopped for a moment, and when he continued his voice was soft: "Like something out of the Sagas. Like Tyrfing come again. When it's drawn in anger the world shakes, it flexes, as though the whole fabric of things *stretched*. You can feel it might just *rip* at any instant."

Alan looked at Reiko, where she stood among her advisors and guards, and what she carried by her side. The hair on the back of his neck bristled a little if he got any closer than this, and he'd heard the stories the others told about what happened when she drew it and called on the great Power of the Otherworld she claimed as her Ancestress.

All the Thurstons nodded soberly as they followed his glance. They

lived in a world where such things were; as their grandparents had en-
dured the Change, so they must accept it for good or ill.

"And now, duty calls," his uncle said.

Órlaith looked at the Capricornian envoys and the evidence they'd laid
out on the table before the monarchs and their closest advisors. The giant
skull of the seagoing crocodile grinned at her with a faint waft of corruption, and some of her followers made protective signs against evil, including crossing themselves among the Christians.

"Forty feet, you say?" she said to the head of the delegation, trying to
imagine the live animal coming at her out of the water.

The Capricornian king's envoy was a woman named Darla Wooton,
dressed in what was evidently the national costume, khaki shorts, sandals
and a sleeveless blue vest-like garment. A broad-brimmed hat bore corks
on dangling strings, from which Órlaith deduced that flies were a real
problem at home.

"Too right," she said. "Thirty-six, to be exact. Your ship fished the
beastie out and kept the skin and the skull, and they thought it weighed
about four tons before the sharks and gulls went to work on it. They get
big, the open-ocean salties, and they've been getting bigger since the
Blackout—"

Which was apparently what they called the Change in her part of the
world.

"—since nobody's shooting them with guns, but that's bloody ridiculous."

She was around thirty—possibly a little less, given the scourging
tropical sun—with sun-streaked brown hair, a wiry build and a face like
a very intelligent rat, with a beak of a nose and receding chin. The two
guards behind her were much bigger, tall rangy-muscular men carrying
broad-bladed spears with round shields slung over their backs blazoned
with a five-petaled rose-like flower, and short heavy chopping swords at
their belts; one was very black-skinned, the other a deeply tanned blond,
but they could have been brothers otherwise.

"Frightening bugger, isn't it?" Wooton said, jerking a thumb at it; apparently the Court of Darwin wasn't long on formality. "From what your Captain Russ said of the way he reconstructed the wreckage, the Koreans chased Moishe's ship—the *Tarshish Queen*—all the way to the Ceram Sea."

There was a map on the table, and she showed a location about a thousand miles north of Australia, a sea of myriad islands from tiny to huge.

"Then they all ran into the lizard with the grin. Your Captain Moishe turned on the Koreans while they were fighting it, and finished off the saltie with a solid bolt. And the last Korean too, burned her to the waterline with napalm shell or firebolt. Your frigate *Stormrider* came across the wreckage a day or two later, the dead saltie floating belly-up and one survivor on the keel of a capsized Korean ship. Gibbering mad, apparently."

"They could talk with him?" Órlaith said, surprised.

Wooton shook her head. "He was a Biter . . . what you lot call Eaters . . . from Los Angeles."

Well, now I know that Johnnie was alive then, Órlaith thought. *The problem is I don't know what sort of trouble he's in* now, *and that's more worrying than it was before. As if hope activates fear.*

The envoy from Darwin gestured to the two catapult bolts lying beside the skull; one was unmistakably the product of Donaldson Foundry & Machine, a well-known Corvallis firm and the supplier Feldman & Sons Merchant Venturers used. The other was cruder, a steel head heat-shrunk on a broken-off wooden shaft.

"Definitely *jinnikukaburi* work, *Heika,*" Egawa Noboru grunted, leaning over to examine it.

And using an extremely insulting nickname the Nihonjin used for their enemies from across the Sea of Japan; it meant roughly *cockroach crawling in human flesh.*

"So," Reiko said. "The last of the *chon* ships which pursued us to Montival are destroyed. My revenge for my father's death continues."

"That was very well done," Egawa conceded. "But our Captain Ishikawa was with them on the merchant's ship, of course."

"Of course, Egawa-san," Órlaith said, hiding her smile.

There's arrogance so sublime it's an odd sort of innocence, Órlaith thought. *And Egawa is a very good fighting man and utterly loyal to his Tennō. And if he's ruthless . . . well, he's fought all his life against an enemy who would eat the flesh from his children's bones, and that's the cold and literal truth.*

"What's really got King Birmo's knickers in a twist is this," Wooton said, pulling aside a cloth that covered a small object beside the catapult-bolts and the man-sized skull. "The saltie was wearing this, on its forearm, forelimb, whatever the fuck you want to call it."

It was an armband composed of ruddy metal, probably aluminum-bronze. On it was a broad circle of some glossy black material, and inlaid on that was a three-armed triskele of gold, with curved writhing arms coming from a central knot.

She heard Alan hiss from the group standing behind her. Órlaith nodded in sympathy; there was a sense of revulsion to that thing, one that made her feel as if her bones had suddenly been filled with ice water pouring off a glacier in the spring.

But not in that good-clean-painful way.

One of Karl's Mackenzies, the young *fioasache*—seeress—Gwri Beauregard Mackenzie gave a pained grunt too. Reiko's hand dropped to the hilt of the Grasscutter. One of the kahunas beside King Kalākaua raised his tabu-staff and began a chant of *pule mahiki,* a prayer to cast out evil spirits.

"Gives me the willies," Wooton said, then stopped and looked from face to face. "Not the only one, eh?"

Órlaith nodded grimly. "That beast didn't attack by accident, I think."

"Fuck me, weaponized salties?" Wooton blurted. "Look, mates, there's something bloody dodgy going on up there in the Ceram. For a long time it was just ships disappearing now and then and we reckoned, what the hell, fuckin' pirates, right? But it's more than that."

"It is," Reiko said in her slow, clear but accented English. "But this is not the same evil *akuma* who works through the *kangshinmu* of our enemies. It sent the beast *against* the *chon* ships, not to help them."

Órlaith nodded. "Or the Power that was behind the Prophet and the

CUT in Montival," she said. "That feels like your enemies, *Heika*. This does not. Well, the Powers that are our guardians are many; we shouldn't be surprised that those who wish us ill are as well. Or that they fall out among themselves."

She put her hand to the long double-lobed hilt of the Sword of the Lady.

"You powerful God, you Goddess gentle and strong, be with me now," she whispered, and drew it slowly. "Threefold Morrigú, Crow of Battle, patron and guardian of my House, spread Your wings about me."

Shock.

The world seemed to halt for an instant. Seeing with the eyes that drank the light of common day, you saw only a yard of marvelously shaped steel . . . but it was never *only* that. The steel and crystal caught the sunlight and refracted it, and there was a glow, something you couldn't be sure you were seeing or only somehow *sensing*.

Órlaith raised it high, then gently lowered the point to the sigil.

Shock.

This time the feeling was sharper, more like the way the Sword felt when she drew it in hot blood for war. There was an intense internal feeling of stress and release like the *snap* of breaking wire as the point touched the yellow sign. A sigh went through the watchers as she sheathed the Lady's gift.

Like a pain you didn't know was there until it's gone, she thought.

Wooton blinked and rubbed her eyes, as if suddenly realizing she hadn't been completely awake.

"I'll be stuffed," she said reverently. "I was right not to touch the bloody thing."

"I think you were indeed," Órlaith said.

Then Órlaith sighed. "It appears my brother Prince John has fallen into a conflict in your part of the world, one no less serious for good and ill than this," she said. "And considering how the *Tarshish Queen* and *Stormrider* ended up in the Ceram, I refuse to think it an accident. Our guardians are also taking a hand here, and giving us a warning."

Reiko looked stricken beneath an iron calm. The alliance with Montival was formally one of equals, but in cold hard fact it was a lifeline that her folk needed if they were not to be gradually ground to powder by superior numbers. If Órlaith decided to change the priorities to put rescuing her brother first rather than fighting the dark Power that ruled what had once been Korea, there was little Reiko could do about it, the more so as there were now strong arguments for it.

Órlaith's hand gripped the hilt of the Sword until her fingers whitened. When she spoke again her normally even contralto voice had gone flat and harsh, with a note of iron:

"But one war at a time. Who tries to be strong everywhere at all times is weak everywhere all the time—"

The senior war-leaders all nodded, as if an unseen hand had moved their heads. That was something they all agreed with down in their souls.

"—and the High Kingdom keeps its oaths. Captain Russ and *Stormrider* and its contingent of the Protector's Guard are a considerable force in their own right, and they can stay in the area and continue the search for the Prince and his companions. We'll deal with the matter before us, and if the situation in the south hasn't resolved itself by then, we'll deal with that in turn."

Órlaith took a deep breath. She was holding the image of a drop of water falling into a pond and the ripples fading. It was a technique she had learned as a method of centering in a visit to Chenrezi Monastery in the Valley of the Sun:

"My brother Prince John is a tried fighting man—"

Of good but not absolutely exceptional quality, she thought.

"—and he's with a shipload of able comrades, and an MRN frigate is looking for him."

And Deor Godulfson is there, which means there's one who knows of the world beyond the light of common day, she thought but again did not say; those around her would be uneasy enough.

"That will have to do for now."

Egawa Noboru rose for a moment, bowed to her, and sat again.

And I feel a little flattered, Órlaith thought, giving a brief nod in return.

The man was not really likeable if you weren't of his own folk and kin, but you had to respect him, and hence his respect was worth having. The more so for knowing he wouldn't readily give it to an outsider unless his own sense of honor forced him to it.

King Kalākaua frowned. "I see your point, Your Highness," he said. "But we of Hawai'i have had good relations with Capricornia for many years. If King John is worried, we should be too. He is a very shrewd man."

"Fair dinkum, Your Majesty," Wooton observed; she'd evidently been here before as her monarch's emissary. "There's no flies on King Birmo. Except when there are, if you know what I mean."

Lord Maugis de Grimmond cleared his throat. "If we could return to the matter the Crown Princess has said is the first priority, I would think a month's rest for the force before moving out would be best."

Admiral Naysmith frowned. "It's not time-critical from a naval point of view. The weather's going to be bad in northeast Asia anyway until well beyond that."

One of Reiko's naval advisors began to reply when a drum throbbed. Everyone looked up; a pair of Hawaiian guardsmen came trotting through escorting a courtier, the same polished young man who'd conducted the Montivallan and Nihonjin parties to their quarters in the palace district. He looked much less relaxed now.

Uh-oh, Órlaith thought, and heard Heuradys say the same thing softly behind her. *It's never good news when someone runs in like that and interrupts his king at council.*

"Your Majesty," he said slightly breathlessly, going to one knee before Kalākaua and pressing his right palm to his heart as he bowed. "A guard-ship has arrived from Oahu. The Koreans have attacked Pearl Harbor! Attacked in great strength!"

Órlaith blinked. Her briefings kicked in; Pearl Harbor was on Oahu, the island most heavily populated in ancient days and hence worst hit by the Change. The Hawaiians had been resettling it over the last genera-tion, and Pearl Harbor was a center of industry—the ships and buildings of the old American navy there provided a bottomless source of steel, aluminum, brass, glass and other materials, and there were foundries and machine shops.

It also included their Royal catapult works, a top-priority military target in any war.

"They attacked without even making demands of us!" Kalākaua exclaimed, clenching a large fist. "They'll regret this! No doubts now—the *Aupuni o Hawai'i* is in this war, to the death!"

Reiko put her hand to her sword-hilt. "And Dai-Nippon fights with you against this treacherous sneak attack!"

"And so does Montival," Órlaith echoed. "We will avenge this infamy."

CHAPTER TEN

BETWEEN WAKING WORLD AND SHADOW

The crooning of the cat ceased. John felt an overwhelming impulse to gasp, as if a smothering weight had been taken off his chest. Then the pain returned, and he dabbed his feet down towards the dusty floor.

Where am I? he thought. *It's like . . . just a room.*

Plaster over thin laths in a style he recognized; you could see how horsehair had been mixed with the plaster as a binder. Wooden boards on the floor, and a window with tattered, yellowed curtains.

He was uneasily aware, even through the pain as he tugged at the bar running behind his neck, that this was a technique his mother's father had used to break men down. A voice like that of his confessor scolded him to save guilt for his own, reasonably abundant, sins. Wallowing in vicarious offenses was a form of laziness and spiritual pride.

—and why . . . how . . . didn't the others keep the enemy from carrying me off? I'm certainly here, wherever here is. Pip wasn't far away when the tower fell . . . I hope she's all right. . . .

He tried to pray again, but there was a clank of fetters. The young man chained to the wall across from him looked to be about his own age, a few years on either side of twenty—you looked older when you'd been beaten and chained up—and likewise with a swordsman's build. Brown hair but a bit lighter than John's, and a strikingly regular face with a slight exotic cast.

John tried to speak, and found that his mouth and throat worked . . . more or less. Unfortunately that also made him conscious of how ragingly thirsty he was.

"Who . . . are you?" he croaked. "Where is this place?"

It took a moment for the man's eyes to focus on John. They were green, with a darker green rim around the outside of the pupils.

"I'm . . . not sure who I am."

John had a musician's ear for language, aided and abetted by a life spent traveling all over Montival with his parents when they were on Progress. It didn't take conscious analysis to spot the dialect:

Boise. Some rural part northeast of Boise City at that. An educated man but not one who's spent much time in town.

The voice went on, a monotone of bewilderment and pain: "Part of me is here. Part of me is there. Part of me is . . . everywhere. Alan. Am I Alan? Or am I just pretending? Or is *he* pretending? Could I know if I was pretending to be me? Everything's mixed up here. Good and bad. Alive and dead. Me and you and him. And *Him*. And *Him!*"

Crazy, poor fellow, John thought. Then: *Of course, enough of this, whatever this is, would drive anyone crazy. St. Michael, aid me—and while you're at it, this man too. Aid us against the snares of the Adversary, you who cast Lucifer down from the ramparts of heaven.*

He could think, but not well or quickly; it was like having a loud buzzing noise in the innermost ear of his mind, making concentration exhausting. Simply thinking *that* through brought extra sweat to his face, dripping down onto the worn boards of the floor around his bleeding toes.

"My ancestor," the man who might be called Alan said. "My ancestor is here. My ancestor is near."

The green eyes met John's brown. Suddenly they seemed deeper, whirlpools spiraling into nothingness. He began to thrash, and there was a smell of dry dust as it stirred and made motes of light in the beams that came through the rents in the curtains. . . .

It smelled dusty—

Then there was a memory. It came suddenly and it was overwhelmingly strong, and it took John instants to realize it wasn't *his* memory. Riding down into a dry valley somewhere ringed by mountains, sagebrush country, he recognized the general type from his travels with his parents and then on his own, but not the specific place. It could have been anywhere inland of the Coast Range. He was a child, eleven or twelve, riding a quarter horse with a couple of dogs at heel and a broad-brimmed hat on his head, and a light bow across the horn of his silver-studded saddle.

The old ranch-house was hidden under the edge of a caprock ridge. It had been well-built once, adobe walls and framed windows, and dead trees showed where there had been a garden, now gone to tumbleweed and thorn and bunchgrass. The boy felt curiosity—the more so as by some freak of preservation the glass windows hadn't been broken, and there were even pre-Change machines, a car on the rims of wheels sunk in the dirt with dust mounded up one side, and a rusted tractor by the charcoal stubs of a barn that had burned at some time.

The boy realized that it might well have stood here since the Change, though he wondered why it had been abandoned—there was good water nearby, enough to be brought by a furrow to irrigate likely-looking land, and plenty of grazing, and firewood not too far away. There was even the remains of a wind-pump by the barn, though it looked decrepit enough to have been abandoned long before the Change. Two or three wooden poles that had brought the wires of the ancient world to this place still stood; one of them had three Harris' hawks "stacked" on its crosspiece, perching on each other's backs in that way those flying pack-hunters used to spot game.

The dogs whined and hung back as he dismounted, dropping the reins to signal the horse to stand. He put an arrow to the bow and made sure his bowie knife was ready to hand as he walked up the steps to the porch and threw his weight against the door. If the place hadn't been salvaged since the Change any number of treasures might be inside.

The smell hit him as he opened the door, ancient and dry but tightly contained in the nearly sealed space, the smell of ancient rot. The boy stared for a moment at the mummified corpses scattered about what had once been a living room, his mind stuttering as he realized what the marks and the bonds and the positions meant. He backed up, swallowing and spitting as cold gummy saliva flooded his mouth, and cold sweat broke out on his forehead. . . .

I have enough bad memories of my own! Why am I remembering someone else's? How did I get chained up like this—

He climbed the three dilapidated flights of stairs, which he had so often climbed before. . . .

Wait a minute. Who am I? John thought, as he *felt* his feet on the worn wooden risers. *Is this a hallucination, or a dream, or what? Where am I really? What am I really?*

The thought was very much like teetering over a canyon, or hang-gliding at Hood River on the Columbia, but without the fun. His parents had once heard of a man who'd gone on a long journey to *find himself*, and had laughed uproariously together and said that if he couldn't find himself at home, he wasn't likely to do it by taking a caravan over the mountains. He hadn't always been satisfied with who and what he was, but it had never been a matter of doubt.

Dreaming. You often think you're someone else in dreams.

The thought calmed him; somewhere he could feel his heart slowing and frantic panting turning to deep breaths.

The man he dreamed . . .

And I'm dreaming I'm someone else dreaming I'm this man too. Someone else is dreaming he's Hildred Castaigne.

. . . knocked at a small door at the end of the corridor.

It opened, pulled so by a mutilated dwarf barely four feet high, and he had only the stumps of ears. They were badly covered by two grotesquely perfect wax prosthetics, strung from a silver wire and painted a blushing pink in total contrast to the jaundice-yellow and fishbelly pallor of the man's face. His eyes were the pale color of frosted lead cast too hot and let cool, but they smoldered. Fresh deep scratches scored the skin of his face, and others in successive stages of healing or infection; all the fingers were missing from his left hand, leaving only stubs that had healed to ragged lumps.

It wasn't the injuries that made John's mind recoil. He knew folk as ugly whose selves made their looks irrelevant. One of his instructors in the lute had been a knight who'd taken a spray of napalm across the eyes from an airburst flame-shell at the battle of the Horse Heaven Hills, and they'd been excellent friends from the first lesson. The thought of the man's face still brought an immediate association of warmth and shared accomplishment even now, though strangers often gave involuntary gasps the first time they saw it.

It wasn't even the odd shape of his totally bald head, lumpy and flattened and drawn almost to a point at the rear.

The eyes, it's something about the eyes.

They gave him an unhinged feeling, as if just looking into them knocked the whole world askew, distorting the angles of things. The second sense of self within him—the man who *dreamed* he was Hildred Castaigne—felt a fascination mixed with dread. Castaigne himself . . . if that muffled wave of sensation was his . . . watched the dwarf with something not far short of love, seasoned with an odd mix of resignation and terror.

The room Castaigne entered was shabby in a dusty, neglected way that was somehow dirty without looking or smelling particularly filthy, things neatly placed in ways that made you confused just looking at them. It smelled of dust, old paper, ink, stale laundry and a not very well cleaned catbox.

Wilde, John thought, one of the bits that floated through the triply shared consciousness he unwillingly inhabited. *The dwarf's name is Wilde.*

Wilde double-locked the door and pushed a heavy chest against it, then came and sat down in a chair with extra-long legs, while peering up into John's face. A black cat retreated under a couch and growled faintly.

He'd handled the furniture effortlessly; he might be small but his shoulders were broad, his chest deep, and his legs stumpy but powerful.

After an unnerving silent interval he picked up a massive leather-bound ledger, handling it effortlessly with his right and the fingerless stump of the left. Another stale gust hit John/Alan/Hildred's face as it opened, and John would have sworn there was something like old fear-sweat as well, the sort of waft you got from an arming-doublet sometimes.

"Henry B. Matthews," Wilde read. "Bookkeeper with Whysot Whysot and Company, dealers in church ornaments. Called April 3rd. Reputation damaged on the race-track. Known as a welsher. Reputation to be repaired by August 1st. Retainer Five Dollars."

He turned the page and ran his fingerless knuckles down the closely-written columns.

"P. Greene Dusenberry, Minister of the Gospel, Fairbeach, New Jersey. Reputation damaged in the Bowery. To be repaired as soon as possible. Retainer $100."

He coughed and added: "Called, April 6th."

The dwarf coughed again and went on: "Listen. Mrs. C. Hamilton Chester, of Chester Park, New York City. Called April 7th. Reputation damaged at Dieppe, France. To be repaired by October 1st Retainer $500. Note.—C. Hamilton Chester, Captain U.S.S. *Avalanche*, ordered home from South Sea Squadron October 1st."

"Then you are not in need of money, Mr. Wilde," Hildred Castaigne said. "The profession of a Repairer of Reputations is lucrative!"

That's a lot of money, John felt/knew, as his mind seemed to translate it into terms of rose nobles. *Sort of middling-merchant guildsman money.*

The colorless eyes looked up at him impassively. "I only wanted to demonstrate that I was correct. You said it was impossible to succeed as a Repairer of Reputations; that even if I did succeed in certain cases it would cost me more than I would gain by it. Today I have five hundred men in my employ, who are poorly paid, but who pursue the work with an enthusiasm which possibly may be born of fear. These men enter every shade and grade of society; some even are pillars of the most exclusive social temples; others are the prop and pride of the financial world;

still others, hold undisputed sway among the 'Fancy and the Talent.' I choose them at my leisure from those who reply to my advertisements. It is easy enough, they are all cowards. I could treble the number in twenty days if I wished. So you see, those who have in their keeping the reputations of their fellow-citizens, I have in my pay."

"They may turn on you," Hildred suggested.

Wilde rubbed his thumb over his cropped ears, and adjusted the wax substitutes.

"I think not," he murmured thoughtfully. "I seldom have to apply, and then only once. Besides they like their wages."

"How do you apply the whip?" Hildred demanded.

Wilde's eyes dwindled to a pair of green sparks. John felt his mind recoil, and even Hildred Castaigne blanched a little inwardly.

"I invite them to come and have a little chat with me," Wilde said in a soft voice.

A knock at the door interrupted him, and his face resumed its amiable expression.

"Who is it?" he inquired.

"Mr. Steylette," was the answer.

"Come tomorrow," replied Mr. Wilde.

"Impossible," began the other, but was silenced by a sort of bark from Mr. Wilde.

"Come tomorrow," he repeated.

"Very . . . very well."

He heard somebody move away from the door and turn the corner by the stairway.

"Who is that?" Hildred asked.

"Arnold Steylette, owner and Editor in Chief of the great *New York Herald*."

He drummed on the ledger with his fingerless hand adding: "I pay him very badly, but he thinks it a good bargain."

"Arnold Steylette!" Hildred repeated, amazed.

Odd, John thought; and he could feel the second man linked to him, the Boisean, agree. *He thinks of a scrivener as if he were a great man, someone of power, not just a hired servant.*

"Yes," said Mr. Wilde, with a self-satisfied cough.

The cat, which had entered the room as he spoke, hesitated, looked up at Wilde and snarled, a deep rumble in its chest. He climbed down from the chair and squatting on the floor, took the creature into his arms and caressed her. The cat ceased snarling and presently began a loud purring which seemed to increase in timbre as he stroked her.

"Where are the notes?" Hildred asked.

His voice was calm, but longing and desire surged through him. The Boisean echoed it, but with an undertone of revulsion.

Wilde pointed to the table, and Hildred picked up a manuscript, blazoned with a title that he whispered aloud with exultation and longing:

The Imperial Dynasty of America.

When Hildred had finished, Wilde nodded and coughed.

"Speaking of your legitimate ambition," he said, "how do Constance and Louis get along?"

"She loves him," he replied simply.

The cat on Wilde's knee suddenly turned and struck at his eyes, and he flung her off and climbed on to the chair opposite Hildred.

"And Dr. Archer! But that's a matter you can settle any time you wish," he added.

"Yes," Castaigne replied.

A sudden image flooded Hildred's mind; John could feel the straight-jacket cramping his arms, strong hands holding him as he convulsed in rage, and the blood and spittle spraying from his mouth as someone—Dr. Archer—approached with a pad of ether-soaked fabric. Then something that was Hildred *imagining:* Imagining the stout middle-aged doctor burning, his skin bubbling and turning black and red cracks of flame bursting through it as his eyeballs ran molted down his cheeks and he screamed and screamed and *did not die . . .*

"Dr. Archer can wait, but it is time I saw my cousin Louis," Hildred said calmly.

"It *is* time," Wilde agreed.

Then he took another ledger from the table and flipped through it.

"We are now in communication with ten thousand men," he said in an abstract tone. "We can count on one hundred thousand within the first twenty-four hours, and in forty-eight hours the state will rise en masse. The country follows the state, and the portion that will not, I mean California and the Northwest, might better never have been inhabited. I shall not send them the Yellow Sign."

A shrill laugh stayed locked behind Hildred Castaigne's lips, though when he spoke it was abstractly:

"A new broom sweeps clean," he said.

"The ambition of Caesar and of Napoleon pales before that which could not rest until it had seized the minds of men and controlled even their unborn thoughts," said Mr. Wilde.

"You are speaking of the King in Yellow," Hildred said, with a pleasure mingled with terror.

A shadow moved through his mind; a figure in tattered yellow robes. John's own memories suddenly grew clearer; the yellow figure on the ramparts of the fantastic coral castle in Baru Denpasar's harbor.

"He is a king whom emperors have served," Wilde said.

"I am content to serve him," Hildred replied.

Mr. Wilde sat rubbing his ears with his fingerless hand. "Perhaps Constance does not love your cousin," he suggested.

Hildred started to reply with a cold surge of venom, but a sudden burst of military music from the street below drowned his voice.

The twentieth dragoon regiment, formerly in garrison at Mount St. Vincent, is returning from the manœuvers in Westchester County, to its new barracks on East Washington Square, he thought, as he moved to look down from the window. *Louis' regiment.*

John's mind looked down as well, and whoever-it-was-from-Boise.

They both saw a good-looking set of horse soldiers in pale blue, tight-fitting jackets, jaunty busbies and tight white riding breeches with a double yellow stripe. Every other squadron was armed with lances, from the metal points of which fluttered yellow and white pennons. The band passed, playing the regimental march; then came the colonel and staff, the horses crowding and trampling, while their heads bobbed in unison, and the pennons fluttered from their lance points.

The troopers rode with what John knew as the English seat; which was odd, since in his experience it was only used for sport—polo. They looked brown as berries though, the way soldiers did after campaigning or at least time in the field, and the music of their sabers against the stirrups, and the jingle of spurs and carbines delighted Hildred.

Castaigne saw his cousin Louis riding with his squadron, a handsome brown-haired young man with an excellent seat, on a mount that would have done for a knight's courser if not a destrier.

Mr. Wilde, who had mounted a chair by the window, saw him too from the way his pale eyes moved, but said nothing. Hildred's cousin turned his head as he rode and looked straight at Hawberk's shop, and Hildred knew the young woman called Constance must have been at the window. When the last troopers had clattered by, and the last pennons vanished into South Fifth Avenue, Wilde clambered out of his chair and dragged the chest away from the door.

"Yes," he said. "It is time that you saw your cousin Louis."

He unlocked the door and Hildred picked up his hat and stick and stepped into the corridor. The stairs were dark. John found he could see more than he sensed Hildred could, even though they were using the same eyes; so could the Boisean. Perhaps it was that they'd spent more time outside in the dark than this city man, in places where you had to pick up subtle clues or trip over a root and plant your face in the dirt. Or just that Hildred's mind was dazzled with savage dreams of glory and power.

Groping about, Hildred set his foot on something soft, which snarled and spat.

Cat, John thought automatically, feeling a slight stab of distress even then—he'd stepped on paws and tails now and then, and hated it.

And then he saw its eyes. Lambent amber, typical enough . . . but there was something else there. He remembered a *song* for an instant, before the memory fled.

Hildred aimed a murderous blow at the cat with his cane, and John felt his own will adding to the strike. It hit the balustrade instead with a jarring impact that shuddered painfully through his wrist into his shoulder, and the beast scurried back into Wilde's room.

Deor stepped back from the wall and lowered the wineglass. Pip did the same and looked at him; the *scop* had turned a little gray.

"What was that about?" she said, when they'd compared notes on what they'd overheard. "It's a conversation about a plot to seize a throne, and some sort of blackmailing scheme too, I think."

"That man . . . the man whose shadow we heard, speaking lines graven in the place whose shadow this is . . . was a . . . *trollkjerring*, they say in Norrheim. One who draws his power from death and fear. The other is his puppet."

Deor frowned, puzzled. "But the puppet . . . it is as if he was more men than one. And there was a shadow . . . a feeling of Prince John."

Thora turned her head sharply from where she waited by the door, and Toa gave a grunt from the window.

"Is John *here*?" Pip said.

Deor smiled.

Rather insufferably, Pip thought.

"Where is *here*?" he said. "We follow a thread through dreams. Dreams that can kill."

"And he's off the stairs," Toa said, cracking the door open a little. "If we're following him, let's go."

CHAPTER ELEVEN

"Fleet to wear in succession," Admiral Naysmith said.

Órlaith shrugged to settle her suit of plate, and as it rattled squinted against the glittering brightness; you generally did, on a sunny day at sea, even when the morning sun was on your left, as it was here. Sailors developed a lot of lines around their eyes; it was one of the marks of the craft, the way burn-scars on the hands were of a smith.

The scent of violence seemed to blow down on a wind from the future, stronger than the offshore breeze, making her feel like a cat whose fur was sparking from a dry wind. She took deep breaths and let them out slowly to keep her mind clear. A hand on the pommel of the Sword helped; she could somehow sense the location of the other ships, and the direction of the wind and the possibilities of movement around and across it for both sides. Nothing that she couldn't have done herself . . .

With more time, training and facilities than she actually had.

Enemy in sight had sounded half an hour ago, and now the slow stately dance of naval battle was in its opening steps, the part that could give way to cataclysmic destruction with shocking suddenness. The creaking song of a big wooden ship sounded as the *Sea-Leopard* came about in a volley of orders and deck crews hauling on the sheet-lines—she was wearing, turning about to come on a new tack rather than beating up, not being in a hurry. That economized on wear and tear at the expense of time.

Sails thuttered and cracked taut, lines and cables hummed their song of power as they caught the force of the wind transmitted through canvas into the frames of the ship, and wood groaned at the stresses. The frigate's deck came upright as her bow pointed downwind for a moment, then canted to starboard as she came about towards the eye of the wind again. The First Mate shouted and pointed with her cane, and the mast-captains relayed the order to their teams as the last adjustments were made to the sheets.

"Thus, thus, very well, thus," Captain Edwards said at the helm, reaching out a hand to touch the wheel. "Steady as she goes, helm."

Admiral Naysmith nodded and said:

"They have the weather gauge on us, but it doesn't look as if they're going to refuse battle," and leveled her telescope to sweep the horizon to the southward as the signals officer had the pennants run up to break out at the mizzen-top. "There must be forty of them."

Just then a message pod whirred down the line from the kite-borne observer currently a wedge-shaped dot a thousand feet up. A signalwoman opened it and handed the contents to the *Sea-Leopard*'s commander. Captain Edwards handed it on to Naysmith.

"Forty-four, Admiral," he said. "And yes, they're coming out to meet us."

Naysmith grunted thoughtfully and looked up at the enemy's observation balloon hanging over the ancient harbor; it was different in detail from what Montival used, but had the general similarity forced on human kind by the laws of nature even in the Changed world, and it would have seen them long ago.

Órlaith looked discreetly over her naval commander's shoulder at the message the observer in the flying wing had sketched. The drawing showed the enemy deploying outside the mouth of Pearl Harbor in a blunt wedge, with the larger ships on the outside and a less orderly gaggle of others within.

"Best choice they have," Naysmith said. "If we catch them where they can't maneuver we'll pound them to burning splinters. They'll probably try to provoke a fleet action and then swarm individual ships in boarding actions."

She grinned like a shark as she snapped the telescope shut. "But we have heavy crews available, and two can play that game."

"Forty-four ships!" King Kalākaua said. "By *Kū-keoloewa*, Kū the Supporter, that's far more than our total naval strength!"

Reiko nodded as they all stepped aside to give the admiral room; she and the Hawaiian monarch were both on the Montivallan flagship, much to the relief of their naval commanders. There was no safe place in a ship-to-ship action, where an admiral was in the front lines as much as the lowliest deckhand pumping at a catapult's hydraulic cocking lines. But the big frigate was as close as you could get to safety as long as the respective rulers insisted on being present . . . which they all did.

And having us all here keeps the lines of command clearer, Órlaith thought. *Naysmith's orders are coming from the same place as the Hawaiian and Nihonjin monarchs. There's no question of their rulers taking orders from my commander. And anyone who wants to think we're instructing Naysmith after a committee meeting is free to do so.*

"Number includes transport . . . transports," Reiko said in her slow careful English. "And they have no shr . . . ships like this."

She tapped her foot on *Sea-Leopard*'s quarterdeck. The six frigates were leading the fleet; some of the smaller Montivallan ships were screening forward, but most—and the Hawaiian and Nihonjin vessels—were behind. This time she was in her own set of Japanese-style armor, the lacquer still showing marks from fights and hard travel—no longer scratched or dented or with frayed cords, in fact lovingly repaired, but the covering slightly brighter where they'd been applied. The crimson chrysanthemum *mon* of her House showed on the breastplate and the brow of the broad-tailed *kabuto* helmet.

"This is more half . . . more than half . . . of their strength at sea, from our intelligence," she said thoughtfully. "To put it where we can with our strength hit it, bad strategy. Very bad. Usually they are not so foolish. Perhaps their intelligence of Montival is poor. Or they are some reason desperate."

Egawa leaned close to her ear and murmured in Nihonjin; he could understand spoken English, but his own command of it was much worse than his *Tennō's*.

"That means Nihon is safe, Majesty, safer than it has been since the Change. That *is* more than half the total *jinnikukaburi* strength. What we have at home can handle the rest, even if they throw everything at us. Simply losing that fleet will cripple the enemy for many years. And if our allies win this battle, nearly all of our own strength will be intact for the final offensive while the enemy are critically weakened at little cost to us. The *kami* favor us with the prospect of a great victory."

She replied in a brusque tone: "The *kami* do favor us, General, for ours is the Land of the Gods. Yet many will die this day, many will be widowed, many children will be orphans, much work of human hands be wasted and leave hunger and want in their wake. It is necessary, but do not exult. We must fulfill our *giri*—"

Which meant roughly the *burden of duty* in her tongue.

"—but do not therefore forget *ninjō*."

Which was *human feeling*, the counterpoint to the merciless demands of duty and obligation. From what Órlaith had been able to gather and what the structure of the language the Sword had taught her in an instant implied, modern Nihonjin thought and much of their poetry turned on the tension between those two. Reiko went on:

"Victory is a means to secure a victorious peace for our people—"

Which was a play on the regnal name she had chosen: *Shōhei Tennō*, Empress of Victorious Peace.

"—so that they may harvest their rice and rear their children in peace free from fear and attack. Success in battle is not an end in itself. The sword must *serve*, even if those who bear the steel *rule*. It is for this reason that duty is heavier than mountains, and the warrior's death lighter than a feather; they are tools to a greater end."

"I bow to your wisdom, *Heika*," Egawa said, and did so.

Well, it's not an accident I like Reiko, Órlaith thought. *And past Tennō may have been puppets of their warlords, but that is most certainly not going to happen while Reiko sits the Chrysanthemum Throne.*

"This is a desperation move," Órlaith said thoughtfully—in Reiko's language, and then in her own. "They are throwing the dice to keep us from entering their home waters, yet they could fight more effectively close to their bases and farther from ours. Something in Korea . . . or near it on the Asian mainland . . . is pushing them to recklessness, I would say."

Reiko made a small exasperated sound. "We in Dai-Nippon have been on the defensive too long, parrying their attacks, or at most retaliating for their raids. Perhaps we overestimate our importance to them, assuming we fill their thoughts as they do ours. We must know more!"

Just then Heuradys came up. She had her shield over her back, and held out Órlaith's.

"Now," she said, in a voice that brooked no argument, and added: "Your Highness," because it was a formal occasion in a way.

The four-foot teardrop shape of plywood and bison-hide and sheet metal bore the arms of Montival with a baton of cadency—only the High King or High Queen could wear them undifferenced. She supposed that she could have had Raven as a quartering, for the Morrigú was the patron of her House, or the Golden Eagle that was her personal totem, but this would do. She took it and slung it over her back too with the guige-strap loose; that way you could slide it onto your left arm with a single shrug and movement.

The twenty pounds of weight was utterly familiar, though the shield was new. Even ordinary mortal swords might last lifetimes, but a shield was fortunate to go through a single afternoon of strong arms and hard blows without being beaten to tatters.

Not that she was probably going to need it. This was formal war, unlike their self-help, deeply-unofficial breakaway Quest to help Reiko find the Grasscutter. Her Household was around her—or rather, down in the break between the quarterdeck and main deck, waiting to rush up to surround her.

Faramir and Morfind had been standing with their hands on their hearts—over their mail-lined jerkins—and heads bowed to the westward as they contemplated *Númenor that was, and Elvenhome that is, and that which is beyond Elvenhome and ever will be,* and a possible trip to the Halls of Mandos.

Their Lakota life-partner Suzie Mika was painting her face with finicky care.

"It'll do," said, looking in a hand mirror; she'd put a bar of black across her eyes, and dotted white lines down her cheeks, and bound her braided black hair back with a neckerchief tied at the rear so that she could put on her light helmet without delay.

"Not gaudy and overdone, like you guys," she added with a grin at the little band of Mackenzie archers that Karl and his brother led.

"Sure, and some just don't understaaand the spiritual significance," Karl Aylward Mackenzie said loftily, exaggerating his lilting accent.

The Mackenzies were painting for war too, but in the fierce primary colors their Clan used, often in stylized forms that showed the face of the individual's sept totem, or sometimes sheer fancy.

Diarmuid Tennart McClintock touched the blue designs tattooed into his face as youths and maidens in his Clan did at their Spear-Taking, when they became adults and Initiates, liable to be called to the levy for war and lawful opponents in duel or feud by the McClintock version of Brehon law. He smiled; in fact, you could say he smirked, and his equally if more crudely tattooed clansfolk jeered in their thick growling accents.

Someone muttered *Clan Wannabee,* and a McClintock replied with *Clan Little Wussie Pleated Skirt,* and each group laughed at the ancient half-serious jokes, both nearly as old as the Change. Then Gwri Beauregard Mackenzie began singing "The Tale of Liath Duv"—Liath the Dark, in the old tongue—which was about an aunt of hers who'd led a band harrying the Prophet's men in the High Cascades a generation ago, and they all joined in the chorus which told how the Fair Folk had favored her.

Beyond them the men-at-arms from the Protector's guard in their black plate armor were being confessed and absolved by their chaplain, kneeling in turn beside him while their comrades made a box around them, leaning on their shields with their backs to their priest to give each some privacy.

They were all settling their spirits in their own way, and making ready to die if needs must. Around them was wrapped the might of Montival's united realms, and it was all pledged to her.

So their shields and their bodies will be between me and danger, she thought. *Or the types that shields and bodies can stop; a catapult bolt or a roundshot or a napalm shell aren't respecters of persons.*

Knowing that there were people—including people she knew and loved, and also absolute strangers, which was daunting in a different way—who'd throw themselves between her and mortal threat without an instant's hesitation had always been part of her life. Before the last six months it had been theoretical, but now she'd seen the blood and the unpleasantly final death.

Remember always your birth means you can break things so easily, Da used to say. Mother too, in different words.

On the one hand, her being here endangered people because the enemy would drive for her—and she suspected they had those who could sense the Sword of the Lady well beyond eye-range.

On the other, looking brave in public and being a symbol like a banner was part of her basic function in life; the Gods knew she probably wasn't going to be making any military decisions today, having an embarrassment of seasoned professionals along. It was rather like being a junior officer: they looked inspiring for the troops while the sergeants did the work. Except that she didn't have to perform a secondary function of stopping spearpoints meant for someone who actually did things.

Heuradys seemed to sense her thoughts. "Mom Two said that having people looking at her all the time was one of the hardest things she had to learn when she moved from being your grandma Sandra's solitary black-ops specialist to field commands. She'd spent all that time hiding and now she had to perform in public. Doing the technical side of things wasn't hard, she had good teachers and a natural talent for it; what she hadn't counted on was a second career as an actress, she said."

"Whereas I was born to the role," Órlaith said softly, and slapped her shoulder—which in plate was rather like giving an affectionate pat to a giant lobster. "Ah, but it's good to have someone I can bitch and whine to, Herry."

"I wouldn't exactly call it *whining*, bitch," she said, in equally quiet tones, and they both laughed. "Not really. Not quite. Though I imagine a lot of peasants and fishermen and blacksmiths might think so."

"A ruler of the ancient Americans . . . I think it was one of the ones carved into that mountain in the Lakota territory . . . said that the definition of whining was talking about a problem without proposing a solution."

"One of the Four Big *Wasicu* Guys of the H̄e Sápa, as Suzie says. Except there *is* no solution here, so you might as well bitch and whine— Excuse me: muse aloud upon the philosophical ironies of your situation."

Órlaith's hand went to the pommel of the Sword of the Lady, as the topsails of the enemy fleet grew larger against the low green horizon of Oahu. She thought she could scent danger coming down the landward breeze, along with an increasing smell of nasty smoke; pillars of black bending towards them showed where the enemy had been methodically destroying buildings and workshops and ships.

"I think it's probably still a better situation than John's," she said grimly. "Only my body's in danger."

Heuradys glanced aside; Reiko was a few steps off, and talking to King Kalākaua, which given the differences in their versions of English required intense concentration.

"You're thinking of—"

Reiko's brother, who had been burned to ash when the Grasscutter sensed his corruption. Or when *Amaterasu-ōmikami* did so Herself, which was even more alarming when you thought about it.

Órlaith swallowed and nodded. "Not exactly. But Da . . . told me once of using the Sword to heal the mind of a magus of the Church Universal and Triumphant, back during the Prophet's War."

Heuradys' brows went up. "It didn't work?"

"Yes, it did work, in a manner of speaking. When it took out the parts of his mind that had been corrupted, it turned him into a child again, in the body of a man in his middle years—a child who could never grow. It scourged out all the parts of him that had been tainted by the Power behind the CUT, and those were most of what makes you . . . *you*."

Her liege knight winced. "A painless death is almost better."

CHAPTER TWELVE

BETWEEN WAKING WORLD AND SHADOW

"**W**e need to know who that man is, and where he dwells," Deor said as they came down from the third floor.

Pip smiled. "I think I know how, too," she said.

Deor's eyes went a little wide as she knocked on the armorer's door.

"Good day," she said as they came through to the chime of the bell above the door, falling back into an exaggerated version of her mother's dulcet tones, without the underlying hint of Townsville dialect she usually had. "Please forgive my intrusion. I am Miss Philippa Balwyn-Abercrombie. Pleased to make your acquaintance, Mr. Hawberk, Miss Hawberk."

The older man looked up, stood, and bowed politely, taking Pip's hand in an abbreviated gesture that wasn't quite kissing it but was visibly one that had evolved from it. His daughter was sitting on the workbench beside him, and he had been comforting her. He was visibly composing himself in a flash as he made his own introductions, and she finished dabbing at her eyes and tucked away her handkerchief.

My goodness, Pip thought. *The fabled stiff upper lip swinging into operation. But he's badly off balance.*

He cleared his throat. "Good day, Miss Balwyn . . . Balwyn-Abercrombie? A relation of the Herefordshire Balwyns, by any chance?"

You could see that he wished the words back as soon as he'd spoken them. Pip thought they must have been reflex, a flashback to the life he'd led before he came here fleeing scandal.

"Remotely. My branch of the family moved to Australia some time ago."

At least the Abercrombies had, in the 1860s. Assuming that had happened in this odd version of history, or cycle of the universe, or whatever it was. Deor might understand it fully, if he wasn't just putting on the Wise Sage, but Pip didn't pretend to. She suspected that it couldn't really be reduced to simple declarative sentences anyway, which bothered her sharp but practical mind.

"May I present my companion, Miss Thora Garwood, and our associate Mr. Godulfson?"

A woman companion and a bodyguard-secretary would make her respectable, if she remembered the mores correctly.

No need to tell him Thora and I are both preggers and looking for the man responsible, Pip thought. *Though what a handy stick to beat John with, and won't I use it, just?*

She *assumed* they were more or less like Victorians here, which might be a mistake, but there wasn't enough time to do anthropology and she'd have to rely on what she remembered from classes and books.

"Ah," he said cautiously. "And this is my daughter, Miss Constance Hawberk."

Then his eyes lit on Toa, apparently slightly surprised to see a gigantic tattooed Maori with a shovel over one shoulder and a box on the other.

"*Tēnā koe,*" the Englishman said.

Which meant a formal hello in Maori; specifically, the way you said it to a single other person.

Toa grunted in surprise and answered: "*Tēnā kōrua.*"

Which was the same thing to *two* people.

"I have traveled in your part of the world too," Hawberk said. "Both Australia and New Zealand. How may I help you? Do you have a matter of armorer's work in which I might be of assistance?"

Deor had bent over the piece on the wooden brace that held it as a shoemaker's lath did leather.

"This is fine work, Mr. Hawberk," he said. "Double-coil on the mail, I see, then alternate rows closed with rivets. Very strong, but a bit less flexible. Even if it's to be a display piece, I'm glad you're not just using butted mail."

Hawberk brightened, with that peculiar expression that someone who loved their work got when hearing it *knowledgeably* praised.

"Pleasant to meet a man who knows mail, Mr. Godulfson," Hawberk said. "Very pleasant. It happens so seldom."

What? But obsessive armor enthusiasts are ten a penny—Pip began to think, then realized: *Ah, nobody wears mail for real here. Bullets. Like those lancers— there's no point, when it can't protect you. Though those bright uniforms are odd, then: you'd think they'd want something inconspicuous, the way scouts do in modern armies.*

"And those are the arms of the Dukes of Burgundy, aren't they, Miss Hawberk?" Pip said brightly, looking at the embroidery she'd set aside. "Though I couldn't say which one."

"Charles the Bold," Constance said shyly.

"Or *Charles the Foolhardy*, Ms. Hawberk," Pip said, and gave her a smile before turning to her father.

"Well, the real reason we dropped by, Mr. Hawberk, is that—it's just a trifle embarrassing—we're traveling in New York and trying to look someone up. And we just missed him here! I didn't realize it was him until after he'd passed us by, for I've never met him, only seen a photo- graph. A Mr. Castaigne."

Hawberk looked at her, then at Deor, as if surprised she was taking the lead in the conversation, then turned to Pip when Deor nodded to- wards her.

"Would that be Hildred, Miss, or his cousin Louis?" he said. "Louis is an officer in the 20th Dragoons."

"Oh, Mr. Hildred Castaigne," Pip said. "He mentioned your shop in one of his letters, and even said where it was located . . . but neglected to note his new address! This was a letter to my father, you understand, who traveled extensively in America and was acquainted with Mr. Castaigne's father. He's corresponded with us, but, ah, over the last six months his letters have gotten a bit . . . eccentric. My father did so wish us to drop by and make sure that everything was, as they say here, OK."

"Eccentric since he was in the asy—" Constance began, then stopped as her father made a gesture.

Pip made herself look wise and discreet; her mother had given her lessons in that, disguised as amateur theatricals.

Never say too much, let the mark fill in the details themselves had been part of the teaching.

"I believe I can be of assistance," he said. "Mr. Castaigne has been ill, and it will do him good to meet friends of the family. He does tend to be too much taken up with his books and his routine."

He looked around, found a scrap of paper and wrote: 80 *Washington Square East* on it.

"This is the address of his rooms at the Benedick," he said.

Pip gave him a glimpse of her dimples. "As in the bachelor in *Much Ado About Nothing?* A nest for those who consider themselves silver-tongued rogues immune to the darts of Cupid?"

He smiled, and so did his daughter; genuinely in her case, Pip thought.

"Yes, it's an apartment for bachelor artists—there are studios on the upper floor."

"Thank you very much, Mr. Hawberk," Pip said, and the others followed through with murmurs of gratitude.

Outside the building they paused, Toa helping to create a bubble of space on the crowded sidewalk. Deor regarded her with pawky amusement.

"I cry hail to you, Captain Pip," he said, with the gesture his folk used as a salute. "I'm a musician, but you played those two like a lute. For one so young, you show much skill in dealing with an audience."

Pip inclined her head, hiding a smile but feeling genuinely flattered. In her experience, men of Deor's persuasion were often better at understanding women—not because they were more womanlike themselves, for they weren't, but because they were less distracted and more able to see you as simply a person and not a set of animated signals for their mating drive. Provided they were smart to begin with, and Deor God-ulfson was very sharp indeed.

Toa snorted. "You should have seen her mum. When she wasn't just chopping people up with those two kukris—ah, now *that* was a pleasure to see. Sort of like one of those machines they use on sugarcane at the mill . . . but she was just about as dangerous when she turned on the charm, straight up. Left people wondering why they'd agreed to sell her their liver for five pence and a pint of the mild and bitter."

They were standing around a food cart of a sort she'd seen in many cities, though in Darwin they reached the status of an art form. This one had an internal charcoal grill, selling various flavored drinks and simple foods. The elaborately braided salty bread thing they called a *pretzel* was particularly interesting, given the way she'd suddenly remembered how ravenous she was.

Pip reached for the bottle of lemonade, then hesitated. "Wait a minute—didn't you say we should refuse food and drink?" she said.

Deor put mustard on the sausage in a bun he'd bought. "Only those offered as gifts," he said. "That creates . . . debt, you might say, which makes for bonds. Where we are now, there's little difference between symbol and reality. Exchange doesn't have the same effect."

Pip looked down at the pretzel. "Why do we need to eat at all?" she said.

Deor grinned again. "Because our minds—the part that make our bodies work, that has an image of our physical selves in it—think we do. Try not breathing! Your body is back on that bed, breathing Baru Den-pasar's air . . . but you'll go blue in the face and faint here, too."

Grimly: "Which is why a blow *here* can hurt you *there*."

"So now we know where this man linked to Prince John lives," Thora said, taking a bite of her own sausage. "What do we do? Break into his house and make him talk?"

Deor shook his head, half-admiringly. "Not so straightforward, oath-sister."

She snorted, chewed and swallowed. "You've used those words to me often enough over the years! And *sometimes* you were right, and sometimes straightforward was better than twisty. What then?"

"The man . . . the shadow of the man that lives forever here in the dream of a mad God . . . is only a finger on the hand of the Power which snatched our John away. Once it becomes fully aware of us and strikes, we will have little time before we return to the waking world . . . or do not. Death is not the worst threat to us, or to the Prince."

Thora signed the Hammer. "Why isn't it already aware of us? If this place is its domain?"

"I am not sure. Perhaps because those Powers who wish human kind well and those who are our guardians shield us; and also because it *is* mad."

He frowned. "I spoke with the High King a few times of the Prophet's War . . . which was also not merely a thing of blades and bows, politics and the contentions of kings. The Power behind the Church Universal and Triumphant . . . and I think behind the dynasty in Korea who sent the men who killed him a generation later . . . is . . . not mad. Malevolent in human terms, yes, and hostile to us, to the whole world of matter. But mainly it is *alien*."

"If it's not mad, it's stupid," Thora said. "*I've* talked with those who were commanders in the Prophet's War too—even with High Marshal d'Ath."

She smiled for a moment. "Now, there's one who should have been a Bearkiller! She's wasted among Associates. They all said that the enemy then, everyone under the CUT's control, just walked up to problems and hit them with a hammer. If the hammer broke, it looked for a bigger hammer. The war was only serious because they had a lot of hammers, including ones that hit us in ways only the Sword of the Lady could parry."

"Neither mad nor stupid, but *alien*," Deor insisted. "From what the High King said, just to operate in our world, in contact with human minds and spirits, was agony to it. It did not . . . does not . . . comprehend us well. He once told me that the Powers said to him that that Enemy was not evil in our sense, not in its own place and time. That was how it manifested in the world of common day, of course."

Toa grunted. "This Yellow Raja, Yellow King, King in a yellow rag-picker's outfit . . . *that* bugger seems pretty evil to me. And I'm not one to say someone's bad just because they're out to kill me. That can be just business, or a difference of opinion, like."

Deor nodded. "This Power we deal with here . . . this King in Yellow . . . it is more *like* us, and understands us better. And it is both mad and evil, in our own sense. Perhaps less powerful than that Other who was the Prophet's patron, but more subtle. This world we see around us—and its future, which we also saw, and the time beyond that—are already full of it, like threads of mold growing through bread."

Pip listened closely, and the pretzel suddenly tasted like ashes for an instant. She chased it with a gulp of lemonade.

Oh, this is *like the Men with Swords and Things with Tentacles,* she thought. *We've been lucky in Oz since the Blackout. Our encounters with this sort of thing have been smaller and more out-of-the-way.*

"That bit we saw first—with the Hell Horse—was the far future of this world?" she said.

"It was a time *after* time, I think. A place . . . or time . . . where all things have collapsed into each other; past and future, good and evil, life and death. A mad God's endless revenge."

Oh, bloody marvelous, she thought with a shudder, and continued briskly aloud:

"So if we're not to grab him and commence with the pointed—and sharp and heavy—questions, what the bloody hell do we do?" she said.

"Follow and observe and think, I would say," Deor said.

John caught something out of the corner of his eye. . . .

No, he thought. *Castaigne did, and someone else did. . . .*

Castaigne had seen four people on the street, moving in a group: two women and two men, one of the latter very large and very dark. Hildred's attention was focused on that one for an instant, frowning in distaste at something he disliked in the man.

I thought they'd all gone to Suanee? ran through his thoughts.

Then he dismissed it and returned to his own thoughts—which were, as usual, mostly about himself and his endless circle of grievances.

I'm trapped with a madman and it's so boring, John thought. Then his mind went clear for an instant: *That was Pip! How can Pip be here? And Deor and Thora and Toa!*

He struggled like a madman himself for a moment . . . and then realized the futility of it. He felt as if he was thrashing about, but nothing *changed.* Yet there was something there, teasing at the edges of his mind. Something like golden threads, two of them, one a bit stronger than the other, spinning out towards Thora and Pip.

That hint of another personality, the Boisean agreed. John felt more . . .

Present. As if I can feel the boundaries between me and the rest of the world. Without everything blurring into everything else for a moment. It's like bobbing about in the water and coming to the surface now and then.

He could also feel how little a man saw of the world around him, and how much was filled in by memory, as if it were a series of pictures ruffled through and held up from little clues. What Hildred Castaigne saw was so familiar to him that it hardly registered at all, just flashes—and all of them were exotic beyond words to John. They passed the place called the Lethal Chamber again, and Castaigne paused.

The door had just closed behind someone who sought it out. John felt pity; suicide was mortal sin, and he prayed for the soul that had abandoned itself. Perhaps the man had been mad, not responsible for what he did. . . .

They were close enough as they crossed the park for the sound of machinery whirring and chunking could be heard—heavy machinery, like a metalworking mill in Corvallis he'd visited once, when his father and mother were cutting the ribbon to celebrate its opening. Gears and flywheels whining, but here they were muffled behind heavy concrete and stone, and with it somehow a *wet* sound that gradually diminished to *rrrrrrr* like a mill grinding bone for fertilizer.

Castaigne didn't consciously notice the sound, but something flowed through him, a dark strength that felt like health but that the ones who shared his mind could instantly feel wasn't. It put an extra spring into the step, though. It felt like *power*, too, and that was more truthful. Like taking some drug that increased your strength now but undermined it in the long run.

As always when he felt power, Castaigne thought of revenge. This time it was the square face of the doctor, the one who'd tended him after his injury. Flashes of that treatment came back to the surface of his mind; it was impossible to tell bloody fancy from dark reality, though he thought the parts about sobbing all alone in a dark locked box were true, and then screaming and trying to flail against the straight confines of it.

This doctor may have earned some of his hate. On the other hand, he seems to have been genuinely trying to help.

Castaigne turned onto a broad north–south thoroughfare that he thought of as *Madison Avenue*. It was flanked by brick mansions, with here and there a taller structure under construction or recently built, mostly of marble and columns in what was apparently the current prevailing style in this city.

Hildred's mind was skipping about as he approached his goal; this experience was showing John how much of the internal monologue you assumed, the mind talking to itself, was an illusion. Or possibly Castaigne was just less coherent than most. Now he was remembering a fall from a horse, the sudden shock of coming loose. That was familiar, but Hildred landed badly, his head striking the stone curb of a pathway in some sort of park. More images after that, of blurred thought and pain in the head and neck and pain, the wretched debilitating misery that came with concussion. John recognized it, and so did the fellow . . .

Passenger, John decided. *We're fellow-passengers.*

Time blurred; then Hildred was sitting across from Dr. Archer in a rather heavy, fussy-looking book-lined office that smelled of print and leather covers, and faintly of disinfectant. A faint muffled howling sounded, like a man screaming endlessly and hoarsely, just on the verge of hearing. It was in the present, if that meant anything; at least it was not one of Hildred Castaigne's memories, and Archer was trying to smile.

"Still determined to settle my hash for me, are you, Mr. Castaigne?"

he said, laughing . . . though from where he stood, John could tell that there was no jest involved.

"Oh, implacably," Castaigne said calmly. "Though it's really a minor matter, in a sense, yet still I do look forward to seeing your debt paid in full."

He brought out a checkbook, indistinguishable from those used in the more advanced parts of Montival, and made out a sum.

"I believe this completes my . . . tuition, Dr. Archer?"

"Most satisfactorily, Mr. Castaigne," the alienist—that was the title on his diploma on the wall—said.

"Indeed, I do owe you a debt of gratitude," Castaigne said.

"Ah!" Archer said, looking interested. "That constitutes progress! How do you conceive of that debt?"

"Why, Doctor, the fall from my horse . . . and the, ah, tuition here . . . has changed my whole character for the better. From a lazy young man about town, I have become active, energetic, temperate, and above all— oh, above all else—ambitious. Not least because my convalescence broadened my horizons."

He reached into the pocket of his jacket and pulled out a slim volume with a cover of soft leather. "For example, I read this. I heartily recommend it to you, Doctor! It will broaden your mind too!"

Archer idly opened the book, then whipped back his hand as if it were red-hot.

"My God," he blurted. *The King in Yellow!*

"The very same," Castaigne said, amusement in his voice. "I remember after finishing the first act that it occurred to me that I had better stop. I started up and flung the book into the fireplace; the volume struck the barred grate and fell open on the hearth in the firelight . . . you see how it is slightly singed? If I had not caught a glimpse of the opening words in the second act I should never have finished it, but as I stooped to pick it up, my eyes became riveted to the open page."

He leaned forward and tapped a finger. "Riveted just here, Doctor. Where the Yellow Sign appears above the words of Cassilda, as Hastur . . ."

Archer's eyes dropped to the point he indicated as Castaigne's voice trailed off. Then they became locked, and sweat broke out on his brow. For perhaps thirty seconds he read, and turned the page with a trembling hand, then wrenched his gaze away.

"This book is illegal; it has been banned throughout the civilized world!"

"Easier to ban in theory than to banish in fact," Castaigne said, with catlike malice. "Though perhaps you should not mention how I have made you a present of this copy."

Archer nodded, absently, as if he had not heard the words with his conscious mind.

Castaigne went on: "When the French Government seized the translated copies which had just arrived in Paris, London, of course, became eager to read it. So it has gone throughout the world; the play is barred out here, confiscated there, denounced by Press and pulpit, censured even by the most advanced of literary anarchists. Yet it spreads."

"It spreads like a disease!"

"Oh, come now, Doctor. You are a man of science, of reason. One who seeks to lay bare the secrets of the human mind, not as poetry or superstition, but as cold fact like engineering or the removal of a diseased appendix! If this play affects men's minds, surely you *must* study it to find out the mechanism by which a mere form of words can unbalance the psyche!"

"Perhaps," Archer said. "Yes, perhaps . . . for science . . ."

With a convulsive gesture he swept the slim book off his desk into a drawer, licking his lips as he shut it away with a small key and tucking the key with trembling fingers into a pocket in his waistcoat.

Chuckling to himself, Castaigne left the doctor sitting at his desk, sweat running down into his starched collar, fingering the key in his pocket and staring ahead with a fixed glare that held an awful hunger.

Hildred chuckled again at the thought of the hunger and of its satisfaction, and made his way back to Bleecker Street, followed it to Wooster, skirted the grounds of the Lethal Chamber, and crossing Washington Park went straight to his rooms in the Benedick.

About what a well-to-do townsman who wasn't married might have, John thought, looking through another man's eyes. *Or the rooms a country knight might keep for visits to Portland . . . not quite enough for a baron, who'd have a bigger entourage.*

The electric lights were fascinating—Hildred took them for granted—but otherwise it was like those of many friends among Portland's artists and musicians. The more successful ones, who weren't living in boarding-houses or their parent's quarters, that was. This Castaigne evidently employed a cook and two housemaids, which was again about what you'd expect. The details were different, of course; the outlines of the overstuffed furniture, the number and type of knickknacks, and the rather florid, Renaissance-derived style of the paintings as opposed to the way the Protectorate's descended from the pre-Raphaelites and Art Nouveau.

One of the housemaids brought out Castaigne's lunch; a rather heavy omelet made with oysters and cream, a tasty seafood soup of clams and cod in tomato broth, rolls and fruit and a mediocre and over-sweet white wine. John found that he could *taste* it all, but for a moment it made him miserably aware that his real body was starving, and then that it was tied in an excruciatingly painful position.

If that is my real body, John thought. *But it's close enough for government work.*

While he ate and read newspapers named the *Herald* and *Meteor* full of local news that was meaningless if you didn't know the context, he looked out his window at the Lethal Chamber on the corner of the square opposite. A few curious people still lingered about the gilded iron railing, but inside the grounds the paths were deserted. He watched the fountains ripple and sparkle; the sparrows had already found this new bathing nook, and the basins were covered with the dusty-feathered little things. Two or three white peacocks picked their way across the lawns, and a drab-colored pigeon sat so motionless on the arm of one of the "Fates," that it seemed to be a part of the sculptured stone.

Then there was a slight commotion in the group of curious loiterers around the gates that captured Castaigne's eye. A young man had entered, and was walking with quick nervous strides along the gravel to the bronze doors. He paused a moment before the "Fates," and as he raised his head to those three mysterious faces, the pigeon rose from its sculptured perch, circled about for a moment and wheeled to the east. The young man pressed his hand to his face, and then with an angry gesture sprang up the marble steps.

The bronze doors swung open to his touch and closed behind him with the ponderous silence of precise balance. The loiterers stared for a few moments, then slouched away, and the frightened pigeon returned to its perch in the arms of Fate.

Again there was that surge of *power*. John found himself praying in silence; not the formal Latin he'd learned later, but the simple words Sister Agatha had taught him as a child.

Holy Mary pierced with sorrows, have mercy on us sinners!

After he finished his fruit and biscuits, Castaigne rose. He utterly ignored the pertly attractive maidservant, who had red hair and an accent a little like a Mackenzie. John didn't think it was that he didn't like women, judging by what he'd thought looking at a picture of a pillowy blond nude on the other side of the dining room; it was more as if nobody else was really *real* to him compared to the imaginings within his own brain.

He rose, put on his hat and went out into the park with nothing in his mind but a walk, which was a relief after most of what he thought about.

John felt as if he was going to sleep, somehow, and that was frightening. He made himself feel more awake, by imagining how his confessor was going to react to all this. What would he say?

That God is giving me His omnipotent view of what a bad man is like, so that I can guard against it? That this is one of the trials He bestows on those who are fortunate in their birth or who He especially loves?

He caught himself just before he thought that if this was proof of God's love, he didn't want it. You did *not* want to think that, even as a joke. He knew in his heart that God did have a sense of humor—his own mental image of the Wedding at Cana was of Jesus with a mug of the (excellent) wine He'd created in one hand, throwing back his head and laughing full-throated at one of the classic bawdy jokes that got thrown around at every wedding since time began. But there were limits.

When he was conscious of what Castaigne was doing again, he'd crossed the central driveway and a group of officers in those fancy uniforms were passing, reminding him of nothing so much as a group of young bucks at Court in Todenangst, senior squires peacocking about with time on their hands as their knights were at work, and nothing on their minds but horses, falcons, tournaments and flirtations.

Or their gambling debts, often enough, he thought with an aching nostalgia.

"Hello, Hildred," one called out, and came back to shake hands with him.

This is Louis, his cousin, John thought.

John could see the resemblance in build and coloring, but there was nothing but easy good-nature in the man's expression, and even in the tilt of his neatly trimmed mustache. He looked like a medium-good fighting man at least, with the slightly pigeon-toed swing to his walk that horse-soldiers got, and thick swordsman's wrists.

He really is like a lot of brainless squires—boring when you talk anything but women and single-minded about even that, full of invincibly ignorant opinions about music, but brave and there's no harm in them. And Hildred wants him dead—or is starting to.

"Just back from Westchester," the cavalryman said. "Been doing the bucolic; milk and curds, you know, dairymaids in sunbonnets, who say 'haeow' and 'I don't think' when you tell them they are pretty."

John felt a flash of sympathy; he'd had the same experience, in his own knight training.

"I'm nearly dead for a square meal at Delmonico's. What's the news?"

"There is none," Hildred replied. "I saw your regiment coming in this morning."

"Did you? I didn't see you. Where were you?"

"In Mr. Wilde's window."

"Oh, hell!" Louis began impatiently. "That man is stark mad! I don't understand why you—"

A flash like white fire ran through Hildred Castaigne's mind, and his cousin actually went a little pale.

"Really, old chap," he said. "I don't mean to run down a man you like, but for the life of me I can't see what the deuce you find in common with Mr. Wilde. He's not well bred, to put it generously; he is hideously deformed; his head is the head of a criminally insane person. You know yourself he's been in an asylum—"

"So have I," Hildred said.

I'd have stepped back and put my hand to my sword-hilt if someone talked to me that way, John thought. *Not the words, at the tone.*

Louis did look startled and confused for a moment, but recovered and slapped him heartily on the shoulder. That made John confusingly sympathetic to Hildred, just for a moment; he hated being mauled that way too.

"You were completely cured," Louis began.

"I suppose you mean that I was simply acknowledged never to have been insane."

"Of course that . . . that's what I meant," he laughed.

Hildred knew the laugh was false; John thought only a deaf man wouldn't notice. Whatever Louis Castaigne was, he was no actor—nor practitioner of any other trade that required getting up in front of an audience. His cousin was torn between contempt and hatred.

If I were no better liar than that I'd still be in a straitjacket! Hildred thought; then he chuckled.

"But that's enough of old, unhappy things," he said. "Where are you going?"

Louis looked after his brother officers who had now almost reached Broadway.

"We had intended to sample a Brunswick cocktail, but to tell you the truth I was anxious for an excuse to go and see Hawberk instead. Come along, I'll make you my excuse."

Hildred turned to follow his cousin's eager step, striding out with his spurs jingling and his riding crop tapping at the top of his high polished black boots. A flash of tawny hair caught John's attention, and frustration nearly drove him into mindless fury as *nothing* happened when he tried to jerk head and eyes around.

Pip! he thought. *Was that Pip? How could Pip and the others be in this place?*

The thought of her made his mind work a little better, less blurred and dull.

CHAPTER THIRTEEN

BETWEEN WAKING WORLD AND SHADOW

"Here he comes," Pip murmured.

They spread out a little and trailed Hildred Castaigne and the man in uniform who could have been his brother and was almost certainly his cousin Louis. They walked directly to Hawberk's shop, and the armorer was outside on the sidewalk, neatly attired in a fresh suit of pale linen sniffing the air.

"I had just decided to take Constance for a little stroll before dinner," he replied to the impetuous volley of questions from Louis. "We thought of walking on the park terrace along the North River."

He nodded to Hildred. "Did you meet the young lady from Australia?"

Hildred looked puzzled. "No . . . from Australia, you say?"

"Yes, she and her party; they said . . ."

He broke off as his daughter emerged, opening her pale mauve parasol against the bright afternoon sun.

"Oh, hello, my dear! Here are Louis and Hildred, by a happy chance."

Pip was watching them in the reflections they made in a shop-window, but even with dust and distortion it was plain how Constance grew pale and then flushed by turns as Louis bent over her small gloved fingers. That was the full I-kiss-your-hand treatment, evidently something special because Constance's blush turned to absolute crimson for an instant.

Good for you, my girl, Pip thought, briefly amused.

Then she caught a glimpse of Hildred's eyes, and felt herself recoil.

And I don't shock easily, she thought.

"Do come with us!" Constance said. "It's a lovely spring evening, just right for a stroll, and I've been shut up in the shop all day."

"I'm desolated, Miss Hawberk, but I was going to dine soon with some friends at my club . . ."

"Nonsense, old man!" his cousin said. "You're coming with us! I know those friends of yours—nothing but blather about revolting French novels. Fresh air will do you good, Hildred."

"Yes, do come, Mr. Castaigne," Constance said.

He hesitated; Pip saw his eyes dart towards his cousin and then back at Constance, and he smiled with a practiced expression, and they all set off.

He wants to keep an eye on them, Pip guessed. *He's not interested in the girl himself, you can tell that by the way he looks at them and holds himself. But seeing them together makes him very, very bloody angry.*

That puzzled her, until she thought of some times she'd had with her disgustingly numerous and even more disgustingly ambitious cousins. Pip was an only child as her mother had been before her, but her paternal aunts and uncles had bred like rabbits . . . and once they weren't children anymore, the offspring had quivered with anxiety and anger whenever it seemed that there was any possibility of her marrying.

Because then Daddy would have an heir for his heir, and they'd be out of the line of succession. Particularly if he does modernize the terminology and make himself King of Townsville. Which makes sense if Mr. Hildred Castaigne intends to make himself a King here, though that seems rather mad. But then again, he is rather mad, what?

Hildred looked jaunty with a flower in his buttonhole, whistling now and then and swinging his walking-stick. Pip envied it a little; it was more like what she usually carried than . . .

This damned brolly, she thought, stopping to look in a shop-window for a moment. *It's useable, but it makes me nervous. You should be able to handle things by instinct in a dustup.*

The others followed her lead; none of them had been specifically trained in how to track someone in a city, but they were all natural hunters and very experienced and none of them was stupid. The rather shabby neighborhood where Hawberk's shop was located—and that of the mysterious Repairer of Reputations—gave way to more prosperous-looking streets, though still insanely crowded by her standards.

Still, that makes it easier to do the tail.

Instants after that, the four they were following got on a large boxy vehicle that slid along the street on rails set into the pavement. For a moment Pip simply stared; then she remembered the similar system they had in Darwin—albeit pulled by horses, not pushed by the legendary force of electricity, which must be what those sparking poles on top running up to the wires slung overhead were for.

Bless a classical education! she thought. *I shall never mock Miss Blandish's Pre-Blackout Sciences class again!*

The driver clucked at them and pointed at a box for fares. Thora reached into her handbag and pulled out a handful of the local currency and offered it, that had apparently been supplied, as their imaginary swords had been changed for equally imaginary—but also legendary—guns.

"Cantcha' read, lady?" the man said in an adenoidal accent, pointing to the *exact change only* stenciled on the glass fare-box.

Then he saw Toa. "And none of his . . ."

His voice trailed off as the big Maori scowled at him, and vanished entirely as Thora flipped him a gold coin. Instead of further argument he cleared his throat and announced to the world:

"Silver Street line—da North River Terrace!"

Pip took a seat where she could see out the large front windows of the vehicle, and keep in view the vehicle Castaigne and his party were on. Theirs lurched into motion with a clatter and an odd whining sound and a smell of ozone, accelerating faster than anything she'd ever been on except a funfair ride where you were pushed up to the top of a slope and then ran down under gravity. Then the speed settled down to something only moderately alarming, about what a good horse could manage for a few miles at a hand-gallop on easy ground, but it went on and on.

"This is like sailing broad reach with a strong steady wind on the starboard quarter," she said.

Deor and Thora were behind her, and Toa was leaning on his shovel, treating swaying effortlessly with the motion of the vehicle. It was nothing much, when you'd ridden out hurricanes in the Timor Sea.

"That's the only thing I can compare it to. Now some of the things Mummy said about life before the Blackout make more sense."

"Yes," Deor said. "Except that you can't count on a favorable wind whenever you want it. That's how they could have cities like this; unfailing machines to deliver the food for all these millions, from many miles away. A delay in getting silk or spices or dyestuff doesn't matter that much except to the pockets of a few, but you have to bake bread every day."

Pip shivered a little. "I've seen the ruins of Sydney," she said. "With the drifts of bones still in the buildings. Everything failed them, in the end."

Seeing a living city like those of the ancient world drove it home.

"Pretty," Thora said, craning her neck to look ahead. "You only see this sort of thing in cities without walls around them."

The car came to a halt with a screech of steel on steel and they disembarked at a little station that was, indeed, pretty; a broad river stretched northward, and there was a pleasantly cool breeze off it. The water was a bright blue riffled with white. Ships whose rigs she knew—brigs, schooners, yachts—shared the water with steam-propelled craft like something out of an ancient book, clumsy ferryboats, their decks swarming with people, railroad transports carrying lines of brown, blue and white freight cars, big liners and tramps, dredgers, scows, and everywhere little tugs puffing and whistling.

"My goodness but it would be convenient to have those things to tow you out of harbor," she said. "The times I've been stuck waiting for a favorable wind in a narrow estuary . . . and that's how we ended up stranded in Baru Denpasar."

Deor chuckled. "The times Thora and I have waited eating up our travel money while captains made excuses for not rowing us out," he said.

"Sitting in port eats money a good deal worse for the one paying the wages and harbor fees," she said, with the iron assurance of someone who'd grown up around merchant skippers, and had briefly been one herself. "But trying to beat up without enough room and getting caught on a lee shore are worse. Now let's find Castaigne."

A row of granite-paved, treelined squares and small parks ran along the riverfront, with landings for ferries and yachts; evidently the business side of sea-trade for this New York was conducted elsewhere, though there were plenty of sailors among the crowds of ordinary city-folk taking the air and enjoying themselves. The merchant crews were unmistakable to anyone who'd ever traveled with the breed, and the military ones all seemed to be in white bell-bottoms for some reason.

Cafés and open-air restaurants were scattered among the trees, and a military band in bright uniforms and plumed headgear was playing from a kiosk on the parapets, the oompah-oompah of a brisk march cutting through the murmur of the crowd.

Pip scanned, working backward methodically from the water and the range of low hills across it. It was Toa who spotted them, but then he had a higher vantage point.

"Over there, by the statue of the Pākehā with the mean mouth and the nasty eyes riding around with a sword," he rumbled quietly, not looking that way and not pointing; people noticed when you did that.

"Let's split up into pairs and meet there," Pip said. "Toa, you trail me and we'll come in from behind—you're the most conspicuous."

"Like a whore at the vicar's tea-party," he said cheerfully, and drifted back.

In an inspired bit of business he occasionally prodded with his shovel at the dirt around trees and in the planters full of bright flowers, as if he were a gardener's helper or something of the sort.

A few of the sailors, mostly the ones most obviously reeling from John Barleycorn or with companions of negotiable affection hanging on their arms or both, gave him hostile glances. Men, especially those who'd had a few drinks, often thought getting beaten bloody in some pointless quarrel would make them more desirable; she'd never quite understood why, since she felt the only reason for fighting was to kill or maim the other party as quickly as possible. None of these was quite drunk enough to pick a fight with a man of Toa's size equipped with a shovel . . . particularly after they'd looked into his eyes for an instant, and got a gut-instinct revelation that he operated in exactly the same way.

Pip tucked her hair up under the bell-shaped hat that had come with the rest of her gear and strolled up behind the statue. It was on a granite base with planters holding rosebushes around it, and benches beyond those, with a bronze plaque set into its side: *General Philip Henry Sheridan 1831–1888*, showing a grim-faced man with a narrow mustache gesturing with a saber. The name teased vaguely at her, something she'd read in a book once, but she couldn't place it.

This side of the statue was in deep shadow, and a little chilly. She sat at one end of the bench that ran around all four sides of it and let her head fall back as if weary, the brim of her hat shading her eyes and the rosebushes leaving a double screen between her and the other side. That not only made her even less visible, it gave her a better chance of hearing what was going on.

Louis Castaigne and Constance were just murmuring sweet nothings as they leaned together under her light sun-parasol, and rather boring sweet nothings at that; he was telling her what a lovely place San Francisco was, and how he'd enjoyed being stationed there, and he made a painfully obvious joke about it being a splendid town for a honeymoon, at which she positively simpered.

If a man said that to me in that you're-my-helpless-little-kitten tone, I'd hit him, she thought. *Rather hard. I suppose these are the Good People, but Christ, I'm almost tempted to rejoice they're in a world that's apparently just been taken over by demons.*

Pip's position put her halfway between the courting couple and Hawberk and Hildred Castaigne, both sitting in the sunshine while the older man smoked a cigar.

Disgusting habit, she thought. *One of the few things I didn't like about Darwin was that so many people there smoke. I suppose because they've got more contact with the islands and the North generally.*

More than half the men she saw were lighting up something or other, mostly pipes and cigarettes, though far fewer of the women. It was worse than Darwin, much worse than Townsville, and infinitely worse than parts of Oz further south, where the habit had largely died out since the Blackout. In one of the few decent things he'd done while she was shadowing him, Hildred Castaigne declined the offer of a cigar from Hawberk. Deor arrived and stood apparently admiring the river from beyond conversational distance, but Pip knew he read lips very well. Thora sat under a flowering tree of some sort, repelling sailors tempted to try joining her with a quelling glare, like Toa not part of the surveillance operation but ready to explode into lethal violence the minute her friend called.

The sun hung low above the woods on an island in the river, and the bay was dyed with golden hues reflected from the sun-warmed sails of the shipping in the harbor. A silent fleet of white-painted warships lay motionless in midstream, recognizable because of the turreted cannon with which they bristled.

Constance turned away from her companion and laughed, a pleasant enough tinkling sound but one Pip found affected. Apparently that was the way women were supposed to do it here; probably they thought an outright guffaw uncouth.

"What are you staring at?" she inquired.

"Nothing—the fleet," Louis Castaigne said with a smile; the sound of his voice was low and pleasant, but Pip felt as if nails had screeched on a chalkboard.

Then Louis began explaining what the vessels were, pointing out each by its relative position to a red fort on a small island in the river. Pip recognized his tone; some men thought displays of expertise were a mate-attractant, like a peacock's tail or starting brawls. She supposed it must work sometimes, or those genes would have been eliminated. Constance hung on his words, and on his arm:

"That little cigar shaped thing is a torpedo boat," he explained.

Torpedo . . . Pip thought. Then: *Ah, those things that ran underwater and exploded against ships. Nasty! Though no more so than a napalm shell from a catapult, I suppose.*

". . . there are four more lying close together. They are the *Tarpon,* the

Falcon, the *Sea Fox*, and the *Octopus*. The gunboats just above are the *Princeton*, the *Champlain*, the *Still Water* and the *Erie*. Next to them lie the cruisers *Farragut* and *Los Angeles*, and above them the battleships *California*, and *Dakota*, and the *Washington* which is the flagship. Those two squatty looking chunks of metal which are anchored there off Castle William are the double turreted monitors *Terrible* and *Magnificent*; behind them lies the ram, *Osceola*."

Constance looked at him with deep approval in her beautiful eyes.

Laying it on a bit thick, dearie? Pip thought. *Is he looking for a wife, or a ewe? Does he know the difference? Are you a ewe or is this some sort of bestiality kinky thing?*

"What loads of things you know about ships . . . for a soldier," she said.

Well, that's a little better.

And they all joined in the laugh which followed.

Presently Louis rose with a nod and offered his arm to Constance, and they strolled away along the river wall. Hawberk watched them for a moment and then turned to Hildred:

"Mr. Wilde was right," he said. "I have found the missing tassets and left cuissard of the *Prince's Emblazoned*, in a vile old junk garret in Pell Street."

"Nine ninety-eight?" Hildred said; Pip could feel the unpleasant smile in his voice.

"Yes."

"Mr. Wilde is a very intelligent man," Hildred said.

"I want to give him the credit of this most important discovery," continued Hawberk. "And I intend it shall be known that he is entitled to the fame of it."

"He won't thank you for that," Hildred said sharply. "Please say nothing about it."

"Do you know what it is worth?" said Hawberk.

"No . . . fifty dollars, perhaps?"

"It is valued at five hundred, but the owner of the *Prince's Emblazoned* will give two thousand dollars to the person who completes his suit; that reward also belongs to Mr. Wilde."

"He doesn't want it! He refuses it!" Hildred answered angrily.

Well, not surprising, if he's gambling for an empire, Pip thought; her mother had always said you should keep lots of liquid, easily portable assets and a trove stashed here or there, *just in case,* as she'd put it. *Though you're being very principled with someone else's money, my bucko.*

Hildred's voice rose a little from that carefully calculated calm: "What do you know about Mr. Wilde? He doesn't need the money. He is rich—or will be—richer than any living man except myself. What will we care for money then—what will we care, he and I, when—when—"

"When what?" demanded Hawberk, sharp fear in his voice as Hildred's grew more shrill.

"You will see," he replied, that flat calm that quivered with unheard tension back again.

Pip rolled her head to the side and peered through the screen of vegetation around the plinth.

Mr. Hawberk did have a rather unexpressive face, but she could catch a glimpse of him blinking rapidly. That was probably his way of running around screaming *dangerous lunatic.*

"No," the dangerous lunatic said, apparently able to read the face of his cousin's prospective father-in-law. "No, I am not mad. Not as the world understands madness."

Though in his position, I might consider the possibility of a hereditary taint, grab Constance and do a quick bunk for Brazil.

"I am not mentally weak; my mind is as healthy as Mr. Wilde's."

Well, the second half of the statement is true, at least.

"I do not care to explain just yet what I have on hand, but it is an investment which will pay more than mere gold, silver and precious stones. It will secure the happiness and prosperity of a continent—yes, a hemisphere!"

"Oh," said Hawberk.

Meaning, Oh, buggery! Pip thought.

"And eventually," he continued more quietly, "it will secure the happiness of the whole world."

And you have the King in Yellow on your side, and it's his idea of happiness. Does that make you less barking mad, or just a super-powerful madman?

"And incidentally your own happiness and prosperity as well as Mr. Wilde's?" Hawberk said soothingly.

"Exactly," Hildred Castaigne said, and smiled or at least showed some teeth.

Hawberk sat in uncomfortable silence for a moment and then said gently:

"Why don't you give up your books and studies, Mr. Castaigne, and take a tramp among the mountains somewhere or other? You used to be fond of fishing. Take a cast or two at the trout in the Rangelys."

"I don't care for fishing anymore," Castaigne answered, without a shade of annoyance in his voice.

Well, that's something we have in common, Pip thought.

She'd been shatteringly bored when her father and grandfather tried to interest her in deep-sea sport fishing. Though she did like grilled Marlin steaks with a nice mango-accented salad.

"You used to be fond of everything," Hawberk continued; "athletics, yachting, shooting, riding—"

"I have never cared to ride since my fall," he said quietly.

"Ah, yes, your fall," Hawberk repeated, looking away in an echoing silence.

"But we were speaking of Mr. Wilde," Hildred said.

"Mr. Wilde," Hawberk repeated. "Do you know what he did this afternoon? He came downstairs and nailed a sign over the hall door next to mine; it read: *Mr. Wilde, Repairer of Reputations. Third Bell.*"

"It is his profession," Hildred said. "For the present."

"Do you know what a Repairer of Reputations can be?"

"I do," Hildred replied . . . with a slight hiss to the tone.

"Oh," Hawberk said again.

Meaning, Oh, buggery!

Louis and Constance came strolling by.

"Do join us!" Constance said. "It is such a lovely day for a walk."

Hawberk looked at his watch. At the same moment a puff of smoke shot from the casemates of the fort in the river, and the boom of a gun rolled across the water and was re-echoed from the highlands opposite.

Pip jumped slightly; the sound had a thudding force that thumped you in the chest, not like anything she'd ever heard before.

A cannon! she thought. *The first one since the Blackout . . . if I were in the real world.*

The flag came running down from the flagpole, bugles sounded on the white decks of the warships with sequences that were eerily familiar, and the first light sparkled out from the Jersey shore with the fascinating hard brilliance of electricity.

Pip rose to follow them, murmuring aside to her companions:

"Apparently Hildred—who's mad as a sackful of cocaine-crazed ferrets, whatever this Dr. Archer who let him out of the booby hatch thinks—sees Louis as standing between him and a throne."

"And Hawberk's daughter as the potential mother of a rival heir," Deor said thoughtfully. "That's less strange than most things in this place. Almost normal, if wicked."

"He'll be out to scrag 'em," Toa put in matter-of-factly, and Thora nodded.

Deor did too. "And there's definitely some link between Hildred Castaigne and John. I think it's through the . . . monarch in the robes."

Best not to say King in Yellow *aloud, then,* Pip noted; the others would have caught it too. *It's a pleasure to work with people who can keep up with you.*

Deor went on in a meditative tone: "A God's mind can contain worlds. What we see here is his dream, and it . . . seeps through, like a leaking cask of poison, wherever he gains a foothold. In a place, in the mind of a man, seeking to twist it to this form."

"As in Baru Denpasar," Pip said.

"And someone wants us to put a spoke in it?" Toa said shrewdly.

No flies on him, either! Pip thought fondly.

"Yes . . . or rather, I think that is the only way we can accomplish what we set out to do. If we weaken . . . him . . . here in his dream, we weaken him everywhere—and weaken the prison in which he has put Prince John."

The streets grew more crowded as the four were walking back into the city, and they could get closer, though Toa trailed behind as guard. Deor and Thora and Pip looked at one another as they caught murmurs from Constance and Louis that included *sweetheart* and *my own Constance.* Which would have been unremarkable . . . except for the way Hildred looked at *them.*

There's something crucial about this, Pip thought. *But bloody hell, I do so wish we could just find John, grab him and go!*

CHAPTER FOURTEEN

John had come to welcome the odd dreams where he was Hildred Castaigne; they were relief from pain, and from the sickening sweetness of the cat's voice, and the bewilderment of the other man, poor bastard. Now . . .

Hildred stood before the steel safe in his bedroom, trying on the jeweled crown.

That has to be one of the ugliest things I've ever seen, John thought.

The Crown of Montival—gold and silver, and filigree work, all made from things wrought from its own earth—was utter restraint by comparison. The Sword was the true symbol of the High Kingdom, in any case.

The diamonds flashed fire as Hildred turned to the mirror, and the heavy beaten gold burned like a halo about his head.

Camilla's agonized scream and the awful words echoing through the dim streets of Carcosa. The last lines in the first act . . .

His mind echoed Hildred's . . . and the Boisean who shared his prison and these dreams. He hadn't read this play, but both of them had, and dreaded it and longed for it at the same time. Hildred shook with the need and the fear, thinking:

I dare not think of what followed—dare not, even in the spring sunshine, here in my own room, surrounded with familiar objects, reassured by the bustle from the street and the voices of the servants in the hallway outside. For those poisoned words have dropped slowly into my heart, as death-sweat drops upon a bedsheet and is absorbed.

Trembling, Hildred took the diadem from his head and wiped his forehead. The thought of Hastur and of his own ambitions went through him, and the memory of Wilde as he had last left him, his face torn and bloody from the claws of that cat . . .

The devil's creature, Hildred thought, and John's mind flashed agreement.

"And what he said—ah, what he said," Hildred murmured.

The alarm bell in the safe began to whirr harshly, and Hildred knew his time was up. But instead of putting the crown back he replaced it on his head and turned defiantly to the mirror.

My eyes, Hildred thought. *So many expressions! Such depth!*

The mirror reflected a face like the one he remembered before the accident, before he read *The King in Yellow*, but whiter, and so thin that it gave him a startled sense of foreignness.

Words hissed from between his clenched teeth: "The day has come! The day has come!"

While the alarm in the safe whirred and clamored, the diamonds sparkled and flamed above the thin, tormented face. A door opened behind him, but he ignored it. It was only when he saw two faces in the mirror that fear and rage flashed through him.

He wheeled and snatched up a long knife from the dressing table, and his cousin Louis sprang back, his face gone milk-pale.

"Hildred! For God's sake, man!"

"Louis?" he said uncertainly, letting his hand fall limp beside him.

"It is I, Louis! Don't you know me?"

He stood silent, a lock he could not have broken for his life's sake holding his tongue, yielding the knife to his cousin's shaking fingers.

"What is all this?" Louis inquired, in a carefully gentle voice. "Are you ill?"

"No," he replied, so softly he probably was unheard. "But it is a fearful thing to fall into the hands of a living God."

"Come, come, old fellow," he cried. "Take off that stupid crown and toddle into the study. Are you going to a masquerade? What's all this theatrical tinsel anyway?"

Hildred cast his eyes down, anger and contempt filling him as Louis failed to recognize the crown for what it was.

Best to humor him. Yet the more proof that I deserve it, not him! he thought.

Hildred let him take it from his hand, and he tossed the splendid diadem in the air, and catching it, turned to his cousin smiling in relief.

"It's dear at fifty cents," he said. "Why, it would put the Pope's tiara to shame if it was real! What's it for?"

Hildred silently took the circlet from his hands, and placing it in the safe shut the massive steel door. The alarm ceased its din at once. Louis watched him curiously, but did not seem to notice the sudden silence.

"That's some biscuit box for a piece of frippery!" he said, as Hildred hunched over the dial to make sure it was hidden as he spun it.

"Come, let's go into the study," Hildred said.

"That's more like it!" Louis replied with a false heartiness.

Louis threw himself on the sofa and flicked at flies with his riding-whip; a flash of anger went through Hildred's mind at it, and at the whole casual, brainless *health* of the man. He wore his fatigue uniform with the braided jacket and jaunty cap, and his cousin noticed that his riding boots were all splashed with red mud.

"Where have you been?" Hildred inquired, though he and John and the nameless Boisean all knew that was what happened when you rode hard through wet ground.

"Jumping mud creeks in Jersey," Louis said. "I haven't had time to change yet; I was rather in a hurry to see you. Haven't you got a glass of something? I'm dead tired; been in the saddle twenty-four hours."

Hildred poured brandy from a bottle, his nose wrinkling at the harsh scent. John's soul flashed sympathy as Louis drank it and grimaced; that smelled like the worst sort of plonk, the sort of stuff you'd expect in a place in Portland or Hood River catering to riverboat crews and bargemen, an odd choice for a wealthy and wellborn man.

"Damned bad stuff," Louis observed. "I'll give you an address where they sell brandy that is brandy."

"It's good enough for my needs," Hildred said indifferently. "I use it to rub my chest with."

I'm surprised it doesn't peel off the skin, or at least kill all the hairs there, John thought.

Louis stared and flicked at another fly with his riding crop, snapping it to a smear on the leg of a table.

He's good, John thought, and . . . somewhere . . . the Boisean agreed. *Very good hand-eye coordination. I'll bet he's a devil with a saber.*

John felt a stab of grief; his father had been able to cut flies in half with a draw-and-strike, and had done it sometimes to entertain his children. The only other person he'd seen do it successfully was Heuradys d'Ath, though she claimed her adoptive mother had been able to do it as well, in her dreadful prime.

Which Da said was true; she was the only person he'd ever seen who was faster than him at his peak. There were more reasons than one that they call her Lady Death.

"See here, old fellow," Louis began, his voice full of a rather forced heartiness. "I've got something to suggest to you. It's four years now that you've shut yourself up here like an owl, never going anywhere, never taking any healthy exercise, never doing a damn thing but poring over those books up there on the mantelpiece."

He glanced along the row of shelves. "Napoleon, Napoleon, Napoleon!" he read. "For heaven's sake, have you nothing but Napoleons there?"

"I wish they were bound in gold," Hildred said. "But wait. Yes, there is another book. *The King in Yellow.*"

He looked his cousin straight in the eye. John could feel how unpleasant the expression was, and from his look Louis realized something of it too.

"Have you never read it?" Hildred asked, that sneer still curling his lip.

"I? No, thank God! I don't want to be driven crazy."

John saw Louis regretted his speech as soon as he had uttered it, but he could *hear* Hildred's teeth grinding as well as feel the sensation. There was only one word which Hildred loathed more than he did *lunatic* and his cousin had just uttered it. A white flash went through his skull, but iron will controlled it.

"Why do you think it dangerous? *The King in Yellow* is only a book, a play . . . and one that has never been performed, at that."

"Oh, I don't know," Louis said, hastily. "I only remember the excitement it created and the denunciations from pulpit and Press. I believe the author shot himself after bringing forth this monstrosity, didn't he?"

"I understand he is still alive," Hildred answered.

"That's probably true," he muttered. "Bullets couldn't kill a fiend like that."

"It is a book of great truths," Hildred said.

"Yes," he replied. "Of *truths* which send men frantic and blast their lives. I don't care if the thing is, as they say, the very supreme essence of art. It's a crime to have written it, and I for one shall never open its pages."

"Is that what you have come to tell me?" Hildred asked.

"No," he said, "I came to tell you that I am going to be married."

For a moment John felt a flailing panic that he was going to *die*, drop down dead as Hildred's metaphorically rotten and practically unhealthy heart simply stopped functioning and carried his unwilling psychic passengers along with him. Then the haze cleared from his eyes, and the man he was—or whose consciousness he rode—managed to draw another breath. It had looked possible to perish of sheer rage there for a moment, though. Would he have been back in the self that hung in the room of pain? Or on his way to Judgement?

Now I realize why Wrath is one of the Seven Deadly Sins, he thought shakily. *And like all of them, it hurts the sinner first.*

"Yes," Louis continued, smiling happily. "Married, and to the sweetest girl on earth."

"Constance Hawberk," Hildred said mechanically.

"How did you know?" he cried, astonished. "I didn't know it myself until that evening last April, when we strolled down to the embankment before dinner."

"Think me mentally infirm if you will, Louis, I'm not stupid and I'm not blind," Hildred said, and barred unseen inner teeth as Louis laughed again. "A blind man could have heard it in your voice, or hers. When is it to be?"

"It was to have been next September, but an hour ago a dispatch came ordering our regiment back to the Presidio, San Francisco. We leave at noon to-morrow. To-morrow," he repeated. "Just think, Hildred, to-morrow I shall be the happiest fellow that ever drew breath in this jolly world, for Constance will go with me."

Hildred smiled and offered him his hand in congratulation, and he seized and shook it like . . .

Like a good-natured puppy, John thought. *He obviously didn't grow up at a court, even one as well-conducted as the one Father and Mother ran, much less a snake pit like the stories about Todenangst in Grandfather Norman's day. He doesn't seem to be long on wits, but hasn't he ever read Shakespeare? That one may smile, and smile, and be a villain . . .*

"I am going to get my squadron as a wedding present," he rattled on. "Captain and Mrs. Louis Castaigne, eh, Hildred? It'll be a brief ceremony— just the Colonel and my brother officers from the regiment at the chapel, but you must come and be my best man! Do say you will, old boy."

"Certainly," Hildred said quietly.

Inside he felt nausea, and a hatred so deep it made the blood beat in his temples with spikes of pain.

"Then I must go," Louis said happily, springing up with a jingle of spurs. "Thank you again, and I'll see you tomorrow."

"There's one thing I want to ask of you," Hildred said quietly.

"Out with it, it's promised," he laughed.

"I want you to meet me for a quarter of an hour's talk to-night."

"Of course, if you wish," he said, somewhat puzzled. "Where?"

"Anywhere, in the park there."

"What time, Hildred?"

"Midnight."

"What in the name of—" he began, but checked himself and laughingly assented. "I won't be sleeping much tonight, in any event!"

Hildred watched him go down the stairs and hurry away, his sabre banging at every stride. He turned into Bleecker Street, and his cousin knew he was going to see Constance.

He waited ten minutes, pacing and muttering—John thought he wasn't even aware he was literally growling part of that time, and muttering disturbing fragments of *The King in Yellow* the rest of it—and then followed in his footsteps, taking with him the jeweled crown and the silken robe embroidered with the Yellow Sign.

Pip felt horribly exposed as she crouched at the third-floor landing of the building that held Hawberk's shop . . . and the offices of the Repairer of Reputations. It was dark now, and stuffy up here, smelling of old wood and plaster and nameless forgotten things sold in shops, and the turned pine dowels of the railing she leaned against were rough and splintery against her shoulder. The turpentine smell of the disused artist's studio they were hiding in once more was strong, and the stale catbox from Wilde's rooms.

And there was a feeling of pressure, not quite like waiting for a ship-to-ship engagement or walking down a jungle trail waiting for a shower of blowgun darts or Iban headhunters trying to remove yours, but more like that than anything else she was familiar with. Something was going to happen, and soon.

I wish I could leave feelings *like that to Deor. But considering where I am . . . for certain values of* am *and* where *. . . it's not surprising.*

And if Wilde opened his door . . .

Fortunately he didn't seem to do that very often. From here she'd extended a mirror—bought as part of a local powder-puff arrangement—on a stick that gave her a good view down the stairwell. The outside doorbell jingled softly. Pip craned her neck, and saw the thin pale-faced form of Hildred Castaigne hesitate for an instant outside the door to Hawberk's armory and then head for the stairs. She snaked backward across the worn boards, rising with swift economy to pad on stocking feet to the door of the old studio next to Wilde's rooms.

"Hildred's here," she said softly.

Toa grunted. "Nobody out back," he said.

Deor nodded and held up one of the wineglasses. Pip walked over to the wall and pressed the glass to it and her ear to the base, while Thora took her stance near the door and put a hand to the *gun* in her bag.

John read:

MR. WILDE,
REPAIRER OF REPUTATIONS.
Third Bell.

As Hildred's eyes flicked across it and his thumb came down on the button and a faint remnant of the chime reached him. The madman's determination had settled into a focus like the edge of a knife. He could see Hawberk moving about in his shop, and he heard Constance's voice in the parlor; John thought he could have learned more, if he'd been in control . . .

Of even my own eyeballs! Well, they're not really mine, *are they?*

—but Hildred hurried up the trembling stairways to Mr. Wilde's apartment, then knocked and entered without ceremony. John recognized the salt-iron-copper smell of blood, like metallic seawater, and so did Hildred and the other passenger in his mind. The sound of a man whimpering in pain was something they'd all heard before too.

Wilde lay groaning on the floor, his face covered with blood, his clothes torn to shreds. Drops of blood were scattered about over the carpet, which had also been ripped and frayed in the struggle. Judging from the fresh liquid look of the blood, it couldn't have been more than a few minutes.

"It's that cursed cat," Wilde said, panting quickly without moving anything but his colorless eyes to the newcomer. "She attacked me while I was asleep. I believe she will kill me yet."

The anger in Hildred's mind suddenly had a focus; setting down the case with the crown and robe, he went into the pantry—past a scuttling of cockroaches among the stale-smelling dishes stacked randomly—seized a hatchet and started searching. When he gave it up and came back to the parlor he found Mr. Wilde squatting on his high chair by the table. He had washed his face and changed his clothes. The great furrows which the cat's claws had ploughed up in his face he had filled with collodion, and a rag hid the wound in his throat.

"I'll kill that cat the moment I see it," Hildred said.

Yes! Please! Before it sings to me again, please kill it! John thought, the force of the sudden passion astonishing him.

Wilde only shook his head and turned to the open ledger before him, reading off name after name. The sums startled Hildred, and some mental alchemy translated them into terms John could understand.

Enough to buy houses and land in a chartered city, or memberships in the guild-merchant in Astoria, he thought. *Or ships* . . .

Calculations of grazing-rights and cattle and horses and wool-clips moved through the back of his consciousness; that would be the Boisean.

"I put on the screws now and then," Wilde explained. "A reputation I repair is one I can destroy, after all."

"One day or other some of these people will assassinate you," Hildred said.

"Do you think so?" Wilde said, rubbing his mutilated ears.

Hildred shrugged. John felt his own mind growing sharper, and as it did it occurred to him how odd the conversations between Wilde and the would-be king were. They seemed so wrapped up in themselves that often they weren't conversing at all, as he used the term; it was more as if they were talking *past* each other, to fragments of their own minds. And they were close confederates in an enterprise both considered of transcendent importance . . . but each was utterly indifferent to the other *as a human being.*

Hildred took down the manuscript entitled *The Imperial Dynasty of America*. The Boisean recognized it, with a start of fear and guilt and blazing desire.

Wait a minute, John thought with newfound clarity. *That means he read it somewhere else . . . in Boise? There's a copy of this in Montival?*

He read along with the madman whose trembling hands turned the pages. When Hildred had finished Wilde took the manuscript and, turning to the dark passage which led from his study to his bedchamber, called out in a loud voice:

"Vance."

Then for the first time, Hildred noticed a man crouching there in the shadow.

How did he expect to catch a cat, *if he couldn't see a man?* John thought, and the other presence concurred.

"Vance, come in," cried Wilde in a flat harsh tone.

The figure rose and crept towards them. "Vance, this is Mr. Castaigne," said Wilde.

Before he had finished speaking, the man threw himself on the ground before the table, crying and grasping at Hildred's feet:

"Oh, God! Oh, my God! Help me! Forgive me! Oh, Mr. Castaigne, keep that man, that *thing,* away. You cannot, you cannot mean it! You are different—save me! I am broken down—I was in a madhouse and now— when all was coming right—when I had forgotten the King—the King in Yellow and—but I shall go mad again—I shall go mad—"

His voice died into a choking rattle, as Wilde leapt and his right hand encircled the man's throat, clenching with brutal power. When Vance fell in a heap on the stained, faded carpet, coughing and retching, Mr. Wilde clambered nimbly into his chair again, and rubbing his mangled ears with the stump of his other hand, turned to Hildred.

"The ledger, please," he said.

Castaigne took it down from the shelf, a little surprised at the weight of the heavy bond paper, and Wilde opened it. After a moment's searching among the beautifully written pages, he coughed complacently, and pointed to the name *Vance.*

"Vance," he read aloud. "Osgood Oswald Vance."

At the sound of his name, the man on the floor raised his head and turned a convulsed face to Wilde. His eyes were suffused with blood, his lips swollen and bitten until they bled.

"Called April 28th," continued Mr. Wilde. "Occupation, cashier in the Seaforth National Bank; has served a term for forgery at Sing Sing, from whence he was transferred to the Asylum for the Criminal Insane. Pardoned by the Governor of New York, and discharged from the Asylum, January 19, 1918. Reputation damaged at Sheepshead Bay. Rumors that he lives beyond his income. Reputation to be repaired at once. Retainer $1,500."

Wilde's cold voice took on a teasing note: "NB: Has embezzled sums amounting to $30,000 since March 20, 1919, excellent family, and secured present position through uncle's influence. Father, President of Seaforth Bank."

Hildred Castaigne looked at the man on the floor with the same disinterested distaste that he had shown the cockroaches.

"Get up, Vance," Wilde said with a purring, threatening gentleness.

Vance rose, his bloodshot eyes on Wilde, his long face doughy and expressionless, save for a thin trickle of drool from the corner of his mouth that he mopped at absently with the sleeve of his jacket.

"He will do as we suggest now," observed Wilde. "I shall read him the history of the Imperial Dynasty."

Hildred stood nodding approval. "Has he become half-witted?" he said. "His eyes are very blank."

"It is of no consequence. Half his wits will suffice for the work we have for him."

The Boisean was growing agitated as Wilde read; John tried to grasp the cause as Wilde's voice came to him in fragments:

"Dynasty in Carcosa . . . the lakes from which power flows through Hastur . . . Aldebaran . . . the mystery of the Hyades . . . Cassilda and Camilla . . . what swims many-armed through the cloudy depths of Demhe . . . Lake of Hali . . ."

At that the other presence, the Boisean, writhed in anguish.

Wilde's voice went on, merciless: "The scalloped tatters of the King in Yellow must hide Yhtill forever. And the dynasty descends to Uoht and Thale, from Naotalba and the Phantom of Truth, to Aldones—"

Then he tossed aside his manuscript and notes. "Then came the Last King, to scourge clean the filth of—"

Castaigne wasn't listening now; the story was graven in his mind in any case. Instead he watched as Wilde threw up his head, his long arms stretched out in a magnificent gesture of pride and power.

Oh, St. Michael protect me! John thought; he knew he was a reasonably brave man, but even in this disembodied state he felt raw terror. *His eyes, they're* glowing *now. They're green and they're glowing.*

At last Wilde finished, and pointing to Hildred cried: "The cousin of the King!"

Castaigne's head was up too. "I am alone worthy of the Imperial Crown of America. My cousin Louis is weak, and he has not received the Yellow Sign nor bowed in worship before Uoht or pledged himself to the King. He must go into exile and remain without an heir, or he must die! Above all, he must not marry Constance Hawberk, for she is the daughter of the Marquis of Avonshire and that would bring England into the question."

"Yes . . . yes, I understand," Vance said; a little blood mixed with the spittle on his chin, from his bitten tongue. "Command me!"

Castaigne took up another bound list, and fanned it open to display the long list of names.

"Each of these men has received the Yellow Sign, which no living human being dares disregard. The city, the state, the whole land, are ready to rise and tremble before the Pallid Mask! The time has come! The people shall know the son of Hastur, and the whole world bow to the black stars which hang in the sky over Carcosa!"

Vance leaned on the table, his head buried in his hands, sobbing dryly. Wilde drew a rough sketch on the margin of yesterday's *Herald* with a bit of lead pencil. Hildred recognized it as a plan of Hawberk's rooms. Then he wrote in his neat hand on a blank sheet of paper.

"This is an accredited warrant of death, from the Eternal Emperor's own hand," Wilde said solemnly, and brought out sealing-wax and seal.

Castaigne signed it with a shaking hand; John saw the scrawl as it appeared, but it took an instant for him to read the Latin because the man who wrote had his attention fixed elsewhere:

Hildred-Rex.

"My first writ of execution," he said.

"But not the last," Wilde said. "As Your Majesty said, a new broom sweeps clean."

He clambered down from his high chair to the floor and unlocking the cabinet, took a long square box from the first shelf. A new knife lay in the tissue paper inside and Hildred picked it up, noticing the glyphs graven into the watermarked steel; one was the Yellow Sign, but the others were unfamiliar and writhed at the edges of his attention. He handed it to Vance, who jerked as if struck with a massive spark as his fingers touched the unpleasantly greasy-looking hilt of carved raw bone; then he handed him the death-writ and the plan of Hawberk's apartment.

"You may go," Wilde said, and Vance shambled out, lurching like a derelict from the Bowery.

The knife gleamed in his hand, but it was curiously hard to see, as if it misdirected the eye.

CHAPTER FIFTEEN

BETWEEN WAKING WORLD AND SHADOW

Deor jerked upright from where he had been leaning against the wall that separated them from Wilde's chambers.

"What?" Thora said.

Pip and Toa waited wordless; Deor looked shaken, his narrow clever face staring and beaded with more sweat than the cool spring night could account for.

"Something has been unsheathed," he said. "A weapon, malignant as Tyrfing. Quickly! We must stop it. The time of testing approaches."

Pip ghosted to the door and looked out through a narrow crack, holding a hand out with fingers spread to check the others until she'd made sure of the way; they didn't have any lights on inside, so the opening would be darkness within darkness, and her eyes perceived the dimly lit hallway as bright. A tall horse-faced man was shambling out of Wilde's rooms.

Weapon? she thought. *What weapon?*

Then there was a glint of steel in his right hand, held down by the side of his leg. She blinked in surprise; yes, that was an inconspicuous location but surely she should have seen it at once? It wasn't as if she was a virgin with respect to matters concerning sharp, pointy-stabby things.

"Man with a knife, heading downstairs," Pip murmured.

"You follow him, I'll take this side," Toa said, climbing out the window above the alley, tossing his shovel onto something that made a dull thug and beginning to clamber down the pipes and iron brackets and folded-up staircases outside.

"I'll lead," Deor said. "It burns like a fire of skulls."

Deor went out the door first; Thora came behind him, and Pip brought up the rear. The darkened hallway was full of shadows, their own monstrous on the stained plaster of the walls. They all moved with the slow tense grace of hunters, or cats; by contrast the blundering steps of Vance were thunder-loud. Deor's stalk grew faster as their quarry almost ran, and Pip followed with an almost inaudible scuff of soft-soled shoes on leather. Both the Montivallans were heavier than she was, Thora by about fifteen pounds and Deor by twice that, but they made no more noise—something that might have annoyed her, if she wasn't focused on the thought of violence to come.

Speaking of which, she thought.

She pulled the slingshot out of her bag and unfolded it with a shake and toss of the wrist that was completely automatic. A semicircular brace at the end of a light-alloy tube now rested against her left forearm, with the pistol-grip of the weapon in her hand and the U-fork for the rubber cords. Those rested under her thumb, and three of the steel ball-bearings were in the palm of her right hand.

She'd inherited the weapon—minus the cords, which had to be renewed periodically—from her mother, who'd also provided instruction in its use. Lady Julianne Balwyn-Abercrombie—Jules to a select few which didn't include her daughter—had rarely raised her voice while doing that, but she had been a perfectionist who could quietly flay worse than any of the teachers at Rockhampton, or even her father's roars and bellows.

Mummy fought her way in and out of half a dozen of the dead cities with this thing, and the kukris, Pip thought. *I don't think she'd think it had fallen into unworthy hands.*

The *damned* brolly was over her back, stuck through the strap that carried her handbag. Vance hadn't struck her as being any sort of a fighting man, but from what Deor had said he was carrying something like a napalm shell with a lighted fuse, and she'd always been properly cautious around *those.*

The stairs made one reversal halfway up each story, with a tiny wedge-shaped landing. Deor raised his hand with the fist clenched as he came to it, and then opened the hand and brought it down horizontal: the near-universal symbols for *halt* and *down*.

That brought them all together, close enough that their clean body odors were noticeable—Thora's had a slightly mealy quality that Pip suspected might be some product of early pregnancy, which was odd when you thought about it, but her sense of smell seemed to be stronger in this not-really-a-place.

I'm being catty. Literally *catty*.

They crouched and peered through the balustrade of the staircase, reminding her of occasions when she'd sneaked downstairs through the hot frangipani-scented nights to peer like this at her parents wrapping presents in the big sitting room of the stationhouse on Tanumgera on Christmas Eve. Which of course was the hottest time of the year in Townsville, though some still made imitation snow out of cotton-bolls for decorations, which she'd always thought absurd.

Vance was hesitating, hidden in the used-bookstore's entrance—there was a *closed* sign behind him, with an odd-looking three-armed sign in yellow on black beneath it. Vance's doughy middle-aged face was gray in a way visible even in this light, and damp with flop-sweat. He looked at the Hawberks' door, then his eyes darted around as if desperately looking for escape.

They fell on the *closed* sign, and for some reason he jerked back as if it were spitting red-hot embers. With three hesitant steps he crossed the hallway to the armorer's front door, and reached for it.

Pip could feel Deor tense, and Thora's hand came halfway out of her bag with the heavy pistol in it.

"Let me," she said very softly. "Quiet."

A steel ball went into the pouch of the slingshot, and she drew just enough to put tension on the rubber. She began to rise and do the quick smooth snatch-and-release that would drive the ball-bearing in a single blurred streak ending in Vance's temple, when Vance pulled his hand back from the Hawberks' door and dashed out into the street.

Deor hissed some curse—literally an Anglo-Saxon one, since his odd little homeland used Old English for religion and emphasis—and bounded down the stairs after him calling on Woden under his breath, with the two women at his heels. There was a yell from the outside and an unmusical clanking sound she recognized with her skin and gut as much as her ears.

Steel on steel, with intent to kill.

The sound made her skin prickle, and her claws slide out—

Wait a bit there, I have claws?

—made her come even more alert, but it didn't cause her any fear. Toa could be asleep under an oxcart after downing three jugs of Bundaberg's best and still handle that shambolic looney called Vance without working up a sweat.

Then they burst out into the darkness, lit by the eerie cones of electric light from the cast-iron standards, and she heard him curse. He had the shovel gripped as he would his spear, and he whirled it over his head and brought it down in a swiping blow that should have left Vance's head hanging by a thread.

Instead the man jerked aside. It didn't look like the tigerish drilled-in agility of a trained fighter; it looked as if the lanky bank-clerk had stumbled. But Toa's strike missed by a hair, and the momentum was so utterly unexpected—impossible enough to freeze *her* for an instant, watching—that it pulled him off balance. Vance's swipe with the knife looked as pig-on-greased-tin awkward as his dodge had been. But Toa bellowed again as he leapt frantically to avoid it, and did—but again only by a hair, and a thin shallow line of blood showed on his ridged belly in a shape that showed he'd have been gutted except for the astonishing swiftness of which he was capable.

Pip shot, a single flexing push with the left hand and pull back past her ear with the right. The ball-bearing was invisible with speed and darkness, though there was a whist of cloven air. They were only twenty feet away. At that distance she could punch the eye out of a rabbit—the vermin were a nuisance all over Townsville's territories and children were encouraged to practice on them—from a galloping horse, much less planted on her feet. The three-ounce ball was a fraction of a second from smacking into the back of the mad clerk's head. . . .

And he lurched around. Her mind gibbered as she saw the ball miss; miss closely enough that it took a patch of skin from the lobe of one ear, so that blood ran down his neck, but not enough to do more than frighten him. He *did* look frightened, his bloodshot eyes blank and glazed, his mouth slack and showing all his wet-sheening teeth, but she didn't think that he was frightened of her, or her comrades.

Deor shouted and threw up his arms, chanting.

Thora pulled a long knife out of her bag, holding it expertly with the thumb against the crosspiece, stabbing up under Vance's nonexistent guard. Toa thrust with the spear/shovel and Pip drew and shot again, this time conservatively at the center of mass—that wouldn't usually kill outright, but it would crack ribs or cause real damage.

The razor-edged head of the shovel went between Vance's arm and his torso, tearing nothing but his coat. It nearly hit Thora, who leapt back with a yell and a twist; that threw her blow off and the point of her knife simply *ticked* from a button on Vance's waistcoat. The steel ball from Pip's catapult struck the shovel-head with a keening *bangggg* sound and skittered off to break a window that tinkled broken glass into the street.

And Thora was backing rapidly, staring incredulously at a slash across her left forearm that dripped red onto the sidewalk.

And she began to *fade*.

"Hold hard, oath-sister!" Deor barked, grabbing her shoulder.

As he did Pip blinked and shook her head. Thora was *there*, but she looked . . .

Transparent. As if there's a bed behind her, and a room with white walls.

And suddenly something else was there too, like a shadow on a screen. The shadow of a huge beast, roaring, its hump-necked ruff brisling. It drifted away, but Thora was solidly among them once more, swearing and winding a cloth strip around the cut on her forearm.

"Anything I should worry about with this wound?" she said.

Toa nodded; the slit in the skin of his belly was thin, but a trickle of blood was soaking the front of his laborer's garments.

"Not poison, but it's a weapon made to sever," Deor said quickly.

"Too right!" Toa said. "Cut this denim stuff I'm wearing right and proper."

Deor gave a hard grin. "Made to cut links, and not only of the body."

Vance had used the moment to back away. Now he turned to dash for escape . . . and then swerved back into the door of the building he'd left.

"Get him!" Deor called.

People were beginning to turn and point, even though the fight had been mostly silent except for scuffles, clangs, curses and a little window-shattering. Pip was glad that the others hadn't used the firearms their swords had translated into; she'd read that guns were loud, but until now she hadn't quite realized *how* loud.

Deor went in on Vance's heels, and the others followed. It was probably only moments before a mob started to gather; Toa seemed to get hostile glances anyway. He thoughtfully kicked the door closed behind him, and Pip went into the hallway on Thora's heels. That let her just see Vance wrench open the door to the armorer's rooms and slip through, slamming it behind him with the click of a Yale-type lock.

"Toa!" Pip called.

She could have just broken the glass pane in the door, but that would mean putting her hand through to get at the Yale . . . and that with a murderous lunatic wielding a cursed and supernaturally sharp dagger on the other side. Pip's menace-gauge said that Vance should have been easy meat for any of the three of them at any time. But whatever possessed the man—and she suspected that *possession* was uncomfortably close to literal truth right now—was a match for them all together.

"Right," he said.

The shovel slammed out into the jamb of the door, and Toa used the leverage of the long handle, the shaft like a straw in his massive hand. There was a popping crunch, and the doorway bounced open with a speed that shattered the frosted-glass centerpiece anyway. A woman's scream came from within in the same instant, and a discordant unmusical *clang*.

Some peripheral part of her consciousness was aware of feet passing by outside in the building's hallway. Whoever it was didn't care that a young woman sounded as if she was being brutally murdered.

Vance was doing his best to live up to that brutal murder definition. Constance Hawberk was falling back before him, screaming and giving every evidence of being a hysterical snowflake . . . except that she was keeping her face to the would-be murderer and holding up a piece of lobster-tail armor between her and the supernaturally keen edge of the knife with a quickness that was very creditable in someone who'd never done anything of the sort before. It clattered and clanged as the madman's blurring slashes landed, leaving deep bright scratches through the black and gold enamel of the Renaissance-style cuirassier's armor, and it could be only instants until the knife found flesh.

Her father had a war-hammer in his hands, snatched up from one of the exhibition suits, and he swung it at Vance with desperate speed. Things seemed to *twist*, and somehow the shaft bounced off Vance's shoulder.

Deor made an odd gesture, as if throwing something at the lunatic.. Thora touched her chest, where the Hammer hung from a cord around her neck, tucked beneath the dress. The single lamp in the room cast her outline behind her on the wall hung with pieces of armor, and the shadow was of a hump-backed bear.

"*Thor with me!*" she shouted; and there was a roar in it, as of the great shadow that stood over her. "*Tyr hold us! Ye Tyr, ye Odhinn!*"

Vance gave a slobbering, gobbling cry, and his hand jerked at Constance as if invisible cords were pulling it towards her heart. Deor was standing with hands upraised, murmuring, with sweat running down his face as if he struggled with a weight greater than mountains. Pip drew and loosed once more as the dagger went *bang* on the armor . . . and Constance went backward over one of the low benches that were scattered about the workroom.

Vance threw himself forward in the full-body leap as if he were diving into water with the knife cocked back for an overarm stab, a move that few ever made in reality—whatever was driving him had finally managed to banish all thought of self-preservation. Constance screamed, which didn't stop her trying to jerk the set of tassets back into position.

Toa abandoned all efforts at his usual surgeon's precision and simply swung his long shovel as if it were a giant flyswatter. Perhaps Thora's prayer had worked, or perhaps whatever was puppeting Vance was so concentrated on its target that it ignored protecting its tool. Enough of the head of the shovel hit him to send him spinning and crash-ing into more of Hawberk's stock-in-trade, falling with a clangor like scrap-iron . . . which of course was precisely what it was. Pip drew and shot three times, and at least one of them hit from the hoarse scream of bewildered pain, though another peened off Toa's shovel.

I don't think he knows what he's doing—bloody literally *doesn't know,* Pip thought.

She surprised herself by feeling a sort of remote flash of sympathy for the man; Philippa Balwyn-Abercrombie didn't consider herself in the least squeamish or sentimental.

"The knife!" Deor shouted. *"Get the knife!"*

Pip drew again; hastily, and not all the way, but the ball thumped into Vance's middle as he struggled up onto his knees, teeth showing and wet with blood. It thudded into his stomach, the impact a little muffled by wool jacket and vest and making him jackknife forward. Constance got a good look at him then, and screamed again; Pip couldn't really blame her.

Something or someone *else* was looking out through the mad accountant.

Constance scrambled backward with feet and elbows, still clutching the scored and dinted tassets. Thora called on the Thunderer again and struck with the battle knife in her hand, one that Pip saw was graven with the Hammer, the steel clashing on the one in Vance's hand and then the blades locking at the guard. Thora used her weight and position to push with all her strength; in the same instant Vance's eyes darted towards

Constance and her efforts to put some distance between her and the madman.

Hawberk stepped between his daughter and the struggle on the floor, a bulldog grimness on his face and the war-hammer in his hands.

Pip took a long breath, drawing it down into the bottom of her lungs, letting it out. Letting tension flow away as the slingshot came up, motion flowing into motion with a calm detachment that was also a focus like a spearpoint.

Thack!

The steel ball smashed into Vance's forearm just below the wrist. His hand spasmed open uncontrollably. Deor jumped forward and stamped his foot down on the haft of the knife as it skittered across the battered hardwood floor.

"The King!" Vance screamed. *"Oh, the yellow tatters of the King! Dog-headed Uoht comes, and He stirs beneath the waves of Hali, and even death shall die!"*

Pip blanched at the sheer shrilling malice in the voice, and Thora seemed to be locked for a moment by a blow as real as it was invisible. Vance scrambled away on hands and knees, dodging Hawberk's strong but clumsy blow with the war-hammer—which forced Thora to dodge as well, lest it land on her foot—and went across the floor like a huge awkward spider. Then he came halfway to his feet, diving out the door in a shambling lunge with his arms swinging like an ape's, grunting gutturally.

Silence fell. Deor reached out quickly and took a black-and-orange armored gauntlet, slid it onto his hand, and picked up the knife. He held it up before his face, studying the glyphs along the steel and grimacing slightly.

Constance and her father were kneeling and holding each other desperately. Hawberk looked up at them as his callused hand stroked her hair.

"Thank you," he said. "Thank you very much."

Then his eyes went wide as he placed them. "It's . . . it's Miss Balwyn-Abercrombie and her people, isn't it?"

Pip made herself smile—the expression sliding off her face was more like a snarl, and she was panting—and nodded.

"Yes," she said. "Glad to be of help to you and Miss Hawberk."

"But . . ."

Hawberk was no fool; and he had a nobleman's lifelong habits of self-possession. Dumb unthinking gratitude was not likely to hold him for long.

"But why were you here when this man burst in? Who is he?"

Pip opened her mouth without knowing what was going to come out; from the looks on the faces of the others, they didn't either but were glad she was the one who was going to say *something*.

"He's under the influence of Mr. Wilde, your neighbor," Pip said. "We believe he is part of . . . a cult, as it were . . . spreading the pernicious book known as *The King in Yellow*—sort of a group of spiritual, ah, anarchists. Known as the *Esoteric Order of Dagon*, among other titles."

Finally I get some use from Uncle Pete's tastes in literature!

"We?" Hawberk said sharply. "*We* believe?"

"A Society of those dedicated to stamping out the madness which that book spreads," Pip said. "Deor—"

Deor held the knife up for Hawberk to examine. He did so with silent intensity, and after a moment recoiled.

"I've seen symbols like that in Paris," Hawberk said, wiping his brow. "Copied in manuscripts relating to the trial of Gilles de Rais."

Constance blanched visibly and stared at her father as he mentioned the notorious medieval mass-murderer and reputed Satanist.

"And in a ruined temple in Gwalior, in India, amid a bas-relief depicting unspeakable rites," Hawberk went on. "I knew Wilde was vicious and probably mad, but this—!"

"We had reason to believe that Mr. Castaigne . . . Hildred Castaigne, that is . . . had fallen under the influence of Wilde and—from the letters I mentioned, please forgive me for being less than totally frank with you—had conceived a mad hatred of his cousin Louis Castaigne, and of Miss Hawberk and yourself. It seems we were correct. Apparently this man who attacked you, this Vance, was their tool—also a member of the cult, and a blackmail victim of Wilde as well. We do know that Wilde is a blackmailer on a huge scale."

Phew! Pip thought. *Those* Men with Swords and Things with Tentacles *books of Uncle Pete's are really coming in useful!* After a moment: *And maybe that's because they're at least partly true? Oh, bugger, I wish I hadn't thought of that.*

Hawberk nodded. "What shall we do?" he said.

"You and Miss Hawberk had best lock yourself in," Pip said. "We'll see to Mr. Wilde, and then no doubt the authorities will take an interest."

Constance began to speak, hesitated, and then said softly, with a tremor in her voice. "And Louis? Louis Castaigne?"

"He's entirely innocent," Pip said firmly, in her best dulcet tones. "Innocent of everything but having a mad cousin, that is, Miss Hawberk."

Even streaked with tears and spatters of Vance's blood, Constance's face blossomed. Pip felt herself smiling as well, and then looked at Deor. The *scop* had an expression of profound sorrow in his eyes as he regarded the girl.

Oh, sod it. This world is . . . not really a world, is it? These people are all part of a dream of darkness. Can we really change that? Even if we kept Vance from killing them, is something bad likely to happen to them anyway?

"And now we'll see about Mr. Wilde," Deor said grimly. "If you don't mind me borrowing this," he added, moving the gauntleted hand. "I don't care to touch this weapon directly."

"I don't blame you, Mr. Godulfson," Hawberk said grimly.

The armorer's brows went up as Deor turned and spoke to Thora in a different language. Pip didn't recognize the rapid-fire sing-song syllables, but Thora put her knife away and pulled out the heavy automatic. She looked at it; then her face smoothed, as she obviously made herself *not* think about the strange archaic weapon. As she did so her fingers moved with the same automatic competence they would have shown with backsword or horse-archer's bow or lance, ejecting the magazine and checking it, reinserting it with a snap, thumbing off the safety and racking the slide to chamber a round.

And evidently I know enough to recognize what she's doing, Pip thought, slightly bemused.

She'd never bothered to learn much about firearms, except that the powders which had pushed slugs and shells out so fast didn't burn explosively ever since the Blackout. Catapults and crossbows she understood intuitively, but apparently it had translated.

Thora tucked the weapon into the belt over her shirtwaist, and checked that it was ready to her hand under the loose thigh-length jacket that completed the outfit. Pip made certain that she could get to her kukris quickly, and pulled a few more ball-bearings out into the palm of her hand.

Constance Hawberk had been looking at them with growing puzzlement. "Thank . . . you again, all of you. And you, Miss Balwyn. I've never met anyone like you, but I'm glad I did."

"You're very welcome. Just doing my bit," Pip said, feeling a little guilty as they filed out into the corridor.

"Now for Wilde," Deor said as the door closed and locked behind them and something heavy was drawn up against it. "Vance isn't important anymore—and Wilde is another step towards Prince John."

"Why couldn't I *hit* the bastard?" Toa said plaintively.

Deor shrugged with a wry smile. "Because we are in a story, my friend; a story about things that once happened. Happened in another place that no amount of physical travel could find, or inconceivably long ago, or both. And the . . . forgive me, I must use a term from my art . . . the *narrative structure* of this story had Vance using this—"

He moved the knife slightly.

"—to kill the young lady and her father. When we disrupted that, it pushed back to restore events to the original . . . plot."

Toa looked slightly alarmed. "This . . . you-know-who bugger . . . *he* was doing it?"

"Not directly," Deor said. "Not yet. For that Power to do so would rip the fabric of this story apart, and this story is very important to It; one source of Its strength. No, what has happened here is that we have . . . written ourselves is the only way I can put it . . . into the story and are turning it towards our own purposes, a little at least. And the *story itself* is fighting us. Events try to reshape themselves towards the original ending."

All right, this is getting even stranger, Pip thought; Thora's snort said something along the same lines.

Then something occurred to her. "These people here . . . they don't know they're characters in a story, do they?"

"No," Deor said. "That is where using the terms of my art, the storyteller's art, breaks down. They are real, and the story is their world which is real to them."

"But if they can't tell they're in a story about something ancient, *how could we?* If we were, that is."

She pinched herself where none of the others could see it. It hurt, and she mildly needed to pee . . . but then, she knew right now that her physical body was lying beside John's and those things had felt just the same back there in the real world, the one where she didn't think occasionally that she was either accompanied by or somehow *was* a lioness.

My head hurts, she thought. *But does that mean anything if pinching myself doesn't?*

Deor began to reply, checked himself, then said: "Best not to think too much along those lines, Captain Pip."

Toa shuddered. "Too bloody right! We've got enough to worry about right now. I wish you hadn't said that, Pip; I have a feeling it's going to come back to me and I wish it wouldn't already, if you know what I mean."

Then something struck him, something closer to his brutally pragmatic nature.

"Won't that happen with this Wilde character, too?" Toa said.

"Probably," Deor admitted.

"Then let's get to it," the Maori grumbled.

They went up the stairs in a quick rush; after the noise of the fight below, stealth was less necessary, or at least less practical.

Deor stopped them outside Wilde's door. "Remember," he said. "Our enemy is not this little man's body. Our enemy is the world around us, trying to make us fail. You are all tested warriors of great skill . . . but you don't need great skill to defeat his *body*. And the greater the skill of your attack, the more things that can go wrong with it. This world, this story, will seize upon each such chance."

Thora nodded. "KISS. Keep it Simple, Stupid. Good advice."

Toa chuckled like gravel in a bucket. "Right you are. A sheila after my own heart. Let's do it, then."

He pulled back the shovel for a blow at the door. Deor coughed, leaned forward and turned the knob. Then he pushed it open sharply, and they lunged through to spread out within.

Wilde was sitting on his high chair, eyes glittering in the dimness of a single tallow candle. He grinned at them, adjusted his pink wax ears, and threw the cat resting on his lap at Deor's head.

CHAPTER SIXTEEN

BETWEEN WAKING WORLD AND SHADOW

The cat stopped singing. John wept with relief; he'd started *wanting* to hear it, and it was starting to *make sense*. His mind babbled, thanks to saints and the Virgin and the Holy Trinity, and to Pip and Thora and Deor and Toa for coming after him—he couldn't recall exactly how he knew that they had, but he did know, and hope was as sweet as water would be on his swollen tongue.

Just knowing that there's something in the universe besides this room and the cat and . . . whoever the man from Boise is, poor bastard.

The cat lashed its tail and hissed, then darted out of the room—the door was open a little, then not. And the absence of the cat *pulled* at him. Suddenly the two of them were . . .

We're with Hildred Castaigne again.

Wilde watched Hildred in silence after Vance left; when Hildred had stepped into the hall he looked back. Mr. Wilde's small eyes were still fixed on him, while the shadows gathered in the fading light. Then he rose, closed the door behind himself as he left and went out into the darkening streets as the fairy-fire of electric lights came on.

They don't even need the gasman who goes around and lights the streetlamps of the richer cities in Montival about this hour.

He stopped in the park by the Lethal Chamber, admiring the shining marble white in the darkness, and the shadowed faces of the Fates.

Hildred noted absently that he had eaten nothing since breakfast, but he was not hungry. John was, and thirsty too. The sensations were muffled since he was feeling Hildred's too, but they were there.

"Sir?"

A man in the tattered remnants of a military greatcoat had been staring across the park at the Chamber, his face thin under the stubble.

Hildred looked at him, and he spoke in a slurred tone, not meeting the younger man's eyes.

"Sir, I have not eaten for two days. I haven't been able to find employment since the war—I fought the Germans in New Jersey—my nerves—the shells, Oh, God, the shells—"

Hildred absently pulled a handful of change from his pockets and dumped it in the man's hand. He took it and looked into Hildred's face as he carefully wrapped the coins in a scrap of cloth, then turned and shambled away without another word.

Hildred waited, as wisps of fog ran through the street and it grew a little chilly. An hour later another beggar approached, and he greeted him with a smile.

That made the man flinch, but he still held out his hand.

"Please, sir, if you could spare some money for food I would thank you and thank God."

Hildred looked at him. "Why do you wish money?"

The man blinked rheumy eyes; he might have been anything from thirty to sixty, and he smelled quite strongly. John's instinctive estimate that he was near the lower end of that range; beggars usually didn't live long lives, mostly having some quirk of mind that kept them from taking care of themselves and earning their keep, and gave them an aversion to letting others help. In Montival anyone could earn enough to eat and a place to sleep if they were willing and able to work, and now that the terrible years after the Change were long past there was usually charity for those who could not. In the Association territories the Church would look after those who had no kin or lord or guild to fall back on, and other realms of the High Kingdom had their own arrangements.

Though that may not be true everywhere. God has blessed us with rich lands and good lordship has let us have the peace that lets each household reap what it sows with none to put them in fear.

"So . . . so that I may eat, sir," the man said.

"Why do you wish to eat?"

"So that I should not die of starvation, sir."

"Why do you fear death?" Hildred said, his voice—and the emotions John could sense—genuinely curious. "Your life is a hell of loneliness and misery and regret for what you have done that cannot be undone, without purpose, promising you only suffering. Why do you strive to keep yourself alive in a world that offers you nothing but pain?"

The man stared at Hildred, the dull unhappiness in it flaring into something more active; he smeared the back of his hand across his bristly chin and mouth, exposing blackened teeth, and tears ran down from the corners of his eyes.

Hildred pulled out a piece of paper from his waistcoat pocket, on which was traced the Yellow Sign, and handed it to him.

"Here. This is infinitely more valuable than money. It will give you purpose!"

The derelict took the paper and stared at it, frowning in puzzlement at first. Then his eyes grew wider and wider.

He's . . . really seeing it, John thought. *And it's telling him things . . . maybe making him think certain things.*

There was an old French poet he'd read once, who'd explained a friend's suicide by saying that he turned a corner one night and came face-to-face with himself, and could not bear it. That came suddenly to his mind as he watched the beggar's face. Too much truth without context could be a deadly lie.

The man turned and stumbled away, still staring at the paper, then mechanically tucked it way. His head turned as if he was hunting for an escape, and then fixed on the statue of the Fates. That froze him for an instant, and then he ran towards the Lethal Chamber. It was an odd motion, as if he were dashing towards it and trying to pull back at the same time, and when he reached the bronze doors his hands went out to the side to hold himself off against the marble. Then they buckled, and the doors swung open and then shut again.

That heavy *chunk* sound came again, and the whirring and grinding. Hildred chuckled softly at the rush of energy he felt, and the faint sufferings of hunger that John had been noticing abruptly went away in a rush of curiously detached nausea—as if he wanted to vomit and had no stomach to do it with, which was more or less *true* and very disturbing to think about.

The electric lights were sparkling among the trees, and the new moon shone in the sky above the Lethal Chamber. Hildred felt a mixture of anticipation and restless boredom that sent him wandering from the Marble Arch to the artillery stables and back again to the lotus fountain. The flowers and grass exhaled a fragrance that John found soothing, as if something had wafted through the barred window of a prison cell. The jet of the fountain played in the moonlight, and the musical splash of falling drops reminded Hildred of the tinkle of mail in Hawberk's shop; there was a little mental jar as John and the Boisean had the same thought at the same time, though it was more natural for them since they'd both worn mail often.

For an instant John had a strong sensation; a mail shirt with a padded backing resting on his shoulder and cinched at his waist, the sort of thing Eastern light horse wore in Montival. It was a memory, but not his and not Hildred's either.

Hildred felt an impatience at the dull sparkle of the moonlight on the water; it brought him no such sensations of exquisite pleasure as when the sunshine played over the polished steel of a corselet on Hawberk's knee. He watched the bats darting and turning above the water plants in the fountain basin, but their rapid, jerky flight set his nerves on edge, and he turned away to walk aimlessly amid the park's trees. The artillery stables were dark, but in the cavalry barracks the officers' windows were brilliantly lighted, and the sallyport was constantly filled with troopers in drab fatigue uniforms, carrying straw and harness and baskets filled with tin dishes.

Twice the mounted sentry at the gates was changed while he wandered up and down the asphalt walk. He pulled a watch on a chain out of a waist-coat pocket—something John had read of in the Regency-era books that were so popular in the Protectorate, especially among gentlewomen—and looked at the dial. It was nearly the midnight hour he'd arranged with his cousin Louis. The lights in the barracks went out one by one, the barred gate was closed, and every minute or two an officer passed in through the side wicket, leaving a rattle of accouterments and a jingle of spurs on the night air. The square had become very silent.

The last homeless loiterer had been driven away by the gray-coated park policeman's kick and prod with his nightstick, the streetcar tracks along Wooster Street were deserted, and the only sound which broke the stillness was the stamping of the sentry's horse and the ring of his sabre against the saddle pommel. In the barracks, the officers' quarters were still lighted, and military servants passed and repassed before the bay windows. It wasn't altogether different from the castle garrisons of men-at-arms John was used to.

Twelve o'clock sounded, the altogether familiar sound of a church's bells. *St. Francis Xavier Cathedral*, Hildred thought. *The new one.*

At the last stroke of the sad-toned bell a figure passed through the wicket beside the portcullis that closed off the interior courtyard of the cavalry barracks, returned the salute of the sentry, and crossed the street into the square and walked towards the Benedick apartment house with the brisk stride of a man who was used to facing disagreeable work.

"Louis," Hildred called.

The man pivoted on his spurred heels and came straight towards his cousin.

"Is that you, Hildred?"

"Yes. You are on time."

Hildred took his offered hand, and they strolled towards the Lethal Chamber.

"It's late, but perhaps that's as well—I couldn't sleep, and at least now I'm not tempted by too many toasts to Constance and her charms, I can't have a sore head tomorrow! By God, Hildred, I keep thinking how lucky I am! And Captain's bars already, you'll note—"

Hildred has a will like iron, John thought. *He's not trying to tear Louis' throat out with his teeth and he wants to, God how he wants to!*

At last they stood under the elms on the Fourth Street corner of the square opposite the Lethal Chamber.

"But I'm babbling," Louis said with a laugh. "What is it that you wanted to speak with me about, old chap? Unless you knew I'd need fresh air and a fresh face."

Hildred motioned him to a seat on a bench under the electric light, and sat down beside him.

And he hates that look . . . the one that's looking for signs of madness. Because he is mad, and down deep he knows it and fears it . . . as he fears and loves the Yellow King. I never really understood how true it is that evil is its own self-inflicted punishment before!

"Well, old chap," he inquired, "what can I do for you?"

Hildred drew from his pocket the manuscript and notes of the Imperial Dynasty of America. The Boisean looked at it with a swirl of contradictory feelings; bitter betrayal seemed to be the strongest of them, oddly enough.

Hildred looked him in the eye and said:

"I will tell you. On your word as a soldier, promise me to read this manuscript from beginning to end, without asking me a question. Promise me to read these notes in the same way, and promise me to listen to what I have to tell later."

"I promise, if you wish it," he said pleasantly. "Give me the paper, Hildred."

He began to read, raising his eyebrows with a puzzled, whimsical air.

Uh-oh. This Hildred hates being patronized. Nobody enjoys it—

A young, artistically inclined Prince with an aversion to boring busywork and speeches in a dynasty of serious warriors and grimly energetic rulers got enough of that. Though his father had sympathized enough to tip him a wink when he ducked out to work on a song instead of giving a speech at the opening of a bridge now and then.

—but most of us don't shake with a need to kill when we get it, even when it's doubly irritating because it's hidden.

As Louis read he frowned, eyebrows contracted, and his lips seemed to form the word *what rubbish!* Then he started and blinked as he came to his own name in the closely written pages, and when he came to Hildred's he lowered the paper, and looked sharply at him for a moment. When he came to the end and read the signature of Mr. Wilde, he folded the paper carefully and returned it to his cousin.

Hildred handed him the notes, and he settled back, pushing his fatigue cap up to his forehead. A flash of memory in Hildred's mind recalled the same gesture with a schoolboy's hat as he walked whistling with a satchel of books over his shoulder on a sunlit day long ago. It was a disturbing element of common humanity in a mind that seemed to be sinking into a sea of chaotic hatred, and then it was gone.

Then he unfolded a scroll marked with the Yellow Sign, but Louis simply looked at it with a show of interest.

"Well," he said, "I see it. What is it?"

"It is the Yellow Sign," Hildred hissed.

"Oh, that's it, is it?" said Louis.

"Dr. Archer used to employ that tone," Hildred said. "But not since I showed him the Yellow Sign . . . and the book."

"You let him know that you own a copy of *The King in Yellow?*" Louis said in alarm.

"Not only that, Louis, I showed him several interesting points," Hildred said with a chuckle that made John swallow convulsively—or at least think of doing so. "He had a very different tone after that, I assure you."

Hildred's voice trembled with triumphant hate for an instant, and then took on a forced calm just as frightening.

"Listen, you have engaged your word?"

"I am listening, old chap," Louis replied in what he probably thought was a soothing voice.

"Dr. Archer, having by some means become possessed of the secret of the Imperial Succession, attempted to deprive me of my right, alleging that because of a fall from my horse four years ago, I had become mentally deficient. He presumed to place me under restraint in his own house in hopes of either driving me insane or poisoning me. I have not forgotten it. I visited him last night and the interview was final. At least from his point of view."

Louis went pale, something visible even in the darkness and under the electric light. He stayed very still, but John and the other man recognized the stillness that preceded action.

"Did . . . you harm Dr. Archer, Hildred?"

"I told you," the other man said impatiently. "I showed him a certain book. He may well harm himself, now."

Hildred made a dismissive gesture. "There are yet three people to be interviewed in the interests of Mr. Wilde and myself. They are my cousin Louis, Mr. Hawberk, and his daughter Constance."

Louis sprang to his feet, lethal menace in his stance. Hildred rose too, and flung the paper marked with the Yellow Sign to the ground.

"Oh, I don't need that to tell you what I have to say," he cried, with a laugh of triumph. "You must renounce the crown to me, do you hear, *to me!*"

Louis looked at his cousin with a startled air, then sighed in relief. "Of course I renounce the—what is it I must renounce?"

"The crown," Hildred said angrily.

"Of course," he answered. "I renounce it. Come, old chap, I'll walk back to your rooms with you."

"Don't try any of your doctor's tricks on me," Hildred cried, trembling with fury. "Don't act as if you think I am insane."

"What nonsense," Louis replied. "Come, it's getting late, Hildred."

"No," the other shouted, "you must listen. You cannot marry, I forbid it. Do you hear? I forbid it. You shall renounce the crown, and in reward I grant you exile, but if you refuse you shall die."

Louis made a forced smile, but Hildred drew a long knife from his sleeve and barred his way.

"Archer has opened his own throat, but there are more knives about this night than that, or this! Ah, you are the King, but I shall be King.

Who are you to keep me from Empire over all the habitable earth! I was born the cousin of a king, but I shall be King!"

Louis stood white and rigid, his eyes full of a terrible surmise. Suddenly a man came running up Fourth Street, entered the gate of the Lethal Chamber, traversed the path to the bronze doors at full speed, and plunged into the death chamber with the cry of one demented.

Hildred laughed until the tears ran down his face; he and John both recognized the man at once.

Vance, John thought. *God pity that poor exiled armorer and his daughter! Mary ever-Virgin, intercede for them!*

"Go," Hildred cried and wept. "You have ceased to be a menace. You will never marry Constance now, and if you marry anyone else in your exile, I will visit you as I did my *doctor* last night. Mr. Wilde takes charge of you tomorrow."

Then Hildred turned and darted into South Fifth Avenue, and with a cry of terror Louis dropped his belt and sabre and followed, boots pounding on the pavement. John heard him close behind at the corner of Bleecker Street, and Hildred dashed into the doorway under Hawberk's sign and into the corridor that gave on their rooms.

The door was closed, but bore the scars of forced entry. Hildred tittered at the sight.

"Halt, or I fire!" Louis cried, but when he saw Hildred dash up the stairs, leaving Hawberk's shop below, he stopped. Hildred heard him hammering and shouting at their door as though it were possible to arouse the dead.

Now I've seen everything, Pip thought, as the cat flew towards Deor's face.

She'd seen cats thrown, of course. Usually they complained, wriggled, righted themselves in midair, landed and streaked off with an air of affronted dignity. This one . . .

"*Watch out!*" she called, and tried to hit it with a slingshot ball.

She missed; she'd been expecting to miss; and the thought that she was probably going to miss made her more likely to miss.

"*Sod this for a game of soldiers!*" she screamed, and pulled out her mother's kukris, the larger in her right hand. "Chop-chop!"

Deor ducked, and the cat sailed by him with its claws outstretched. Deor moved then, quick and certain, but his slash with the glyph-graven knife was directed *above* the shabby black feline. It screamed, and so did Wilde. Toa's shovel came down like a giant cleaver, and the little man swayed aside and leapt to the floor as it crushed the custom-made chair into splinters.

"Call on your protectors!" Deor said sharply.

Pip shrieked and raised her kukris. "*Well, if you're going to protect me, get on with it!*"

. . . and suddenly her paw lashed out at the cat.

Paws? some part of her thought. *Now I have paws. Four paws. And I'm walking on them. It's like being on springs! I could jump a hundred feet! I can smell everything and it's bright as day in here! I can move like lightning!*

Most of her was just thinking that the little beast smelled *wrong*, as if it had been dead too long to eat without actually being dead, something that you definitely would *not* eat unless you were very, very hungry. It was a Bad Thing, bad enough to make her ignore the fascinating meadowlark flittering around the room, and even the great shaggy she-bear. They were busy with the other Bad Thing, anyway, the one that smelled like an ape . . . as much as the cat smelled like a cat, at least.

And though it was ridiculous she knew they were members of her pride. The bird was her brother and the bear was her sister—they were even bearing to the same male, and there was nothing more sisterly than that. Even the giant ratty thing was a relative; in fact, he smelled rather like a sire. Not *her* sire, but definitely *A* sire. They were all hunting together, though it was also like a standoff between two different prides over territory where you snarled and leapt and showed your claws and teeth.

No, more serious, more like fighting a pack of hyenas to protect the cubs, she decided.

The plate-sized claw-edged disk on the end of her forelimb flashed through the air and slapped down with a force that might have broken a buffalo's neck, the claws gouging into the dried wood in a shower of splinters. Her awareness was tightly focused yet broad at the same time; she could see the bear's paw-swipe at the ape-thing, almost as fast as hers and even more powerful, and the way something bright flashed with the meadowlark's beak, and the bush rat's chittering menace from the door, blocking the way out.

The Bad-Thing-cat tried to scuttle between her forelegs, hissing. Pip-lioness sprang straight up, her arched back nearly reaching the ceiling, twisting lithely in midair to come down with all four paws aimed at the cat. Space itself seemed to twist in turn, and somehow the cat was *not* where she landed, her three-hundred-odd pounds of healthy young lioness making an audible but padded *thump*. Her hind paws instantly fastened into the floor-boards by weight and claw-lock and torqueing against them she struck in a boxing motion, *slap-slap-slap-slap* fast enough to make the air hiss. The tip of one claw just touched one haunch of the frantically dodging cat, and a little tuft of black fur arced through the air with a curve of red dots.

Blood smells bad too, Pip-lioness' nose told her.

The cat screeched. The lioness' teeth were barred like twin curved saws of ivory and a racking snarl sounded through the room, under the basso growl of the she-bear. The meadowlark sang a song of magic and battle that Pip understood even though there were no words in her mind, and the words were in another tongue than the one her ape-self knew:

> "—lord of the host of heroes
> Who undaunted fight on Vigrid plain
> All-seeing saw his own death
> At the end of Time
> On Earth's last day
> And whispered this
> To his bright blade—"

Everything slowed. Pip-lioness' breath smoked in the sudden cold. Things flashed before her eyes—raven-wings circling a single blue eye that saw everything that ever was or would be, ash-leaves fluttering from a cloak lined with blue, a gray beard and the thrust of a spear that cut like the rushing passage of time. She could smell a wolf, and smell goats—but overpowering, goats bigger than buffalo—and the haft of a hammer clanged against the iron gloves of a red-bearded giant as chariot-wheels rumbled like thunder. By the door a tattooed brown giant laughed with a sound of volcanoes and earthquakes and the tsunamis that crush all before them, in his hand a massive fishhook-shaped weapon that sank into the fabric of the universe and *pulled* with world-shaking might.

The redbeard's Hammer reached out and touched it, and the figures shared a fighting grin. A winged circle turned over all, and a single piercing trumpet-note sounded.

The ape-thing turned and scuttled for the door. Even Pip's lioness soul had been daunted by the half-seen, half-sensed figures about her, but from them flowed power that made the one true path to strike part of bone and sinew. Her claws flashed out—

And she was kneeling on the floor, panting, wheezing, while Wilde lay bleeding at her feet. The blood-dripping kukri in her right paw—

"*Hand,*" she muttered to herself. "God, but that was a vivid hallucination—"

—was outstretched towards the dying man. She must have hacked across his throat . . .

Thora grinned at her. "Look at the wound, Pip," she said.

Pip did. That jagged tear was *not* what the honed steel in her hand would produce.

"He's dying anyway," Pip said, wiping the steel on the hem of her skirt.

It wasn't as if these were really her clothes, though she did step back from the spreading pool that was near-black in the dim light.

"That's what counts," she said coolly.

Thora nodded, and touched her chest where the amulet lay again.

"Thanks, my old friend," she said . . . and Pip knew she wasn't addressing anyone here. "I'll make a *Blót* when I can."

Toa grunted from the doorway, his face and massive forearms sheening with sweat as if he'd grappled with forces strong enough to have up-rooted oaks.

"Someone coming up the stairs, bloody fast!" he said.

"Quick!" Deor snapped.

He bent and grabbed Wilde by the collar and dragged him backward from the room and into the corridor beyond. The knife in his hand moved in a curious pattern around the dying man's head, then dipped into the blood and drew runes in a semicircle about him.

"Through here!" he said. "Thora, Pip, together—feel the bond that unites you to Prince John."

Pip did, feeling a little self-conscious about it. And there *was* a feeling of connection; but it didn't lead anywhere in particular as far as she was concerned.

"Here!" Deor said, his head turning with an intentness like a hunting wolf.

They followed him down the dark corridor, leaving the light of the tallow candle behind. The next room was lined by books and papers, dim shapes in shadow. One wall had a bare space, and on it was hung a plaque that bore a three-armed yellow sigil on black, twisting in ways that made her eyes want to slide away and focus on it at the same time. Deor advanced on it with the knife held before him, and used the knife to flip the plaque off the wall. It shattered, and Pip felt an obscure sense of relief, as if some physical pressure she hadn't been conscious of until that instant was removed.

And now she could see the wall better. "Look," she said. "See the gap between those two bookcases?"

Deor tried to feel into it, but his hand wouldn't fit. She stepped over and ran hers in; it was tight, but she could just feel a line down the plaster beyond.

"Wilde had small hands—smaller than mine, but there's definitely something there. I'd say that bookcase is concealing a door. It must pivot on the other side. Toa, watch our backs."

The big man had good eyes, but huge hands and fingers like muscular sausages.

Thora, Deor and Pip began tracing the outlines of the mahogany shelves. Pip's fingers found a rough spot.

"Help me take these bound files off here!" she said. "I'd wager there's a catch here somewhere."

Behind them, the door to the outer room slammed open.

CHAPTER SEVENTEEN

BETWEEN WAKING WORLD AND SHADOW

John felt an inner dizziness, and the world contorted around him, making him feel as if he were about to pitch forward on his face . . . when he didn't have one, and was bound upright back where he *did* have one. He was here and there, spinning, the fabric of things buckling like the buffeting of huge blows or a raging storm through existence rather than sea and air—only the typhoon that the Grasscutter had raised in Westria came close to the cataclysmic violence he sensed.

Hildred's mind blazed like a burning jewel, but something was tugging at the connection between them. Wilde's door was open, and Hildred burst through crying:

"It is done, it is done! Let the nations rise and look upon their King!"

Wilde wasn't there, and the first jar of worry dampened the flow of maddened joy. Hildred went to the cabinet and took the diadem from its case, the diamonds and fretted gold glistening blue and yellow in the dim light of the tallow candle, and then drew on the white silk robe, embroidered with the Yellow Sign.

"King!" he muttered. "At last I am King, King by my right in Hastur, King because I know the mystery of the Hyades, and my mind has sounded the depths of the Lake of Hali. *I am King!*"

His mind moved gloatingly to the first gray pencilings of dawn, and how a tempest brewed which would shake two hemispheres. Visions of shouting crowds and ranked guards and men and women kneeling before a throne possessed Hildred as he threw up his arms in exultation.

Then a man groaned. John and the Boisean with him both recognized the sound of someone badly wounded, too badly hurt to scream, but Castaigne was simply puzzled by it, and by the smell of blood—he did recognize *that*, and vague fleeting memories of hunting trips and hanging a deer up to drain while the dogs nuzzled at it and ate the offal went through him.

He seized the tallow dip and sprang to the door to the hallway, sheltering the guttering flame. The cat passed him like a demon, and the tallow dip went out, but the long knife flew swifter than she, and he heard her screech; John and the Boisean recognized the heavy tugging feel of a steel edge ramming into meat and bone. For a moment the sound of her tumbling and thumping about filled the darkness, and then Hildred lighted a lamp and raised it over his head.

Wilde lay on the floor with his throat torn open. The unwilling co-hosts of Hildred's mind recognized the ragged tear of an animal's claws, and the word *tiger* went through them in unison. At first Hildred thought his mentor was dead but as he looked, a green sparkle came into his sunken eyes, his mutilated hand trembled, and then a spasm stretched his mouth from ear to ear.

For a moment terror and despair gave place to hope, but as Hildred bent over him his eyeballs rolled up in his head, and he died with the usual twitching squalor and stink.

"My Crown, my Empire! Oh, Master, no!"

John had noticed steps behind him, but Hildred hadn't in his agony of soul, an agony that shook John even though he realized how richly it was deserved. Hands seized him from behind, and bound him despite a struggle that left his veins standing out like cords. His voice shrieked wordless hate, and he sank his teeth into a wrist below a blue uniform jacket's cuff, worrying it until the man screamed, too, and staggered away with blood spurting from a torn artery. It ran down Hildred's teeth and chin too and across the silk of his robe. It tasted hot and salt and metallic as he fell to the floor and struggled in futile jerks against the handcuffs and the boots.

He saw Hawberk then, and behind him Louis' ghastly-pale face, and farther away, in the corner, a woman, Constance, weeping softly.

"Ah! I see it now!" he shrieked. "You have seized the throne and the Empire. Woe! *Woe to you who are crowned with the crown of the King in Yellow!*"

His mind spun down to blackness, and John heard a familiar voice shouting:

"John! Johnnie! Wake up!"

Cords of silver and gold pulled at him, pain and relief and hope more bitter than either. He opened his eyes.

"I've got it!" Pip said. Then: "John! Johnnie! Wake up!"

There was a prison stench as the stretch of wall swung back. A lamp burned dimly, high on the windowless wall, and a chain from an overhead bracket ran to a thick bar. That ran behind Prince John's back, between the crooks of his elbows, with his hands bound in front of him and the balls of his feet just touching the dirty boards below. Another man sat manacled to the wall not far away.

"Wait—" Deor began, then swore and followed her.

The others crowded in, and the hidden door swung shut. John looked at her, his honey-brown eyes dull.

"You almost look . . . real . . ." he said.

"I am real, you bloody fool!" she snapped. "Toa, hold him!"

Muffled through the door and the books and papers on the other side came shouting and a high frenzied shrieking. Toa put an arm around John's waist and lifted, enough to take the strain of the rope, and Pip flicked out her kukri in two precise chops. The weapon had started as a peasant's tool in Nepal, used for everything from cutting kindling to settling disputes with the neighbors; her mother had gotten these from a Gurkha veteran she'd adventured with after the Blackout, a sort of uncle-mentor. The heavy back-curved blade was fine steel and it snicked through the heavy sisal with a *thack-thack-thack* as she moved it with snapping precision, then struck the point into the floor and took John in her arms, lowering him gently.

"Water, somebody," she said.

A hand—she didn't notice whose—put a bottle in her hand; it was lemonade from the street cart, but that would do. John's lips were cracked and his face gaunt and heavy with brown beard just getting to the end of the bristly stage, but his eyes cleared as they met hers.

"Ah!" he said, taking his lips from the bottle. "Holy Mary, Mother of God, that was good. Pip . . . Thora . . . Deor . . . Toa . . . thank you! But what are you doing here? Where *is* here?"

It's the dream of a mad God, Pip thought, then took pity on his bewilderment—that was apparently literally true, but not what he needed to hear.

She closed her eyes for a moment, feeling herself shuddering in relief. *We found him!* she thought, and it was as if a weight had been taken off her very bones.

Admittedly they hadn't rescued him yet, or themselves; they were stuck in a very bad place. But half-done was well-begun.

Deor spoke with a briskness that was more soothing than a gentler tone would have been:

"My Prince, you were abducted in the moment of victory. You remember that?"

"Yes . . ." he said, frowning. "The Pallid Mask . . . and there was some local ghoulie working with him—Rangda, I think I heard her called. She . . . well, she looked to me like a woman with white hair only her face was . . . sort of like a beast, with fangs. . . ."

Pip blanched, and saw that the others did too. "Rangda? The demon queen of the *Leyaks*?"

I really wish things in folktales would stay there! On the other hand, I just turned into a lion . . . except this is all a collective dream . . . oh, bugger.

"If that's what she is," John said, draining the rest of the lemonade. "She had this mob of little . . . things with her. Like pygmy humans, with faces like a withered apple and big eyes. And blowguns."

"Kuro-i!" Deor said.

They all looked at him, even Thora. He shrugged. "I collect tales. The kuro-i are goblins of a sort. Haunters of the deep jungle, takers of heads; not quite human, and full of malign hatred towards our breed. Some of the scholars I've spoken with in Bali thought they were a memory of a tiny folk who first inhabited the island world before true men came south in their canoes very long ago."

John nodded, and then winced as he tried to shrug his shoulders. Pip and Toa gripped them and began to knead, both familiar with injuries and their care. John went a little white around the lips, but stifled the groan that tried to burst out between clenched teeth. When he could speak he went on:

"And the Pallid Mask was there. Like the one in the mask we fought in Baru Denpasar's harbor, but not . . . quite the same . . ."

The man chained to the wall stirred, clanking his fetters. John nodded to him. "This man's one of ours, from Montival. Boise, I think—I'll tell you about that later. We need to take him out of here."

At their hesitation—and Pip's unspoken thought that they had enough to do with John—the young man's face firmed.

"House Artos doesn't leave their own behind."

"Fair enough," Toa said, and walked over to the man. "Who're you, mate?"

The man's face turned up. "I'm . . . I'm not sure. I think . . . I think I'm from Boise, as he says. I think I was taken here when . . . when . . . when I read a book. But I don't know."

Deor moved over, knelt, and looked the man in the eye. Now that she had a chance, Pip's brows went up—that was a handsome man, more so than almost any she'd ever met. Something very lost and sad about him, though; and that was not the type who'd ever attracted her, even if John hadn't been right here.

She felt a hand grip hers, and looked down into John's eyes. His smile quirked up one corner of his mouth, and they shared something wordless. Toa snorted and moved back a little, rolling his eyes but smiling fondly himself. Deor's hiss brought her back to the moment, and to the one who'd shared John's imprisonment.

"This is a great evil," he said quietly, moving his free left hand in a gesture she knew drew a rune in the air, though she hadn't the slightest idea what it meant.

"Part of this man's being has been rent away and imprisoned here, while the rest is . . . split, in the waking world. So that he is neither here nor there, and so is enslaved in both, without even fully knowing it—and so cannot fight it."

John moved, and she helped him sit upright, working his hands doggedly and wincing as he did so.

"He seemed a good enough sort," he said. "We . . . it's hard to explain . . . there was this man named Hildred—"

The four rescuers exchanged a glance.

"And this man here and I, we were somehow seeing things through his eyes sometimes. As if we were riding in his mind."

John smiled again. "And I got to know him fairly well, even though he doesn't know his own name."

He shuddered, and a haunted look came into his eyes. "And there was this *cat* . . . I hope it doesn't spoil cats for me forever . . . anyway, let's get him out of those bonds. I'm not leaving anyone *here*."

Pip looked, peering through the gloom. "Can't pick those, I'm afraid. They're not locked, they're riveted—see there? A soft-iron rod put through and then peened over with a hammer. You'll not get that open without a cold chisel or a good hard metal-file; it's how slavers fasten coffles in the hold of a ship fitted out for it so that they can't get loose."

Thora looked at her. "That's true," she said neutrally. "How exactly did you find out?"

"Mummy told me, and she had a broken set of them, it's still over the mantle back in Tanumgera Station. She and Uncle Pete and Aunt Fifi took a Suluk corsair that had been raiding in Sulawesi once, and they had the devil of a time getting the fetters off the cargo."

"What did they do with them?" Thora asked.

"The fetters? Threw them overboard, mainly, with the pirates wrapped inside yelling their heads off. Oh, the cargo; took them home. And got a nice little reward from the sultan there: cloves, mostly, and some really good coffee, miles better than the Papuan variety. The Darwin and East Indies Trading Company has a factory there now."

Deor thought for a moment and nodded. "Can you break these chains?" he said to Toa.

The big man walked over to the Boisean, whose handsome features were suddenly alive with hope.

"Well, I can rip 'em out, if I have to," Toa rumbled. "Looks like mild steel, and not too thick."

John seemed to be recovering quickly; he estimated the strength of the thumb-thick links and shaped a silent whistle of respect.

Toa examined the edge of his shovel-spear. "Better yet . . . you got good nerves, mate?" he asked the man sitting on the floor.

"Right now, yes. Even *hell* yes," he replied.

"Good-o. Put your hands up above your head on either side of that staple the chain's run through. That's right. Keep the chain tight, backs of yer hands flat on the plaster. Now, let's hope me eye's in, eh?"

He grinned like a friendly ogre, eyes and teeth white in the gloom, and drew the massive tool-weapon back. Then he whipped it forward, and back again for another strike in the space of one ordinary breath, precise as a machine-tool in a foundry. There was a hard *ting* sound, twice repeated, and the man slumped forward as the chain was split—a single link now dangled from each of the cuffs. He held up his hands before his face in wondering joy.

"Thank you, friend," he said softly.

Toa grinned. "Welcome," he said cheerfully, then wiped his forehead. "Took more graft than I thought it would—must be getting old."

Deor shook his head. "Those were more than chains. They were symbols. Remember where we are! You did more than break metal."

"I want to get back to where things make sense," John muttered.

Pip opened her mouth to reassure him, then remembered what lay between them and where they'd started . . . and remembered what awaited them when they woke up on that bed.

Then she gasped. There was a sense of pressure, as if things creaked around her without noise.

"Gather," Deor said, his thin clever face drawn. "*Something* wakes. It is part of this place, but beyond the appearances we see, from deeper down in the . . . the structure. And it comes in wrath."

He paused, seeming to see beyond the grubby, cracked plaster and lath of the walls.

"It *hunts*."

Thora and Toa lifted the man he'd just freed under the arms and dumped him unceremoniously near John. Deor looked at the long knife he still held in the gauntleted hand.

"Fitting," he said, and began to inscribe a circle around them, alternating a precise line with runes. "This blade was meant to sever that which is connected."

Toa stood easily with the shovel held loosely in his hands; the long shaft and his long arms put the door easily within his reach.

"Quiet out there, but we shouldn't overstay our welcome," he hinted broadly.

John looked up at Pip. "This is going to be an embarrassing bit in my *chanson* about all this," he said.

"What, because I rescued you?" she said. "Well, made a good beginning on it."

"No, that's fine. It's because I haven't told you I love you or asked you to marry me yet," he said. "I'll have to be careful or I'll look like a cad, and we can't have that, can we? Marry me, my beloved, and make me the luckiest man on Earth!"

Pip sighed. "Damn you, John Arminger Mackenzie, I thought I was immune to charming musicians! All right, take the three words as said, and . . . doesn't your mother have any say in who you marry?"

"Not a word," he said cheerfully. "In any case, I don't have to go home for a while yet. My sister's High Queen in three years, but *I* don't inherit the Lord Protector's throne until my mother passes . . . and she's only forty-five."

He crossed himself. "God and His mother and all the company of the Saints preserve her."

"Amen!" Pip said. "Plenty of time to fossick about, then."

Wait a minute. Did I just agree to marry him? Pip thought suddenly. *Well, I suppose I did. I'm going to have to watch this one; he's a charmer!*

Their hands met, clasped and squeezed.

"We must retrace our steps," Deor said as he worked. "Remember that your gear will shape itself to your surroundings and your own wishes. And remember your protectors . . ."

He looked at John. "Yours is Raven, my Prince; She above all others wards your House. And yours . . ."

The Mist Hills scop looked at the anonymous man they'd rescued.

"Yours, I think, is Coyote, man of many names and none. A strong Power, but a chancy one. Call on no God you are not sure of."

"Hold on—wouldn't what we did here change what those other places were like?" Thora said. "We were traveling back along the history of this world."

"It's not that simple, oath-sister," Deor said. "This is a story many times retold, and each telling a cycle of the universe, from the void of Ginnungagap to the fires of Sutr at Ragnarok. What comes later is . . . may be . . . the product of many, many retellings, not of a single one. We're deep in a . . . a sheaf . . . of cycles that this Power here dominates."

"Do you actually understand what you just said, old friend?" Thora asked.

"No. I don't think even the High King did ken it fully," Deor said frankly. "Perhaps Lady Juniper, if she'd had the Sword as well. Or perhaps only a God might, and while I sing of them, I'm as mortal as any in Midgard."

"The next part is likely to be sort of alarming," Pip said to John. "But it ought to get you out of those ragged pants, at least."

"I hope it gives me a metaphorical bath," he said.

"And I wasn't going to say a *thing*, darling!"

The blue-green eyes of the nameless Boisean were starting to glow a little with hope; it probably wasn't something he'd had much of before.

Deor completed his work and stood back, looking at it critically. "Not as elegant as Lady Juniper's work, but it will have to do."

There were voices outside the hidden door, and crashing sounds, as if someone was knocking books onto the floor. Toa flashed a look at Deor, and the scop nodded, drew a deep breath and shouted.

And the world changed.

CHAPTER EIGHTEEN

BETWEEN WAKING WORLD AND SHADOW

For a moment John Arminger Mackenzie felt nothing but sheer relief. It was as if everything that had happened since the tower fell at the siege of the Carcosan fort had . . .

Not never happened, he thought, reveling in the feeling of health and strength and youth. *Just happened long ago and I'm fully recovered.*

The Boisean was looking more cheerful too—understandably so, since the fetter-cuffs were gone. He was dressed—

We all are, John thought.

—in a tough-looking uniform of yellow-brown khaki, with plenty of pockets and pouches, and found himself carrying a rifle.

So am I, John thought.

Information poured through his mind, and the memory of it kicking against his shoulder and the feel of cartridges stripping out of a clip into the magazine under his thumb, all as familiar as using a bow or a crossbow. All of them had them, except Deor, who had a massive revolver in a leather holster at his waist. Thora and Pip had *Medical Corps* in badges on their shoulders, and Toa had a nonsense-word in the same place: *Suanee Auxiliary Force*. It was all visible, though only just; the light came from cracks in the wall, and it was as red and flickering as an open fire in the hearth.

Then the rest of what was around him really sank in. The air stank of burning and rot, and the room was canted—the floor buckled, but the walls out of true in ways that suggested the whole building had been knocked off its foundations and twisted. The only thing he knew that could do that was an earthquake, but that didn't seem to be what had happened, somehow.

"Let's get out of here," Deor said, coughing in the smoky haze that filled the room.

"Right," Toa said.

He slung his weapon over his back—on second glance it wasn't a rifle, and the *translation* supplied machine gun, a name he belatedly recognized from his studies—and began to press on the spot where the door's outline rested. For a long moment nothing happened except the Maori's long exhalation of breath as he strained motionless, like a statue labeled *effort* in some allegorical set piece.

Just before John thought they'd have to look for something to act as a battering-ram or a lever, Toa gave a long guttural:

"Huuuuuuh!"

There was a long crackle and crunch, and the door swung outward. Deor pulled the long knife from his belt in one gloved hand and pushed forward, with Thora flanking him. John fumbled at his rifle.

Pip noticed. "Just imagine you're drawing a sword," she said, and coughed as she worked the bolt of her own weapon. "Or loading a crossbow."

John did, and felt his fingers move automatically through a series of motions that brought a *click-clack-clunk* sound, and a knowledge of what the weapon he gripped could do, and how to do it. He raised it almost to his shoulder, ready to snap-shoot. It wasn't altogether unlike a regular crossbow, except that he knew there were ten more rounds in the magazine and that all he needed to do was work the little side-lever again each time his finger pulled the trigger.

Plaster gritted under his boots, and then glass amid a heavy stink of medicinal alcohol as they went into the next room.

"This was a study, a room for books, when we came through," Pip said. "Part of Wilde's chambers. I think that was long ago by local reckoning, generations."

It had shelves around it now as well. They held glass bottles and flasks, with *things* in them. John swallowed and let his eyes slide out of focus as he realized that most of them had been bits of people. A sign on one wall advertised *Conversation Pieces* and *Devotional Objects*.

"There's a body in the corridor," Thora said.

They all followed. The man was lying down curled into a ball, sur-rounded with a sticky pool of dried blood and other fluids; John thought the man had been dead for four or five days, though there hadn't been as many insects as he'd have expected, mostly flies drowned in the pool. It was unpleasant, but he'd seen worse.

Then he looked a little more closely. All the man's hair had fallen out, except a patch over one ear, and there were bubbly lesions and sores over much of the visible skin. It didn't match any disease he knew of, but there were no other signs of violence. He'd crawled here, puked and bled—from every orifice—and then died with his hair falling out and teeth falling out and skin sloughing away.

"Leave it," Deor said.

Thora nodded. "We haven't the time. Whatever killed him, our best chance is to keep going. When we get back, we'll be . . . in our real bodies again."

Pip murmured in his ear. "Though what happens to us here can *hurt* our real bodies. Through the soul to the flesh; psychosomatic, the old word for it was."

They went out through another room of ghastly things in glass bot-tles, or their smashed remnants glittering on the floor like stars of red fire, and out into a new corridor. That had more light, because most of the roof and attic above had been smashed off the house, though parts had fallen in. Thick black soot like snowflakes filtered down slowly, and more black was above, like low clouds underlit by fire.

"You came to me through *this*?" John said. "Thank you!"

Pip shook her head. "It . . . it wasn't like this then. I think whatever happened was just after we came through this . . . this version of 1998."

"The year of the Change?" he said.

Deor paused as he clambered over a pile of wreckage, testing each piece of footing. "It's a time that resonates across the cycles, I think," he said. "Catastrophes cluster around it. Now quickly. We must reach a point where we can make the next step, and soon. This is not a good place to be."

"You don't bloody well say! And here I thought I was our Queen of Ironic Understatement," Pip said dryly.

John felt himself almost grin as they clambered over the pile of shattered timber and splintery lath and roofing tiles and brick. They found the remains of a staircase and descended it one by one, sticking close to the wall. John found himself covering their back-trail on one landing, rifle to his shoulder and the Boisean close behind him facing the other way.

"She's your intended?" the man asked.

"Evidently," John said quietly.

"I think . . . I think I have someone. She's tall and fair-haired . . . I think. But I don't know her name any more than I do mine. I'm . . . I'm thinking a bit better, but it won't come *clear*."

"Well, we're headed back to the real world, friend," John said. "St. Michael, aid us! And when we're there, you'll have a friend."

He slapped the man's shoulder; they hadn't actually spoken much, but they'd shared more than human beings generally could.

"Front door clear," he heard Thora call.

There was a rending crash. "Now it's really clear," Toa said.

"Quickly!" Deor said again.

The first floor was more intact, and hence darker. After a few glimpses of the stores to either side, John was rather glad of that. The children's toy-shop with the dolls in a lynching game titled *Catch Him and Run Him Up* wasn't the worst of it by any means, or the Pallid Mask masks. Half the front façade of the building had slumped down, but Toa had heaved a load of brick and timber out of the way.

Thora looked back at it after she'd wheeled through. "Well, if you want to be *crude*," she said, with a taut grin.

The street outside was half-covered by cones of collapsed buildings, some burnt-out, some still smoldering or sending flames and plumes of smoke into the lowering sky. A little farther away he could see the remains of much taller buildings, ones that reminded him of the giants that still stood in some parts of Montival. Some were on fire with flames pouring out of their endless rows of windows; others were shells of scorched girders; many had fallen into one another, like giant dominos scattered by the fist of some titanic child. You could see that the blow had landed north of here, running towards them in a wave of heat and force.

For a moment John's memories blurred his sight; that day on the deck of the *Tarshish Queen* when he'd seen Reiko dancing an invocation to her Ancestress on the shore of Topanga, and the moment when her outflung arm and the Grasscutter Sword had brought down the wrath of *Amaterasu-ōmikami*. He'd seen that wall of force sliding towards him, tossing aside the substance of Ocean itself and crushing Korean warships like toys made of matches under a knight's armored boot. This must have been even worse, worse than the anger of a Goddess.

Then, flatly: "Look out."

What Thora had warned of looked picayune by comparison, but deadly enough to a few lone strangers like them—and you couldn't die deader than dead. The figure at the head of the crowd was dressed in a hooded robe of yellow tatters and for a heart-stopping moment . . .

"No, that's just someone dressed like him," John decided, going to ground behind an up-tilted block of concrete.

"Leading a mob of rotting lunatics carrying sticks with heads on them," Pip replied. "Are they the undead, or what?"

"No, not dead," Deor said, after he signed the air with a rune. "Not quite, not yet—and easier to deal with because of it."

"Oh, I *so* do not want to understand what you just said," John muttered.

"Dead people are usually fairly easy to deal with; you just need a shovel, or some dingoes," Pip pointed out, articulating something John had not wanted to say because he suspected he might not like the answer. "Or the ants, if you're patient."

"Where we are . . . not necessarily," Deor replied.

I was right. I don't like that answer.

Meanwhile they'd all gone to ground. There was plenty of cover, though John had to suppress a yelp when his elbow came down on an ember hidden under the omnipresent ash. Meanwhile, the crowd was getting closer, more visible, and he profoundly wished they hadn't. Whatever had killed the man in the corridor they'd just left had bitten these folk too. Hair had fallen out in patches, *bleeding* patches, and more understandable burns mixed with something that had singed them like acid and made skin hang in tatters over weeping sores. Clothes were ragged and stained with fluids and blood; one woman staggering in the front rank had eyes that had turned blood red and clutched a child obviously long-dead. Teeth showed long and dry in gaping mouths, where gums bled and fell away.

I'm glad we can't smell anything but smoke and burning, John thought, uneasily aware that the ruins below him had plentiful bodies tumbled amid brick and metal and wood—a burnt, blackened hand protruded not far away.

Every second or third of the hundreds of walkers carried a stick or pole bearing a head—mostly human, though he saw a scattering of cats and dogs and one horse.

"And they're heading straight for us," Pip said. "Turn them or run, chaps, one or the other."

"Too many to fight—" Thora began.

Crack.

The sound was loud and sharp, and one of the mob staggered and fell.

"Gunshot!" Deor said.

That was something nobody in the world had heard since the year of his father's birth, forty-six years before. Except that this place was not in or of the world to which he'd been born.

Another fusillade of the cracks, and another that was like an endless series of the same sound jammed together. It was coming from the right on the street that joined the one they and the crowd shared, at a T-junction less than a hundred long paces ahead. Dozens fell, then scores and more.

A vehicle jolted into view, with men—it was all men—in the same uniform they wore—firing rifles and a machine gun from its bed. The last survivors of the crowd broke and fled, shambling away and being gunned down from behind.

Tense silence gripped John and his comrades. He squinted through the fire-shot gloom, and saw that the troops were only a little less tattered than the mob they'd slaughtered. They jumped down from the truck and advanced on the bodies and the wounded, clipping long knives below the barrels of their guns. An officer led them, staggering and laughing and weeping and shrieking incoherently as he emptied his revolver into the bodies. His men stabbed and hacked. . . .

"I think they're cutting out the hearts and eating them," Thora said.

Others dropped their pants and threw themselves on the twitching bodies. The Boisean made a retching noise from beside him and raised his rifle.

"Wait—" John began, then cursed and brought his rifle to his shoulder. *Crack.*

It punched back into his shoulder with a hard solidity. He was a fair archer and very good with a crossbow; evidently whatever had translated him here *translated* that as well, for him and the others. He worked the bolt again and again, letting the muzzle fall back down and the sights settle. Toa was firing his heavier weapon too, short bursts of *braaaap . . . braaaap . . . braaapp.* In the firelit darkness the weapons spat blade-shaped tongues of yellow flame from their muzzles as they shot.

John let his fingers reload the weapon, pulling the bolt back and pressing clips of cartridges from the pouches at his belt into the magazine well. His senses were stretched in alertness, but some part of his mind that had been listening to all those grizzled veterans was appalled by the firepower this little group had spat out. Things he'd read in pre-Change books made more sense now, how soldiers in the ancient world had spent so much time *hiding.* He was used to a world where when men fought they usually did it in masses and blocks, and at arm's length after charging through a shower of missiles that might or might not wound and kill you through your armor and shield if they chanced to hit.

"We must travel some miles from here," Deor said, when the enemy were all dead. "It will be better if we take that . . . horseless vehicle."

John mentally cursed himself. They all knew the concept of horseless carriages and wagons, and he'd seen refurbished pre-Change vehicles running on big windup springs used as a rich man's plaything. Usually only a few elders who'd been grown before the Change were interested in that sort of thing, of course. One mill-owning magnate in the city-state of Corvallis had shown off just such a toy to the Royal family on a visit when he was fourteen, and had let him drive it sedately around a blocked-off street. There had been a tear running down the man's seamed, white-bearded cheek as they climbed out, and a four-horse hitch of Percherons had come back to tow it home.

It was just that you didn't think of them in terms of anything *practical*, like going somewhere important fast. For that you used horses, one way or another, or sails on water.

"Well, it won't come here by itself," John sighed, and led the way, rifle at half-port.

None of them were squeamish, but they all looked away from the mutual massacre around the motor-truck; except for Toa, who stopped to administer an elephantine kick.

"That 'un was trying to reach for his gun," he explained. "Somehow I don't fancy lying wounded in the street around here if I can avoid it."

The truck had a towing-hitch at the rear, seats in an open body, and *44th Battery* stenciled on its side, over the sigil of the Yellow Sign; he presumed it had been designed to pull some explosive equivalent of field catapults. The motor under the hood at the front was making a steady ticking sound, which was a relief.

They stopped and looked at each other as John climbed in the open side.

"You know how to use one of these, Johnnie?" Pip asked curiously.

"Not really, but—" He explained about the spring-driven replica. "That's as close as anyone around today, I think . . . anyone under seventy years old, that is. Órlaith was bored, but I thought it was interesting."

Deor and Pip climbed in beside him as he slid behind the wheel; Thora and Toa and the Boisean went in the open space behind, where they had a broader field of view and could cover the sides with their weapons.

"Good-oh you know how to drive these things, Johnnie dearest," Pip said cheerfully.

"Ah—yes," John said, smiling brightly and remembering his father and mother telling him to look confident for others even when he wasn't.

I remember how I made the wind-up toy move, he thought. *And those controls were rigged up to make it work just like a pre-Change automobile, so that rich old bastard could relive his childhood with a* stick-shift. *The problem is that this thing doesn't have the same controls except for the wheel. All right, there are three pedals on the floor, so one should be the clutch, one should be the accelerator, and one should be the brake . . . I think I can figure this out, but by the* Saints *we're sort of pressed for time!*

As if to punctuate the thought there was a shot from the bed of the truck, and the *clink-clack* sound of Thora working the bolt of her rifle. A tentative tap at the leftmost pedal made the engine roar; that must be the accelerator. He crossed himself, pulled out his crucifix and kissed it— whenever you thought yourself the uniquely unfortunate victim of circumstances, a brief glance at the Man of Sorrows was a good idea for putting things in perspective—took a deep breath, and worked the lever by his side with the knob on it.

"You got him, mate!" Toa cried enthusiastically, as the truck lurched backward and hit something with a grisly crunch.

"Well, you meant to do that, eh?" Pip murmured.

"Of course!" John said as he stamped on the brake—it *was* the brake, thank God—and shoved the lever back where it had been before.

Logically, if it had gone backward when he pushed it *this* way, the forward gears must be the other way. From the worn and battered and faded indicators, there were three. Hopefully the nearest meant *ahead slow.*

There was a bestial howling from behind them, from many throats. Toa's weapon chattered, shatteringly loud, and Thora shouted:

"Now would be a good time, Johnnie!"

Squeezed beside him Pip twisted and looked back through the open space and into the body of the truck, and presumably at whatever was behind it. She blanched, which made John want to gibber in panic; Philippa Balwyn-Abercrombie wasn't the sort who blanched on small provocation.

A deep breath, and he stepped on the clutch and pushed the lever forward, then transferred his foot to the accelerator. Yells followed as the vehicle lurched forward with a grinding, clanging clash of machinery from under the hood, seeming to stagger as it built up speed. Some force pushed him back against the hard rest behind him, like going over the crest of a rise in a fairground roller-coaster. The wheels lurched and banged over bits of rubble in the roadway, tossing everyone from side to side—the cramped quarters in the front were an advantage now, though Deor cursed in Old English as he was nearly thrown out.

John eased off on the accelerator and wrenched at the wheel to avoid a head-high pile of bricks, then back again to dodge a smoldering tree-trunk, then up onto the sidewalk and a clanging contact with some cast-iron something.

"Left! Left here!" Deor shouted.

Crack.

Pip fired her rifle at something he hadn't seen as he dragged at the wheel to turn them left down a broader road and then frantically right to avoid another cone of slumped wreckage. The left wheels of the truck rode high, and John yelped as he felt the vehicle beginning to tip. Behind him Toa bellowed and leapt to the left side, a *thud* he could feel through the steel fabric beneath him, and the truck slammed down on all four wheels again as it came to a—relatively—uncluttered stretch of roadway.

Then a figure crashed into the bumper of the truck and vaulted over it, lying full-length along it and beginning to crawl towards him. The face was mostly red eyes and gray teeth, the skin around them scorched black and weeping red from a network of cracks. The knife clenched between the broken teeth was long and crusted brown.

"Bugger!" Pip said crisply, as John gave a wordless yell.

Pip and Deor fired simultaneously, she bracing her rifle on the top of the dashboard and Deor extending his pistol. John couldn't tell if one hit or both, but the man grinning around the stained steel of the knife jerked upright as half his head splashed away, then fell over backward. The wheels thumped over him, and John concentrated on driving—that and coughing up black phlegm, stained from the rain of ash all around them.

"I wonder what's in this damned ash," Pip said.

"I don't," Deor said bluntly. "And we would die of it if we had to stay here long."

John kept his attention on the half-buried street, and was thankful of it as Pip made disgusted noises and Deor grew more and more silent; Toa was swearing in half a dozen languages, and Thora the same, though in different ones.

This city died of more than a blow from the sky, John thought. *That may have been a cleansing.*

The sky grew darker, and tendrils of mist rose. Before long it was a clinging mist that hid everything, growing closer and closer to his face. At last he braked the truck and stuck the lever back into the middle position.

"I can't drive this thing any farther," he said.

"You are right," Deor said. "More than you know. We must pass through this. To . . . another place."

Pip grimaced in the dimness. "Back to where we went into the fog?" she said.

"Yes," Deor said.

Oh. She told me that, John thought. *I thought she must be exaggerating. Now I'm horribly afraid she wasn't.*

They piled out of the truck and began walking behind Deor into the mist. John couldn't see anything beyond six paces away, which was just enough to make all of them visible. He coughed again, and noticed that the snow-like fall of black ash had stopped, and that less of it was crusted over the pavement under his feet. Then it wasn't pavement anymore. . . .

John opened his mouth to ask Deor what was happening, hesitating to interrupt the chanting he could hear the scop murmuring under his breath. Then something went through him like a flash of white fire. And there were voices screaming . . .

He stumbled to a halt, bracing himself instinctively on the point of his kite shield. . . .

Wait a minute. I'm in full plate! he thought.

It was so infinitely familiar that he hadn't noticed. And his lungs felt free of the poison he'd been breathing for hours. He took a deep breath, noting that the visor of his sallet was up, and looked at the others. Pip was back in her white shorts and singlet and round black hat, twirling her double-headed cane in relief, and Toa had his huge spear and fiber loincloth-belt. Deor was in his own folk's dress, with the mail and round shield, and Thora in a Bearkiller A-lister's cataphract armor. The man he'd been imprisoned with was in the full fig of a Boisean light cavalryman, with captain's bars on the collar of his mail shirt.

"I think I just had a vision of . . . Hell," John said.

"Close enough, as you Christians conceive of it," Deor said grimly, glancing around himself.

John looked at the Boisean: "You're probably wearing an ID tag, if that uniform's any guide, friend. Take a look."

The man did, pulling out a leather thong from beneath the mail and the quilted gambeson beneath it.

"Alan!" he said, tilting it to read it by the light of moon and stars . . . which were suddenly overhead. "Alan Thurston!"

He was no fool, and noticed how the others froze; specifically, how Deor and John and Thora did. Pip and Toa looked almost as puzzled as he.

"Do you know me?" the man—Alan—said.

Deor said cautiously: "The ruling House of the United States of Boise is named Thurston," he said. "And . . . you could be of that kin."

John looked at him and mentally stepped back to analyze. *He could be, by his looks,* he decided.

Back in the ancient world, those who were visibly descended from the folk of Africa below the Sahara had been called *black*. Old Lawrence Thurston, the first General-President of Boise, had been one such, as well as an officer in the old American army; so had the first Count of Molalla, whose grandson Sir Droyn was a liege knight of Órlaith's and a good sort, though a bit of a prig in John's opinion.

Lawrence Thurston's wife, though, had been of a stock mostly European in blood, and so had the wives of his sons Martin and Frederick; the distinctions of the old world meant little in modern times, as opposed to more realistic and well-grounded concerns like your faith, clan, tribe, city-state, family allegiances or ties of lordship. John had known Frederick Thurston's children all his life—they were much of an age with him, and their father was a close friend and comrade-in-arms of his parents from the Quest of the Lady's Sword, as well as ruler of a major member-realm of the High Kingdom.

Alan Thurston, on the other hand, he knew only by his name and that of his mother, Juliet, widow of the dead traitor Martin.

"If you're one of *those* Thurstons, your uncle Frederick is General-President of Boise," John said.

Pip gave him a sharp glance from under her bowler hat; she'd heard the unspoken complications he'd left out. Alan—it was good to have a name for him—grinned.

"Well—" he began happily.

"Hsst!" Toa said, his full-featured face probing the area around them.

John stopped letting the familiar and for once oh-so-welcome weight of the armor distract him and looked around. What he saw was a roadway stretching into the distance, under starlight that was somehow wrong, and a vague reddish background glow that came from everywhere and nowhere. The roadway was pockmarked and gashed by years of untended weather, but also crowded with boxy automobiles and motor-trucks.

So were the immediate verges, and they'd all been struck by some monstrous blow of fire and blast from the rear; some looked almost melted. Thorny scrub grew over many, and over the bleached, charred skeletons of dead trees about. He thought he could see the roofless snags of a farmhouse and barn in the middle distance.

The air smelled dry and dusty, with an odor of rust and old, old rot, wind soughed through the scrub, and things skittered through the under-brush. Otherwise there was a profound, tense quiet. No birds, and not even many of the buzzing and chirping insects.

"This is what happened after the last place we were?" he asked.

My head hurts trying to figure this out, he thought. *Give me the waking world any day! There, all you have to worry about is evil magic and things like the Sword of the Lady and the Grasscutter.*

"Not exactly," Deor said. "Or I think not wholly. This is part of the dream of the thing we fight—the King in Yellow. His memory of all his victories and triumphs. It feels . . . stronger than the last time we came past, to reach you, my Prince. As if that King wakes, and wakes in anger."

John stopped in mid-reply as Toa wheeled about again. There was a creaking metallic sound, rusty metal moving on metal, then squealing as joints long melded together broke free.

"Move!" Deor said, and led the way, Saxon broadsword naked in his hand and Hraefnbeorg's raven on his shield.

And Odhinn's bird, John thought uneasily. *Not a comfortable ally, the Lord of the Gallows whose daughters reap men on the bloody field so that they may fight again at Ragnarok. I'm bound for a different destination . . . hopefully.*

His lips moved in prayer as he trotted along beside the scop:

"Sancte Michael Archangele, defende nos in proelio, contra nequitiam et insidias diaboli esto præsidium. Imperet illi Deus, supplices deprecamur: tuque, princeps militiæ cælestis, Satanam aliosque spiritus malignos, qui ad perditionem animarum pervagantur in mundo, divina virtute, in infernum detrude. Amen."

The words were comforting in the language of the liturgy or in common English:

Saint Michael the Archangel, defend us in battle, be our protection against the malice and snares of the Adversary . . .

"Amen," Pip echoed him.

He glanced at her, slightly surprised, and she grinned in the dimness and shrugged.

"I'm Catholic too, sweetie—Anglican Rite. Not overly pious, but there's no doubt whose help we need now, is there?"

Behind them Toa gave a yell and lashed out with his great spear, sweeping it in a half-circle that ended in a thudding and a dry crunching sound.

Just ahead of them John saw movement behind the dusty, cobwebbed darkness of a car's window.

"What's happening?" he yelled; the smell of ancient rot was stronger.

"Draugur!" Deor said. "Aptrgangr, again-walkers, hungry for the blood and flesh of the living."

I had to ask! John's mind gibbered at him.

"You've dealt with this?" Pip asked.

"No," Deor said. "Nor any living man in the world of common day, I think. But I know them from the lore I learned in Norrheim and Iceland."

"What do we do about 'em?" Toa said. "Bit past their sell-by date from what I saw, doesn't seem like stabbing will get the job done."

"There are many ways to slay Draugur," Deor said. "But right now . . . remember they can die again! Smash their bodies or cripple them. And do as the Prince did; call on any guardian or aid you may have."

John brought his shield up, and then suddenly noticed that it seemed to be *glowing*. He bent his head for an instant to look at it, and saw that instead of the usual arms of Montival with a cadet's baton it bore a plain red surface with a white cross—a Crusader's cross. And that was lit, slightly but unmistakably. He forced himself to calm, taking one deep breath after another:

"Haro, Portland!" he shouted.

Shadowy figures were skulking around them, more rising by the moment. At first he thought they were the same grotesquely disfigured survivors he'd seen in the city they'd just left. Then one moved into a patch of dim light, and he saw its face, the fluttering rags of clothes stiff with the liquids of long decay, the tufts of hair on mummified skin and unclean bone, and the eyes . . .

Even faced with mortal peril he flung the shield up before his face rather than look into those eyes. Toa retched, an astonishing response from a man who seemed to be carved from strength and fury. Alan murmured aloud, awestruck:

"That is not dead which can eternal lie.

And with strange aeons even death may die."

Deor's voice belled. "Woden! Ha, Woden, Lord of the Slain, be with us! *Keep moving!"*

Thora moved up beside him, shield raised. "Overrun," she barked. "Strike as if they had torso armor!"

John knocked his visor down; he could see just enough through the vision-slit, but hopefully no more than that. They braced and then leapt off their back feet in a stamping run, shoulders tucked into the shields. Deor and Alan guarded their flanks, with Pip in the center to deal with anyone . . . or anything . . . that got through, and guard Toa's back while he held the rear. What skill and courage could do they would do. That left purity of heart. . . .

But I'm a miserable sinner! John thought as he prepared for impact. *I just want to get on a ship with Pip and go introduce her to Mother!*

His shield rammed into a body with his weight behind it, something he'd done a thousand times in practice and a few in real fights these last few months. It felt *wrong*, and so did the crunch that followed; too dry, too fragile and it stank like an opened grave. He overcame his impulse to stab around the side of his shield. . . .

Wait a minute, the reasoning part of his mind thought. *That . . . thing . . . just collapsed.*

Fingers like twigs clawed at him, not one of them strong . . . but there were so many, half-glimpsed in the darkness. Like a rustling forest of un-death hungry for the living. He hacked into the side of a knee and half-wheeled and cut through a tattered neck. The . . . things that had once been people . . . he'd cut dropped away, and more stepped in.

John kept moving and smashed his shield into another dry and rotting face. This time there wasn't any doubt. Suddenly the walking thing was just honestly dead, and fell in a tangle. He hopped over it and smashed again, with the same result.

And I hope if there are souls involved, they're set free, he thought.

"Haro, Portland! Holy Mary for Portland!" he shouted. *"Órlaith and Montival!"*

"Thor with me!" Thora barked as her backsword flicked in economical strokes. *"Yuk-hai-sa-saaa!"*

"Bugger this!"

That was Pip; in the same instant her cane's serrated head went *crack* into a skull covered in thin rags of hair and skin. That worked too, and she'd hacked through a spine with the kukri in her other hand at the same time, moving as gracefully as a dancer in the dimness. Alan Thurston was working in a crouch, shield up and saber slashing for knees and ankles.

He caught occasional glimpses of Toa's spear flashing in sweeping arcs, and Deor's shout echoed:

"Ho, la, Woden!"

He thought the figures around the Mist Hills man were moving more slowly than the others, and stumbling more. The Saxon broadsword reaped, and John remembered uneasily who . . . Who . . . was also Lord of the Gallows-Tree, and of the Slain.

"The Power that wards you is strong indeed, Prince," the scop panted, a flash of teeth beneath the nasal bar of his helmet. "But there is more than one at work for us today."

John was glad he was getting help; and very glad he was in full armor. He kept his sword back in the man-at-arms position—hilt-forward and over his head—and used mainly his shield, ramming with the surface and chopping with the edges.

Something seemed to *change*. They were still stumbling down a road in the darkness, but it had never been paved—this was more like a country road back home, though more rutted and with less gravel than most places would have tolerated. Perhaps in the CORA lands, where they had trouble agreeing on whether the sun rose in the east or west, much less who should contribute graders and horses and workers to keeping up the roadways.

John stumbled to a halt and leaned on his shield and panted, wheezing and coughing, knocking up the visor of his sallet so that he could see better and, more important, get that extra mouthful of air. The night breeze cooled his sweat a little, and he could see that all five of them were on their feet.

He could also see behind them, and it didn't look in the least like the place they'd just been. Instead the white dirt of the road shimmered in the darkness, winding off into an empty countryside of rolling hills and copses of trees. It was ordinary-looking country, if not anything quite like what he'd seen before. Perhaps parts of the Willamette in the far south, or the Chehalis valley if you subtracted the mountains . . .

It doesn't stink, either, John thought. *He took a deep breath. But there's something . . . off.*

"Is everyone hale?" Deor said.

They gathered around. Pip had a bleeding scratch on one forearm; he helped her clean and bandage it. Toa had a mark on one massive calf, and he examined it while leaning on his spear and turning up the leg.

"Sodding thing *bit* me," he said. "And that was *after* I cut it in half."

"Let me look at that," Deor said, kneeling. "I'll cleanse it. Best not to let this fester, considering what teeth they were that bit. Worse than a lion."

Whatever he used made Toa give a mild grunt, which meant it probably hit like a red-hot cauterizing iron.

"What's this?" John asked. "This place, I mean."

He had the usual canteen at his belt, and he handed it around and took a welcome swallow of tepid, metallic-tasting water.

"It's a *bad* place," Toa said, with a frightening grin—the tattoos on his face were supposed to look terrifying, and they did, especially in this reddish un-light. "But I think it's one we went through on the way in."

"We are deeper into the mind of the . . . Power that rules here," Deor agreed.

"Deeper in to get out," Pip agreed, working her fingers. "Dammit, that hurts!"

"Bad for the flawless complexion, too," Thora said.

She said it with a smile . . . more or less. Her own face had a weathered handsomeness, but it also showed every year of an adventurous thirty-five spent knocking around an implausible amount of the Changed world in Deor's company. None of the great *chanson de geste* that told of the paladins of Charlemagne had the hero accompanied by his current intended and very-recently-ex-girlfriend.

Which means either the chanson *were heavily edited, or the jongleurs didn't know what the hell they were talking about, or I'm not the hero of this song,* John thought.

"Oh, on the contrary, dear Thora, a few scars are wonderful icebreakers in some situations."

Thora hadn't been going out of her way to make things more awkward. Or less, for that matter. There seemed to be something they knew that he didn't, too—it was in the way Pip's fair brow rose, and the ironic quirk to Thora's grin.

I'm getting tired of other people knowing things I don't.

"Let's walk," Deor said. "The steps are symbolic; but here, symbols have power."

They did. John slung his shield on his back and trudged along behind him, with Pip at his side; she was whistling a song she told him was "Advance Australia Fair" when he asked. Sweat started up, though it wasn't particularly warm or cold; if you moved in armor, you sweated—and the sweat stayed next to your skin. Even if it was very cold, you sweated and then the sweat chilled you the moment you stopped; of course, if it was hot and sunny the armor got too hot to touch, and you grilled like a fish wrapped in damp straw matting and dropped into a pit of hot coals.

Oh, that was brilliant, John, he thought: now he felt hungry.

"What is it that you and Thora aren't telling me?" he said after a while; Toa began to laugh.

When John stared at him, the big Maori laughed even harder. "Oh, no, mate, not a bleedin' chance. I know better than to stick my ghoolies in the mangle, you bet your arse I do."

Pip just raised a slim blond brow. "Oh, come now, Johnnie. Thora and I have the greatest respect for each other—"

Thora chuckled and raised a gauntleted thumb; he realized that they actually did. He didn't think they liked each other much—the thought of what it would be like for him if they were friends was enough to make him blanch—but they certainly respected each other's abilities. You would have to be stupid or blind not to respect Thora Garwood's capacities, or Philippa Balwyn-Abercrombie's . . . and neither of the ladies were stupid in the least.

Unless you count being involved with me, he thought mordantly. *Which got them here, wherever here really is. If it really is.*

Unexpectedly, Toa spoke again: "You should tell the lad. Wouldn't be fair if it all went tits-up and he'd never got the word, like."

"He'd get all protective," Thora said.

"Nah," Toa said. "Lady, he's no fool. We're here . . . but we're really not, you know?"

Pip and Thora exchanged one of those disturbing looks, and Thora shrugged in a clatter of armor. Pip cleared her throat.

"You're going to be a daddy, sweetie," she said.

Thora was fighting down a grin as he nearly tripped, and looked wildly between them.

"Who . . . who . . . who . . ."

"I wouldn't have thought your totem was an owl," Thora said, letting the grin out. It was remarkably evil.

"He's a Raven," Deor cast over his shoulder. "You can see the shadow of the wings on him. Well, think who his father was, and Who his father met and knew. The Crow Goddess . . . and others."

He seemed to be enjoying the conversation far too much, and to find the whole complicated business of men and women rather amusing.

"Put the poor bastard out of his misery," Toa urged.

The silent communion between the two women ended with Thora nodding and making a sweeping gesture that said: *Go ahead.*

Pip bowed and pointed at her, and Thora made the same gesture.

"It's her," they said in chorus.

Distantly, John heard a clatter. Then he realized it was the clatter of his own plates as he fell. Two faces looked down at him in concern, then cleared. The grin on Pip's face was, if possible—

"Our prepotent sire has fainted," she said. "All those Victorian novels they made me read at Rockhampton Girls Grammar School finally come in useful, or would if I had any smelling salts . . . I wonder what smelling salts *were*?"

"And remember," Thora said. "Toa was right. Our real bodies aren't here."

They each gave him a hand and heaved him upright; getting up in sixty pounds of armor wasn't all that difficult when it was well-distributed all over your body, but he felt as if he'd been hit behind the ear with the proverbial sock full of wet sand.

"How . . . how . . ."

This time both women laughed instead of grinning. "Oh, Johnnie, do you really need to ask that question?" Thora asked.

Pip sighed. "The oldsters say rubber products just aren't as reliable as they were before the Blackout . . . the Change."

Thora's tone grew pawky. "Don't worry, Johnnie. I'll look after it— literally."

He felt an ignoble rush of relief, because if she'd appealed for his aid and acknowledgement he wouldn't in honor have been able to deny it to her . . . and his child . . . and . . .

Oh, God pity me and forgive my weakness, the complications!

Fortunately Bearkillers, even the Catholic ones, didn't look on such matters the same way Associates did. He hadn't a clue how Deor's folk did, but the scop didn't seem too disturbed.

"And so will I for the babe," Deor said, and paused to look him in the eye. "On that you have my word as a Godulfson. My oath-sister's child shall be as mine."

A wry grin. "It's the closest I'll come to being a father—closer than I expected, in fact. My brother the lord of Mist Hills has offered us land. If—it's an if the size of mountains—we make it safely back to Montival, we're going to take it of him, put an end to our wanderings save for visits in the neighborhood and raise horses and grapes. And it's out of the way, and likely will be even when you've a fine son or strapping daughter twenty years from now. Eventually the child will have to know her heritage. But what I can do until then, I will do."

John managed to wheeze: "Thank you," as they took up the trudge again. "You're a man I would trust with that."

It could have been much worse; if the women had both been Mackenzies, they might have expected him to move in with the pair of them, a thought which evoked feelings of horror and horrified attraction at the same time.

"And don't worry. I won't tell your mother if you don't want me to," Thora said.

"Neither will I," Pip said.

He hadn't thought of it in those terms, and felt another rush of relief *before* the fear, which was odd but seemed to make sense. His mother most assuredly *was* Catholic and *was* an Associate, and in her way notably pious. Bringing home a wellborn Anglican Rite bride like Pip was one thing, even if they'd had to find a priest on their own and arrived with wedding bands and a baby. A royal bastard on the other hand . . .

Oh, God, the political complications! I hadn't thought of that! Why does fun have to be so serious?

Anonymous Nobleman X wouldn't have to worry; a gift to the mother, possibly some patronage down the road, and that was it. The second in line to the High Kingdom and the heir to the Protectorate . . .

Visions of court faction in his middle years sprang into his mind and made more sweat run into the lining of his helmet and his arming-doublet.

"I warned her too, Your Highness," Deor said.

"It was an accident!" Thora said.

Deor smiled at her, then sobered. "Best indeed if nobody beyond us four . . ."

He looked at Alan and continued pointedly: "Us *five* ever knows. Men could die on bloody fields and houses burn otherwise."

The Boisean smiled crookedly. "I barely know my own name right now, sir," he said. "And besides . . . if this is where you say it is, who would believe anything I said I'd learned here? For what my promise is worth, I'll keep my peace . . . and even I don't know what it's worth."

Deor laughed. "You have a point, Alan of Thor's Stone."

John flogged himself back to alertness; in a way it was almost fortunate he was in this place of peril and horror.

Almost.

CHAPTER NINETEEN

BETWEEN WAKING WORLD AND SHADOW

After a while a horse-drawn cart approached them, growing from a dot in the dim distance until it was visibly a four-wheel vehicle. That was reassuringly familiar, though at home he'd have expected two horses, and it was making an odd whining noise, not what you got from ungreased wheels. The driver looked roly-poly; as they drew closer John realized that he was *round* except for the cloth-cased stick-limbs, and the same lemon-yellow color as the tunic and hood he wore. He looked at them and giggled as he drove by; once he was close you could see that the harness was sewn onto the beast, which wasn't exactly a horse. But it wept blood and whimpered as it pulled.

The rear of the cart was a cage of iron bars. John saw the faces of children behind them, and started forward with his hand on the hilt of his sword as they stared at him through the bars.

"Wait, Prince!" Deor said. *"Wait!"*

The scop's hand closed on his shield-arm and dragged him backward. That jerked him back from the bars just as the boneless fingers reached for him and the angelic lips parted to show rows of needle-teeth.

"Children!" the driver of the wagon chuckled, in a liquid burbling tone . . . and in an Old French that John alone of their party could speak. "Be good. Be *gooooood!*"

And laughing like water gurgling in a sewer he lashed the not-horse into a shambling trot.

"This way," Deor said. And: "Appearances are dangerous here, as we go deeper. This is where all things collapse together, and that mixing is ill indeed."

They walked on, like walking in a dream . . . except that John knew it wasn't *his* dream, or the dream of anything human. Though he had a disturbing sense that it might have been once, in some inconceivably ancient cycle of the cosmos. A file of figures appeared, human this time, and linked by a rope around their waists; they were chanting and flogging each other with barbed whips as they walked, the blood running down into the rag loincloths twisted around their waists. Every dozen paces the whips would change hands. None of them looked up as the five adventurers passed, and John could see that their eyes were sewn shut; the first in the line probed his way forward with a stick. Beyond them in the field a plow went by, pulled by men, or things more or less like men, and guided by a horse . . . or something more or less like a horse.

Light showed ahead, brighter than the cindered sky yielded. The road made an abrupt left turn on the edge of a cliff, or a line of low steep hills. Thora whistled tunelessly as she looked down, and the rest of them came up.

Several hundred feet below was a vast panorama of land furrowed and fissured with what after a moment John recognized as field fortifications—the relatives of those he'd helped lay out for the siege of the Carcosan fort in Baru Denpasar. These snaked out as far as the eye could see, though, two opposing lines . . . or two opposing sets, for each was line after line of trench, connected with zigzagging communications trenches running vertically to the front. The whole was pockmarked with craters, some old and crumbling and flooded, others rawly new—and as he watched a spark light snapped and earth flew skyward, with a long rolling boom following close on its heels. Rusted barbed wire spread in coils and belts across the land between the trenches, and figures hung on it. For the closer ones you could see them twitch, and hear their thin hopeless mewling. Hints of movement beneath them showed where rats the size of cats scuttled and fed and dragged their full bellies through the muck.

Wisps of green mist floated over the landscape, and a hint of it set them all coughing more than the stink of death had. Faint in the distance whistles sounded, and suddenly the empty-looking trenches threw up hordes of men in steel helmets and drab-colored uniforms, scrambling up assault ladders and running forward. He thought they carried rifles with long knives affixed, though it was hard to be sure; there was a faint tacka-tacka-tacka sound and windrows of them fell. More snaps of fire and fountains of dirt, and men and pieces of men were tossed up in the black poplar-shapes of dirt.

Bugles sounded, thin and endless. When they ceased there was quiet again, save for the cries of the wounded. Two flags flapped not far apart, their staffs driven into the dirt by the hands of falling men. Both were featureless gray tatters.

"I don't think we want to go that way," John said thoughtfully, keeping the shiver out of his voice. "I think that's a battle, and that it's been going on a long long time."

"Like the *Einherjar*, but without honor or joy or hope," Thora said with a shiver.

"And to think I ran away from home because I was bored," Pip muttered. "I'll write a book about it—*Pregnant In Hell* would be a good title."

Everyone chuckled, and they kept going. Now and then Deor would halt at a crossroads, chant and close his eyes and point one way or another. Once they had to cross a section of hard-paved road, twelve lanes wide and crowded with automobiles—looking very much like some sections of pre-Change highway he'd seen, except that they weren't ruins and were all running. And totally motionless, bumper to bumper. The five companions all coughed and gagged at the acrid stench of the air they had to breathe. The jammed road extended out of sight in either direction, shimmering with heat, eternally motionless.

One glimpse through a bloodied windscreen where hands beat and

beat and beat was enough, and he kept his head down and hurried with
the others.

At last they came through the outskirts of a town, one that plucked at
the strings of his memory. It was a quaint-looking place, with steep-pitched
roofs and cobbled streets and overhanging balconies, and the odd elm and
chestnut tree along its narrow ways. Folk in clothes a little like those of an
Association town hurried past, wimpled housewives with baskets of loaves,
besmocked artisans, a jongleur strumming on a lute . . .

"Stop!" a voice cried shrilly from a window several stories above them.
"Stop! Stop! *Stop!*"

Each shout was accompanied by a thudding blow. At the fourth a
naked woman with *something* dangling from her jaws ran out on the bal-
cony, then leapt up and scaled the brick of the wall as agile as a monkey.
She was laughing around whatever it was, and there were streaks of red
down her chin and breasts.

The mind of the Yellow King, John thought.

The really disturbing thing about it wasn't that he was in the mind of
a mad demon . . .

No, that is *disturbing*, John thought. *That is* very *disturbing.*

What was *even more* disturbing was that he wasn't sure he was just
seeing images, part of the Yellow King's imaginings. He was pretty sure
that the people in that strange version of New York had been just that,
people. People who were somehow trapped here forever, or at least until
the Day of Judgement. He didn't know how the theology of it all worked,
but he did know this was a fair working facsimile of damnation.

At the center of the town was a lopsided square leading down to a
river, with a tall building topped by a spire like a church, and on its top
the three-armed Yellow Sign.

"I don't like this," Deor began.

John bit back a: *No shit! I don't either!*

Deor meant something specific. Light pulsed through the stained-glass
windows of the not-church, along with chanting—a guttural chorus he

couldn't quite make out. Then the great carved doors swung open and he could:

"*Uoht! Uoht! Uoht!*"

Worshippers came out in a boiling mob; or at least he thought it was a mob, until he realized that they were dancing, a jerking chaotic mass that moved to the drone of pipes and the maddeningly irregular pulse of a drum. The dancers were naked save for bestial masks, all distorted; a raven with a curved beak, a bull's-head with antlers, a rabbit that wept tears of red. They lashed each other as the flagellants on the road had, and their screams melded into the music.

"*Uoht! Uoht! Uoht!*"

After the dancers came more naked figures chained to a wheeled platform with barbed links, their faces painted white on one side and black on the other, scrambling forward on their hands and knees. A tall black pillar sat in the middle of the platform, and its head had been carved into . . .

It's not really like a dog, John thought.

He *liked* dogs, and found their faces appealing in a dopey, enthusiastic, childlike fashion. Dogs were more honest than men, too. They didn't pretend to like you if you treated them well, they actually did, and would treat you as if you were their blood kin and liege lord rolled into one.

It looks more like a bat. There's a reason the old painters used bat-faces for demons. This looks like the Adversary trying to copy a dog.

Whoever had carved it knew their work. The needle teeth weren't too regular, and they had stains the way a working carnivore's did. The broad ribbed ears and the flared convoluted nostrils were delicately pink veined in crimson and black, and the black bristly hairs of the muzzle seemed to almost bristle. . . .

They did. The eyes opened, and they were as black as the bristling fur. The pupils were like . . . No, they *were* the three-limbed Yellow Sign, but they were alive, and full of wicked intelligence and a living will to harm that struck like a hammer of hot wind. The columnar . . . body? Was it bending, mistlike?

"Uoht! Uoht! Uoht!"

The votaries screamed the name. John realized his mouth was open and he was making small mewing noises, rather like this grandmother's Persian cats when they were unhappy with a thunderstorm or catapult-practice in Castle Todenangst. The difference was that he *knew* that running back and forth moaning wouldn't do him any good at all. But it was so tempting!

"Now that we've been formally introduced to Mr. Uoht, let's run like buggery!" Pip said crisply, her melodically accented soprano steady. Then she muttered: "At least there aren't tentacles."

Whatever that means, John thought. *Well, it's nice to know the mother of my children*—even then the words brought an odd mixture of pride and something quite like fear—*has plenty of courage to pass on. At least as much as I!*

"Fuckin' second the motion," Toa rasped; he had his spear up and was backing away step by step. "Bad doggie!"

"Down to the water," Deor said. "Toa, Thora and Pip, you lead and get us a boat ready. Prince John, Alan, with me."

That was sensible; Pip was a highly competent ship's captain, Toa was her second in command, and Thora had spent a lot of time on boats. She was also a ferociously able fighter—not that Pip wasn't formidable too, but Thora was equipped and trained for a straight-on slugging match in a way she wasn't. One look at Toa was usually enough to intimidate, though you couldn't be sure here, and he was also one of the strongest men John had ever met and like an otter in the water.

But I really wish it wasn't so sensible for me to hold the rearguard. Roland won immortal fame at Roncevalles and died there . . . on the other hand he'd be dead now anyway, wouldn't he? Buck up, John. This part will sound good in the chanson. It's good I've been sharing my musical plans with Deor—he could make it if . . . if necessary.

The votaries were more or less ignoring the five of them, as most of the people . . . sort of people . . . here had. The dog-bat-thing wasn't. It seemed to have a little trouble finding them, for which John thanked God the Father, the Son and the Holy Ghost; also the Virgin and the whole bright company of the Saints—literally, and wished he could work the rosary that lay against his skin under the arming doublet.

And maybe that's why it can't find us easily, John thought. *God's hand is over us. I'm not worthy . . . but who is? Praise God for His infinite mercy!*

He tried not to think of Who else might be involved; he didn't . . . or wasn't supposed to . . . believe the Aesir did things like that, and he didn't even know what Powers Alan Thurston called on, and he had probably never even heard of those Toa's people followed if they weren't Christians.

The three formed up shield-to-shield; John was in the center, as the man with the heaviest armor and biggest shield.

An honor I could do without, he thought.

Aloud he said quietly: "Friends, I always hated the training in walking backward in armor. The sergeants-at-arms laughed at the squires every time we tripped and fell, and that hurt worse than the bruises. Perhaps I was a little hasty. It teaches you to be graceful about your exits; as a musician, that's a valuable skill. And I'd really like to get off the stage here before they start booing and throwing things."

"You dance well, too," Deor said with a chuckle. "What a shame your tastes are so conventional otherwise, my liege."

"Let's do this," Alan said.

John knocked down his visor and raised the shield. Back a step, and a step. Uoht's yellow gaze moved as the column of mist slid forward, pivoting, and the force of it was like a hot blow, like being trapped in your coffin and smelling your own body rotting. He hunched his shoulder into the shield, the way you did when weapons beat on it. The feel of comrades to either side of him kept him steady; he could feel his father's hand on his shoulder, too, his mother's eyes full of love and pride at his knighting, as he came out of the chapel after the vigil.

"Back a step," Deor said. "And back . . . and back . . ."

Something was keeping those eyes from really seeing them, but that only enraged the . . . whatever Uoht was. Slaver drooled in long threads from the fangs, and the thin lips moved—he had a horrible suspicion that it was shaping words.

Then he grunted, and heard Deor and Alan make almost the same sound. Something had hit him, impalpable but strong, and his mind vanished in a blaze of pain for an instant. His next step backward was involuntary, and he braced himself as if leaning into a storm-wind, a blizzard in the Cascades. The pillar drifted towards him. As it did the world dimmed and *thinned*. As if it were a screen, and behind the screen . . .

A tower on a hill, amid a wasteland of tumbled mud and beneath a cindered moon and behind *that* the spires of a city. More dog-headed pillars, all of them turning to look at him . . .

John pushed with his mind, as if he were back on the squire's training-field, ramming his shield against a pole set on a weighted skid, trying to budge it with his legs churning.

"Back," Deor said again, more hoarsely this time. "Back a step . . ."

The deep nostrils flared, hunting for a scent. A sound came from between its jaws, a deep humming sound. It grew louder and louder, jarring, and suddenly the teeth in his jaws hurt. A warm trickle started from his nose, running salt over his lips—the distinctive metallic tang of blood. Blood was running down the faces of the worshippers too, as they capered and shrieked:

"Uoht! Uoht! Uoht!"

The note grew deeper, and the hilt of his sword was growing hot in his hand, beneath the leather palm of his armored gauntlet and the wrapping of bison rawhide and silver wire on the weapon. He wasn't sure if a material weapon could cut Uoht anyway . . . except that Deor had explained convincingly that this wasn't actually a material place, despite the irritating itch that he couldn't scratch in a delicate place. His very material self was sleeping in a bed in a beach-house in Baru Denpasar with Pip and Thora beside him.

He pushed away that distracting thought. The pressure against his shield was building, building. The same sense of weight seemed to be squeezing at his temples, constricting like a knotted cord until he felt his eyeballs start to bulge. They retreated step after step, his sabatons skidding on the smooth granite cobbles of the street. The smell of mud and water grew stronger. . . .

"Got the boat!" Pip called.

"Run!" Deor wheezed, like a man throwing down an impossible weight. *"Run!"*

John wheeled, and almost fell to his knees as the pressure increased. But now he wasn't trying to resist it, and his feet seemed to fly over the stones. Ahead the road sloped into the water, and a boat was waiting—with Toa throwing the mooring-post it had been chained to into it, having apparently torn it out of the ground by main force. Pip was aboard, shipping a steering oar, and Thora helped the big Maori as he fell to pushing it forward.

The union of their straining effort started the twenty-foot, double-ended hull moving just as the three men arrived. John managed to sheath his sword as he ran—fortunately it was hard to stab yourself in the hip or groin in full armor—and pitched the shield ahead of him to fall with a hard clatter in the bottom of the boat. His hands clamped on the gunwale, and he joined the others in running it down the slope and into the water.

"Alan first!" she called, going by their positions.

The Boisean rolled over the gunwale and into the boat and scrambled on all fours towards the bows.

"Now Deor . . . now John . . . Thora . . . Toa!"

John was knee-deep in the water when she called his name, feeling it pouring into his greaves. He leapt and pushed, grunting against the weight of body and armor and wetness, rolling into the sopping bottom of the boat and shuddering-glad he hadn't pushed the rail under the surface. Someone heavy landed on top of him, and he gave a protesting *ooof*!

"Get for'ard and out oars. Move your arses, all of you!" Pip shouted.

No, Captain *Pip shouted that,* his mind thought, as he scrambled to obey and a large foot landed in the small of his back.

The oars were loose in the bottom of the craft. They all grabbed one and shoved it through the thwarts; John was the second-slowest, with Alan hanging back a fraction of a second to see what they did. He wasn't a total novice at oars, though; Boise did have lakes, and a few big rivers, and presumably he'd gone fishing now and then.

Though I wouldn't want to eat anything caught in these *waters.*

"Captain!" Deor called. "Take us downstream!"

John could see back behind them; it was an advantage of running away while rowing. It was a big river, not on the scale of the Columbia but comparable to the lower Willamette, say a long bowshot and a half across. The *thing—*

Wasn't there anymore? They all rested on their oars for a moment.

Or at least I can't see it, John thought as the village faded into the darkness.

He muttered a sincere prayer—the sincerity of his prayers in general was improving, though he thought the cost was a bit excessive—of thanks. The others did as well, in their varied fashions.

CHAPTER TWENTY

BETWEEN WAKING WORLD AND SHADOW

"Bloody glad to see the last of . . . whatever that was," Pip said from the tiller of their hijacked boat.

Gnomically, she added: "I'm never going to sneer at Uncle Pete's taste in fiction again."

Deor was at the oar just sternward from John; he handled himself on boats and ships with the workmanlike competence he showed at most things besides music, where he shone to a degree that made John a little envious—though when you added in fifteen years more experience . . .

"What *was* that thing? The . . . demon, I suppose it was?"

Deor shrugged his shoulders, and his mail shirt rustled and clinked. "I don't know," he said.

"You're an honest man, Deor Godulfson," Pip called—she was less than ten feet away.

Deor laughed, a little hoarsely. John realized he must have been shouting the commands to move back step by step, shouting against the muffling power that had nearly crushed them into paste.

"I think," he said, "that it is part of the . . . story, the story of the Yellow King. Perhaps an avatar or emissary of that Power, perhaps a great servant, like the Pallid Mask. What worries me is that it sensed us. Now the Power will seek to see."

"Speaking of which—" Alan said.

A man was standing on the bank of the river, laughing, with his arms stretched over his head. As they passed they saw his empty, bleeding eye sockets and that each hand held an eyeball in its palms. They turned and followed the boat as it drifted past . . .

"Enough jawing," Pip said in that crisp tone of command that seemed to operate directly on your nerves. "If we need to get downstream, let's go."

That's not the way Father did it, or Mother does . . . but it works, John thought. *She has what they had, the Baraka, the thing that rulers need.*

"Toa, give us the stroke," Pip said. "This boat deserves a good one, it really flows with the water."

The Maori did, in his growling bass, and they all fell into the rhythm of it:

"E pari ra koe te tai,
Whakaki ana mai
Nga ngutu-awa.
Hui nga ope au
Ki te tai uru.
Aue! Tiaia!
Aue! Koia hoki.
Hūkere, Waikato!
Aue, ku-umea!
Tūpara, Tūpara,
Tūpara, Waikato!
Tōia, e!"

John could feel the silken smoothness of the way the boat cut the low riffles of the river's current, and leapt to the stroke of the oars. When Toa finished Pip took it up; he guessed it was the same chant in English, because it had the feel of something translated, an alien rhythm:

"Flowing there is the ocean tide,
Surging towards me,
Filling up the mouth of the river.
Gathering are the armies

At the sea of the west.
Now dip the paddles!
That's it! Come along!
Harder, faster, O Waikato!
Oh, a long, strong stroke!
Now quickly, quickly!
Quicker, Waikato!
Pull away O!"

Rowing in armor wasn't as easy as in ordinary clothes, but wasn't impossibly difficult either—you could do acrobatics in a good suit of plate if you were strong and experienced, and the set his mind had conjured was the same as he usually wore, one made of chrome-alloy steel by master-craftsmen. It *felt* the same, which meant he just clanked a bit as he swayed forward and back pulling on the oar.

"Where are we going?"

"The place we came in when we left . . . Baru Denpasar, the world, the *real* world," Pip said. "Which only Deor can find, of course, so please don't get eaten by any monsters, eh? The only thing I've found here I like are Johnnie and this boat."

"I will do my best, my lady Captain," Deor said.

"The place with the Hell Horse," Pip added. "Which we evaded by running as fast as we could."

John half missed a stroke. "Are . . . you sure that's what it was?" he said.

Pip grinned at him. "No, lover; it just fit the way you described it. But if I was sure, I'd have seen it, and then I'd be dead, now wouldn't I?"

More soberly: "Though that seems to be a bit less . . . definite, around here."

"Here, I think," Deor said, looking over his shoulder. "Where that road meets the water, by the dead oak."

Pip leaned on the tiller, and they all stroked their oars more slowly. An instant, and the keel of the boat grated on gravel and mud. John brought his oar in with the others—you had to be careful or you could clout someone in the head doing that—and leapt over the side, his feet in the water once again. All of them put their shoulders to the hull and ran the boat up on the shore, more out of reflex than anything else.

Deor stopped as the others spread out on the dirt road that wound uphill from the river's edge. John looked back as he slung his shield over his back. The front of the boat was intricately carved, in a way that he avoided looking at too closely, but set into the worked wood was the grinning skull of a cat, old bone bleached until there was only a hint of ivory in the white. Green stones had been inset in the eye sockets.

Deor touched it and went silent for a moment. "It spoke to me," he said.

Pip snorted. "What did it say? Meow?"

Deor looked at her. "No, my lady. In speech without words, said without ceasing . . . *Hurts, hurts, make it stop, I am a good cat, hurts, mother, mother, hurts make it stop.* There is a spirit trapped in this vessel, and it has been for a very long time."

Pip glanced away, scowling and swallowing. John put his hand to his sword, but before he could draw Toa lashed out with the steel-shod butt of his spear, quick as the flick of a frog's tongue after a darting fly, hunting from its lily pad on a summer's day. The bone exploded into dust. John put his hand to the weathered boards of the boat's hull. Did it feel different, or was that his imagination?

Well, it'll feel different when I compose the chanson, he thought.

And then noticed the gaps in the planks. And had they been so frayed and proud-grained before? He put his shoulder to it on impulse, and it felt lighter as it slid out onto the dark river and settled almost immediately, listing as the water gurgled through the gaps in the long low hull.

Up from the river, and then they walked on a featureless dirt road through scrubby countryside; when they had come a little way it was as if the road extended forever in each direction, but now there was a hint of warmth to the air, a rankness of scent.

"It feels like a borderland here," John said, turning his head but finding nothing to prompt the thought.

"Yes. I see it now," Deor said. "A silver thread, running with light. We are close, close."

They walked and walked, or the landscape flowed backward around them. John could sense something himself, a pulling. At times he was walking down a darkened road, with the familiar weight of a sword at his side and his shield upon his back. Then it was more as if he were flying in a dream beside a meadowlark whose song wove around his, and his feathers were black and his heavy beak keen and dark eyes, over a road where a great she-bear shambled and a golden lioness walked and a bush rat skittered through the scrub, all aggression and stretched senses. Then he stumbled, and was on foot again.

"Make yourself feel and walk like a man," Deor said, staggering himself. "There is always the risk of losing yourself, in this place, I think. It eats at the boundaries of things; between life and death, good and evil, this world and others. And we are sought, sought."

"Bloody good thing we're almost home, then," Pip said.

Thora and Toa laughed, at the same moment and almost in the same tone, though one was a rumbling bass and the other an alto.

"That's the time you have to be most careful," Thora said.

"Too right," Toa agreed. "Let's push the pace a bit. Walk-trot-walk . . . if you gents weighed down with all the ironmongery can keep up?"

Mist gathered. On a hill in the middle distance a tall fire burned, and figures whirled around it.

"I recognize that," Pip said. "Oh, and I wish I didn't."

"They're dancing," John said. "That's odd music—bagpipes and drums of some sort . . ."

"No!" Deor said sharply. "Don't listen! And don't watch that dance; you don't want to know the meaning of it!"

It was hard to tear his eyes away. The dancers were so tall and the twisting of their twig-like fingers traced such patterns . . . and the other figures bound in the heart of the fire, their cries were—

Alan Thurston grabbed him by the edge of his pauldron and shook him sharply.

"You were starting to leave the road," he said.

"Thanks!" John said, taking off his helmet to wipe the palm of a gauntlet over his face. "I think you did me a good turn there."

Alan shrugged, his haunted eyes dark. "You were the first thing I'd seen in a really long time that I didn't immediately not want to see, Prince," he said. "I figure I owe you a debt."

They struggled on. A ruined church . . . possibly a church . . . stood not far from the road, with tumbled gravestones about it. The mist cleared and gave them a better view. Deor grimaced.

"Those are not names on the stones," he said, jerking his head towards the cemetery. "Those are runes, though not mine. Glyphs of binding and confinement. And that is not a place for the bodies of the dead . . . not as we understand death."

He took off the armored gauntlet and laid down the knife they'd seized from the madman in the ancient city. Alan Thurston stepped forward and took both.

"Figure this will work better than my saber," he said.

Deor nodded. "Though be careful of it, my friend."

Then he produced a drum . . .

Where from? John thought. Then: *Probably better not to ask.*

. . . and began to tap on it. As he did, John heard something beneath that rhythmic throbbing; hooves on stone. Slow, and dragging and irregular; a counter-music to the pattern and purpose of the drum. Deor's face went pale beneath his weathered tan and the not-light of the cindered black stars above them.

"The Hell Horse," Pip said, her face whey-white under the sun-kissed gold.

Deor drummed and chanted, thick drops of sweat rolling down his face. After a moment he paused:

"I must go first, to bring the rest of you through, as I came here first," he said.

A meadowlark flitted past and was gone, but the thutter of the drum persisted . . . or was that only the beat of his heart.

John stiffened and raised his shield. "That's right," he said. "Then Pip and Thora, then Toa, then—"

"Then you, and then me," Alan Thurston said.

Pip looked mutinous for a second, but Thora nodded.

"He's right, sister," she said. "It's got to be that way."

She looked at him. "You're a brave man, John. May your White Christ be with you."

"But—" Pip began.

"No time to argue. Go!" John said.

No! No! Get me out of this awful place! he gibbered inwardly.

"Johnnie—" Pip began, and the lioness snarled and took a soaring leap and was gone.

The she-bear roared, and was gone.

"Look after Pip," John said tightly. "She's tough as nails herself, but she's going to need help with the baby."

Toa nodded soberly. "Promised her mum I would, long ago," he said. "Don't like scarpering on you, mate, but—"

"A man lives by his oaths," John said. "You . . ."

The big man was gone. John looked at Alan. "Well, it's just the two of us again," he said; they shook hands. "Bare is brotherless back, as your uncle is fond of saying."

The other man's handsome face split in a smile. "It's a good saying. Would I like him, my uncle?"

John nodded. "He's . . . solid. My father said that about him—that his oath was his bond, and you couldn't want a better comrade or better friend."

He grinned. "Including a better friend when you're trying to keep a fire going in a blizzard and down to your last stick of jerky—they went through some rough times together, when they were our age and on their Quest."

"Rough as this?" Alan said, trying to see through the gathering trails of mist.

"I don't think so."

The thought was oddly cheering. He'd grown up in that towering shadow, and this last little time lived with the grief of its massive absence.

"I think he'd be proud of you," John added. Softly: "And Father would be of me. Yes, I think he would."

It didn't make him less afraid, but it did make it easier to control that twisting feeling under his breastbone. The clopping sounded louder, even as the pulse of the drum continued. He crossed himself, kissed his crucifix and spoke softly:

"O God, I am heartily sorry for having offended Thee, and I detest all my sins because I dread the loss of Heaven and the pains of Hell; but most of all because they offend Thee, my God, Who art all good and deserving of all my love. I firmly resolve, with the help of Thy grace, to confess my sins, to do penance, and to amend my life. Amen. Hail Mary, full of grace . . . Lady pierced with sorrows . . . intercede for me, Lady, now and at the hour of my death. And as You are also a mother, intercede for Thora and Pip. Throw Your mantle about them and the innocent lives they bear."

The slow, dragging beat of the hooves came closer and closer, thudding on dirt, clattering hard on stone among the graves. Alan whipped the glyph-graven knife through the air, wrist-loosening circles until the cloven air hissed.

"Come on, you ambling glue pot!" he shouted. "This'll work on you!"

Then, sotto voice: "Come on, Deor, get us out!"

The brush between them and the graveyard rustled.

"*Haro, Portland! Holy Mary for Portland!*" John said, bringing his cross-blazoned shield up just under his eyes and his sword overhead hilt-forward.

Something came out of the brush towards them. John thought it was a horse—but it was accompanied by a wave of feeling. A sick tiredness, a weariness that made his very bones ache and seem as if they were about to crumble. He might have lain down, if it had been worth the trouble, but it wasn't. Nothing was.

The blunt point at the bottom of his teardrop-shaped shield thumped into the dried mud of the roadway. He couldn't be bothered to bring it up. Why? It didn't matter. Nothing did, in a life that was just a futile struggle against the day when—

Alan clanged the steel rim of his shield into John's shoulder.

"Not today!" John snarled, pulling his own shield back up again. "Thanks, buddy!"

"Just thought you were getting tired of holding up that piece of a barn door," Alan said.

The weariness drew back a little. Then it fell on him like an avalanche coming down Mount Hood—he'd been in one of those once, on a skiing holiday when he was in his teens, and he'd been buried for half an hour until his father and mother led the party that dug him out. Even that icy, battering, smothering darkness that choked and moved without giving anything to push against hadn't been as bad as this.

He found himself on one knee and jerked the shield up; in that position it could cover you right over your head.

"Hail . . . Mary . . ." he choked out as Alan gave a wordless shout and cut with the knife.

John's shield blazed, the cross overwhelmingly bright. And that light was blue, the blue of a summer's sky, the blue of a mother's eyes, the blue of sunlit sea.

He was falling, into something infinite and soft and full of comfort.

CHAPTER TWENTY-ONE

King Kalākaua looked on soberly as the first flat thudding *crack* of a ship's catapult sounded to the north, shading his eyes with a broad hand against the bright morning sunlight.

It was too far to see the blur of a bolt or roundshot, though the flaming cover of a napalm shell would have been visible. Órlaith reflected that he'd probably been on ships of his own navy that saw action against corsairs and pirates; she'd been on Feldman's *Tarshish Queen* when it shot its way out of San Francisco Bay a few months ago, against Haida raiders and Korean warships just like these.

"This is . . . a lesson," the Hawaiian monarch said, adjusting to the gentle pitch and roll of the *Sea-Leopard*'s quarterdeck with the ease of a lifetime's practice. "We could not have fought off this attack by ourselves."

One of his commanders stirred, and he looked at the man. "Yes, General Alika, perhaps if we had not welcomed the Montivallans and Japanese the Koreans would not have attacked us. But perhaps they would—this fleet, this army, came in the same week that the others arrived. It must have been in preparation for months, traveling towards us for a long time."

He shrugged his broad taut-muscled shoulders, most of which showed beyond the straps of his light cuirass.

"And if we let fear of attack stop us from making friendships as we please, are we a sovereign kingdom, a free people, or the slaves of those who master us with threats?"

"I am sorry, Your Majesty," the scar-faced older man said. "It is just . . ."

He nodded towards the pillars of smoke coming from Oahu to the north. There was a faint reek of it now, a somehow sour scent of fires burning things not meant for the flames.

"Yes, much wealth won by sweat and work has been lost and will have to be rebuilt. And the blood of our people—I hope most were able to escape to the mountains, but every hour we wait more will be killed or worse."

Órlaith gave him a sympathetic nod. She knew that Montivallan soldiers and sailors would die in the coming fight, or be maimed and go halt or blind or handless all their lives afterwards, and it hurt. Yet they were all here carrying blades, herself with them and sharing their peril. They were here because they wished it—for honor's sake, or for their given oaths; for a lord they loved or comrades dearer than life who they would not see go into danger alone, or an abstract sense of duty, or any number of causes down to simple callow boredom with endless days spent staring up a plow-horse's arse or hauling nets.

When you took up the spear you gave yourself up to the sacrifice, as one who went to the Dark Mother consenting and with open eyes. She herself made that choice every day.

But Kalākaua knew that his folk were meeting death and fire in their own homes, and that his land lay waste beneath an invader's heel. That had to be hard, hard. The lord and the land and the folk were one, and the lord of the land was bound to the spirits who embodied both. In a very real sense, for a true ruler harm to the people or land was like a blade in your own flesh; even the thought of it made her skin crawl. She exchanged a glance with Reiko and thought she saw the same knowledge in her dark eyes. They inclined their heads to each other, in a communion no others they knew could share outside the closest of their own blood kin.

Her left hand gripped the hilt of the Sword of the Lady. That sense of communion with her followers was there, the *knowing* that felt as every one of them was a presence, and the calculus of force and speed and wind and wave that moved them. And she could sense what Reiko bore—a storm of fire and air locked in steel by a will beyond that of humankind.

More faintly, more diffuse . . .

Wrath, she thought, glancing at Kalākaua again.

Power and wrath, an anger that could grind the bones of earth to dust and raise the sea to moving walls. He was a kindly man, she judged, but his were a folk as wild in war as they were easygoing in everyday life, a people whose ancestors had hunted shark for sport, diving naked in the waters with only spears for weapons, and sailed the breadth of the Mother Ocean in their canoes undaunted by typhoon and raw solitary distance. The Powers that shaped and guarded them were likewise strong and wild.

Kāne and Pele and mighty Kū of the Battles walk today.

And over the enemy, a flat black louring, like a window into . . . not blackness, not as night or even the interior of an unlighted cave was black. A doorway into *nothing,* into a world at the end of all things that could drink the death of a universe and spend eternities chewing the stale tag ends of thought about . . . nothing but itself. Her father had described that to her in his tales of the Prophet's War, but the words . . . didn't have the metallic *taste* of it, the sense of utter motionless cold and a nullity that lived and hated and hungered.

"Orrey?" Heuradys said softly.

Órlaith started and shook her head. Her liege knight's eyes were a lionlike amber, but just for an instant there was a hint of gray, and a crested helm and a bitter spear and a shield marked with a Gorgon's head. That was the Lady she worshipped as her second mother had before her, the wise and crafty Defender of the City whose emblems were the owl and the olive.

"Things are a bit raw right now, Herry," she said, equally softly. "Normally I'm fine with leaving the Otherworld on the other side of its Veil, and dealing with the light of common day. But not *this* day, and that's part of my work too."

"Nice to know you're not just a pretty face," Heuradys said, and Órlaith grinned thanks for the little jest.

Naysmith stiffened. "What the devil?" she said, looking at the latest message from the kite-observer and then through her own glass. "They're not opening out into line! They're *all* heading straight for us! That's . . . suicide."

She turned to the signaler. "Flanking ships advance. Captain Edwards, take in sail. If they're willing to stick their heads into a sack, we'll oblige them."

CRACK!

Sea-Leopard heeled under the recoil of her broadside of twenty-four-pounder catapults. The roundshot slashed out, invisible except as blurred streaks, and the Korean warship coming in on the port quarter seemed to stagger in the water. Órlaith could *hear* the crunching sound of the cast-steel globes racking into the timbers of the enemy ship. Splinters flew skyward amid screams. At least it wasn't napalm shell or firebolt; two more of the enemy ships burned like torches not far behind them and sent the black slanting pillars of their funeral pyres into the sky, but this one was too close to risk setting it afire. Pumps were jetting water over the *Sea-Leopard's* decks anyway, and down the thin sheet metal that guarded the wooden hull. Special squads waited with the foam-gear that could extinguish chemical fire.

More screams of pain and mortal terror came from the waist of the Korean craft, where several of the heavy metal balls smashed through the gunwales and went through ranks of men kneeling behind them. Men too tightly packed to dodge even if they'd had time.

What flew skyward from those impacts wasn't splinters, except from a few of the polearms the soldiers carried. It was parts of men, and if you looked closely you could see that they *splashed* as much as breaking.

"For what we are about to receive . . ." some Christian with a sense of humor said.

The metallic twangs from the enemy ship were fewer in number; six, she thought. And subtly different, probably because the engineering tradition behind their design was. Natural law set the limits for what the students of the mechanic arts could do, but styles differed from nation to nation within those bounds. The massive fabric of the ship shuddered a bit, and something flashed by overhead too fast to see. Bits fell—severed ends of rope, and a block-and-tackle that caught in the netting overhead. Shouts sounded harsh as orders were barked and the topmen cleared the rigging above, with their clasp knives in their teeth.

Then the frigate's broadside cut loose again; she could see in her mind the crews lunging up and down at the handles of the cocking mechanisms below, and the grunts as the shot were levered into the troughs. The enemy ship was only a few hundred yards away now, within long bow-shot, and there was an explosion of spray and splinters as the heavy metal struck at the waterline. The bow jerked down as water flooded in, rammed home by the forward momentum of the ship. Then the thick stay-lines that held the foremast in place and transmitted the force of the wind to the hull snapped, writhing across the deck like thigh-thick whips with bone-cracking force.

The tall mast was a composite, smaller timbers fitted and bound together with shrunk-on hoops, not a single trunk like the *Sea-Leopard*'s Sitka spruce sparage. It was nearly as strong, but when it failed . . . as its writhing bend showed it was about to do . . .

"Duck!" Órlaith shouted crisply; petty officers were echoing it all the way down the hundreds of feet of deck.

She suited action to words by knocking down her visor and going to one knee with her shield up.

The enemy ship's mast shattered like one of the fabled bombs of the ancient world. The huge strain on the length of it turned into energy in motion as splinters and chunks scythed outward. Heuradys stepped in front of her, as several of Reiko's samurai did with her; the *Tennō* merely looked down for a moment and put an armored forearm in front of her face as she knelt.

The mast cracked like a whip as it disintegrated too; like an endless succession of whips, in fact. About a second later something went *bang!* into Órlaith's shield, hard enough to rock her backward. Whatever it had been went over the side spinning hard enough to look like a disk as it flew. There were screams and curses from spots where sharp wood hit flesh or blunt pieces struck with bone-cracking force, and more purposeful shouts as stretcher-bearers and surgeon's assistants hurried to bandage and rush the wounded below to the lazaretto and the waiting doctors.

They all came back to their feet afterwards; Kalākaua had a bleeding gash on his right forearm, but he worked the fingers to make sure nothing important had been damaged, and submitted impatiently as a Montivallan medic dusted it with antiseptic powder and bound it up tightly.

"My apologies, Your Highness," Admiral Naysmith said. "I didn't anticipate this."

"You couldn't, Admiral," Órlaith said. "It's suicidal, in the usual military . . . naval . . . terms. But the enemy are playing a different and longer game. I wish I'd realized that before we started. How long?"

Naysmith glanced to both sides. "Half an hour before the flanking elements grind their way through the enemy screens; possibly as little as fifteen minutes, possibly as much as three-quarters of an hour. Until then we're on our own except for what comes up from behind us."

That was the armed merchantmen crammed with troops. Alan Thurston was back there . . . probably wishing he was up here.

"We'll just have to break the trap open from the inside, then," Órlaith said cheerfully.

Two more Korean ships came on, parting to pass the sinking one to either side; another was approaching from the same angle on the starboard bow. None of them stopped to pick up men from the dismasted ship as it listed to port and went down by the head. It might not go all the way down, since wooden ships were inherently buoyant and very hard to sink, but it would be awash quite soon.

Captain Edwards barked orders, and the hands at the wheel turned it slightly as the watch-officer pointed with her cane. The same commands set the deck-crews hauling and ran up from the mast-captains to the tops, and buntlines adjusted the hang and cant of the sails. Everything was stripped down to a minimum, fighting-sail as it was called, just the biggest in each the four tiers. The strong linen canvas glistened silvery in the bright sun, wet down enough to make its fibers swell to catch the least breeze, as well as making it less—a little less—likely to catch fire.

One of the many joys of naval battle, Órlaith thought. Great swaths of burning cloth dropping on your head.

"We're only going to get one broadside on each side off when they come in, ma'am," Edwards warned the admiral.

Naysmith's hand clenched on the hilt of her cutlass, probably without thinking of it. She'd fought on river barges as a young ensign during the campaign up the Columbia and Snake during the Prophet's War, as well as against pirates and Haida corsairs since, all along the misty forested archipelagoes that stretched down the coast of Alaska towards Kamchatka.

"They're sacrificing their fleet for a crack at this ship," she said. "Over to you, Captain. This is a ship-to-ship engagement now."

She gave a bleak smile. "Ship to ships, rather."

He nodded, gave a considering look at the approaching ships, and said:

"Load grape. Guns to fire as they bear." Then to Órlaith: "Your Highness, if you'd care to take command of your meinie?"

That meant her personal followers; it would also be safer off the quarterdeck, though nowhere was really safe in a boarding action—even going and sitting on the ballast down by the keel increased your chance of drowning. Órlaith nodded and made herself take breaths that were deeper and a little faster than reflex would have made them, building a reserve against extremity. The other monarchs and their personal guards silently formed up with her as she clattered down the companionway from the quarterdeck to the break beneath it, where the long sweep to the forecastle began.

Not many heads turned her way as they arrived. The sailing-crew was busy or waiting with tense focus for orders. Half-pikes and boarding axes, glaives and bucklers and quivers of crossbow-bolts were racked around the masts and against the inside of the thick four-foot metal-sheathed bulwarks that edged the deck. A final working party was scattering sand on the Douglas-fir planks. Órlaith grinned tautly at the sight.

So our feet won't slip in the blood. I remember back in Westria . . . you could see the red flowing out of the enemy's scuppers like water.

She gave her own folk a brief smile and nod, then looked back up. The enemy ships were shockingly close, and more were coming in behind them. Beyond to either side flame bellowed into the sky, and masts shook and fell; the enemy were using their transports as living shields to slow the Montivallan frigates coming to the rescue of the flagship. That was like putting puppies up against hunting mastiffs, but each one-sided fight delayed them.

"Prepare to receive boarders!"

That was Captain Edwards' voice from the quarterdeck, amplified through his speaking-horn.

"Fire as you bear!"

CRACK . . . CRACK . . . CRACK . . .

That was the big catapults cutting loose and their throwing arms smacking with shattering force into the rubber-padded stopping plates. Right on the heels came a malignant hiss. The load wasn't roundshot; it was boiled-leather tubes full of thousands of eyeball-sized lead balls. Collars at the end of the throwing-trough stopped the tubes when the catapults were loaded with grape, but the balls kept right on going, through the scored paper that secured them.

The balls crackled like hail when they hit something hard, with a *thunk* when it was metal. When they hit flesh, it was more of a wet slapping. They scythed through the crowds of enemy fighters waiting to make the jump to the Montivallan frigate amid a chorus of startlement and agony.

"Down!" Heuradys barked.

The lighter sounds of the enemy's deck-mounted catapults sounded.

The knight clamped a hand on the backplate of Órlaith's armor and used it to jerk her head lower. Something went *whirt* overhead, like a giant arrow . . . which was what it was, a bolt from something that her people would have called a springald. Blocks and tackle and cables fell from overhead, as the sickle-shaped heads of the bolts cut through the rigging. So did half a sailor trailing a spray of blood that splashed across the ribbed steel of her sabatons where they rested on the deck.

His eyes blinked three times in astonishment before the face went slack.

Ah, Mother-of-all receive him in the Summerlands, Órlaith thought. *I wish I hadn't seen that. It's not the sort of furniture you want in your mind, coming back in dreams or idle moments.*

Then a huge grinding roar as four of the Korean warships crashed into the *Sea-Leopard*, two each amidships on either side, and two more at the bows. The great ship staggered in the water, and half the crew fell as the deck pitched. Órlaith braced herself with the lower point of her shield and stayed upright. A hard clarity filled her, where she seemed to see everything at once, *know* everything at once.

Grapnels flew and tangled in the frigate's rigging, dozens of them, or crunched their points into the bulwarks. Heaved tight, they held the ships together. Crewfolk rushed to hack at them with axes and cutlasses, but the last yard of each hawser was wound with steel rope, and sparks flew where the weapons struck. Arrows came up in clouds from the decks of the enemy ships, or down from sharpshooters in their rigging. Everyone who could tucked themselves under the inward slant of the bulwarks, or raised bucklers in protection. Many of the arrows struck the maze of hawser and rope in the rigging, or the sails, or masts and spars or the netting. Plenty got through, and more lofted with that ugly hissing sound massed archery made.

Órlaith put her shield up above her with a quick punching twist of her left arm; two shafts rammed into it and through the sheet metal of its facing with *punk-punk* sounds, into the bison-hide and plywood of its core, feeling like a pair of hard sharp pushes.

Karl Aylward Mackenzie had a bleeding cut on one leg just below the knee and the hang of his kilt. He examined it, shrugged, and snarled:

"And it's two can play at that game! Mackenzies—take the ones in the rigging, the others are dropping their shafts blind!"

"We are the point—
We are the edge—
We are the wolves that Hecate fed!
We are the bow—
We are the shaft—
We are the darts that Hecate cast!"

The clansfolk chanted as they drew their great yellow yew bows, aiming upward at the enemy snipers in their posts high above their decks. Men fell shrieking or quiet, or dropped and hung from the rope-slings they'd secured themselves with. The catapult crews were pouring up the companionways from the gun-deck beneath, their personal weapons in their hands, rushing with the Marine contingent to the bulwarks. Boarding ladders were raised high on the enemy ships and toppled forward, thudding down with the thick slightly curved spikes—at home in Montival they called them raven-beaks—on their undersides striking into the bulwarks to hold them.

"Juche! Juche! Juche!"

The Korean war-shout burst from a thousand throats in barking unison; the Sword told her it meant something like *by our own efforts* or *on our own,* but with a dark overtone of *we alone are fit to live* that felt a little . . . green, as if it were a new shoot of meaning from an older word.

And a snarling brabble of: *"Jug-ida! Jug-ida!"* which hardly needed translation: *Kill! Kill!*

The first wave reached the tops of the boarding ramps where they ran up from the lower decks of the smaller Korean ships. Before her Karl Aylward Mackenzie barked:

"On me! The boarders to the left!"

Longbow shafts flicked out, barely visible over the short distances, over the heads of the two ranks of Protector's Guard men-at-arms before them; the first were kneeling, the second in a low wide-legged stance, both with their big kite shields up in an overlapping fortress. Sir Droyn Jones de Molalla stood on their right flank, his sword out and motionless hilt-forward over his plumed helmet.

Morfind and Faramir and Suzie Mika were using their short recurve saddlebows on the same targets. Through the vision slit of her sallet's visor she saw a man at the front of the nearest boarding ramp take an arrow in one eye and pitch forward bonelessly. Half a dozen others fell in the same moment, bodkin-point arrows smashing into faces and through the light chain or studded-leather armor most of the enemy wore. One sank only a handspan as it met the tougher lamellar cuirass of an officer, but he staggered as it sprouted from his chest and didn't notice the boarding pike that slammed seven inches of sharpened metal through his throat . . . or at least didn't notice it until far too late.

As he fell, the hundreds of crewfolk crouching under the bulwards rose and leveled their crossbows and fired. At close range the brutal power behind the pile-shaped heads of the bolts would send them even through a knight's armor. Against the more lightly-clad Koreans they were like spikes bashed through softwood, and some of them went right through bodies and limbs and into the man behind. The other half of the sailors struck with glaives and half-pikes, stabbing or trying to knock the boarders off the narrow planks and into the water.

Órlaith could feel the attack waver, that impalpable balance when blind determination to rush forward or die began to be poisoned by doubt springing from warrior to warrior. Then another figure came aboard at the bows—not in the spiked, flared lobster-tail helmets of the Korean elite warriors, but in a tattered motley of strings and tufts of cloth, with a three-pronged gold headdress on this head and cords masking his face.

A hand-drum thuttered in his hand as he wailed and chanted. Órlaith could feel the dark threads that connected the magus to the enemy host, and the impact of the snarled command that sent them forward. More ran

up the boarding-ramps, throwing themselves bodily on the waiting points
to clear the way for those behind. .

"Kangshinmu!" Reiko barked.

That was the enemy's own term for their adepts, the instruments of
the Power that ruled and drove them.

Their eyes met. Then they faced the enemy and put their hands to
their blades and drew.

Shock.

The world flexed as the Sword of the Lady gathered the light and
shone like crystal and silver.

"Órlaith and Montival!" rang out.

"Tennō Heika banzai!" from Reiko's followers. "Banzai! *Banzai!"*

To the eye, the Sword of the Gathering Clouds of Heaven was steel
lightly chiseled and inlaid with gold. Part of it *was* steel shaped by human
hands and had a human history, albeit one that stretched back into
quasi-legend. The gold . . . wasn't.

It was the Sun itself; it was *Amaterasu-ōmikami's* being stretching into
the world of human kind. Faintly, Órlaith's ears heard a roar as of incon-
ceivable fires as the Grasscutter was drawn for war. Existence stretched,
as if the weapon was too *real* for the story that contained it. Was that
Reiko, or a nine-tailed fox that reared back with its fur bristling and white
teeth barred, the Ghost Fox that shared her name?

The cold black hatred from the *kangshinmu* struck the light of the twin
Swords; nothing physical happened, in a way, but the enemy rushed forward in a wave that matched their master's thought. The Montivallans
and their enemies met them, and Órlaith felt as if her feet were dancing
with the spirits of Air as the Lady's Sword rose to defend Her people. . . .

Órlaith staggered as the world became hard and firm once more. Black
threads seemed to writhe in the *kangshinmu's* shattered skull, and then the
Grasscutter finished what the Sword of the Lady had begun.

Reiko went to one knee, the Grasscutter outstretched in the classic
follow-through to the *ten-uchi* strike. Where a man had been, there was

only floating ash, dust that vanished with a sigh of wind. Silence fell like a ripple spreading out from them, the roaring crush of battle fading. The enemy shrank back, blinking as if they were men waking from a dream, and weapons clattered to the deck.

"Accept surrenders!" Órlaith shouted. "I'll have the heads of anyone who kills those who've thrown down!"

She switched to *Chosŏn-ŏ*. "Throw down your weapons and you will be spared! We have no desire for your blood."

The need to do that brought her fully back to the world of common day, to the slaughterhouse stinks of blood and dung. She heard Reiko echoing the command in *Nihongo*, and Kalākaua doing likewise. There were plenty of all three folk within hearing, since the *Sea-Leopard* now lay at the center of a drifting mass of ships, Korean and Montivallan and Hawaiian and Japanese lashed together into one raft of death.

Órlaith felt her hand shaking slightly as she sheathed the Sword. A stagger brought Heuradys' arm beneath hers, supporting. She turned, her mind stuttering with the struggle between exhaustion and the things that needed to be done, dully wondering where the blood that coated the whole right side of her armored body came from.

Then the world brightened. Alan Thurston was near behind her, along with many more from the transports who'd come over the quarter-deck and plunged into the melee. His mail shirt was red-daubed too, and he had a rather odd-looking fighting knife in one hand . . . a hand in an armored gauntlet like a knight's, not the leather glove Boisean cavalry favored.

Their eyes locked as the blade was raised. Dimly, somewhere, she heard Heuradys' shout of alarm and the beginning of the blurring speed of a draw-and-strike, hampered by the press of bodies and Órlaith's own body. Then his eyes changed.

"No," he said clearly. "Prince John freed me, and not for this. I choose otherwise. I shall do as I choose, not you, King of Nothingness. For the first time in my life I am one and whole, and that one knows what he must do."

The knife seemed to fight him as he turned it and drove it up under his own ribs. He fell just beyond her reaching fingers and lay; she knelt beside him and bent low as he struggled to speak.

"Light . . ." he said. "I wish . . ." and died.

Distantly, she heard a voice: "Where's the *knife?*"

CHAPTER TWENTY-TWO

"Don't stop! Don't you dare stop!" Philippa Balwyn-Abercrombie said.

Deor's hands moved on the drum, despite the sweat and exhaustion and stubble on his face. A light breeze off the sea moved the gauze of the curtains, but brought little relief from the hot night. Moths with gaudy wings fluttered around the single lamp that cast a slight pale-yellow light from the top of the dresser, giving off the hot fruity smell of burning palm oil. It was the dark of darkest night, about two hours before dawn, and the others looked nearly as ghastly; she felt ghastly. . . .

And John just lay there, his breathing as regular as the *shsssshhshs* of the surf on the beach not far away. Ruan Chu Mackenzie wiped his face and dribbled a little water between his lips, then went and did the same for Deor without interrupting his movements. The skill of his hands was the same with both men—the young Mackenzie took his duties as a healer very seriously; they were part of his religion, from what she'd gathered. If there was an extra tenderness and anxiety in his smile for the scop, who could blame him?

Not me, thought Pip. *I'm just now realizing how much I . . . well, yes, it's bloody well love . . . how much I love John.*

She'd been waiting for anything else so long that it took her a double heartbeat before she realized that John's eyes were open. The wax-mask immobility of his face, so much worse than mere sleep or even unconsciousness, turned back to *life*. Confused bewildered life, eyes darting around the room and obviously wondering where he was, but *life*.

You don't know what you've got till it's gone.

There was a saying to that effect, or it might be a song. That was even more true when you thought something was gone and then you got it *back*. She lunged forward, but Toa stepped in and plucked her into the air with one huge arm that pinned hers to her waist as well.

"Wait a bit, Cap'n," he said. "Make sure, like, after all the shite we saw in that . . . other place."

Deor dropped the drum and staggered. Then he stepped forward and gripped John's head between his hands, looking deeply into his eyes.

"Yes," he said after a minute, walking backward and half-falling into a rattan chair that creaked under his lean weight. "Yes, that's him."

Thora knelt beside the chair and put her arm over his shoulders. "Well done, old friend," she said gently. "Well done and very well done, oathbrother."

Ruan knelt at his other side, offering a mug of water; Deor seized it and drank, coughed, drank again with a long sigh.

Toa released her, and Pip scrambled to John's side, cradling his head. His hazel eyes sought hers.

"It was . . . so bright," he murmured, still distant. "So bright . . . so kind . . ."

Then they snapped into focus on her. "Thank you, Pip. Thank you. You came for me in that awful place."

"I need you, damn you," she said, and kissed him. "You're the only man I've ever met who doesn't bore me!"

"Let me get up," John said, and she helped him.

He staggered a little and felt . . .

"I'm hungry," he said. "I could use a steak."

They all laughed . . . but Ruan suddenly stopped. "What's this?" he said.

"*No!*" Deor barked. Then: "I'm sorry, my heart, but that is a thing of peril. And it should not be here."

A knife was suddenly lying on the floor. A rune-graven blade that the four of them all remembered. They looked at each other in silence, until John spoke:

"Shit," he said crisply.

There was a growing clamor outside, voices raised in shouts. A man in the glittering dress and cloth-of-gold sarong of Baru Denpasar's royal court burst through.

"A ship has come, a great warship!"

John forced himself upright, and hobbled out to fling the slatted shutters wide despite the aches and twinges of a body long disused, as if age had struck him before his time. A ship was standing in towards the entrance to Baru Denpasar's harbor, a three-master with the Crowned Mountain and Sword of the High Kingdom of Montival fluttering from the mizzen. A frigate he recognized . . .

"*Stormrider!*" he shouted.